DENIS DIDEROT (1713–1784, the son of a master-cutler who wanted him to follow a career in the church. He attended the best Paris schools, took a degree in theology in 1735 but turned away from religion, and tried his hand briefly at law before deciding to make his way as a translator and writer. In 1746, he was invited to provide a French version of Ephraim Chambers's *Cyclopoedia* (1728). The project became the *Encyclopédie* (1751–72), intended to be a compendium of human knowledge in all fields but also the embodiment of the new 'philosophic' spirit of intellectual enquiry. As editor-in-chief, Diderot became the impresario of the French Enlightenment. But ideas were dangerous, and in 1749 Diderot was imprisoned for four months for publishing opinions judged contrary to religion and the public good. He became a star of the salons, where he was known as a brilliant conversationalist. He invented art criticism, and devised a new form of theatre which would determine the shape of European drama. But in private he pursued ideas of startling originality in texts like *Supplément au voyage de Bougainville* and *Le Rêve d'Alembert*, which for the most part were not published until after his death. He anticipated DNA, Darwin, and modern genetics, but also discussed the human and ethical implications of biological materialism in fictions—*La Religieuse*, *Le Neveau de Rameau*, and *Jacques le fataliste*—which seem more at home in our century than in his. His life, spent among books, was uneventful and he rarely strayed far from Paris. In 1773, though, he travelled to Saint Petersburg to meet his patron, Catherine II. But his hopes of persuading her to implement his 'philosophic' ideas failed, and in 1774 he returned to Paris where he continued talking and writing until his death in 1784.

DAVID COWARD is Emeritus Professor of French Literature at the University of Leeds. He is the author of studies of Marivaux, Marguerite Duras, Marcel Pagnol, Restif de la Bretonne, and *A History of French Literature, from 'chanson de geste' to cinema* (2002). For Oxford World's Classics, he has edited nine novels by Alexandre Dumas and translated Dumas *fils*' *La Dame aux Camélias*, two selections of short stories by Maupassant, and two by Sade, and Beaumarchais' *Figaro Trilogy*. Winner of the 1996 Scott-Moncrieff Prize for translation, he reviews regularly for the *Times Literary Supplement*.

OXFORD WORLD'S CLASSICS

*For over 100 years Oxford World's Classics have brought
readers closer to the world's great literature. Now with over 700
titles—from the 4,000-year-old myths of Mesopotamia to the
twentieth century's greatest novels—the series makes available
lesser-known as well as celebrated writing.*

*The pocket-sized hardbacks of the early years contained
introductions by Virginia Woolf, T. S. Eliot, Graham Greene,
and other literary figures which enriched the experience of reading.
Today the series is recognized for its fine scholarship and
reliability in texts that span world literature, drama and poetry,
religion, philosophy and politics. Each edition includes perceptive
commentary and essential background information to meet the
changing needs of readers.*

OXFORD WORLD'S CLASSICS

DENIS DIDEROT

Jacques the Fatalist and his Master

Translated with an Introduction and Notes by
DAVID COWARD

OXFORD
UNIVERSITY PRESS

OXFORD
UNIVERSITY PRESS

Great Clarendon Street, Oxford OX2 6DP

Oxford University Press is a department of the University of Oxford.
It furthers the University's objective of excellence in research, scholarship,
and education by publishing worldwide in

Oxford New York

Auckland Bangkok Buenos Aires Cape Town Chennai
Dar es Salaam Delhi Hong Kong Istanbul Karachi Kolkata
Kuala Lumpur Madrid Melbourne Mexico City Mumbai Nairobi
São Paulo Shanghai Taipei Tokyo Toronto

Oxford is a registered trade mark of Oxford University Press
in the UK and in certain other countries

Published in the United States
by Oxford University Press Inc., New York

First published as an Oxford World's Classics paperback 1999
Reissued 2008

British Library Cataloguing in Publication Data

Data available

Library of Congress Cataloging in Publication Data

Diderot, Denis, 1713–1784.
[Jacques le fataliste et son maître. English]
Jacques the fatalist and his master / Denis Diderot;
translated and edited by David Coward.
(Oxford world's classics)
Includes bibliographical references.
I. Coward, David. II. Title. III. Series. Oxford world's
classics (Oxford University Press)
PQ1979.A65E5 1999 843'.5—dc21 98-31240

ISBN 978-0-19-953795-2

17

Typeset in Ehrhardt
by Alliance Phototypesetters, Pondicherry, India
Printed and bound in Great Britain by Clays Ltd, Elcograf S.p.A.

CONTENTS

INTRODUCTION

The Age of Enlightenment

The eighteenth century was the self-proclaimed Age of Enlightenment. In England and particularly France, a concerted attack was
launched on old ways of thinking which had at their centre the theology of the Christian Church. Already by 1700, cosmopolitan citizens
of the Europe-wide 'Republic of Letters' had begun to dismantle the
belief that God was the mysterious creator and curator of the universe
and all that lies therein. They no longer raised their eyes to heaven but
began to scrutinize the world around them. What they saw was order:
days which followed nights, tides which rose and fell, seasons which
came and went. They observed that what was true of the external
world seemed also to be true of human beings, even of whole civilizations, for everything has its season, is born, and dies.

Reluctant at first to jettison God, they persevered in their suspicion
that the cosmos was a gigantic, physical, self-perpetuating, orderly
system. They called it 'Nature' and began to subject it to analysis,
starting from the premiss that the universe was an enigma only because
the human brain did not understand it. Through science and philosophy, its secrets could be unlocked. By proving mathematically that
the planets hold their stations by the principle of gravity, Newton did
more than make an important discovery: he made the first discovery of
the New Age. Nature had been made to yield up a great mystery. Surely
it was only a matter of time before other principles, no less mighty,
would emerge and dispel the darkness of human ignorance. Observation and experiment replaced surmise and speculation, and conclusions were valid only until they were overtaken by new evidence and
new conclusions.

Thus was born the scientific optimism of an age which came to believe that everything was explicable. For if there were laws which
governed external nature, it was reasonable to assume that there were
also laws which controlled the world of man: physical laws governing
his body, and social, political, economic, and moral laws controlling his
collective affairs. Instead of bowing to a divine order which could not

be questioned, human beings need only to ask enough questions to acquire a complete understanding of Nature and Man's place in it.

But understanding was not enough. Knowledge arms and empowers, and with the power conferred by new discoveries, there grew a missionary spirit which identified a specific objective: human happiness. Reason was not to be pure, but applied. Knowledge was not to be disinterested but useful, an agent of change and not an end in itself. Fired by a belief no less strong than the old faith in a benevolent God, the new rationalists proclaimed a brave vision of the future. By rejecting the superstitious hold of revealed religion and accepting his place in Nature, Man could perfect both himself and his environment, inherit a demystified world, and inhabit a society where oppression, injustice, crime, and poverty ceased to exist.

Those who led the crusade, the *philosophes*, were for the most part disseminators rather than discoverers of knowledge. In modern terms, they were committed intellectuals, not conceptual philosophers. They shared methods, beliefs, and goals, but they were often divided among themselves on major questions. Not all believed, for instance, that it was necessary or indeed possible to discard God the Creator, since God imposed a moral dimension on Nature which otherwise was impersonal and a stranger to justice. But they also faced opposition from outside, from Church and State which persecuted them, from the satirists who mocked their endeavours, and from public opinion which, being wedded to the old ways, reacted conservatively to their calls to think boldly. Few were spared inconvenience, and some were jailed and forced into exile.

Two centuries on, it is less possible to believe that the age of true Enlightenment will ever dawn. With every answer we find, new questions arise and the unknown retreats steadily before our forward march. But the knowledge revolution of the eighteenth century was real. It shifted the direction of human enquiry and made intellectual curiosity not merely respectable but a duty. While the assault on Nature's secrets still goes on, many ongoing campaigns were begun in the eighteenth century and some have long since been won, from inoculation to town-planning, and they have changed our world. Marx owed much to the utopian socialists of the *ancien régime* and Darwin to the early transformists who believed that all life emerged from the sea, while the Enlightenment's concern with the nature of consciousness would lead directly to Freud.

Many laboured devoutly in the cause, but four names stand out. Voltaire's legacy was resistance to authority and, above all, the message of tolerance: the freedom to believe, think, and speak. Child-centred education, the democratic principle, and the rights of the individual are traceable to Rousseau. Montesquieu not only invented sociology but helped provide the insurgents of Britain's American colonies with a constitution. Until recent times, no such sweeping claims have seemed possible for Denis Diderot, though between the two world wars, Marxist theorists attempted to turn him into the prophet of anti-individualist, social morality, the unsung herald of communist obedience. It was a role which hardly suited his ebullient personality, which historians of ideas have always defined as his major weakness. Diderot had bright thoughts on everything but he has been accused of spreading himself too thinly, of being too curious, too diffuse, too inconclusive. His contemporaries would have agreed with this estimate. In his lifetime he was known as *Le Philosophe*, the official cheerleader of the French Enlightenment, the editor of its mouthpiece, the *Encyclopédie* (1751–72), the champion of the new *drame bourgeois*, a sound trencherman, and an indefatigable talker and raconteur. Yet they saw only the tip of a very large iceberg, for Diderot kept a tight rein on his boldest ideas, out of prudence, arguing with himself in the privacy of writings which were not published until after his death. It is only in the last half-century that Diderot has finally emerged as the most original and intellectually stimulating of all the *philosophes*, as well as the most human.

Denis Diderot

Diderot was also the most Parisian of the *philosophes*, though he was born at Langres in Champagne, in 1713. His father, Didier Diderot, had followed a family tradition more than a century old by becoming the town's master-cutler. His mother, Angélique Vigneron, was the daughter of a tanner, though the Vignerons, by supplying the Church with clergymen, were also long-standing servants of the community. One of Angélique's brothers officiated at her wedding in 1712, and another was appointed canon of Saint-Mammès, Langres Cathedral, in 1721.

Didier Diderot was a kindly man, well respected in the town and God-fearing, as the destiny of his four surviving children suggests.

While Denise (b. 1716) remained at home and looked after her parents, Angélique (b. 1720) took the veil and Didier-Pierre (b. 1722) entered the Church. Denis too was intended for an ecclesiastical career, and the family had hopes that he might eventually succeed his uncle, the canon. Accordingly, he was sent to the Jesuit college at Langres in 1723 and, in 1726, he was tonsured in preparation for his clerical life to come.

In the event his uncle died in 1728 and his post at the cathedral was lost. Undaunted, Denis's father, who still had high hopes for his son, took him to Paris to continue his education. As the *collège* system allowed, he attended classes at a number of schools, completing his secondary education with the Jesuits at Louis-le-Grand but also studying philosophy at the Collège de Beauvais and the Jansenist Collège d'Harcourt. He was an able pupil, though not always amenable to discipline, and to his regular studies he added a passion for mathematics and Greek language and literature.

He was awarded his MA (roughly equivalent to the modern *baccalauréat*) in 1732 and proceeded to read for a degree in theology at the Sorbonne—Diderot was the only *philosophe* to receive a university education—which was awarded in 1735. Duly armed with his diploma, he applied for a living, was unsuccessful, and less strong now in his faith and probably already addicted to Paris, he abandoned all thought of ecclesiastical preferment, much to his father's chagrin. In 1736 he took up law and began working as a clerk in a lawyer's office. He lasted a year. Informed of his son's lack of enthusiasm for his legal studies by a cousin, Frère Ange, a Carmelite monk whom he had asked to keep an eye on him, Didier Diderot cut off his allowance and Denis disappeared into the bohemian world of the capital. Little is known of his life between 1737 and 1740, though hints from his later correspondence suggest that he was stage-struck, tried in vain to learn to dance, and lived from hand to mouth. His mother secretly sent him small sums of money which he supplemented by giving private mathematics lessons and writing sermons for clergymen. He also read widely and taught himself English from a dictionary.

In 1741 he found employment with another lawyer, toyed with the idea of returning to the Church, and then fell in love with Anne-Toinette Champion who drove out all thought of a religious vocation. Though Anne-Toinette's mother had blue blood in her veins, she had lost her fortune and made her living as a laundress. Didier Diderot, still hoping that his son would make a brilliant career in the Church, was appalled. In January 1743 he refused to permit such a marriage and arranged for Denis to be confined, for his own good, in a monastery near Langres. He escaped in February, pursued by Frère Ange, returned to Paris, and married Anne-Toinette in November. He did not inform his parents and his father discovered the truth only in 1749, by which time his mother was dead. Diderot regretted the deception and, despite their differences, father and son remained close.

Diderot was no more faithful to his wife than he had been to religion, and he came to regret his marriage, which produced five children of whom only one survived, Angélique (b. 1753), on whom he doted. In 1746 he began a liaison with Mme de Puisieux, an occasional novelist, which flattered his social aspirations but made heavy demands on his purse. It was not the last of his extramarital affairs.

By this time his philosophy was beginning to take shape. As a student he had accepted the world-view of Descartes, who saw the cosmos as the rational product of a divine intelligence. But, like many of his generation, he saw the force of the criticisms of Cartesianism made by Voltaire in the *Lettres philosophiques* (1734, first published in English as *Letters Concerning the English Nation*). Descartes's description of the universe as a sea of ether in which planets formed like swirls and eddies could not be sustained in the face of Newtonian mathematics, while his argument that we are born with innate ideas had been clearly overturned by John Locke, who concluded that when we come into the world we are as blank paper upon which the hand of experience writes. Diderot's interest in English empirical thinkers steadily led him away from the God of Christian theology towards a broader deism which dispensed with the Bible as the authorized source of our knowledge of things, and established 'God' as a less specific creating and presiding principle. His first published essay, the *Pensées philosophiques* (*Philosophical Thoughts*, 1746), argued against both scepticism and atheism, but also denounced the irrationality and intolerance of established religion. His attack on miracles, fanatical priests, and the 'superstition' of faith did not endear him to the authorities, who ordered the book to be burnt by the public hangman.

But now Diderot was starting to be noticed. He had begun writing reviews and articles on mythology, physics, the fine arts, and mathematics for the leading literary journal of the time, the *Mercure de France*. He had also translated, for money, Temple Stanyan's *History of Greece*, the *Universal Dictionary of Medicine* by Robert James, and the English philosopher Shaftesbury's *Essay concerning Merit and Virtue*. In 1746 he was approached by a publisher named Le Breton who invited him to adapt Ephraim Chambers's *Cyclopoedia, or Universal Dictionary of Arts and Sciences* (1728) into French. The following year he and the mathematician Jean le Rond d'Alembert became joint editors of a venture which, from these modest beginnings, would turn into the embodiment of the philosophic creed: the *Encyclopédie raisonnée des sciences, des arts et des métiers* (*Analytical Encyclopedia of the Sciences, Arts, and Crafts*), which was published between 1751 and 1772.

For the next two decades Diderot devoted most of his waking hours to organizing, defending, and editing the *Encyclopédie*. He recruited contributors in all fields: religion and the arts, mathematics, astronomy, physics, and chemistry, together with the newer life sciences (natural history, biology, medicine, psychology) and social sciences (law, politics, economics). True to his conviction that knowledge should be useful, he also included articles on technology, practical crafts, and manufacturing processes, for 'poets, philosophers, orators, government ministers, soldiers, and heroes would go naked and want for bread without the artisan whom all despise'.

The *Encyclopédie* was intended to be not merely a compendium of knowledge in all fields but an affirmation of the new philosophic belief in applied Reason. In practice, this meant missing no opportunity to defend freedom of thought against the despotism of politics and the obscurantism of religion. Thus, even the learned and apparently innocuous article devoted to 'Shrewsbury' turns into an attack on clergy who use the pulpit to lead the faithful by the nose for their own selfish, sectarian ends. The *Encyclopédie*'s 60,600 articles eventually filled seventeen folio volumes of letterpress, and the plates a further eleven. It was a treasury of subversive erudition with which, said Carlyle, 'only the siege of Troy offers some faint parallel'. The Church rightly saw it as a destabilizing influence, took up the challenge, fought it persistently, and succeeded in having it banned in 1759, though by sheer persistence and some help from well-placed sympathizers Diderot overcame the opposition. In many ways the embattled publishing history of the *Encyclopédie* is as revealing of the struggle for Enlightenment as its contents. Diderot, as both its manager and intellectual driving force, was always in the thick of the struggle.

While d'Alembert, the pure mathematician, ploughed narrow furrows, Diderot's intellectual curiosity led him from pure philosophy to mathematics, from the natural sciences to such practical arts as paper-making and silk-production. As Voltaire remarked: 'He passes from the heights of metaphysics to the weaver's loom and thence to the theatre.' But even before the first volume appeared, Diderot received a warning of how dangerous ideas could be.

By 1747 he had outgrown Voltairean deism and discovered Spinoza, who provided a means of closing the gap between the two kinds of matter, the one divine, the other base, which ancient philosophers had first identified. Spinoza argued that there is no difference between mind, a manifestation of the divine, and matter, as represented by the creations of nature. Spirit and matter are thus reconciled in a single substance—which he called God—shaped by forces which must lie outside it. It followed that since we are dependent on causes outside us, we can have no real volition, that the greatest good is knowledge of God's will, and that wisdom lies in acceptance. Diderot was taken with this solution to the problem of the duality of matter, though he saw no reason to retain God even as a hypothesis. To his mind, Spinozism was essentially determinist: all creation is the product of the unavoidable laws which govern the universe and organizes matter into pre-programmed forms.

Diderot pursued this principle in the *Lettre sur les aveugles* (*Letter on the Blind*, 1749), where he argued that our knowledge of the world is determined by the information delivered by our five senses. Locke had already claimed that what we know of the world derives exclusively from information supplied by the senses without which we would know nothing at all. We see, hear, smell, touch, and taste and use the data to negotiate paths through our environment and form ideas about it. We learn to distinguish near and far, sweet and bitter, rough and smooth, and on the sole basis of the impressions we receive, acquire the ability to like and dislike, and thus to judge, choose, and ultimately act. Conception follows perception, and ideas, having physiological roots, are no more innate than they are divine. Knowledge, mind, and spirit are products of the mechanical operations of the material body. Diderot took the implications of Locke's sensationalism and described a system in which God was an irrelevance.

If the basis of his atheistical materialism was solidly established, it did not go unnoticed in official quarters. The authorities, who already anticipated future trouble from the editor of the *Encyclopédie*, decided it was time to act, and in July 1749 ordered him to be confined in the Chateau de Vincennes as the author of, among other works, a licentious novel, *Les Bijous indiscrets* (*The Indiscreet Jewels*, 1748) and the *Lettre sur les aveugles*. His detention was short-lived and not unpleasant—he was allowed to work and receive visits from his wife and friends like Jean-Jacques Rousseau—but it was an experience he had no wish to repeat. Though he would fight the battles of the *Encyclopédie* tenaciously, he was not a particularly brave man and he capitulated, agreed to behave, and was released on 3 November. Thereafter he trod warily, though until 1753 he took his scientific atheism several stages further without being incommoded. After that date, however, until 1778 he kept his most radical musings to himself.

Diderot thus became a closet rebel while his fame grew as the embattled editor of the *Encyclopédie*, a brilliant conversationalist, and a star of the Paris salons, where in two weeks, said Edward Gibbon, 'I heard more conversation worth remembering than I had done in two or three winters in London'. His life revolved around his work (in addition to editing the *Encyclopédie*, he also contributed 5,000 articles to it), his daughter Angélique, and a select group of friends, mainly writers and intellectuals, who included d'Alembert, Jaucourt, the largest single contributor to the *Encyclopédie*, the sensationalist philosopher Condillac, Grimm, editor of the exclusive, handwritten, and subversive journal the *Correspondance littéraire*, the materialist d'Holbach, and Rousseau, who eventually quarrelled with everyone. In 1756 he met Sophie Volland, who was unmarried, well-to-do, rather plain but well-read, and with her he enjoyed a thirty-year relationship which may or may not have been physical, but was certainly a meeting of two sprightly minds. He became interested in the theatre, established the principles of a new kind of drama, and composed two plays to illustrate his theories. In 1759 he wrote the first of his *Salons*, which laid the ground-rules for modern art criticism, and in the early 1760s began exploring the possibilities of fiction.

It was a full but uneventful life. In the age of the Grand Tour, he showed no enthusiasm for travel and rarely strayed from Paris. He rented a summer house at Meudon, a few miles down river, returned to Langres in 1759 for his father's funeral, stayed in the country with colleagues like d'Holbach and friends like Mme d'Aine, and journeyed from time to time to see the Volland family near Saint-Dizier, some 200 km east of the capital.

But wherever he went he was good company, as his gossipy, whimsical, and sometimes coarse correspondence reveals. To the Great he was respectful but never obsequious, while with his friends he was open and spontaneous, trading anecdotes and ideas and revelling in the antics of 'originals' like 'le Père Hoop', a sardonic Edinburgh doctor named Hope who had been adopted by his circle. He ate and drank too much and wrote frankly of his ailments: a bad melon, he reports, has turned him into 'a man who no longer possesses the key to his backside'.

His professional life was punctuated by crises: his defence of the *Encyclopédist* abbé de Prades, whose work had been condemned as casting doubt on Christian miracles, in 1751, which brought him into conflict with the Church; d'Alembert's defection from the *Encyclopédie* in 1757; its banning in 1759; its publisher Le Breton's surreptitious censoring of articles in 1764, which Diderot regarded as treachery. But he survived them and meanwhile remained devoted to his friends, began new if rather wordy love affairs, and worried about the education of his daughter for whom, always an attentive father, he found a suitable husband in 1772. After 1766, as the pressures eased, he acquired a degree of financial independence which allowed him to devote more time to his private speculations.

The *Encyclopédie* had not made him rich. Over twenty-five years it earned him 80,000 livres (about half a million sterling in modern values). But in 1767 Catherine II of Russia, an admirer, settled an annual pension on him of 1,000 livres and for 15,000 bought his library, which would revert to her on his death. In 1773 he broke the habit of a lifetime and travelled to Saint Petersburg with half an idea that he might persuade Catherine to permit free speech, reduce the power of the aristocracy and the clergy, curb the police, encourage middle-class enterprise, and educate the peasantry. But the Tsarina had little time for his 'paper ideas' and, after a stay of five months, somewhat chastened, he began the long journey back to Paris, where he continued to talk and write. He died in 1784, over lunch, while reaching for the cherry compote.

Diderot's Fiction

Diderot's curiosity was universal and the range of his knowledge immense. It encompassed biology, cosmology, perception, and linguistics, and explored disciplines (molecular physics, microbiology, genetics) which did not even exist in his day. He was fascinated by manual crafts and gadgetry (he anticipated the typewriter), but was equally at home exploring the philosophical implications of human physiology and the ethical implications of his scientific materialism. He had a gift for intuitive, lateral thinking, and many accepted principles of modern science, linguistics, and aesthetics seem little more than confirmations of his startlingly educated guesses. But he also provided art criticism with a vocabulary, laid the basis for modern European drama, and wrote fictions which seem closer to the French *nouveau roman* of the 1950s and the postmodern novel of the 1990s than to the fiction of his own day.

The first and least innovative of these, *Les Bijoux indiscrets* (1748) was written—in a fortnight, his daughter said, and for money—in the fashionably 'oriental', licentious style. Mangogul, an 'African' monarch, acquires a magic ring one turn of which will induce 'the frankest part of a woman' to speak the truth about its owner's amorous adventures 'in a loud, clear, and intelligible voice'. Thirty trials fail to produce a single instance of wifely fidelity. In addition to this traditional satire of women, Diderot fires equally conventional barbs at doctors, pedants, and the clergy. But he also plays with 'philosophic' ideas—materialism, tolerance, and the relativism of moral values—and frames his fiction as an illustration of the experimental method of intellectual enquiry: Mangogul is set the task of verifying, by accumulating evidence, the proposition that women are faithful. It is also clear that *Les Bijoux indiscrets* was intended to win friends for the *Encyclopédie*. Wise Mangogul and his constant, intelligent mistress Mirzoza are ciphers for Louis XV and Mme de Pompadour, whom Diderot hoped to rally to the cause of Enlightenment. He did not impress the King—the novel was included among the titles for which he was imprisoned in 1749—but succeeded rather better with Mme de Pompadour, who was to prove a good friend to the *philosophes*.

Diderot did not return to fiction for a dozen years. Yet it was inevitable that he would. As a writer, he was committed to stories and made extensive use of anecdotes even in his soberest disquisitions, not merely to lighten the tone but because they were true, the raw data of experience. He made very free with the lives and opinions of his friends and acquaintances, whom he regarded as suppliers of experimental evidence from which inferences might be drawn: invented stories would falsify the conclusions. As a gossip, he was also committed to talk. In company he talked to others; alone at his desk he talked to himself, using dialogue both as a form of disputation and exposition. From there to the theatre was the first logical step, though his two plays, *Le Fils naturel* (*The Natural Son*, 1757) and *Le Père de Famille* (*The Father of the Family*, 1758), melodramatic and sentimental celebrations of middle-class values, were failures.

He began by dismissing the two dominant forms of theatre: tragedy, because the anguish of kings and princes had little to say about 'modern conditions'; and comedy, which derided the follies of the middle class, the most 'useful' part of society. His own plays featured upright merchants and promoted the values of honesty, hard work, family, and tolerance. They were not well received in Paris, but his theory of the *drame bourgeois* was to influence the whole course of European drama. Beaumarchais was convinced by it, as was Lessing in Germany, and a direct line may be drawn from Diderot through Romantic drama (at least insofar as it too mixed its genres) to the 'social' theatre of Dumas *fils* and 'realists' like Ibsen, and thence to the 'problem' plays of the twentieth century.

Though he backed his own practice with reflections on staging and a fascinating essay on the nature of acting, the *Paradoxe sur le comédien* (*The Paradox of the Actor*, 1773) he did not persist with his theatrical experiments. But he did learn from them that if created characters are to convince, they must be made, in some way, true. As a playgoer, he would sometimes cover his ears and try to follow the action by what he saw. For while words convey consciously intended meanings, body-language discloses hidden motivations and reveals more of a character. If dialogue is a strength of all Diderot's fiction, so are mime, gesture, and stage directions, which fill in the picture. He was even prepared to halt the action and paint a 'tableau' (a technique borrowed from his art criticism) which allows readers to see—that is, receive sense impressions of—the pose, expression, and gestures of his characters from which they may draw their own conclusions.

But the immediate spur to his return to fiction was Samuel Richardson, whose novels took France by storm in the 1750s. Diderot admired *Pamela* (1742) and *Clarissa Harlowe* (1748) because they projected the same kind of middle-class values which he himself approved. But he was even more startled by Richardson's skill in creating the illusion of truth, for the truer the fiction the more compelling the message it conveys. In 1762, in an *Éloge de Richardson*, he identified a great discovery.

By recording a turn of phrase or a tone of voice, by drawing attention to a gesture, a look, a detail of dress, Richardson seemed to show life itself in action. Instead of stating in words that Lovelace is a wicked man, he showed him committing wicked actions, so that the reader is able to perceive and judge in fiction as he perceives and judges in life. This systematic use of 'small, authentic details' was to remain at the heart of Diderot's concept of literary realism. In 1770 he divided fiction into three types: the epic and allegorical (Homer, Tasso), the amusing (the tales of La Fontaine or his own *Bijous indiscrets*), and the 'historical', by which he meant novels like *Don Quixote* and, to be sure, *Clarissa*, which express truth by making us own what the novelist has imagined on our behalf. He asked his reader to consider the sculpted head of a woman. The conventional aesthetics of beauty required it to have regular features, eyes set well apart, and with good bone structure. The result is abstract Woman. But add a wart to the nose or a scar to the cheek and it becomes 'the head of the woman who lives next door'. Such views clearly set him at odds with contemporary French fiction, which did not imitate life but other novels.

By 1770 he had been writing dialogues, scenes, and open-ended fictions—'novels' and 'stories' are hardly the right terms for his experiments with narrative—for a decade. Yet he had begun in a distinctly Richardsonian vein. *La Religieuse* (*The Nun*) started life in 1760 as an elaborate joke played on the kindly Marquis de Croismare, who had become concerned by the fate of a young woman forced to take the veil against her will. Diderot counterfeited letters from 'Soeur Suzanne' and, to maintain the hoax, produced what he claimed was her own grim account of her sufferings: the pressures from her family, the cruelty to which she is subjected, the lesbian love of which she becomes the unwitting object, the hostility of the ecclesiastical authorities, and finally her escape, which restores her freedom but brings new miseries and, ultimately, death. There are no naughty nuns of the libertine tradition here, and none of the facile anticlericalism which opponents of the Church regularly directed against the convent system. Indeed, Diderot goes out of his way to complicate motive and situation. Suzanne is no rebel but a good Catholic who happens not to have a vocation. She is cloistered, she is told, because her family cannot afford a marriage portion for her, but in reality because she is illegitimate: she is made to assume her mother's guilt and expunge her father's shame. But Suzanne is not the only victim. The three Mothers Superior she encounters are protected neither by their beliefs nor by authority: the first loses her faith; the second is possessed by a latent sadism which flourishes in an environment rich in the opportunities to exercise it; and the third goes mad, obsessed by visions of hellfire. Diderot shows the suffocation of the human spirit, not through dramatic action but through the minutely chronicled interplay of characters who are brought to life by a revealing gesture, a turn of phrase, and the 'little, authentic details' he had admired in Richardson. For *La Religieuse* may have begun as a joke, but it ended up by being 'true' at several levels. Just as the characters are dressed in habits and mannerisms which Diderot took from his observation of people, so the fate of Suzanne relies on well-documented case-histories: his own sister had died, mad, in a convent in 1748. Diderot's realism has a strong documentary edge to it.

Though *La Religieuse* was intended to be anticlerical, it is also a political fable, for it contains a warning that tyranny crushes tyrants as surely as it destroys their victims. But it further raises the question of free will, for it shows how little control Suzanne and those around her have over their lives in the constraining world of the convent. This theme is explored further, from a different perspective, in *Le Neveu de Rameau* (*Rameau's Nephew*), which Diderot began in 1761 shortly after meeting Jean-François Rameau, the bohemian nephew of the great composer. Diderot was fascinated by Rameau, who is unreliable, dishonest, and as slippery as an eel, but also lucid and engaging. Rameau refuses to accept responsibility for what he is and does, on the grounds that no one is in a position to judge him, since neither the circumstances and consequences of the actions we judge are fully known to us nor is our judgement of them consistent. More importantly, Rameau is not what he would like to be. He is tormented by his own failure, which he blames on Nature. The gifts he was born with are not the gifts he would like to have. He cannot bear the thought that his uncle, a dismal man whom he despises, should have been given a genius for music while he has only a gift for mimicry. He knows that he can never become the great artist he longs to be, for he lacks the necessary 'fibre'. He is good at things which he disdains but, however hard he tries, can never do the things he admires. As a philosopher, he cannot deny that the path we follow in life is the effect of the constitution and qualities which Nature equipped us with. But this fatalistic argument does not satisfy Rameau, who cannot accept the mediocrity which prevents him being what he wants to be. Rameau, like Suzanne, has no choice.

Diderot pursued these philosophical issues in a handful of short tales and dialogues which deal with the ethical and practical implications of his materialism. The opinion we form of others is always faulty because, since we can never know all the facts of a case, we invariably rush to judgement. But we also go wrong when we misinterpret data or overestimate our ability to direct events. In *Ceci n'est pas un conte* (*This is not a Story*), the love Mlle de la Chaux feels cannot be translated into happiness, however hard she tries, while the heroine of the tale of *Madame de la Carlière* requires eternal vows in a world that is based on change. Tales written in the same ink (about the ambiguous Père Hudson or Mme de la Pommeraye, who discovers that she cannot control the chemical relationship between other people) are incorporated into what was to be Diderot's most ambitious attempt to find a *modus vivendi* for predestined mortals in an unfree world: *Jacques le fataliste*.

Fatalism

The Fatalism of the title should not mislead. It has nothing to do with the 'fate' and 'destiny' of popular horoscopes, nor with the gods of ancient Greece who presided capriciously over human life, nor the pagan Wheel of Fortune which raised mortals high before bringing them low, nor Christian Providence which is God's plan for creation. Diderot's fatalism is in reality biological and psychological determinism, a complex philosophy which is not explained but assumed. He uses fiction to examine its ethical implications and asks a practical question: how may a convinced determinist reach an accommodation with a world in which he has no freedom?

As we have seen, his early Deism was overtaken by an interest in the life sciences which was to condition all his subsequent thinking. Finding no evidence to support the view that there are two kinds of matter, one divine, the other base, he concluded that there is only matter. But if matter was not divine, neither was it so very base. Since it is the matrix of all creation, it must contain the essential characteristics of life: it is therefore sentient and capable of movement. The universe is made of aggregations of matter formed by the mechanical interaction of chemically charged particles. The diversity of created life-forms implies that they are grouped in different ways in different types and species. The difference between a man and the statue of a man is that human molecules are organized around a central nervous system, whereas marble, whatever outward form it takes, will always be a crude aggregate.

At first Diderot had been able to reconcile materialism with a creator. Yet the weight of evidence supported the conclusion that matter was eternal, not created, and that life renewed itself. Biological materialism thus led directly to atheism, for God was no longer needed to explain the origins and diversity of life-forms. Everything that exists is the product of molecular chemistry in a universe which is in a state of perpetual flux. The process operates by the principle of cause and effect, since all created life is the product of a prior event: creation. But materialism is also compatible with a hierarchical chain of being, which demonstrably runs from inert stone through plants, animals, and Man. The next step was to demonstrate how the movement and sensibility implicit in each molecule become the building-blocks of human consciousness.

Man is the best example of the process which turns clay into thinking matter. But what is 'thinking'? Diderot found the answer in perception. As we have seen, his interest in sensationalist psychology enabled him to define all thought as the product of the senses. The *Lettre sur les aveugles* argues that just as a blind man's knowledge of the world is limited by his sightlessness, so ours is hampered by the handicap of having only five senses. Had we a hundred, what might we not know? Data from the senses stimulate nerves as a note struck on a keyboard sets other strings vibrating, or as the fly that lands in the web alerts the spider. The central nervous system is the carrier and facilitator of understanding, memory, ideas, the imagination, and affectivity, and the brain is the seat of consciousness. The difference between the genius and the imbecile, saint and sinner, is constitutional, for we are what our sense-processing system allows us to be. Man, to all intents and purposes is a thinking machine.

But the view that molecules are eternal and life a function of matter raised difficult questions. If the universe is entirely mechanical, the concept of human will is an illusion, for it means that man is pre-programmed by his physiology and shaped by the particular environment which acts upon it. Moreover, if there is no God, what basis is there for morality? Without a God to define what is good and what is evil, and without free will to choose between them, can we honestly claim to have a hand in shaping what we are? In a letter to the lawyer Landois in 1756, Diderot was not optimistic. We cannot override our systems or break the chain of cause and effect. We are permanently marked by the necessary structure of things, like a piece of cloth from which the creases can never be ironed out.

Yet this was not Diderot's final answer, for he came to believe that we can enter the chain and affect outcomes. We already possess simple tools, such as the telescope, which boost our perception—and therefore knowledge—of things. But at a deeper level, the vast reading he undertook as editor and contributor to the *Encyclopédie* enabled him to add a pre-Darwinian coda to his biological materialism. The first 'transformist' philosophers began by recognizing that nature is in a state of constant flux, and argued from fossil and other evidence that each species is a development of a single model, marine in origin, which has survived through the elimination of unviable 'monsters'. All life-forms were once something else and will continue to evolve, which means that the chain of being is not fixed but subject to change. Diderot saw that by tapping into nature's processes we can begin to harness them. Indeed, mankind, by domesticating animals and improving plant strains, has been actively engaged for centuries on just such a project. Effects will continue to spring from causes, but causes can be manipulated. In other words, human will and human intelligence can become part of the chain and turn natural change into progress.

Human beings are not, therefore, the powerless playthings of uncontrollable forces. Nature can be known and disciplined, and human physiology itself can be altered. Diderot anticipated DNA, genetic engineering, and cloning (and saw the ethical problems which go with them), and foresaw biochemical and clinical approaches to states of mind. But if redesigning Man is a long-term process, his environment can be altered more quickly: the social will has the power to modify the iron law of survival. A moral dimension may thus be added to our world through relativism, a social code of ethics which curtails our liberty only when it impinges on the rights of others. Economics should not be left to market forces nor politics to despots, for the consequences of both are unpredictable. But a regime which spread the benefits of collective living more widely was achievable through human will, though Diderot did not think equality was a feasible goal.

He thought it impossible to legislate away the right-wing bias of natural selection which favours the strong.

Though such developments were clearly long term, the process had begun. History suggests that civilizations are ruled by three distinct codes. Diderot believed that the superstition of the *loi religieuse* was discredited beyond return, that the *loi naturelle* remained inescapable, but that the *loi civile* offers scope for progress. Society can help the ill and the old, it can promote the freedom and justice denied to the heroine of *La Religieuse*. It could, if it chose, educate the ignorant, comfort the needy, abolish slavery, and thus mitigate the law of the jungle. Individuals will always be trapped by their bodies, but they can become free as citizens.

The originality of Diderot's vision emerges very clearly when set against dilemmas which face humanity at the end of the twentieth century. Since 1953, when Watson and Crick decoded the molecular structure of DNA, the biological sciences have redefined life in chemical terms. The moral discourse of religion, social doctrines such as Marxism, psychiatry, and behavioural psychology have all been undermined by the new genetics. Just as genes predispose us to cancer, so they can be held accountable for criminality. How we live and die, how we behave, what we are, is determined for us by the particular structure of the double helix. Diderot had no access to the technology which unpicked the mechanics of the process, but he already saw that body and mind are matter, that whole societies behave like aggregations of molecules—in a word, that biology is fate.

Genetic manipulation raises broad ethical questions, not to mention the problem of human survival. For if we annex the processes of nature, we may so distort the ecosystem that we disrupt it with unforeseeable consequences. But there are dilemmas also for the individual: what should I think of my selfish neighbour when I know that selfishness is an effect of a cause which is not a person but a gene? The term 'free will', once the preserve of theologians and philosophers, is back on our daily agenda.

Diderot may not have seriously considered the possibility, unthinkable to the science of his day, that man might enter the chain so enthusiastically that he would destroy it. But he was aware of the threat his biological and psychological determinism represented to human individuality, and wondered if anything would be gained—except more efficient wars—from conflicts which pitted a thousand molecularly enhanced soldiers against another thousand men programmed for fighting. But in *Jacques le fataliste* he set out to examine how a rational man can live with the consequences of 'fatalism'.

Jacques the Fatalist

Jacques le fataliste bristles with datable allusions to events and people which indicate that it was probably written over nearly two decades, between possibly as early as 1762 and 1780, the bulk of it probably being complete by the time of Diderot's visit to Catherine of Russia in the winter of 1773. Though during his lifetime it had a limited circulation in the handwritten *Correspondance littéraire* which Grimm sent to patrons throughout Europe, it was not published until after the Revolution, in 1796, being judged (like *La Religieuse*, which also appeared in that year) to be too inflammatory for the *ancien régime* authorities.

The starting-date is by tradition associated with Diderot's meeting, at the beginning of 1762, with Laurence Sterne, who sent him the first six books of *The Life and Opinions of Tristram Shandy*. Diderot, who read English, found the book delightful, pronouncing its author 'the English Rabelais'. But whatever plans, if any, he originally had for *Jacques* must have changed in 1765 when Sterne published Book VIII, containing the episode of Corporal Trim's knee which was to provide Diderot with the framework for his own narrative. Diderot's debt to Sterne has often been exaggerated, and his own disclaimer (p. 238) can be accepted. True, Jacques shares a Christian name with Trim (who was baptised James Butler), and is as voluble. But although Sterne touches upon questions which also preoccupied Diderot, he was more interested in the processes of his own mind than in fatalism.

Even so, Sterne provided Diderot with a practical demonstration of the art of digression and a vindication of the view (which must have been music to Diderot's ears) that 'Writing, when properly managed, . . . is but a different name for conversation' (*Tristram Shandy*, Book II, Ch. 11). After Richardson, Sterne came as a culture-shock. *Clarissa* is a novel of illusion whose carefully chronicled realism creates a parallel universe in which the reader is encouraged to believe totally. *Tristram Shandy* constantly subverts the illusion of fiction and, by talking constantly to his reader, Sterne makes him an accomplice to a different kind of literary experience. Here, he says, is not what happens in fiction but what really happens in life. If we believe him, it is because we are drawn to his affable, spontaneous voice and the candid way he takes us into his confidence. Diderot, who keeps telling us that 'this is not a novel', is no less honest in admitting that he is not omniscient and, though much less whimsical than Sterne, insists that he is not an 'author' and strikes a pose as a firm but avuncular tease with a twinkle in his eye. Having paid tribute to Richardson in *La Religieuse*, Diderot now entered into the spirit of Shandyism.

But Sterne is not the only ghost in Diderot's machine. From Cervantes he learned that when a master and his servant are sent travelling, they function best as opposite sides of an argument, and from Rabelais he took the lead which helped him express the surreal side of his mind. He borrows a fable from La Fontaine to make a point, and does more than quote the odd line of Molière: the methods of Merval the moneylender are those of Harpagon in *L'Avare*, while Père Hudson's intoning of the Angelus to get rid of unwanted visitors recalls Tartuffe's use of religious observance to escape unwanted attention. Montaigne furnishes him with a justification for using the *mot juste*, even though the *mot* in question might be indelicate. But more is involved than literary theft or pastiche. At the turn of an anecdote Diderot pauses to rewrite books and plays by other people, Goldoni's *Bourru bienfaisant*, for example, or Collé's *La Vérité dans le vin*, to bring into the open a truth that was implicit in the original.

If *Jacques le fataliste* draws on multiple sources at a time when the novel as a genre was still fluid and seeking a shape, it also relies heavily on real events and people, as the large number of Explanatory Notes at the end of this volume indicates. It is not, however, a documentary novel in the accepted sense. Battles, old theological squabbles, and occasional society personages stray into the narrative, but reference to public events (the unrest following the poor harvests of 1768 and 1769, the furore caused by Maupeou's attempt to reform the *parlements*, the widespread use of police informers) is infrequent and indirect. What loom much larger are small incidents drawn from Diderot's own observation. The pining dog who symbolizes love, and the street scene which might do as a subject for Fragonard both started in letters to Sophie Volland in 1760—and it is likely that these are not the only examples. As to people, the text is littered with passing references to eighteenth-century notables: Julien Le Roy, the watchmaker; the stone doctor Frère Cosme; Tronchin the physician; the anti-Jansenist Bishop of Mirepoix; Gallet, the drunken poet; Mandrin, the highwayman; and a clutch of forgotten writers. Some known personally to him, and others derived from hearsay, are given more prominence and become pegs on which to hang an argument. While he found Le Pelletier of Orléans in a book and Guerchy (the model for Jacques's Captain) in the social chronicle of his day, Père Ange at least shares a name with the Carmelite monk who spied on him as a young man, and Père Hudson bears more than a passing resemblance to a cleric of equally dubious reputation whom Diderot had met. He was acquainted with Mlle Pigeon, and may even have known the Poet of Pondicherry.

The effect of so much name-dropping is to anchor the narrative in a world that is not so much historically but intimately true. We may need to consult the historical record to learn that Gousse is based on an engraver who drew plates for the *Encyclopédie*; but the specifics are not important, for we recognize his type. Thus Diderot draws us into his private world which turns out to be already familiar to us. It matters little, therefore, if the chronology of his references is jumbled and the route his travellers take is unspecified. Realism—in spite of his attention to 'little details' of speech, gesture, and dress—was not his primary aim. By drawing so consistently on real people and authentic events, he stakes his claim as a writer of 'truth' and measures out his distance from mere novelists who invent mere fictions. It is this aspect of Diderot's Shandyism which readers have found most disorienting.

Diderot does not hide his disdain for fiction which, if not a lie, is certainly untrue. He is openly dismissive of the epistolary novels of Madame Riccoboni and the abbé Prévost's fondness for the clichés—shipwrecks, bandits, and other thrilling perils—of romance. 'This is not a novel,' he declares, and he warns us that, however fond we are of stories, especially love stories, he will not do what 'storytellers' do. He has no truck with beginnings, middles, and endings (he supplies us with three of the latter and leaves us to choose), and raps the reader smartly on the knuckles for demanding the facile ploys which novelists use to keep the pages turning. In a novel, the cloud of dust Jacques and his Master see behind them would hide the approach of furious bandits. Here it is just a cloud of dust. Diderot constantly denies what we expect from stories—that they give us a privileged knowledge of people and events which is not available in life—and makes a point of confessing that he knows no more than his reader. We never learn for sure if Jacques's Captain is dead, nor are we told why the landlady, who tells a better story than innkeepers' wives do, has come down in the world.

Of course, the omniscient novelist would not leave us wondering. But he would also make our judgements for us. Diderot, on the contrary, leaves his stories and characters hanging. Our initial sympathy for Madame de La Pommeraye turns into horror when she shows her claws, and we are increasingly drawn to the Marquis des Arcis, the cruel seducer who becomes a victim. Père Hudson may be a scoundrel, but we are not allowed to forget that he returns his lax abbey to pious religious rule. Whereas fiction peddles the predictable, Diderot, faithful to his sensationalist principle that things are better shown than merely affirmed, offers information for us to interpret. *Jacques le fataliste* is thus less a novel than an exercise in perception, and Diderot less an 'author' than a signwriter who provides clues for us to interpret. The constant interruptions are not there simply to provoke but to allow emotions to settle: when the tale is resumed, the perspective has altered and with it our opinions. The major lesson to emerge is that people do not change, but we do not see all of them at any one time and the idea we form of them and their conduct is therefore dependent on our own shifting viewpoint.

It is a lesson that Jacques knows already, and he constantly drives it home to his Master who wants stories and answers, just as we do. His Master complains and grows testy, just as we do, for there seems much to complain about. *Jacques le fataliste* is an unmade bed of a book, as Diderot cheerfully admits (p. 185). It is a tissue of tales, anecdotes, and philosophical asides which has no form or structure. It is less a novel than an extended and disjointed conversation between two thinly drawn protagonists, into which Diderot inserts chance meetings with other characters who, for the most part, appear once and never return. We become interested in the story of Madame de La Pommeraye, but once she has served her purpose she is heard of no more. Nothing seems planned, everything happens by chance, and more adventures are begun than are concluded:

1. As Jacques and his Master ride along, they are involved in a series of adventures: they spend a night in a bandit-infested inn; Jacques recovers his Master's watch and his wallet; his Master's horse is stolen, etc.;

2. Jacques begins to tell the story of his love-life;

3. He tells the story of his brother;

4. They arrive at an inn where they hear the tale of Madame de La Pommeraye and the Marquis des Arcis, who is staying at the inn;

5. Jacques tells the story of his duelling Captain;

6. They set out accompanied by the Marquis des Arcis, who tells the story of Richard, his secretary, and le Père Hudson;

7. When Jacques succumbs to a sore throat, his Master tells the story of his love-life and the villainy of the Chevalier de Saint-Ouin;

8. The Master meets up with the Chevalier, kills him, and runs away. Jacques is arrested and imprisoned in his place;

9. Diderot offers three separate versions of the conclusion of Jacques's loves, of which the third seems to carry most weight, though it reads like a novel—a paradox which should put us on our guard: Jacques is freed from prison by bandits who one night raid the very chateau belonging to Desglands where both his Master and Denise happen to be. Jacques saves the chateau, is hailed as a hero, and is re-united with his Master and Denise. He marries her and lives, if not happily, then at least contentedly, ever after.

The outline is complicated enough, but to have a full idea of the book we would need to add Diderot's literary and philosophical digressions, count the number of times Jacques begins his own history before being interrupted and diverted into somebody else's, separate the brief anecdotes from longer, more disciplined tales, and distinguish between scenes of Paris high society (in the Madame de La Pommeraye episode and the tale told by the Master), the religious background to Hudson's predatory activities, and the rustic setting where Jacques loses—more than once—his virginity.

We should also need to consider the political charge Diderot inserts into his sprawling narrative. The strange chateau which his travellers briefly visit is a veiled denunciation of a regime dominated by aristocratic privilege and hostility to new ideas, just as the quarrel at the inn where the Master orders Jacques downstairs is a crushing comment on the relationship between the King and the Paris *parlement*. More central, however, is the question of how Jacques stands in relation to his Master. Here the servant who, like Figaro, asks how many masters are fit to be valets, seems in control. Yet though his name evokes the *jacqueries*, or peasant uprisings, which some in the 1770s already feared as a threat to the political order, Jacques is no rebel. His superiority lies not in his greater capacity to lead but in his ability to interpret the signs and make sense of disorder. The struggle between him and his Master is not based on class but on the distinction between political power and knowledge, between the state and philosophy. Jacques has no desire to be rid of his Master, without whom he would be reduced to silence, which is the only fate he fears. Provided his Master is prepared to acknowledge his intelligence, he is happy to have 'the thing' and for his Master to go on having the 'name'.

Yet not all is confusion in *Jacques le fataliste*. Even though Diderot's travellers have no named destination, their journey is a strong narrative thread to which we are regularly returned after being distracted by the innumerable encounters, conversations, and adventures which occur along the way. Strangely comforting too, once we have been educated to accept it, is the voice of Diderot who intervenes constantly, suggesting variants, discussing the implications of what we have witnessed, and never wearying of reminding us that this is not a novel and that we should learn to think for ourselves: Diderot himself turns into an extra character who carries us along on the back of his quick mind and unfailing good humour. He indulges his irony at our expense, asking our questions for us and anticipating our expectations, but he is a gentle bully. He can be earnest but is never dull, for he tells very good jokes, some of them—like the fable of the Knife and the Sheath—distinctly off-colour. He pokes mild fun at doctors, priests, human foibles, and pretentious literary styles, has a good line in comedy, both high and low, and never lets the pace flag: there is always a surprise waiting around the next corner. But it is the tumbling ebullience of his mind which is hardest to resist.

Along with his century, but for a more specific reason, he was suspicious of the imagination and, as in all his fictions, invented little but worked systematically from observation and 'truth'. It is because *Jacques le fataliste* is a montage of real people and events, a patchwork picture of life rooted in truth, that it acquires its credibility as an experiment. The opening paragraph asks questions which do not have answers except in the philosophy Jacques has inherited from his Captain, who believed that every bullet has its billet. From there, Jacques, by the kind of association of ideas which will recur throughout his travels, thinks of his knee, how he got his wound, and thence along the chain of events to the time he fell in love, a circumstance he was no more free to avoid than the musket-shot on the field of battle. For Jacques is well aware of the problem of free will: 'the calculation we do in our heads and the calculation that's already been done in the Great Ledger in the sky, are two very different calculations. Do we control our destiny, or does destiny control us?' (pp. 10–11). Diderot does not keep us waiting long for the answer: 'We think that we are in charge of our destiny, but it's always Destiny that's in charge of us' (p. 26). He dispenses as quickly with the question (to which the Master would like answer) of who compiled the Ledger. Jacques, like his Captain, would not give a 'brass farthing' to know, since knowing would not stop him breaking his neck in the hole into which it was written his horse would throw him. Diderot thus does not try to prove the existence of the Ledger nor to explain it. His purpose is to show how a convinced fatalist may live with the knowledge that 'everything is written on high' without collapsing into despair or abandoning all moral sense.

In the event, Jacques copes well. He behaves 'like you and me', which is to say that he has appetites, shows initiative, prefers charity to injustice, and sometimes acts foolishly, though he certainly talks more than most of us. If he remains cheerful, sane, and positive, it is because he makes good use of his brain. Whereas his Master has habits of mind as ingrained as his routine with his watch and snuffbox, Jacques does not reach for hasty judgements but is prepared to wait upon events. The repetition of his 'usual refrain' is not an expression of stoic resignation but a simple recognition of a fact. He does not fear 'what is written on high', for experience has taught him that what is written may work as much to his advantage as against him. But more important, he uses his powers of observation and deduction (the philosophic tools of enquiry) to interpret the signs. He learns that being deposited under a gibbet is not an omen but an event which has a rational explanation. He consistently uses his knowledge of people and things to negotiate his way through his life, for which he takes responsibility. Jacques was not fated by nature to be a successful fatalist: he survives fatalism by making the most of the gifts nature has bestowed upon him. He vindicates Diderot's belief that human beings are rational creatures who make decisions which, though they may be wrong, are always conscious. Jacques is a triumphant demonstration of Diderot's view that philosophical necessity is no threat to human happiness, and the best answer to those who equate destiny with doom. *Jacques le fataliste* is a celebration of life which is never dull, rarely threatening, and always interesting.

It is also, in formal terms, a hybrid and difficult to classify. Is it a novel, a critical parody of the techniques of fiction, a ragbag-ful of anecdotes and stories by a writer who was good over short distances but lacked the stamina to structure a complex narrative? Or is it perhaps a dramatic dialogue, which makes it closer to a loose form of theatre? It was first turned into a play in 1847 and Francis Huster's *Les Amours de Jacques le fataliste* was successfully staged in 1971. The vengeance of Madame de La Pommeraye has been used by half-a-dozen playwrights (including Sardou), and was the basis of a film, *Les Dames du Bois de Boulogne*, directed by Robert Bresson in 1946, with a screenplay by Jean Cocteau. Or should it be seen as a philosophical exemplum or perhaps as an episodic *conte philosophique* in the manner of Voltaire's *Candide*? But however it is categorized, *Jacques le fataliste* seems less a work of its own time than of ours. It has been called a forward-looking 'anti-novel', an anticipation of the post-war *nouveau roman* which also dispensed with beginnings, middles, and ends and rejected the psychological props of realistic fiction. The closest comparison is offered by Samuel Beckett's *Waiting for Godot* (1953), which also shows two characters with no past who wait in an indeterminate landscape for a revelation about the nature of existence. But in its fondness for pastiche, story, and unfinished business, it also clearly qualifies as a distinctly postmodern text.

Diderot, however, is quite specific about his book. He distances himself from the novel, rejects allegory, and observes: 'The reader who takes what I write for the truth might well be less mistaken than the reader who concludes that it is a fable' (p. 12). Diderot's business is with truth. He teaches us how to judge truly by showing us a world which is rooted in truth. The minutiae of living and the infinite variety of people are graphically caught by his attention to the 'little details'. But it is not only the external world that is true. He also projects the inner truth about himself, and from it a multidimensional self-portrait emerges. In their different ways, Jacques is Diderot, his Master is Diderot, and Diderot steps on to his own stage, a sharp teller of teasing tales, with a mischievous twinkle fixed permanently in his eye. Whatever label is ultimately attached to *Jacques le fataliste*, Diderot dominates his creation, an engaging, provoking, artful master of the revels.

A Note on Money

1 liard = 3 deniers
1 sou = 4 liards (later 6)
1 livre (or franc) = 20 sous
1 écu = 3 livres
1 louis = 8 écus

NOTE ON THE TEXT

Jacques le Fataliste was written, with revisions and additions, between possibly as early as 1762 and 1782. It appeared first in fifteen parts in the handwritten *Correspondance littéraire* between November 1778 and June 1780. Four significant additions appeared in the July issue and others in 1786. The imperfect serialized version was used by Friedrich Schiller for his translation of the Madame de la Pommeraye episode in 1785, and by Christlob Mylius, who translated the whole text into German in 1792. The first French edition, also based on what had appeared in the *Correspondance littéraire*, was published in 1796 and was not superseded until a manuscript copy, with corrections in Diderot's own hand, sent to Catherine the Great with the rest of his library in 1785, became available in the Diderot archive at Saint Petersburg in the 1970s. As the fullest and most correct of the known versions, this has since then been used as the basis of editions by Jaques Proust (Paris, 1972), Simone le Cointre and Jean Le Galliot (Geneva, 1976), Paul Vernière (Paris, 1978), and most recently by Laurent Versini in volume 2 of his five-volume edition of Diderot's major works (Paris, 1994–7). It is this text which has been used for the present translation.

SELECT BIBLIOGRAPHY

Among the many general surveys in English of Diderot's century, see Robert
Niklaus, *A Literary History of France: the Eighteenth Century, 1715–1789*
(London 1972), Haydn Mason, *French Writers and their Society, 1715–1800*
(London 1982), and, for a succinct introduction to the current of thought,
J. H. Brumfitt's *The French Enlightenment* (London, 1972). John Lough's *The
Encyclopédie* (London 1971) is a comprehensive guide to the aims, achieve-
ment, and history of the flagship of French *philosophie*.

The indispensable guide to the many studies devoted to Diderot and his
work is Frederick A. Spear's *Bibliographie de Diderot, Répertoire analytique
international* (Geneva, 2 vols., 1980 and 1988), which has been regularly up-
dated in the periodical review, *Diderot Studies* (Syracuse University Press,
1961–), an invaluable source of useful information and opinion.

The most recent biography is Laurent Versini's *Denis Diderot, alias Frère
Tonpla* (Paris, 1996), though the fullest account remains Arthur Wilson's
Diderot (Oxford, 1972). Other biographies in English include Lester Crocker,
The Embattled Philosopher: A Biography of Denis Diderot (East Lansing,
Michigan State College Press, 1954) and P. N. Furbank's excellent *Diderot: A
Critical Biography* (London, 1992). Short introductions are given by Otis
Fellows, *Diderot* (Boston, 1977) and Peter France, *Diderot* (Oxford, 1983).
Longer studies include Carol Blum, *Diderot: The Virtue of a Philosopher* (New
York, 1974), John Hope Mason, *The Irresistible Diderot* (London, 1982),
Geoffrey Bremner, *Order and Chance: The Pattern of Diderot's Thought*
(Cambridge, 1983), and D. Brewer, *The Discourse of Enlightenment in
Eighteenth Century France: Diderot and the Art of Philosophising* (Cambridge,
1993).

For a survey of Diderot's fiction, Roger Kempf, *Diderot et le roman* (Paris,
Seuil, 1964) is still useful. The major studies of *Jacques le Fataliste* are
J. Robert Loy, *Diderot's Determinist Fatalist* (New York, 1950); Jacques
Smietanski, *Le Réalisme dans Jacques le Fataliste* (Paris, 1965); Stephen
Werner, *Diderot's Great Scroll: Narrative Art in Jacques le Fataliste, Voltaire
Studies*, 128 (1975); a feminist reading by Jeannette Geffriaud Rosso, *Jacques
le Fataliste: l'amour et son image* (Pisa and Paris, 1981); and Geoffrey
Bremner's short guide *Diderot: Jacques le Fataliste* (London, 1985). A. G.
Fredman's *Diderot and Sterne* (New York, 1955) remains the fullest study of
the links between *Tristram Shandy* and *Jacques*.

Among the many articles devoted to Diderot's novel, the following consider
specific aspects of the text: Michel Delon, 'Mme de la Pommeraye, Mme de
Merteuil, même combat', *Europe*, 637 (May 1982), 200–3; Peter France,

'Jacques or his Master? Diderot and the Peasants', *British Journal of Eighteenth Century Studies*, 7 (1984), 1–13; Carlos Fuentes, 'El secreto de Diderot', *Quimera*, 49 (1985), 54–63; Jean Garagnan, 'Diderot et la génèse de *Jacques le Fataliste*', *Studi Francesi*, 27 (1983), 81–2; Jean-Marie Goulemot, 'Figures du pouvoir dans *Jacques le Fataliste*', *Stanford French Review*, 8 (1984), 321–33; Michael O'Dea, 'Freedom, Illusion and Fate in Diderot's *Jacques le Fataliste*', *Symposium*, 39 (1985), 38–48; Jack Undank, '*Jacques le Fataliste* and the Uses of Representation', *Modern Language Notes*, 101 (1986), 741–65; and, in *Diderot Studies*, Lester Crocker, '*Jacques le Fataliste*, an "expérience morale"' (3 (1961), 73–99), Ernest Simon, 'Fatalism, the Hobby-horse and the Aesthetics of the Novel' (16 (1973), 253–74), Donal O'Gorman, 'Hypotheses for a New Reading of *Jacques le Fataliste*' (19 (1978), 129–43), and Ruth M. Mésavage, 'Dialogue and Illusion in *Jacques le Fataliste*' (22 (1986), 79–87).

Further Reading in Oxford World's Classics

Miguel de Cervantes, *Don Quixote de la Mancha*, tr. Charles Jarvis, ed. E. C. Riley.

Denis Diderot, *This is Not a Story and Other Stories*, tr. and ed. P. N. Furbank.

Samuel Johnson, *The History of Rasselas*, ed. J. P. Hardy.

Laurence Sterne, *Tristram Shandy*, ed. Ian Campbell Ross.

Voltaire, *Candide and Other Stories*, tr. and ed. Roger Pearson.

—— *Letters Concerning the English Nation*, ed. N. Cronk.

A CHRONOLOGY OF DENIS DIDEROT

1713 5 October: birth of Denis Diderot at Langres, first child of Didier
Diderot (1675–1759), a master cutler, and Angélique Vigneron
(1677–1748), a tanner's daughter. There followed Denise (1715–97),
Catherine (1716–18), Catherine (II) (1719–35), Angélique
(1720–48), who took the veil and died mad, and Didier-Pierre
(1722–87), a strict churchman who could not tolerate his brother's
atheism.

1723 Enters the Jesuit college at Langres.

1726 22 August: receives the tonsure, the first step towards an
ecclesiastical career.

1728 Autumn: moves to Paris to continue his education at the Collège
Louis-le-Grand, the Jansenist Collège d'Harcourt, and the Collège
de Beauvais.

1732 2 September: Master of Arts.

1735 6 August: awarded a bachelor's degree in theology but, after
applying unsuccessfully for a living, abandons his plans for a career
in the Church and takes up law, with the reluctant approval of his
father.

1737 Abandons law and makes a meagre living as a private tutor, translator, and supplier of sermons to the clergy. Frère Ange, at Diderot's
father's request, keeps an eye on him.

1741 Contemplates entering the seminary of Saint-Sulpice in Paris, but
falls in love with Anne-Toinette Champion (1710–96).

1742 Meets Jean-Jacques Rousseau.

1743 January: His father refuses to allow him to marry Anne-Toinette
and has him detained in a monastery at Langres, from which he
escapes a month later. 6 November: marries Anne-Toinette secretly
in Paris. Publication of his translation of Temple Stanyan's *History
of Greece*.

1744 Birth of Angélique, who lives only a few weeks. Meets Condillac and
begins following a course of lectures in surgery.

1745 Translates Shaftesbury's *Essay on Merit and Virtue*.

1746 Beginning of a liaison with Mme de Puisieux which lasts until 1751.
Invited by the publisher Le Breton to translate Ephraim Chambers's
Cyclopoedia (1728). Meets d'Alembert. June: publishes *Pensées
philosophiques* (*Philosophical Thoughts*) anonymously; it is banned in
July. Birth of François-Jacques-Denis. Ordination of Didier
Diderot

1747 June: denounced by the curé of Saint-Médard as 'a most dangerous
      man', he is watched by the police. 16 October: becomes joint-
      director, with d'Alembert, of the *Encyclopédie*.

1748 Publication of his first novel, *Les Bijous indiscrets* (*The Indiscreet
      Jewels*). His sister, Angélique, dies in her convent. October: death of
      his mother.

1749 24 July–3 November: imprisoned at the Château de Vincennes for
      publishing the *Lettre sur les aveugles* (*Letter on the Blind*). There he is
      visited by Rousseau. On his release, he meets d'Holbach and
      Grimm.

1750 June: death of François-Jacques-Denis. October: birth of Denis-
      Laurent, who dies in December. Distribution of the Prospectus of
      the *Encyclopédie*.

1751 18 February: *Lettre sur les sourds et muets* (*Letter on the Deaf and
      Dumb*). 1 July: publication of volume I of the *Encyclopédie*.

1752 January: volume II of the *Encyclopédie* which, together with Volume
      I, is banned by the Royal Council. The Prades affair brings him into
      conflict with the authorities. Police raid Diderot's house. He entrusts
      other manuscript to Malesherbes, the government minister in charge
      of the Book Trade, for safekeeping.

1753 November: Volume III of the *Encyclopédie*. 2 September: birth of
      Marie-Angélique, his fourth and only surviving child. December:
      Pensées sur l'interprétation de la nature (*Thoughts on the Interpretation
      of Nature*). Not wishing to provoke the authorities, he publishes no
      more radical works until 1778.

1754 Volume IV of the *Encyclopédie*. Begins following a course of
      chemistry lectures.

1755 Volume V of the *Encyclopédie*. Moves to the rue Taranne, where
      he lives until shortly before his death. First of many con-
      tributions appear in Grimm's *Correspondance littéraire*. July:
      meets Sophie Volland (1716–84), who may have been his mistress
      for a time, and with whom he corresponded regularly for many
      years.

1756 May: Volume VI of the *Encyclopédie*. 29 June: Diderot's letter to
      Landois on determinism.

1757 February: publication of the play *Le Fils naturel* (*The Natural Son*)
      and the *Entretiens avec Dorval* (*Conversations with Dorval*), a discus-
      sion of the play and of Diderot's views on drama. March: beginning
      of the quarrel with Rousseau. November: Volume VII of the
      Encyclopédie.

1758 D'Alembert states his intention of withdrawing from the
      Encyclopédie. October: Diderot breaks with Rousseau. November:

the play *Le Père de famille* (*The Father of the Family*) and the *Discours sur la poésie dramatique* (*Discourse on Dramatic Poetry*).

1759 March: the permission to print the *Encyclopédie* is withdrawn. 3 June: death of his father. September: the *Encyclopédie* is condemned by Rome. Writes the first of his nine *Salons* (detailed accounts of the major art exhibitions in Paris, the last completed in 1781) for the *Correspondance littéraire*.

1760 February–May: correspondence with the Marquis de Croismare, which becomes the starting point for *La Religieuse* (*The Nun*). 2 May: first performance of Palissot's satirical play *Les Philosophes*, which attacks him and the other leading *philosophes*.

1761 February: *Le Père de famille* is performed in Paris. Writes the *Éloge de Richardson* (*Eulogy of Richardson*), published in 1762. April (?): meets Jean-François Rameau, nephew of the composer. September: revises the last volumes of the *Encyclopédie*.

1762 6 August: the *parlement* orders the expulsion of the Jesuits. Works on *Le Neveu de Rameau* (*Rameau's Nephew*). D'Holbach introduces him to Laurence Sterne, who promises to send him the first six volumes of *Tristram Shandy*. The first of the eleven volumes of plates which accompany the *Encyclopédie* appear: the last is published in 1772.

1763 Quarrels with his brother who, since 1745, had considered him the Antichrist. Meets David Hume.

1764 October: Meets David Garrick. November: Is furious to learn that his publisher Le Breton has secretly censored articles of the *Encyclopédie*.

1765 Reconciled with d'Alembert, but Rousseau rejects his overtures. 1 May: Louis XV grants him permission to sell his library to Catherine II of Russia for 15,000 livres and an annual pension of 1,000 livres. She allows him to use it during his lifetime: it will revert to her only on his death. Autumn: reads volume VIII of *Tristram Shandy* which contains the story of Trim's knee. Resumes, or more probably begins writing *Jacques le fataliste*.

1766 Subscribers receive the remaining volumes (VIII–XVII) of the *Encyclopédie*.

1767 Diderot's brother appointed canon of the cathedral at Langres.

1769 August–September: writes *Le Rêve de d'Alembert* (*D'Alembert's Dream*). Falls in love with Mme de Maux.

1770 Writes a number of tales and dialogues, including *Les Deux Amis de Bourbonne* (*The Two Friends of Bourbonne*).

1771 Writes the *Principes philosophiques sur la matière et le mouvement* (*Philosophical Principles Concerning Matter and Movement*) and reads a version of *Jacques le fataliste* to a friend. 26 September: *Le Fils naturel* staged in Paris. Diderot withdraws it after one performance.

1772 March: *Essai sur les femmes* (*Essay on Women*). September: finishes two stories, *Ceci n'est pas un conte* (*This is Not a Story*) and *Madame de la Carlière*. Marriage of Angélique to an ironmaster, Caroillon de Vandeul.

1773 11 June: leaves Paris for Russia. 15 June–20 August: stays at The Hague, where he revises *Le Neveu de Rameau*, *Jacques le fataliste*, and an article which would be published as *Le Paradoxe sur le comédien* (*The Paradox of the Actor*). 8 October: arrives at Saint Petersburg.

1774 In Russia, he works on various writings dealing with politics, physiology, and materialism. 5 March: leaves Saint-Petersburg, reaching The Hague on 5 April, where he remains until 15 September. Arrives in Paris on 21 October.

1776 A dialogue on atheism, the *Entretien d'un philosophe avec la Maréchale de **** (*Conversation of a Philosopher with the Maréchale de ****) appears in Métra's *Correspondance secrète*.

1777 Continues his collaboration (1772–80) with the abbé Raynal in the *Histoire des deux Indes*, writes a comedy, *Est il bon, est il méchant?* (*Is he Good, is he Wicked?*), and further revises *Le Neveu de Rameau* and *Jacques le fataliste*.

1778 November–June 1780: publication in serial form of *Jacques le fataliste* in the *Correspondance littéraire*.

1780 Revises *La Religieuse*, also serialized in the *Correspondance littéraire*, and expands his *Essai sur les règnes de Claude et de Néron* (*Essay on the Reigns of Claudius and Nero*, 1778), his major political work.

1781 July: reads *Jacques le fataliste* to his wife and probably makes further additions to the text.

1783 29 October: death of d'Alembert.

1784 22 February: death of Sophie Volland. The news is kept from Diderot, who is recovering from an attack of apoplexy. 15 July: moves to the rue de Richelieu. 31 July: death of Diderot. He is buried (1 August) in the church of Saint-Roch. 9 September: Catherine II sends 1,000 roubles to Mme Diderot.

1785 Friedrich Schiller translates the Mme de la Pommeraye episode of *Jacques le fataliste* in *Die Rheinische Thalia*. This text is translated back into French by J.-P. Doray de Langrais in 1792 as *Exemple singulier de la vengeance d'une femme* (*Strange Case of a Woman's Vengeance*). 5 November: Diderot's library and manuscripts arrive in Saint-Petersburg.

1792 *Jacques le fataliste* translated into German by Christlob Mylius.
1796 Publication of *La Religieuse* and *Jacques le fataliste*
1805 Goethe publishes his translation of *Le Neveu de Rameau*.
1825 *Jacques le fataliste* is banned by the Paris police and the following
       year copies of the book are destroyed as an 'outrage to both public
       and religious morality and to the common decencies'.

JACQUES THE FATALIST
AND HIS MASTER

How had they met? By chance, like everybody else. What were their names? What's it to you? Where were they coming from? From the nearest place. Where were they going? Does anyone really know where they're going? What were they saying? The Master wasn't saying anything, and Jacques was saying that his Captain used to say that everything that happens to us here below, for good and for ill, was written up there, on high.

Master. That's saying a lot.

Jacques. My Captain also used to say that every bullet shot out of the barrel of a rifle had its billet.*

Master. And he was quite right.

After a brief pause, Jacques exclaimed: 'The innkeeper and his inn can go to hell!'

Master. Why would you want to see a fellow man consigned to Hell? It's not Christian.

Jacques. Because while I'm getting drunk on his rotgut wine, I forget to water the horses. My father notices. He gets angry. I shrug my shoulders at him. He picks up a stick and lays it across my shoulders a touch hard. A regiment was passing on its way to camp at Fontenoy. I enlist out of pique. We reach our destination and battle commences...*

Master. ... and you stop the bullet that's got your name on it.

Jacques. You guessed. Got it in the knee, and God knows what adventures, happy and unhappy, followed that shot. They all hang together exactly like the links in a chain, no more and no less. For instance, if it hadn't been for that shot, I don't think I'd ever have fallen in love, or walked with a limp.

Master. So you've been in love?*

Jacques. Have I been in love!

Master. And all on account of a shot from a rifle?

Jacques. All on account of a shot from a rifle.

Master. You never mentioned it before.

Jacques. No, I don't think I did.

Master. Why was that?

Jacques. Because it could not have been said before nor after this moment.

Master. And that moment has now come and you can speak of being in love?

Jacques. Who can tell?

Master. Take a chance. Make a start.

Jacques began to tell the story of his loves. It was after lunch. The weather was sultry. His Master nodded off. Night came upon them in the middle of nowhere: they were lost. The Master fell into a terrible rage and freely set about his servant with a whip and the poor devil said at every thwack: 'That one was apparently written up there too...'

You see, Reader, I'm into my stride and I have it entirely in my power to make you wait a year, two years, three years, to hear the story of Jacques's love affairs, by separating him from his Master and making the both of them undergo all the perils I please. What's to prevent me marrying off the Master and telling you how his wife deceived him? or making Jacques take ship for the Indies? and sending his Master there? or bringing both of them back to France on the same vessel? How easy it is to make up stories! But I'll let them off lightly with an uncomfortable night, and you with this delay.

The new day dawned. Now they're on their horses again and on their way.

Where were they on their way to?

That's the second time you've asked that question, and here's the second time I answer: What's it to you? If I get launched on the subject of their travels, you can kiss the story of Jacques's love affairs good-bye... They rode on in silence for some time. When the both of them had got over their pique, the master said to his servant: 'Well, Jacques, where were we up to with the tale of your loves?'

Jacques. I think we'd got to the rout of the enemy army. They run away, we run after them, it's every man for himself. I stay put on the battlefield, buried under the dead and wounded who were very numerous. Next day, I was thrown into a cart along with a dozen others to be taken to one of our field hospitals. I tell you, sir, I'd say there's no wound hurts more than a wound in the knee.

Master. Come, come, Jacques, don't exaggerate.

Jacques. No, by God, I'm not exaggerating, sir. There are ever so many bones in the knee, and tendons and all sorts of bits and pieces they have names for, though I don't know what they are.*

A kind of country bumpkin who was following them on a horse, carrying a girl behind him, and had overheard them, now spoke up, saying: 'The gentleman is quite right.' No one knew at whom this 'gentleman' was aimed, but it went down very badly with both Jacques and his Master, and Jacques said to the tactless interloper: 'Mind your own business.'

'I am minding my own business. I'm a surgeon, your honours, and I shall now demonstrate...'

The woman riding behind him said: 'Doctor, let's be on our way and leave these gentlemen alone. They don't want to have anything demonstrated to them.'

'Certainly not,' said the surgeon, 'I intend to demonstrate and demonstrate I shall.'

Whereupon, turning round for the purpose of his demonstration, he jostles his passenger, makes her lose her balance, and tips her on to the ground where she lands with one foot caught in the tails of his coat, and her petticoats clean over her head. Jacques dismounts, frees the poor creature's foot, and pulls her petticoats down. Actually, I couldn't say if he started by pulling her petticoats down or by freeing her foot, but if we can judge the state of the woman by the shrieks she uttered, she had hurt herself quite badly. Jacques's master said to the surgeon:

'See where demonstrating gets you!'

And the surgeon replied: 'See what happens when you won't let people demonstrate!'

And Jacques told the woman, who was either still lying where she had fallen or had been set on her feet again: 'Cheer up, girl, it's not your fault, nor the doctor's, nor mine, nor my master's, because it was written up above that today, on this road, at this very hour, the doctor would shoot his mouth off, my master and I would behave very rudely, you would get a knock on the head, and we'd all get a glimpse of your backside.'

What couldn't I make of this episode if the fancy took me to reduce you to tears! I'd make the woman someone important: I'd make her the niece of the curé of the nearest village, I'd rouse all the men in the parish, I'd get ready to show lots of fighting and sex, for, truth to tell, the girl was very shapely under those nether garments, as Jacques and his Master had noticed. Love never wanted a better opportunity! Why shouldn't Jacques fall in love a second time? Why shouldn't he turn out a second time to be the rival—even the preferred rival—of his Master?*

You mean it had happened once already?

You're always asking questions! Don't you want Jacques to go on with the tale of his loves? You'd better let me know, once and for all: is that or is that not what you would like? If it's what you want, let's get the girl back up on the horse behind the surgeon, send them on their way, and return to our two travellers.

This time it was Jacques who spoke. He said to his Master:

Jacques. That's how it goes. You've never been wounded in your life, you've never known what it's like to be shot in the knee, and yet you tell me, who's had a knee shattered and walked with a limp since I was twenty, that...

Master. You may be right. But that damned surgeon is the reason why you're still lying in that cart with your comrades, miles from the hospital, far from being cured, and a long way from falling in love.

Jacques. You can think what you like but the pain in my knee was unbearable. It was made even worse by the hardness of the cart where I was lying and the potholes in the road, and every jolt made me scream in agony...

Master. Because it was written on high that you'd scream out?

Jacques. Of course it was. I was losing blood fast and I'd have been a dead man if the cart, which was the last in the line, hadn't stopped outside this cottage. There I asked to be let off and they laid me on the ground. A young woman who was standing by the door of the cottage went inside, then came back out again almost at once with a glass and a bottle of wine. I gulped down one, two glasses in short order. The carts in front of ours moved off. I was about to be picked up and put back with my comrades, but I clung for dear life to the woman's skirts and anything else I could get hold of, and said I refused to get on board again, and that if I was going to die I'd sooner do it where I was rather than a couple of miles further on. As I said this, I passed out. When I came to, I found I'd been undressed and was lying in a bed which stood in one corner of the cottage, and standing over me were a peasant, who was the master of the house, his wife, who was the woman who had helped me, and several young children. The woman had dipped one corner of her apron in vinegar and was dabbing at my nose and temples.*

Master. Oh you wretch! You villain! I can see where all this is leading, you swine!

Jacques. No sir, I don't think you see anything of the sort.

Master. Isn't this the woman you're going to fall in love with?

Jacques. If I did fall in love with her, what would be so strange in that? Are we free to decide whether or not to fall in love? And even if we were, do we have the power to behave as though we weren't? If it was written on high that I would fall in love, then I could have told myself everything you are about to say now—and boxed my own ears, banged my head against the wall, torn my hair out—and everything would still have turned out exactly the same and my benefactor would have been a cuckold.

Master. But if we follow the logic of your argument, then no crime we commit can ever be followed by remorse.

Jacques. The objection you raise has rattled my brains more than once. But for all that, however much I dislike the thought, I always come back to something my Captain used to say: 'Everything good or bad that happens to us here below is written on high.' Sir, do you know of some way of rubbing out what's written up there? Can I stop being me, or failing that, can I behave as though I were not me? Can I be both me and somebody else? And has there been a single instant since the time I came into the world when this was not the case? You can go on about it as much as you like and your arguments may be perfectly sound, but if it is written in me or up there that I shan't agree with them, there's not much I can do about it.

Master. There's one thing puzzling me: would your benefactor have been a cuckold because it was written on high, or was it written on high because you would cuckold your benefactor?

Jacques. Both were written side by side. Everything was written down at the same time. It's like a great scroll that unrolls a bit at a time.

Now, Reader, you can imagine how far I could extend this discussion of a topic that's been talked about and written about a great deal for two thousand years without anyone being any the wiser. If you feel the tiniest bit obliged to me for what I've just told you, you should be infinitely grateful for what I haven't said.

While our two theorists were arguing and not agreeing, as some-times happens with Theory, night drew on. They were traversing a part of the country that was never very safe and was even less so at that time as a result of maladministration and poverty, which had resulted in a huge increase in the criminal population.* They stopped at the most sordid inn imaginable. Two trestle-beds were put up for them in a room that had been formed by partitions that gaped on every side. They asked for supper to be served. They were brought pond-water, black bread, and wine that was off. The innkeeper, his wife, their chil-dren, and the servants all had a sinister look about them. From the room next door they could hear the uproarious laughter and rowdy carousing of a dozen highwaymen and footpads who had got there first and commandeered all the eatables. Jacques took it all very calmly. The same could not be said for the Master, who strode anxiously around the room while his servant wolfed down a few chunks of black bread and pulled faces as he sank a couple of glasses of bad wine. This was the stage they were at when they heard a knock at the door. It was a servant, forced by their insolent and dangerous neighbours to bring our trav-ellers a plate heaped high with the bones of a chicken they had picked clean. Jacques lost his temper and reached for his Master's pistols.

'Where are you going?'

'Leave this to me.'

'I asked you where you're going.'

'I'm going to show that rabble what's what.'

'You do realize there are a dozen of them?'

'I don't care if there's a hundred of them—exactly how many makes no difference if it's written on high that there aren't enough of them.'

'Go to Hell, you and your damned refrain!'

Jacques breaks free of his Master's grip and bursts into the room full of cut-throats, a loaded pistol in each hand. 'At the double, time for bed,' says he, 'I'll blow out the brains of the first man who makes a move!' It's clear from Jacques's voice and manner that he means it, and the ruffians—who valued their lives just as highly as law-abiding people do—get up from the table without saying a word, undress, and go to bed. The Master, not knowing how the episode would finish, quaked as he waited for him to come back. Jacques returned loaded with all the robbers' clothes. He'd taken them in case they felt tempted to leave their beds. He had put out their light and double-locked their door, the key of which he had hung over the barrel of one of his pistols.

'Now, sir,' he said to his Master, 'all that remains to be done is to barricade ourselves in by pushing our beds against the door, and then get a peaceful night's sleep.'

He set about moving the beds and, while he was doing this, he gave his Master an unvarnished, succinct account of his mission.

Master. Jacques, you're a devil of a man! So you believe...

Jacques. I neither believe nor disbelieve.

Master. But what if they'd refused to go to bed?

Jacques. That was impossible.

Master. Why's that?

Jacques. Because they didn't.

Master. But what if they get up?

Jacques. It'll turn out this way or that.

Master. If... if... if... and...

Jacques. If, if! If the sea boiled, as the saying goes, a lot of fish would get cooked. Now look here, sir, a few moments ago you were convinced I was in great danger, though nothing was less true. Now you're convinced you are in great danger, and nothing is possibly more false. Everybody in this inn is afraid of everybody else, which only goes to show how stupid we all are.

And so saying, he undressed, got into bed, and went to sleep. His Master, taking his turn to gnaw a crust of black bread and drinking a glass of the vinegary wine, kept his ears open for any sound, watched Jacques snoring, and muttered: 'He's a devil of a man!' Then, following his servant's lead, the Master also stretched out on his palliasse, though he did not sleep as well. At first light Jacques felt a hand shaking him: it was his Master, who called to him in a whisper:

Master. Jacques! Jacques!

Jacques. Wassamarrer?

Master. It's light.

Jacques. Could be.

Master. Come on, get up!

Jacques. Why?

Master. So we can make a quick getaway.

Jacques. Why?

Master. Because it's not safe here.

Jacques. Who can tell? And who knows if we'd be any better off some place else?

Master. Jacques?

Jacques. Oh, Jacques! Jacques! Look, sir, you're the very devil of a man!

Master. You're the one that's the devil of a man! Oh come on, Jacques, please...

Jacques rubbed his eyes, yawned several times, stretched his arms, got out of bed, dressed in his own good time, moved the beds back, left the room, went downstairs, found the stables, saddled and bridled the horses, woke the innkeeper who was still asleep, paid the bill, held on to the keys to both rooms, and then they were off.

The Master wanted them to ride out at a fast trot. Jacques preferred to go at walking pace, as was consistent with his philosophy. When they'd got a fair way from the sordid inn where they'd stayed the night, the Master, hearing a clinking noise coming from Jacques's pocket, asked him what it was. Jacques said it was the keys to the two rooms.

Master. But why didn't you hand them in?

Jacques. Because they'll have to break down two doors—our neighbour's, to let them out, and ours, to get their clothes back—and that'll buy us some time.

Master. Very good, Jacques. But why do we need to buy time?

Jacques. Why? Damned if I know.

Master. And if you want to buy time, why are you crawling along like this?

Jacques. Because, since we can't read what's written on high, we never know what we want or what we're doing, and because we follow our fancy which we call Reason, or our Reason which as often as not is a dangerous kind of fancy which can either turn out quite well or very badly. My Captain believed that prudence is an assumption we make which says that experience justifies regarding present circumstances as the cause of certain future effects which we can only hope or fear will happen.

Master. And did you understand what he was talking about?

Jacques. Of course. In time, I got used to the way he used to go on. But, he would say, who can claim he ever has enough experience? Has the man who reckons he has more than enough never been duped? Furthermore, is anyone capable of knowing the full extent of his present circumstances? The calculation we do in our heads and the calculation that's already been done in the great ledger in the sky, are two very different calculations. Do we control our destiny, or does destiny control us? How many carefully laid plans have failed in the past, and how many will fail in the future? How many crazy schemes have succeeded, and how many will succeed? That's what my Captain told me over and over again after the fall of Berg-op-Zoom and Port-Mahon,* and he went on to say that prudence could not guarantee that things would turn out well, though it was a comfort and an excuse when they turned out badly. Accordingly, he slept as soundly in his tent on the eve of battle as he did in barracks and went into action exactly as he would go to a ball. He's the one you'd have said was a devil of a man.

Master. Can you tell me the difference between a man who's mad and a man who's wise?

Jacques. Of course, why not? A madman... just a minute... is a man who is unhappy. So it follows that a man who is happy is wise.

Master. And what do you mean by a happy man and an unhappy man?

Jacques. That's easy. A happy man is somebody whose happiness is written on high. It follows that somebody whose unhappiness is written on high is an unhappy man.

Master. And who was it who wrote down all this happiness and unhappiness up there, on high?

Jacques. And who made the great scroll where everything is written? A captain who was a friend of my Captain would have given his small change to know the answer to that one. My Captain wouldn't have given a brass farthing, nor would I. For what good would it do me? Would it help me to avoid falling into the hole where I'm fated to break my neck?

Master. I think it would.

Jacques. Well I don't, since there'd have to be an incorrect entry in the great scroll which contains the truth, the whole truth, and nothing but the truth. I mean, would 'Jacques will break his neck on such and such a day' be written in the great scroll, and then it turned out that Jacques didn't break his neck? Can you conceive how that could be possible, whoever compiled the great scroll?

Master. There's a great deal more that could be said on that subject...

They'd got this far when they heard, some distance to their rear, a noise and shouting. They turned to look and saw a gang of men armed with poles and pitchforks heading straight for them as fast as their legs could carry them. Now, you're thinking that these were the men from the inn, the cut-throats and servants we mentioned. You're thinking that when it was morning, the doors with no keys had been broken down and the robbers had concluded that our two travellers had de-camped with their effects. Jacques certainly thought so and muttered: 'Damn the keys and damn the whim or reason which made me bring them with me. Damn prudence, etc., etc.!' You're thinking that this small army is about to set about Jacques and his Master, that there'll be a bloody battle, with much laying on of sticks and many pistols fired. And there would be too, if I so chose. But then you could say farewell to the truth of this narrative and goodbye to the story of Jacques's loves.

Our two travellers were not pursued. I've no idea what happened at the inn after they left. They simply carried on their way, still plodding along without knowing where they were going, though they had a fairly clear idea of where they wanted to go, warding off boredom and fatigue by silence and idle talk as is the wont of those who travel by foot, and sometimes too of those who stay sitting where they are.

It must be obvious by now that I'm not writing a novel, since I am not doing what a novelist would not fail to do. The reader who takes what I write for the truth might well be less mistaken than the reader who concludes that it is a fable.

This time, it was the Master who spoke first, and he opened the pro-ceedings with his usual refrain: 'Well now, Jacques, what about the story of your loves?'

Jacques. Now where was I up to? I've been interrupted so many times that it might be as well if I started from the beginning again.

Master. No need. When you came to after passing out on the doorstep, you were lying in a bed in the cottage surrounded by its en-tire population.

Jacques. Ah yes. The first priority was to get hold of a surgeon, and there wasn't one for miles round about. The paterfamilias told one of his children to get on a horse, and sent him off to the nearest inhabited place. Meanwhile, the materfamilias heated a quantity of rough wine and tore an old shirt of her husband's into strips; my knee was fo-mented with the wine, smothered with compresses, and wrapped in bandage. A quantity of sugar that had been rescued from the ants was added to some of the wine used for the poultice and I gulped it down. Then I was told to be patient. It was late. All present sat down and had their supper. And then they'd had their supper. But the boy hadn't come back, ergo no surgeon. The father began to get cross. He was a naturally unpleasant man. He snapped at his wife and he found fault with everything. He sent the other children to bed with a flea in their ear. His wife sat on a bench and took up her distaff.* He strode up and down and, as he strode up and down, he kept nagging away at her: 'If you'd gone to the mill like I told you...' and he ended his sentence with a nod of his head in the general direction of my bed.

'I'll go tomorrow.'

'You should have gone today like I told you... And what's keeping you from collecting up the last of the straw in the barn?'

'I'll do it tomorrow.'

'We're getting to the end of what we've got, and you'd have been more damned use if you'd collected it up today, like I told you... And that pile of barley in the hayloft that's starting to go off, I'd bet good money you've not given a thought to turning it.'

'The children did it.'

'You should have done it yourself. If you'd been minding your own business in the hayloft, you wouldn't have been standing by the door.'

But then a surgeon turned up, followed by another, and then a third who arrived with the little boy from the cottage.

Master. So you were as well supplied with surgeons as Saint Roch was with hats.*

Jacques. The first one wasn't at home when the boy turned up at his house, but his wife had contacted the second and the third had come with the boy.

'Ah! evening all, fancy seeing you here,' the first one said to the others...

They'd all come as fast as they could. They were hot and they were thirsty. They all sit down round the table, which still has its tablecloth on. The woman goes down to the cellar and comes back up with a bottle. The husband mutters under his breath: 'But what the devil was she doing standing on the doorstep?' They drink up, they talk about the various ailments then going the rounds, they start listing their patients. I groan. I'm told: 'Be with you in a moment.' When the bottle's empty, they ask for another, which would be knocked off the account for my treatment, then a third, and a fourth, all to be knocked off the bill, and as each new bottle arrived the husband repeated what he'd said at the start: 'But what the devil was she doing standing on the doorstep?'

Just think what another author might have done with those three surgeons—their talk when they were on to the fourth bottle, their vast numbers of miraculous cures, Jacques's impatience, the husband's bad temper, what our rustic sawbones said as they gathered round Jacques's knee, their several opinions—one claiming Jacques would die if they didn't cut his leg off pretty damn quick, another opining that the bullet had to be removed together with the little bit of trouser that had gone in with it, that way the poor devil's leg could be saved. Meanwhile, you would have seen Jacques sitting on his bed, looking sadly at his leg and bidding it a last goodbye, just as one of our generals, flanked by Dufouart and Louis, was observed to do.* The third surgeon would come out with such inanities that they'd start squabbling among themselves and, proceeding by way of curses, would quickly have come to blows.

I'll spare you such things—you can find stuff like that in novels, in comedies written by the ancients, and in your daily dealings with other people. I mean, when I heard the husband say of his wife: 'But what the devil was she doing standing on the doorstep?', I was reminded of Molière's Harpagon when he's talking about his son and says 'But what the devil was he doing on the ship?'* and realized that it's not enough to be true, you have to be amusing too, which is the reason why people will go on saying 'But what the devil was he doing on the ship' forever, while what my character says here, 'But what the devil was she doing standing on the doorstep?', will never become anybody's catch-phrase.

Jacques did not behave towards his Master with the same reticence I show you. He did not omit the smallest detail, though in so doing he ran the risk of sending him to sleep a second time. It wasn't the most skilful of the three surgeons but the most forceful who finally saw off the others and claimed the patient.

Now you're not, I hear you say, going to brandish lancets under our noses, slice into living flesh, let blood flow freely, viz., show us a surgical operation? Think about it: would that be in good taste? Oh very well, let's skip the operation—but at least you will allow Jacques to say to his Master, as he in fact did: 'Ah, sir! It's an excruciating business, having a shattered knee put back together again!', and also give his

Master leave to answer, as before: 'Come, come, Jacques, don't exaggerate.' Though there's one thing I wouldn't dream of keeping from you for all the money in the world, which is this: no sooner had Jacques's Master given him this very rude reply than his horse staggers and falls down, his knee comes into contact with a pointed stone, and he immediately starts screaming: 'I'm dying! My knee's broken!' Though Jacques, the kindliest soul imaginable, was genuinely fond of his Master, I should very much like to know what was going through his mind, if not on the spur of the moment, then at least when he had checked that the fall had done no serious damage, and whether he was able to suppress a momentary twinge of secret exultation prompted by an accident which would teach his Master what it was like to have an injured knee. But there's also something else I'd like you to tell me, Reader: would his Master have preferred to have been injured, even if more seriously, in any other part of himself than his knee, and was he more hurt in his pride than in his body?

When the Master had partly got over the fall and the pain, he remounted and gave his steed five or six good digs with his spurs. It went off like a bullet, as did Jacques's, for between the two horses there was the same fellow-feeling as between their riders.* They made two sets of friends.

When both horses were winded and had resumed their normal pace, Jacques said to his Master: 'Well, sir, what do you reckon to it?'

Master. Reckon to what?

Jacques. A bang on the knee.

Master. I share your opinion. It's one of the most painful things there is.

Jacques. A bang on your knee in particular?

Master. No, no. On yours, on mine, on anybody's knee the whole world over.

Jacques. But sir, you haven't really thought about this. Believe me, we can only feel sorry for ourselves.

Master. Rubbish!

Jacques. If only I could express myself as well as I think! But it was written on high that I'd have thoughts in my head but that the words wouldn't come.

Here Jacques proceeded to lose himself in abstract notions which were rather subtle and quite possibly true. He tried to make his Master see that the word 'pain' is meaningless in itself, and that it only begins to acquire a content when it makes us remember a sensation which we ourselves have previously experienced. The Master asked him if he'd ever had a baby.

'No,' said Jacques.

Master. And do you believe that childbirth is very painful?
Jacques. Oh yes.
Master. Do you feel sorry for women in labour?
Jacques. Very.
Master. So you sometimes feel sorry for someone other than yourself?
Jacques. I feel sorry for all those who wring their hands, tear their hair, and yell their heads off, because I know by experience that no one does those things unless they're hurting. But when it comes to the specific pain felt by women when they give birth, I'm not sorry at all, since, thank God, I don't know what it's like. But getting back to a pain which both of us do know, the story of my knee which has turned into the story of your knee as a result of your fall...*
Master. No, Jacques, say: the story of your loves which have become my loves as a result of my past sorrows.
Jacques. So there I am, trussed up, feeling a little better, with the surgeon departed and my hosts gone and in bed. Their room was separated from mine by nothing more than a partition made of slatted lathes covered up by grey paper on which a few tinted prints had been stuck. I wasn't asleep and I heard the wife say to her husband: 'Leave me be, I don't want a bit of fun. That a poor man dying on our doorstep...'

'You can tell me all about it afterwards, woman.'

'No, I won't have it. Look, if you don't stop that, I'm getting up. I don't fancy it, I'm feeling too low.'

'If you're going to make a great song and dance about it, more fool you.'

'I'm not making a song and dance, it's just that sometimes you're so rough... it's just... it's...'

After a fairly short interval, the husband said: 'Look, woman, you must see now that as a result of your misplaced sympathy you have landed us in a pretty pickle. We're going to have the devil's own job getting out of it. It's been a bad year, we've hardly got enough for ourselves and the children. Corn's a terrible price. There's no wine. It wouldn't be so bad if I could find work, but all the rich people are cutting back. The poor haven't got anything to do. For every day you get taken on, you're four days laid off. Nobody's paying what they owe and anybody who's owed money is now so heartless it makes you want to give up. And this is the moment you choose to bring this man into the house, a total stranger, who'll stay for as long as it pleases God and the surgeon—who'll be in no hurry to cure him, for these surgeons make illness last as long as they can—somebody who hasn't a penny and will double, triple our outgoings. So, woman, how are you going to get this man off your hands? Go on, speak. Say something sensible.'

'Who can talk sensibly to you?'

'You say I'm bad-tempered, that I'm always telling you off. But who wouldn't be bad-tempered? who wouldn't tell you off? We had some wine left, not much, in the cellar, but God knows at what rate it'll go down now! Those surgeons got through more last night than we and the children drink in a week. And your surgeon, who doesn't come cheap as you can imagine, who's going to pay him?'

'Yes, you're absolutely right, and because we're poverty-stricken, here you go getting me in the family way, as if we didn't have enough kids already.'

'Rubbish!'

'It's not rubbish. I feel sure I've fallen on.'

'That's what you always say.'

'And I've never been wrong when my ear itches afterwards. It's itching like mad now...'

'What does your ear have to do with it?'

'Get off me! Leave my ear alone! Leave me alone, man, are you crazy? You'll only make it worse for yourself.'

'No, no, I haven't had it since last midsummer's eve.'

'If you do it, you'll land us in... and then a month from now you'll go on at me as if it was all my fault.'

'No, no.'

'And nine months from now, it'll be even worse.'

'No, no!'

'And it'll be what you wanted?'

'Yes, yes!'

'You won't forget? You're sure you won't say what you said all the other times?'

'Yes, yes!'

And that's how a man who is furious with his wife for giving way to a charitable impulse moves from No, no! to Yes, yes!

Master. That's exactly what I was thinking.

Jacques. Now clearly, the husband was hardly being consistent, but he was young and his wife was pretty. People never have more children than when times are hard.*

Master. The poor breed like rabbits.

Jacques. One child more doesn't make much difference to them, since it's the parish that feeds them. Anyway, it's the only pleasure that doesn't cost money. They console each other by night for the disasters that happen by day... Still, what the man said was absolutely right. As I was mulling this over to myself, I suddenly felt an excruciating pain in my leg and cried out: 'Aaargh, my knee!' And the husband cried: 'Oh, wife!' And the wife shrieked: 'Oh, husband! But that man's there...'

'Well, what about him?'

'Maybe he can hear us.'

'Let him.'

'I won't be able to look him in the face in the morning.'

'Why not? Aren't you my wife? Am I not your husband? What's a husband got a wife and a wife a husband for, if not...?'

'Ow!'

'What's the matter now?'

'My ear!'

'What's wrong with your ear?'

'It's itching worse than ever.'

'Go to sleep. It'll pass.'

'I can't sleep. Oh, my ear, my ear!'

'Your ear, your ear, you're always on about your ear!'

I won't tell you what went on between them, but the wife, after whispering 'my ear, my ear' several times in rapid succession, ended up stammering in broken syllables, 'my... ear', and followed up 'my... ear' with, well it's hard to say exactly, but taken together with the silence that ensued, it led me to suspect that the itch in her ear had been satisfactorily soothed in one way or another. It made no odds to me—I was glad, though I suspect she was gladder.

Master. Jacques, I want you to put your hand on your heart and swear that this isn't the woman you fell in love with.

Jacques. I swear.

Master. Pity.

Jacques. Maybe it's a pity, maybe it isn't. You seem to think that women who have ears as ticklish as hers are only too ready to listen?

Master. I believe that is written on high.

Jacques. And I think that's written after the entry that says they never listen to the same man for long and that they're pretty well inclined to listen to the next man who comes along.

Master. That could very well be the case.

And then they immediately launched into an interminable argument about women, one saying they were good and kind, the other that they were spiteful and nasty, and they were both right. One said stupid, the other said intelligent, and they were both right. One said deceitful, the other loyal, and they were both right. One said tight-fisted, the other said generous, and they were both right. One said attractive, the other said ugly, and they were both right. One said they gossiped, the other that they were discreet; one said candid, the other two-faced; one said they knew nothing, the other that they knew a great deal; one said chaste, the other said promiscuous; one said mad, the other sane; one said they were tall and the other said they were short—and they were both right.

After this argument, with which they could have circled the globe without running out of things to say or agreeing, they were overtaken by a storm which obliged them to hurry on their way...

Where to?

Where? Reader, you and your curiosity are terrible nuisances. What's it matter to you? If I said Pontoise or Saint-Germain, or Notre Dame de Lorette or Saint Jacques of Compostella, would you be any the wiser? If you insist, I'll tell you they were making their way towards... yes, why not?... towards a huge castle over the gate of which was written this inscription: 'I belong to no one. I belong to everyone. You were here before you arrived and you will still be here when you've gone.'

And did they go inside the castle?

No. Because unless what was written was wrong, they were already there before they arrived.

But at least they left?

No. Because unless what was written was wrong, they were still inside after they'd gone.

What did they do there?

Jacques said what it was written on high he would say, and his Master said whatever he liked, and they were both right.

What sort of company did they find inside?

Mixed.

What did people say?

Some truth and a lot of lies.

Were there any clever people?

Where are there not clever people? There were also a lot of people asking impertinent, tomfool questions whom everybody avoided like the plague. What shocked Jacques and his Master most the whole time they walked around...

So they walked around?

That's all anybody did, except when they were sitting or in bed. What shocked Jacques and his Master most was to discover that a score of rogues had taken over the best rooms where they stayed all the time, on top of each other. They claimed, against both common law and the true sense of the inscription, that the castle had been bequeathed exclusively to them as their property. With the backing of a handful of fat-arses in their pay, they had imposed this view on a large number of other fat-arses who were also in their pay, that is, who were ready for a small sum to hang or murder anyone who dared contradict them. Even so, at the time Jacques and his Master were there, some were still bold enough to do just that.

Were they punished for it?

Depends on what you mean.*

Now you'll say I've gone off at a tangent and that, not knowing what next to do with my travellers, I've lurched into allegory, which is the common refuge of arid minds. Very well. I'll draw a line under my allegory, and for you I'll sacrifice all the rich implications I could pick out of it, I'll agree to anything you want—but only on condition that you won't make my life a misery any more by arguing about where Jacques and his Master finally passed the night, about whether they got to a large town and slept with whores, or spent it with an old friend who gave them a right royal welcome, or took refuge in a hostel of mendicant friars where they were given an uncomfortable room and were put on short commons for the love of God, or stayed in a grand country house where they lacked the bare necessities in the midst of stunning opulence, or whether the next morning they debouched from an expensive inn where they were made to pay through the nose for a meagre dinner served on silver plates and a night spent in beds with musty damask curtains and damp, creased sheets, or whether they were given hospitality by a village priest as poor as the mice in his church, who scuttled around his parishioners' backyards scrounging the wherewithal to give them an omelette and a fricasseed chicken, or whether they got drunk on excellent wines, ate a sumptuous dinner, and went down with terrible indigestion in a rich Cistercian abbey. For although any and all of this might seem possible to you, Jacques did not think so: the only possibility was what was written up there, on high. But what is true is that from whatever location you choose for them to put their best foot forward, they'd not got twenty yards before the Master (who nevertheless, according to his custom, had taken his pinch of snuff) said to Jacques: 'Well now, Jacques, and what about the tale of your loves?'

Instead of answering, Jacques cried: 'The hell with the tale of my loves! I've gone and left...

Master. What have you left?

Instead of answering, Jacques turned all his pockets out and searched everywhere, but in vain. He had left their travelling wallet under the head of his bed, and no sooner did he confess as much to his Master when his Master cried: 'The hell with the tale of your loves! I've gone and left my watch hanging from the mantelpiece!'

Jacques did not wait to be asked twice but immediately turned his horse round and resumed his steady pace, for he was never in a hurry, and returned to...

The great big castle?

Certainly not. Just go back to the different possible and not-possible locations in the list aforementioned and choose whichever you think best suits the circumstances.

Meanwhile, the Master continued on his way, which meant that Master and servant were separated and I'm damned if I know which of them I want to stick with. If you want to go with Jacques, you'd better be warned: looking for the wallet and the watch might turn out to be such a long and complicated business that it might be ages and ages before he joins up again with his Master, the only person he'll confide in, and then you can say goodbye to the story of his loves. If you ditch him and let him go off by himself to look for the wallet and the watch and decide to accompany the Master, then your manners would be perfect, but you'd be very bored: you have no idea what the man's really like. There's not a great deal going on in his head. If he happens to say something sensible, it's either because he's remembered something someone else said or has blurted it out on the spur of the moment, without thinking. He has two eyes just like you and me, but most of the time you can't tell if he's using them to look with. He's not asleep but he's not quite awake either. He just exists—that's his normal state—like an automaton. He rode on, turning round from time to time to see if Jacques was coming. He dismounted and walked. He remounted, proceeded for a mile, dismounted again and sat on the ground, with his horse's reins looped round his arms and his head resting in both hands. When he got tired of this position, he got up and looked into the distance to see if he could make out Jacques. No Jacques. Then he lost patience and, none too sure if he were talking out loud or not, said: 'The villain! the dog! the knave! Where's he got to? What's he up to? Does it take this long to fetch a wallet and a watch? I'll tan your hide, that's for sure, I'll give you a damned good leathering!' Then he felt for his watch in his waistcoat pocket but it wasn't there, and went to pieces, for without his watch, without his snuffbox, and without Jacques, he didn't know which way to turn, for they were the three mainsprings of his life, which he spent taking snuff, looking to see what time it was, and asking Jacques questions, though not necessarily in that order. Deprived of his watch, he was therefore reduced to his snuffbox which he kept opening and shutting all the time, just as I do when I'm bored. The amount of snuff left in my snuffbox each night is in direct proportion to how much I've enjoyed myself during the day, or alternatively the inverse of my boredom. I do urge you, Reader, to familiarize yourself with these terms which are borrowed from geometry, because I find them precise and shall make extensive use of them.

Well? Had enough of the Master? Since the servant is not coming to us, shall we go to him? Poor Jacques! Even as we speak, he was woefully exclaiming: 'So it was written on high that on the same day I'd not only be arrested for highway robbery and on the point of being marched off to jail, but also be accused of seducing a young woman!'

Now, as he'd been making his slow way back to... the castle? no, to wherever it was they'd spent the night... he overtook one of those itinerant pedlars called packmen who called out: 'Your honour, garters, belts, ribbons to hang your watch on, the latest line in snuffboxes, fancy trinkets, rings, watch-fobs. What about this watch, sir, a watch, a fine gold watch, engraved, got a double case, like new...'

To which Jacques replied: 'I'm looking for a watch, but not that one...' and he went on his way, still at walking pace. As he went, he thought he could see it written on high that the watch the pedlar had offered him and the watch belonging to his Master were one and the same. He turned back and said to the packman: 'Friend, let's have a look at that watch with the gold case, I've a fancy it might be the very thing for me.'

'By God,' said the packman, 'I'd be surprised if it wasn't. It's handsome, very handsome, made by Julien Le Roy.* It's only just come into my hands, I got it cheap, so I'll let it go for a song. Lots of little deals that turn a small, quick profit, that's my line. But there's not much doing now, times is hard, and I shouldn't think another bargain like this will drop into my lap for another three months. You look a likely sort of gent to me, and I'd sooner you had the benefit of it than somebody else.'

While they'd been talking, the man had put his pack on the ground, opened it, and produced the watch which Jacques recognized instantly. He was not the least surprised, for just as he never hurried, so nothing ever surprised him. He looked at the watch: 'Yes,' he thought to himself, 'this is it.' To the packman he said:

'You're right, it's handsome, very handsome, and I know it's genuine.'

Whereupon he put it into his waistcoat pocket and said to the pedlar: 'Thanks a lot, friend.'

'What d'you mean, thanks?'

'This watch belongs to my Master.'

'I don't know nothing about your Master but that there watch is mine. I bought it and paid good money for it,' and, seizing Jacques by the collar, he set about trying to get the watch back. Jacques got to his horse, grabbed one of his pistols, and, pressing the barrel against the packman's chest, said: 'Clear off, or you're dead.'

Thoroughly scared, the packman released his grip. Jacques got on his horse, and as he went on his plodding way towards the town he said to himself: 'That's got the watch back, now let's see about the wallet.'

The packman hurriedly did up his pack, loaded it on his back, and set off after Jacques shouting: 'Stop thief! Stop thief! Help! Murder! Help! Help!...'

It was harvest time* and the fields were full of workers. They all dropped their sickles and gathered round the pedlar, asking where the thief was and which way the murderer had gone.

'There he is, that's him over there!'

'What? Him that's dawdling along, heading for town?'

'That's the man.'

'Come off it, don't be daft, that's not how a robber makes a getaway.'

'But that's what he is, he's a robber, I tell you. He threatened me and stole a gold watch.'

The crowd didn't know which to believe: the shouts of the packman or Jacques's leisurely progress.

'Look, lads,' said the packman, 'I'll be ruined if you don't give us a hand. That watch is worth 30 louis if it's worth a penny. You've got to help, he's getting away with my watch, and once he puts his spurs to his horse, that's my watch gone for good.'

Now if Jacques wasn't close enough to hear the shouting, he had an excellent view of the mob that had gathered, though he did not increase his pace. By promising them a reward, the packman persuaded the peasants to rush off in pursuit. So now behold a multitude of men, women, and children running after Jacques shouting: 'Stop thief! Stop thief! Murder!' while the packman followed as close behind them as the pack he was carrying permitted, also yelling: 'Stop thief! Stop thief! Murder!'

They reach the town—for it was indeed in a town that Jacques and his Master had spent the previous night: I've just remembered. The townspeople come out of their houses and join forces with the peasants and the packman, shouting in unison: 'Stop thief! Stop thief! Murder!' They all catch up with Jacques at the same time. As the packman makes a leap at him, Jacques unleashes a jab with his boot that lays him out flat on the ground, though he still goes on bawling: 'Rogue, villain, swine, give me my watch back! And even if you give it back, that won't stop you getting hung!'

Jacques, keeping a cool head, harangued the crowd which kept growing bigger all the time: 'There's a justice of the peace here, so take me to him. There, I'll prove that I'm no thief and that this man could very well be. Yes, it's true I took a watch off him. But the watch belongs to my Master. I'm not entirely unknown in town. When we got here the evening before last we stayed with the Lieutenant-Governor, who's an old friend of his.'

If I didn't mention earlier that Jacques and his Master had travelled by way of Conches* and spent the night under the roof of the Lieutenant-Governor there, it's because it's only just come back to me now.

'Take me to the Lieutenant-Governor,' said Jacques, and so saying he dismounted. He stood out in the middle of the procession, him, his horse, and the packman. They march on and arrive outside the gates of the Lieutenant-Governor's house. Jacques, his horse, and the packman go inside, with Jacques and the packman keeping firm hold of each other by the lapels. The mob stayed outside.

And what was Jacques's Master doing in the meantime? He'd nodded off on the side of the road, having looped over one arm the reins of his horse which was cropping the grass around his sleeping form within the circumference dictated by the length of the reins.

The instant the Lieutenant-Governor set eyes on Jacques, he exclaimed: 'Why, it's not Jacques, is it? What's brought you back here by yourself?'

'My Master's watch. He left it hanging from the corner of the mantelpiece and I've just found it in this man's pack. I also left our wallet under the head of my bed. If you give the order, it will be found too.'

'Let's hope that's written up there on high,' said the Justice, and thereupon he summoned his servants. Immediately the packman pointed out a large, surly-looking specimen who had only recently entered his honour's service, and said: 'He's the one who sold me the watch.'

The Justice looked very stern and said to both his footman and the packman: 'The pair of you deserve to be sent to the galleys, you for selling the watch and you for buying it.'

To the footman he said: 'Give this man his money back and get out of my livery at once.'

To the packman he said: 'You, clear out of these parts, and quick about it, if you don't want to hang around here permanently—from a gibbet. You both ply a trade which will bring you nothing but trouble. ... And now, Jacques, let's see about your wallet.'

The maid, who had appropriated it to her own use, now appeared without needing to be called. She was a tall girl, and rather comely.

'It's me, sir, I got the wallet,' she said to her master, 'but I never stole it, he give it me.'

'I gave you my wallet?'

'Yes.'

'Maybe I did, but I'll be damned if I can remember doing so.'

The Justice said to Jacques: 'Come now, Jacques, you can spare us the details.'

'But sir...'

'She's pretty and willing, I see that.'

'Sir, I swear...'

'How much was there in the wallet?'

'About nine hundred and seventeen livres.'

'Oh, Javotte! Nine hundred and seventeen livres for one night! That's far too much for you. And for him too. Give me the wallet.'

The tall girl gave the wallet to her master, who took a six-franc crown out of it. 'There,' said he, tossing her the coin, 'that's for services rendered. You're worth more, but only to someone other than Jacques. You could earn twice as much every day of the week with my blessing—but don't do it under my roof, understand? As for you, Jacques, look smart, jump on your horse, and get back to your Master.'

Jacques bowed to the Justice and left without another word, though he said to himself: 'The cheek of that damned girl! The minx! So it was written on high that another man would sleep with her and that Jacques would foot the bill? Still, Jacques, take heart. Haven't you done pretty well to have rescued your wallet and your Master's watch with a minimum of fuss and bother?'

Jacques gets back on his horse and makes his way through the crowd which had gathered at the gate of the Lieutenant-Governor's house. But since he felt extremely put out that so many people believed he was a thief, he covered his embarrassment by taking the watch from his pocket and looking to see what time it was, and then dug his spurs into his mount, which was not used to such treatment but went off like a bullet all the same. Jacques's custom was always to give it its head, for he found it was just as difficult to try to stop it when it was galloping as to make it go faster when it was walking. We think that we are in charge of our destiny, but it's always Destiny that's in charge of us, and Destiny for Jacques was everything which concerned or came into contact with him—his horse, his Master, a monk, a dog, a woman, a mule, a rook. And so his horse galloped off with him in the direction of his Master, who had nodded off by the side of the road with the bridle of his mount looped over his arm, as I've already said. Actually, when I said it, the horse was on the end of the bridle. But when Jacques arrived the bridle was still there but the horse was visibly not on the end of it. It would appear that some ne'er-do-well had crept up on the sleeping rider, carefully cut the bridle, and gone off with the animal. The noise made by Jacques's horse woke the Master, whose first word was: 'Why aren't you here, you dog, I'll give you such a...' But then he gave a huge yawn.

'Go ahead, sir, yawn your head off,' said Jacques. 'Where's your horse?'

'Horse?'

'Yes, where's it got to?'

The Master, suddenly becoming aware that someone had stolen his horse, was about to lay into Jacques with a will (and the bridle), but Jacques said: 'Easy does it, sir, today I don't feel like letting my hide get tanned. You hit me once and I swear that if you do it again I'll be off like a shot and leave you here by yourself.'

This threat immediately took the wind out of the fury of the Master, who said in a calmer voice: 'What about my watch?'

'Here it is.'

'And the wallet?'

'It's here.'

'It took you long enough.'

'Not all that long to do all the things I did. Listen and I'll tell you. I went, got into a fight, roused all the peasants in the fields, caused a riot in town, got taken for a highwayman, was led before the justice, was questioned twice, almost got two men hanged, had a footman dismissed and a maid turned out of doors, and was found guilty of sleeping with a strumpet I'd never seen in my life, though I had to cough up for the pleasure. Then I came back.'

'And while I was waiting for you, I...'

'While you were waiting, it was written on high that you'd fall asleep and that someone would steal your horse. Well, sir, don't let's give it another thought, the horse is lost and gone. Maybe it's written up there that it will be found.'

'My horse! My poor horse!'

'You can moan from now until the middle of next week, but it won't make it any more or less gone.'

'What are we going to do?'

'You can get up and ride behind me. Or if you prefer, we'll take our riding boots off, sling them over the saddle, and proceed on foot.'

'My horse! My poor horse!'

They set off on foot, with the Master exclaiming from time to time: 'My horse! My poor horse!', and Jacques enlarging generously on the bald account he'd given of his adventures. When he got to the point where he was accused by the strumpet, the Master said: 'Jacques, is it true you never slept with the wench?'

Jacques. Quite true, sir.

Master. But you paid her?

Jacques. That I did.

Master. There was one time in my life when I came off worse than you.

Jacques. You paid up after spending a night...

Master. Exactly.

Jacques. Aren't you going to tell me about it?

Master. Before we start on the story of my love-life, we've got to get to the end of yours. So now, Jacques, what about your loves? I assume they were the first and only loves of your life, notwithstanding the episode with the servant of the Lieutenant-Governor of Conches, for even if you had slept with her, it wouldn't necessarily mean you were in love. Men sleep with women they don't love every day of the week, and don't sleep with the women they do love. But...

Jacques. Well? But? What is it?

Master. Oh my horse!... Jacques, dear Jacques, don't be angry. Imagine you were my horse and just suppose I'd lost you. Now tell me, wouldn't you think the better of me if you heard me wailing: 'oh Jacques! poor Jacques!'

Jacques smiled and said:

Jacques. I had, I think, got to what my host was saying to his wife the night after my knee was poulticed up for the first time. He and his wife got up later than usual.

Master. I can believe it.

Jacques. When I woke up, I parted my bed-curtains carefully and observed my host, his wife, and the surgeon standing by the window, having a whispered conference. After what I'd heard during the night, I had no difficulty guessing what they were talking about. I coughed. The surgeon said to the husband: 'He's awake, comrade. Go down to the cellar and we'll take a drop—it steadies the hand. Then I'll remove the dressing and see what's to be done next.'

The bottle was full then it was empty, for in medical parlance 'take a drop' means finishing at least one bottle, and the surgeon came over to my bed:

'What sort of night did you have?' he said.

'So so.'

'Give me your arm... Good, pulse not bad, not much sign of a temperature. We'd better take a look at this knee. Come here, my girl,' he said to my hostess, who was standing at the foot of my bed behind the curtain, 'and give me a hand.'

The wife called one of her children.

'I don't need a child here, I need you. One false move now and we'll have enough work for a month. Come closer.'

The wife came closer, her eyes lowered.

'Take his leg, the good one, I'll take care of the other. Gently, gently. To me, a bit more my way. Now lad, turn over, just a quarter turn to your right, no, right I said, and there we are.'

I gripped the mattress hard with both hands and clenched my teeth, with the sweat pouring down my face.

'Now lad, there's no way of doing this gently,' said he.

'I've noticed.'

'Right then. Woman, let go of his leg, get his pillow, bring that chair nearer, and put the pillow on it. That's too near, a bit further back. Now lad, give me your hand, grip hard. Woman, go round the side of the bed next to the wall and get hold of him under the arms. That's very good. Comrade, is there anything left in that bottle?'

'No.'

'Come and take your wife's place and she can go and get another... Good, fill it right up... Woman, leave your husband where he is and come over here by me.'

The wife called one of her children again.

'Hell and damnation! I told you before, we don't need children for this. Kneel down and place one hand under his calf. You're trembling, woman, as if you've been up to no good. Come on, pull yourself together. Now place your left hand under his lower thigh, there, just above the bandage... Good!'

Then the outer stitches are cut, the bandages unwound, the dressing removed, and the wound exposed. The surgeon feels above it, below it, all round it, and every time he touches me he mutters: 'Ignoramus! dolt! clod! And he calls himself a surgeon! This isn't a

leg that needs cutting off. It'll last as long as the other one, I guarantee it.'

'Will I get better?'

'I've made lots of patients better.'

'Will I be able to walk?'

'You'll walk.'

'Will I limp?'

'Ah, now that's a different matter. God, lad, don't be so impatient.
Aren't you grateful to me for saving your leg? Anyway, if you do limp,
it won't be much. Fond of dancing, are you?'

'Very.'

'You may not walk quite as well, but you'll be a better dancer for it...
Woman, heat up some of that wine for the poultice... No, let's have the
other stuff first, just a wee glass, it'll help the bandages go on.'

He drinks. The hot wine is brought, my knee is bathed with it, the
dressing is reapplied, I'm put back to bed, told to sleep if I can, and my
bed-curtains are drawn. The opened bottle is polished off, another is
brought up, and the surgeon, the husband, and the wife start whispering again.

Husband. How long's all this going to take?

Surgeon. A long time... Your health!

Husband. How long exactly? A month?

Surgeon. A month! Make it two or three or four, who can tell? The
kneecap is chipped, the femur, the tibia... Your good health, my good
woman!

Husband. Four months! Mercy on us! Why did we take him in?
What the devil was she doing standing on the doorstep?

Surgeon. My very good health! I did a good job there.

Wife. Don't start all that again, husband. Last night you promised
you wouldn't. Just be patient, you'll get over it.

Husband. All right then, but you tell me what we're going to do with
him. As if it wasn't a bad year...

Wife. If you want, I'll go and see the priest.

Husband. If you go anywhere near him, I give you a damned good
hiding...

Surgeon. Whatever for? My wife goes to see him all the time.

Husband. That's our business.

Surgeon. I drink to the health of my goddaughter. How is she by the
way?

Wife. She's fine.

Surgeon. Raise your glass, comrade: to your wife and mine. They're both good women.

Husband. Yours is smarter than mine. She'd never have been so stupid as to...

Wife. There's always the Sisters of Charity.

Surgeon. Don't be daft, woman! You can't put a man in a nunnery! There's a small problem with that, though it's not as small as a finger... But let's drink a health to the nuns, fine women all.

Wife. What small problem?

Surgeon. Your husband won't let you go to the priest, and my wife won't let me go anywhere near the nuns... But what about another drink, comrade, maybe it'll give us an idea. Have you questioned the man? Perhaps he's got money.

Husband. What, a soldier have money?

Surgeon. A soldier has a father, a mother, brothers, sisters, relations, friends, he must have somebody... Let's have another drink. Now stand back and leave this to me.

Such, verbatim, was the conversation that took place between the surgeon, the husband, and the wife. But since I'm in total charge here, just think how different the mood would have been if I'd substituted a nasty character for one of these good people. If I'd done that, Jacques would have seen himself (or been seen by you) on the point of being manhandled out of bed, dumped on a road, or left in a ditch.

Why not killed?

No, not killed, I'd have sent for somebody to come to the rescue. That somebody would have been a soldier from his company— but that would have reeked with the stench of *Cleveland*.* Truth! truth!

But truth, you'll say, is usually cold, ordinary, and flat. For example, the account you've just given of the way Jacques's knee was bandaged may be true but is it interesting? It's not.

Agreed.

If a writer is to be true, then he's got to be cast in the mould of Molière, Regnard, Richardson, or Sedaine*—truth has its interesting side, which a writer will latch on to if he has genius.

If he has genius, I grant you. But what if he doesn't?

If a man doesn't have genius, then he shouldn't try to write.

But what if a man is unfortunate enough to be like a certain poet I once packed off to Pondicherry?*

What poet's that?

This poet... but look here, Reader, if you keep on interrupting me and I interrupt myself like this, what will become of the story of Jacques's loves? Take my advice and let's drop the poet. So, the husband and his wife stepped to one side...

No, no. Let's have the story of the poet from Pondicherry.

The surgeon crossed over to Jacques's bed...

Tell us the story of the poet from Pondicherry! Let's have the story of the poet from Pondicherry!

One day, a young man came to see me. Young men come to see me every day of the week... Look, Reader, what's he got to do with the travels of the fatalist Jacques and his Master?

Give us the story of the poet from Pondicherry!

After the usual polite, courteous comments about my intelligence, my genius, my taste, my benevolence, and other remarks which I never believe a word of, although people have been making them to me for twenty years, and quite sincerely for all I know, the young poet produces a sheet of paper from his pocket.

'These are some of my poems,' said he.

'Poems?'

'Yes, sir, and I was hoping you might be good enough to give me your opinion of them.'

'Do you like the truth?'

'Yes, sir, it's what I ask of you.'

'You shall have it.'

Just hold it there. You're not stupid enough to believe that a poet will come to you expecting the truth?

Yes.

And you'd give it him?

Certainly.

Straight from the shoulder?

Oh, yes. However kind your motives, dressing the truth up is always the crudest form of insult. When you think it through, it means: 'you are a rotten poet and, since I clearly don't believe you're man enough to stand the truth, you're also a pretty feeble specimen.'

And being frank has always worked?

Almost invariably... So I read the young man's poems right through. Then I said:

'Not only are these poems bad, they make it obvious to me that you'll never ever write any good ones.'

'Then I shall have to write bad ones, because I can't stop writing poems.'

'That's a terrible curse! Have you any idea, sir, what misery it will bring you? Neither the gods nor men nor critics have ever forgiven mediocrity in poets: Horace said that.'*

'I know.'

'Are you rich?'

'No.'

'Are you poor?'

'Very.'

'And you are determined to add the affliction of being poor to the ridiculous folly of being a bad poet? You'll waste the whole of your life and one day you'll be old. Old, poor, and a bad poet. Come, sir, that's nothing to be.'

'I can quite see all that, but I can't help myself.'

(At this point Jacques would have said: 'It was written up there, on high.')

'Have you any family?'

'I do.'

'How are they situated?'

'They're jewellers.'

'Would they be prepared to help?'

'Perhaps.'

'Well, then, go and see your parents and put it to them that they might set you up with a bagful of gems, then get on a ship and take yourself off to Pondicherry. You can write bad poems during the voyage. When you get there, you'll make a great deal of money. When you've made your fortune, you can come back and write all the bad poems you want, only don't give them to a publisher: you should never bring ruin on anyone.'

It was about twelve years after I gave the young man that advice that he turned up one day. I didn't recognize him.

'It's me, sir,' he said, 'the man you told to go to Pondicherry. I went and there I made a hundred thousand francs. Now I'm back and I've taken up writing poems again. I've brought some for you to see... Are they still bad?'

'As bad as ever. But you've made a decent provision for your future so I can't see why you shouldn't go on writing bad poems.'

'That's exactly what I intend to do.'

The surgeon crosses over to Jacques's bed. Jacques doesn't give him time to speak but says: 'I heard everything.'

Then turning to his Master, he added...

He was about to add but his Master stopped him. He was tired of walking and sat down by the side of the road, with his head to one side, watching a traveller approaching on foot, with the bridle of the horse he was leading looped round his arm.

Now, Reader, if you're thinking that this horse is the horse that was stolen from Jacques's Master you'd be wrong. That's how it would happen in a novel sooner or later, in this way or in another. But this isn't a novel, as I think I've already told you and now repeat. The Master said to Jacques: 'Do you see that man coming this way?'

Jacques. I see him.

Master. Looks like a good horse he's got there.

Jacques. I was in the infantry. I don't know anything about horses.

Master. I was an officer in the cavalry and I do.

Jacques. So?

Master. I want you to go and ask the man if he'd let us have the animal. We'll pay, of course.

Jacques. That's silly, but I'll go. How much do you want to pay?

Master. Up to a hundred crowns.

Telling his Master to take good care not to fall asleep, Jacques goes on ahead to meet the traveller, suggests buying his horse, pays for it, and leads it back.

'Well, Jacques,' said his Master, 'you have your presentiments but I too, as you see, have mine. It's a fine animal and no doubt the man swore there's absolutely nothing wrong with it. But when it comes to the matter of horses, all men are horse-traders.'

Jacques. In what matters are they not horse-traders?

Master. You ride it. I'll ride yours.

Jacques. Very well.

So now both of them are mounted again. Jacques adds:

Jacques. When I left home, my father, my mother, and my god-father each gave me something according to their modest means. I also had in reserve the five louis my older brother, Jean, gave me when he set out on his ill-fated journey to Lisbon.*

Here Jacques started to blub and his Master began telling him it had all been written on high.

Jacques. That's true, sir, and I've told myself that many, many times. Even so, I still can't help blubbing.

Whereupon Jacques starts sobbing and boo-hooing twice as hard and his Master takes a pinch of snuff and looks at his watch to see what time it is. Holding his horse's bridle in his teeth, Jacques wiped his eyes with both hands and then went on:

Jacques. With the five louis from Jean, the money I got for enlisting and what my parents and friends gave me, I'd put by a small stock of cash and hadn't touched a penny of it. So as things turned out, it was just as well I had my little savings to fall back on, wouldn't you say, sir?

Master. You couldn't have stayed much longer in that cottage.

Jacques. Not even if I paid.

Master. But why did your brother go to Lisbon?

Jacques. I've got the distinct impression that you're deliberately trying to stop me sticking to the point. If you keep asking questions, we'll have circled the entire globe before we get to the finish of the tale of my love-life.*

Master. What's it matter provided you go on talking and I go on listening? They are the two most important things, aren't they? Why criticize me when by rights you should be thanking me?

Jacques. My brother went to Lisbon to get away and find peace and quiet. Very clever was my brother Jean, and that was his downfall. He'd have been much better off being a dimwit like me. But it was written otherwise up there, on high. It was written that a Carmelite monk who came to the village once each season asking for eggs, wool, flax, fruits, wine for the monastery, would be put up in my father's house, that he would lead my brother Jean astray, and that my brother Jean would take his vows and become a monk.

Master. Your brother Jean was a Carmelite?

Jacques. Yes, sir, a discalced Carmelite.* He was energetic, intelligent, with a quibbling cast of mind: he was the village lawyer. He could read and write, and when he was still a boy spent his time deciphering and copying old parchments. He worked his way up through all the jobs of the order, starting as porter then moving on to cellarer, gardener, sacristan, assistant bursar, and treasurer. The way he was going, he'd have made all our fortunes. He provided the wherewithal for two of our sisters to get married—and good marriages they were—and a number of other girls in the village too. He couldn't walk down the street without fathers and mothers and children coming up to him or calling out: 'Good day to you, Frère Jean! How are you, Frère Jean?' When he went into a house, God's blessing entered with him, that's for sure, and if there was a daughter there without a husband, she'd be married two months after his visit. Poor Frère Jean! Ambition was his undoing.

The bursar of the monastery, whose assistant he'd been made, was old. The monks said afterwards that Frère Jean had got it into his head that he would succeed him when he died, and with this in mind he made a shambles of the deed-room, burned all the old ledgers, and concocted new ones to replace them, so that when the old bursar finally died, the devil himself wouldn't have been able to find his way through the mess he'd made of the community's papers. If anyone needed a document, he could waste a month looking for it, and even then it never materialized as often as not. In the end, the other brothers realized what Jean was up to and why. They took a grave view of it all and Frère Jean, instead of becoming bursar as he'd assumed, was put on bread and water and disciplined until he gave the index to his records to somebody else. Monks can be very unforgiving. When they'd got all the information they needed out of Frère Jean, they made him a hod-carrier in the distillery where they made their Eau des Carmes.* So Frère Jean, once treasurer of the Order and assistant bursar, was reduced to humping charcoal! Frère Jean had his pride and couldn't come to terms with his fall from power and splendour. He decided to take the first opportunity that came along to extricate himself from a situation which he found humiliating.

It was then that a young monk arrived in the monastery. He was considered to be the order's brightest star in both the confessional and the pulpit. His name was Père Ange.* He had lustrous eyes, a handsome face, and arms and hands to delight a sculptor. He began preaching, he gave confessions galore. The old priests were deserted in droves by the women in the congregation who flocked to Père Ange instead. Every evening before Sundays and feast days, Père Ange's confessional was besieged by penitents of both sexes while the older fathers were left to

kick their heels in their empty booths, which made them very cross...
But it would be less depressing, sir, if I abandon the story of Frère Jean
and took up the story of my love-life again.

Master. No, no. I'll just have a pinch of snuff and a look at what time
it is, and then you can carry on.

Jacques. Oh very well, if that's what you want.

But Jacques's horse had other ideas. All at once, it gets the bit between its teeth and jumps into a ditch. Jacques grips hard with his
knees and yanks the reins, but to no avail. The stubborn animal scram-
bles up from the bottom of the ditch and starts climbing for dear life up
a hillock where it comes to a dead stop. Jacques looks round him and
finds himself under a gibbet.

Now another author, Reader, would not pass up the opportunity to
have a corpse hanging from the gibbet and make Jacques recoil with a
grief-stricken shock of recognition. If I said that's how it happened,
you might believe me, for stranger things can happen, though that
wouldn't make it any truer. The gibbet was in fact untenanted.

Jacques waited for the horse to stop blowing. It then came back
down the hillock of its own accord, scrambled back across the ditch,
and deposited him at the side of his Master who said: 'Jacques, you
gave me an awful fright! I thought you'd get killed... But you're not listening. What are you thinking?'

Jacques. About what I saw up there.

Master. And what did you see?

Jacques. A gibbet. Gallows.

Master. Damn! It's a bad omen. But remember your philosophy: if
it's written on high, then whatever avoiding action you take, you'll still
be hanged, my lad. And if it isn't written on high, then your horse is a
liar. That animal may not be inspired but it's liable to get ideas of its
own. I'd be careful if I were you.

After a moment's silence, Jacques rubbed his brow and shook his
head, as a man does when trying to chase away unpleasant thoughts,
and then suddenly resumed his tale:

Jacques. The older monks got together and decided, whatever the
cost and by whatever means it would take, to get rid of the young up-
start who was humiliating them. Do you know what they did?... Sir,
you're not listening.

Master. No, no, I'm listening. Carry on.

Jacques. They bribed the porter, who was an old rogue like themselves. The old rogue accused the young monk of taking liberties with one of his women penitents in the monastery parlour, and swore on his oath that he'd seen him at it. Perhaps it was true, maybe it wasn't, who can say? But the funny thing was that the day after the accusation was made, formal proceedings were begun against the prior by a surgeon who had not been paid for medicines he had supplied and visits he had made while treating the said villainous porter for a dose of the clap... Sir, you're not listening and I know what it is you've got your mind on. I bet it's that gibbet.

Master. I can't deny it.

Jacques. I look up and I find you staring at me. Do you think I look sinister?

Master. No, no.

Jacques. That means yes, yes. Well, if I scare you, we'd best go our separate ways.

Master. Don't be silly, Jacques, you're not thinking straight. Aren't you sure of yourself?

Jacques. No, sir, I am not. Who is sure of himself?

Master. Every upright man. Are you saying, Jacques, good, honest Jacques, that back there a moment ago the idea of crime didn't scare the wits out of you? But come, Jacques, let's drop this discussion. Get back to your story.

Jacques. As a result of the libel or slander put about by the porter, all and sundry felt they were entitled to do all sorts of wicked, nasty things to poor Père Ange, who started to break under the strain. At this point, they called in a doctor who they bribed. He certified that he was mad and said it would do him good to go away and fill his lungs with the air of his native heath. If it had been mooted that he be simply sent away or locked up, it could have been managed quite easily. But among the pious females who thought the sun shone out of him, there were several great ladies who needed to be handled carefully. They were told all about their confessor in tones of hypocritical concern.

'Alas! poor Père Ange! He was the leading light of our community!'

'Why, what's happened to him?'

This question met with a deep sigh and eyes raised to Heaven. If further questions were asked, they were answered by lowered eyes and silence. To this playacting was sometimes added: 'O God! Woe are we!... He still has lucid moments... flashes of genius... He may get over it, but there's not much hope... What a loss to the faith!'

Meanwhile, the harsh treatment got worse. They tried everything to bring Père Ange to the state it was claimed he was in, and it would have worked too if Frère Jean hadn't felt sorry for him. What else can I say? One night, we were all fast asleep. We hear a knock at the door. We get up and in walk Père Ange and my brother, both in disguise. They spent the following day in our house and the next, at first light, they decamped. They went with their pockets well lined, for as he embraced me Jean said: 'I've married off all your sisters. If I'd stayed in the monastery for another couple of years, the way I was going, you'd have ended up one of the biggest farmers round about. But that's all finished now, I've done all I could for you. Goodbye, Jacques. If things turn out well for Père Ange and me, you'll know it.'

Then he slipped into my hand the five louis I told you about, plus another five for the latest village girl he had found a husband for. She'd just had a chubby boy who resembled Frère Jean to a T.

Master [*with his snuffbox open and his watch back in his pocket*]. Why did they go to Lisbon?

Jacques. To be there for the earthquake* which couldn't happen without them. They went to get crushed, buried, and burned, as was written on high.

Master. Ah, that's monks for you!

Jacques. Who'd give tuppence for the best of them?

Master. Don't talk to me about monks.

Jacques. Have you had dealings with them too?

Master. I'll tell you all about it some other time.

Jacques. But why are monks so obnoxious?

Master. I think it's because they're monks... Anyway, let's get back to your loves.

Jacques. No, sir, let's not.

Master. Don't you want me to know all about them any more?

Jacques. Of course, but destiny doesn't. Haven't you noticed that the minute I open my mouth, the devil starts meddling and something always comes up that cuts me short? I'll never finish the story, I tell you, it's written on high.

Master. Try all the same.

Jacques. But if you were to start the story of your love-life, perhaps that would break the spell and then mine would move along more quickly. I've got a notion that the one depends on the other. You see, sir, I sometimes get a feeling that destiny's talking to me.

Master. And do you always think it's a good idea to listen?

Jacques. Of course. Remember the day it whispered to me that your watch was in the pack on the pedlar's back?

The Master started to yawn, and as he yawned he gave his snuffbox a tap with one hand, and as he tapped his snuffbox he looked into the distance, and as he looked into the distance, he said to Jacques: 'Can you make out something over there, on your left?'

Jacques. Yes, and I'll wager it's something that doesn't want me to continue with my story nor you to begin yours.

Jacques was right. Since whatever it was they could see was coming towards them and they were going towards it, the fact that both were advancing towards each other from opposite directions abridged the distance between them. Soon they saw a coach draped in black drawn by four black horses swathed in black cloths which covered their heads and reached down to their hooves. Behind them walked two servants in black and the rear was brought up by two others, also dressed in black, each riding a black horse caparisoned in black. In the driving seat was a black-clad driver, with a hat pulled well down and, wrapped round it, a long crêpe that hung over his left shoulder. The driver's head was hunched forward, he held the reins slackly so that he seemed less to be leading his horses than being led by them.

Our two travellers have now drawn level with the hearse. Immediately Jacques gives a shriek, falls rather than dismounts from his horse, tears his hair, and rolls on the ground, shouting: 'It's my Captain! my poor Captain! it's him! there's no mistake! that's his coat of arms on the door!'

For inside the hearse there was a long coffin, and over it was draped funeral cloth, and on the funeral cloth lay a sword and a sash, and at the side of the coffin walked a priest, intoning from a prayer-book which he held in his hand. The hearse continued on its way. Jacques followed it weeping and wailing, the Master followed Jacques cursing, and the servants confirmed to Jacques that this was indeed the funeral cortège of his Captain who had died in the neighbouring town, whence his remains were being conveyed to the resting-place of his ancestors. The Captain, since being deprived by the death of another soldier, a friend of his who was also a captain in the same regiment, of the satisfaction of fighting a duel with him at least once a week, had gone into a melancholy decline which had killed him in a matter of months.

Jacques paid his Captain his due tribute of praise, regrets, and tears. Then he apologized to his Master, got back on his horse, and they went on their way in silence.

But for God's sake, Mr Storyteller, you ask, where were they going?

And I answer: for God's sake, Reader, does any of us know where we're going? Where are you going? Do I have to remind you what happened to Aesop? His master, Xanthippus,* said to him one evening in summer, or maybe winter, for Greeks bathed all year round: 'Aesop, go down to the baths and if there aren't too many people there, we shall bathe.'

Off Aesop trots. On the way, he is stopped by the Athenian street patrol.

'Where do you think you're going?'

'Where am I going?' replies Aesop, 'I really have no idea.'

'You don't know? Then it's jail for you.'

'There!' said Aesop. 'I was right when I said I didn't know where I was going. I wanted to go to the baths and here I am on my way to jail.'

Jacques followed his master as you follow yours. His Master followed his master just as Jacques was following him.

But who was Jacques's Master's master?

Come, come. Is any of us short of a master in this world? Jacques's Master had a hundred masters if he had one, just as you do. But among the many masters of Jacques's Master, there couldn't have been a single master who was any good, since he kept changing them every day.

That's because he was human.

Human and passionate, like you, Reader. Human and curious, like you, Reader. Human and always asking questions, like you, Reader. Human and a damned nuisance, just like you, Reader.

And why did he ask questions?

Good question! He asked questions to learn and to quibble, like you, Reader.

The Master said to Jacques: You don't seem in the mood to resume the story of your love-life.

Jacques. My poor Captain! He's going now where we are all headed, though it's amazing he hasn't got there long before this. Oh! Ah!

Master. Why, Jacques, I do believe you're crying. Let your tears flow freely, because now you may shed them without shame. His death releases you from the strict proprieties which constrained you while he was alive. You no longer have the same reasons for withholding your grief as you then had for concealing your felicity. No one will seek to put upon your tears the same interpretation which might have been put on your happiness. Everything is forgiven those who grieve. Moreover, at this time, we are perforce revealed as either caring or unforgiving and, all things considered, it is better to stand accused of human frailty than to be suspected of indifference. I would rather your sorrow were freely expressed, for then it would be less anguished. I would have it extreme, for then it would have a shorter term. Remember, and with increase, what he was: the acuteness with which he plumbed the deepest questions, the subtlety he brought to the discussion of the most delicate issues, his solid sense of the true priorities which ensured he kept his mind fixed firmly on the most important problems, the generous light he threw on the most arid subjects, the supreme art he deployed as the champion of those who stood accused: his humanity gave him quicker wits than self-interest or egoism ever gave the guilty, and he was hard only on himself. Far from trying to excuse the trifling faults he committed, he was more intent than his worst enemy on magnifying them, and was keener than an envious rival to cast doubt on his own virtues by subjecting them to a rigorous analysis of the motives which might have unwittingly prompted them. Set no limit on your grief other than that which healing time alone prescribes. Let us submit to the universal law of things when we lose a friend, as we in turn shall submit when it is pleased to deal with us. Let us accept, unsorrowing, the sentence which fate pronounces on them, as we shall accept unresistingly the decree which it will issue against us. The duties of friends do not cease with the rites of burial. The earth which is still fresh at this moment will settle over the ashes of the man you loved so tenderly, but your heart will keep his memory alive.

Jacques. Sir, that's very fine, but what's it got to do with anything? I've lost my Captain, I'm grief-stricken and you come out, like a parrot, with a slice of funeral oration written by some man or other, or maybe by a woman to another woman who has just lost the man she loved.

Master. Actually, I think it was written by a woman.

Jacques. And I think a man wrote it. But whether it was a woman or a man, I repeat: what the devil's it got to do with anything? Do you think I was my Captain's mistress? My Captain, sir, was a fine, upstanding man and I have always been as straight as a die.

Master. But Jacques, who's arguing with you?

Jacques. In that case, what did you mean by declaiming consoling words spoken by some man to another man, or by one woman to another woman? If I keep asking, perhaps you'll tell me.

Master. No, Jacques, you'll have to work it out for yourself.

Jacques. I could spend the rest of my life trying and I still wouldn't guess—it would take me until the Day of Judgement.

Master. Jacques, I had the impression that you were listening carefully while I was speaking.

Jacques. Just because something is absurd doesn't mean we shouldn't pay attention.

Master. That's true, Jacques.

Jacques. I almost burst at the bit about the 'strict proprieties' which constrained me as long as my Captain was alive and from which I was released by his death.

Master. Excellent, Jacques. I have achieved what I set out to do. Tell me, was there a more effective way of consoling you? You were crying. Now, if I'd got you to talk about the person for whom you were grieving, what would have happened? You'd have blubbed a great deal more and I'd only have added to your misery. I sidetracked you twice: first, with my ludicrous funeral oration, and secondly, with the little argument that followed. Come now, admit that the thought of your Captain is now as far away as the hearse taking him to his final resting-place. Consequently, I think you could resume the story of your loves.

Jacques. I think I could too. 'Doctor,' said I to the surgeon, 'do you live far from here?'

'A good mile at least.'

'A decent-sized house, is it?'

'Fairly decent.'

'Have you got a room to spare?'

'No.'

'What? Not even if I paid, and paid well?'

'Oh, if you paid and paid well? That puts a different complexion on it, lad. But you don't look to me as if you could pay, let alone pay well.'

'That's my business. And would I be well looked after in your house?'

'Very. My wife's been nursing the sick all her life, and my eldest daughter keeps all comers in line and can change a dressing as well as I can myself.'

'How much would you want for bed, board, and care?'

The surgeon scratched an ear then said: 'For bed... board... care... But who'll be responsible for paying me?'

'I'll pay every day.'

'Now you're talking...'

Sir, I don't think you're listening.

Master. No, I wasn't, Jacques. It was written on high that on this occasion, and it may not be the last, you'd talk and no one would listen.

Jacques. If a man doesn't listen when another person is talking, then either he's not thinking anything at all or else he's thinking about something which isn't the same as the thing the other person is saying. Which were you doing?

Master. The second. I was thinking about what one of the servants in black riding behind the hearse was telling you, that the death of your Captain's friend had deprived him of the pleasure of fighting a duel at least once a week. Did you make anything of that?

Jacques. Of course.

Master. To me it's a puzzle, and I'd be obliged if you'd explain it.

Jacques. But what the devil is it to you?

Master. Not much, but when you talk it seems you want people to listen, no?

Jacques. That goes without saying.

Master. Well, in all honesty, I won't be able to pay attention as long as that incomprehensible statement keeps buzzing round inside my head. Please, put me out of my misery.

Jacques. Very well. But you must at least swear that you won't interrupt any more.

Master. No interrupting, I swear.

Jacques. Well this was the way of it. My Captain, a good man, a man of honour, a man of merit, one of the ablest officers in his regiment, but eccentric and unpredictable, had met and become friends with another officer in the same regiment, who was also a good man, a man of honour, a man of merit, as able a soldier as he and just as eccentric and unpredictable.

Jacques was about to begin the story of his Captain when they heard a large body of men and horses coming up behind them. It was the same gloomy hearse coming back the way it had gone. It was escorted by...

Excise men?

No.

Mounted constables?

Possibly. But whoever they were, the cortège was preceded by the priest in cassock and surplice who had his hands tied behind his back, the black-clad driver, with his hands tied behind his back, and the two servants in black, also with their hands tied behind their backs. Who was the most surprised by this? Answer: Jacques, who cried: 'My Captain! My poor Captain isn't dead! God be praised!' Whereupon he turns his horse, gives it both spurs, and gallops back to meet the supposed funeral procession. He had got to within thirty paces of it when the Excise men, or possibly the mounted constables, fix him in their sights and shout: 'Stop! Go back the way you came, or you're dead!' Jacques pulled up short and paused to listen to what Destiny was saying in his head. He thought he could hear Destiny say: 'Go back the way you came,' which was what he did. His Master said: 'Well, Jacques? What is it?'

Jacques. I've really no idea.

Master. Why not?

Jacques. I don't know that either.

Master. You'll see, those men will turn out to be smugglers who filled the coffin with contraband. They've been betrayed to the Excise by the same rogues they bought the goods from.

Jacques. But how come they used this coach with my Captain's coat of arms on it?

Master. Or perhaps it's a kidnapping. They've hidden a body in the coffin, who knows, a woman, a girl, a nun. Just because there's a shroud doesn't mean there's a corpse.

Jacques. But why the coach with my Captain's coat of arms on it?

Master. You can explain it whichever way you like, but do finish the tale of your Captain.

Jacques. You still want to know the tale? But maybe my Captain's still alive.

Master. What's that got to do with it?

Jacques. I don't like talking about living persons because now and then you are made to blush for the good things and the bad things you've said about them—for the good they go and spoil and for the bad which they make up for.

Master. Avoid empty eulogies and don't be bitter and censorious. Just tell it the way it is.

Jacques. That's not easy. A storyteller has a personality, a point of view, standards, and passions which lead him to exaggerate or understate. Just tell it the way it is, indeed! That's something that probably doesn't even happen twice in one day in any large city. Besides, is the listener any more impartial than the speaker? No. Which accounts for the fact that in a large city it scarcely happens twice in any day that people really hear what is being said to them.

Master. Hell's teeth, Jacques, with such notions as those you might as well ban the use of tongues and ears altogether and stop people saying anything, hearing anything, and believing anything. In the meantime, just be yourself and speak as you find. And I'll be me and listen ditto.

Jacques. But if there's hardly anything we say that's heard the way it's intended, there's far worse: it follows that there's hardly anything we do that is judged by what we had in mind when we did it.

Master. I doubt if there's another head beneath the vast canopy of heaven that's stuffed as full of paradoxical notions as yours.

Jacques. Where's the harm? Paradoxical isn't necessarily the same as false.

Master. True.

Jacques. My Captain and I were passing through Orléans. All the talk of the town was of something that had just happened to a Monsieur Le Pelletier,* a good citizen fired with such charitable zeal for the poor that having, as a result of extravagant alms-giving, reduced his own very considerable fortune to less than a modest competency, he next proceeded to knock on doors seeking in other people's pockets the donations which he could no longer find in his own.

Master. And do you think there were two ways of looking at this man's behaviour?

Jacques. No, not among the poor. But nearly all the rich people without exception thought he was mad, and matters almost reached the stage where his relatives tried to have him stopped for dilapidating the family fortune. While we were partaking of refreshment at an inn, a crowd of idlers collected around a man who liked the sound of his own voice—he was the local barber—and were saying: 'You were there, tell us how it happened.'

'Willingly,' said the resident oracle, who never passed up the chance of holding forth in public. 'One of my customers, Monsieur Aubertot, whose house is just opposite the chapel of the Capuchins, was standing outside his front door. Monsieur Le Pelletier goes up to him and says: "Monsieur Aubertot, will you give me a little something for my friends?" Friends is what he called the poor, as you know.

' "No, Monsieur Le Pelletier, not today."

'Monsieur Le Pelletier pressed him: "If only you knew the person on whose behalf I ask you to be generous! A poor woman who has just been brought to bed and does not have a rag to wrap the child in."

' "I can't help."

' "Or there's a girl, young and pretty, who can't find work and wants for bread. Your liberality could well save her from a disorderly life."

' "I can't help."

' "Or a workman who lived by selling his labour. He's just fallen off some scaffolding and broken a leg."

' "I can't help, I tell you."

' "Come now, Monsieur Aubertot, show some compassion—you'll never have another opportunity to commit a more commendable action."

' "I can't help and I won't help."

' "Good Monsieur Aubertot! Kind Monsieur Aubertot!"

' "Monsieur Le Pelletier, please leave me alone. When I want to help, I'll not need to be asked."

'And so saying, Monsieur Aubertot turns his back on him, goes through his door, and into his shop where Monsieur Le Pelletier follows him. He follows him from the front of the shop into the back of the shop, from the back of his shop into his private quarters. There, Monsieur Aubertot, losing patience with the repeated demands of Monsieur Le Pelletier, slaps his face.'

At this point, my Captain suddenly gets to his feet and asks the oracle: 'And he didn't kill him?'

'No, sir. Do people go round killing each other like that?'

'But he slapped his face, by God! Slapped his face! So what did he do?'

'What did he do after getting his face slapped? He put a twinkle in his eye and said to Monsieur Aubertot: "That was for me. Now what do my friends get?"'

When they heard this, all present expressed their admiration with the exception of my Captain, who said to them: 'This Monsieur Le Pelletier of yours, gentlemen, is a shameless poltroon, a coward, a chicken-hearted wretch. Even so, his honour would have been defended by my sword if I'd been there, and your Monsieur Aubertot would have been lucky to come out of it minus his nose and both ears.'

The barber said: 'I see, sir, that you wouldn't have given the man who committed the offence sufficient time to acknowledge that he was in the wrong, throw himself at Monsieur Le Pelletier's feet, and offer him his purse...'

'Certainly not!'

'You're a soldier and Monsieur Le Pelletier is a Christian man. You both have different views about slaps on the cheek.'

'The cheeks of all men of honour are the same cheek.'

'That's not quite the view taken in the gospel.'

'The gospel is in my heart and my scabbard. I know no other.'

Jacques. I don't know where your gospel is, sir, but mine is written on high. Each one of us takes insults and blessings in our own way. And it's more than likely that we don't even judge these things the same way at two different moments of our lives.

Master. So? What of it, you garrulous oaf!

Whenever Jacques's Master lost his temper, Jacques would shut up, start musing, and would often not break his silence until he came out with a remark linked to what was going on in his head but entirely unconnected with what they had been talking about before—rather like reading a book when you've skipped a few pages. This is precisely what happened now when he said: 'You see, sir...'

Master. Ah! you've recovered the faculty of speech at last. I'm delighted for both our sakes. I was beginning to get as bored with not hearing you speak as you were with not speaking. So fire away.

Jacques. You see, sir, life is a series of misunderstandings. There are the misunderstandings of love, the misunderstandings of friendship, misunderstandings in politics, money matters, the Church, the bench, business, wives, husbands...

Master. Oh, just forget your misunderstandings and try to see that you'll be committing a crude blunder yourself if you now launch into a moral disquisition when what we're dealing with is a matter of historical fact only. Now, what about the story of your Captain?

Jacques was about to begin the story of his Captain when for the second time his horse suddenly veered to the right, left the road, whisked him off across a long, level plain, and a good mile later, stopped abruptly under a gibbet...

Under a gibbet? Depositing its rider under gibbets is an odd way for a horse to behave.

'What can this mean?' said Jacques. 'Is Destiny trying to tell me something?'

Master. No doubt about it, Jacques. Your horse has obviously got second sight. But what's frustrating about all prognostications, visions, and warnings from on high that come via dreams and apparitions, is that they are completely useless, for they won't prevent what's going to happen from happening. I advise you to make peace with your conscience, Jacques, settle your affairs, and fire away as quick as you like with the story of your Captain and the tale of your love-life. I'd be sorry to lose you before I heard them all the way through. And even if you were more worried than you are, what good would it do? None at all. What fate has decreed, as spelled out twice by your horse, will be accomplished. Look, do you have restitution of any sort you should make to anybody? Entrust me with your last wishes and rest assured that I'll see they're carried out to the letter. If you've stolen anything from me, I give it to you, only ask God for forgiveness and in the time we have left together, which may be long or short, don't steal anything else.

Jacques. It's no good. I look back over my past and I can't see anything it in that would interest human justice. I've never killed nor stolen nor ravished.

Master. That's too bad. Taking the broad view, I'd sooner your crime was already in the bag than still to be committed, for obvious reasons.

Jacques. But sir, maybe I'll be hanged not for anything I've done but for something somebody else has done.

Master. It's possible.

Jacques. Maybe I won't be hanged till after I'm dead.

Master. That too is possible.

Jacques. Maybe I won't be hanged at all.

Master. Unlikely.

Jacques. Maybe it's written on high that I'll just be there when another man is hanged, and who knows, sir, where that man is now, whether he's somewhere hereabouts or far away?

Master. Listen, Jacques, just settle your mind to being hanged, since fate has decreed it and your horse says so, but don't be impertinent. Let's have no more of your infernal speculations. Just get on with the story of your Captain and be quick about it.

Jacques. Don't lose your temper, sir. There's many an honest man who's been hanged—it's one of the misunderstandings of the legal trade.

Master. All these misunderstandings are highly irritating. Let's talk about something else.

Jacques, somewhat reassured by the different ways he had found of interpreting his horse's prediction, said:

'When I joined the regiment, there were two officers more or less equal in age, birth, seniority, and merit. My Captain was one of them. The only difference between them was that one was rich and the other wasn't. My Captain was the rich one. Their affinity was bound to give rise either to close friendship or the strongest antipathy. In the event, it gave rise to both.'

Here, Jacques paused, as he would again on several occasions during the course of his narration every time his horse's head swivelled to the right or to the left. So, picking up where he had left off, he repeated his last sentence, as if he had hiccups.

Jacques. In the event, it gave rise to both. There were some days when they were the best of friends, and others when they were deadly enemies. On days when they were friends, they sought each other out, greeted each other with open arms, embraced, shared their troubles, their pleasures, their needs. They took each other's advice on their most private affairs, family matters, their hopes, fears, and plans for promotion. But when they met the next day, they would look each other haughtily in the eye, call each other Sir, make flinty remarks, reach for their swords, and fight. If one of them was wounded, the other would rush to his friend's side, shed hot tears, beat his breast despairingly, go with him to his quarters, and remain at his bedside until he was fully recovered. A week, two weeks, a month later, it would start all over again, and then you'd have the sight of two good men... yes two

excellent men, two loyal friends, each liable to be killed by the other—
and the one who died would not be the more to be pitied of the pair.

They had been warned several times that their behaviour was
bizarre. I myself, having my Captain's permission to speak freely, said
more than once: 'But sir, what if you killed him?' At this, he would
begin to sob, cover his eyes with both hands, and run around his room
like a mad thing. Yet two hours later, either his friend would bring him
back bleeding or he would do the same for his friend.

But neither my remonstrations... neither my remonstrations nor
the remonstrations of other people had the least effect. There was only
one thing for it: they had to be kept apart. The War Minister was informed of their singular determination to persist in oscillating wildly
between these two extreme and opposite poles. My Captain was made
adjutant in a garrison elsewhere, told to take up his duties with immediate effect, and was expressly ordered never to leave his post. A
separate order restricted his friend to company barracks... Damn, this
blasted horse will drive me mad!... The orders had no sooner arrived
from the Minister when my Captain, saying he merely wished to show
his gratitude for the favour he'd been shown, galloped off to court, said
that he was rich and that his friend, who was poor, was equally deserving of His Majesty's indulgence. He said the posting he had just been
given would be a fitting reward for his friend's loyal service, that it
would make good his want of fortune, and that he himself would be
only too happy if this were done. Since the Minister had no intention
other than to keep these two bizarre men apart, and because generous
actions invariably strike a responsive chord, it was decided... Damn
the beast! Keep your head straight, will you?... it was decided that my
Captain would stay with the regiment and his friend would take up his
command elsewhere.

The moment they were separated, each realized how much he was
going to miss the other. Both fell into a state of profound melancholia.
My Captain applied for six months' leave so that he might return to fill
his lungs with the good air of home. But when he's ten miles or so from
his barracks, he sells his horse, disguises himself as a peasant, and
heads for the garrison where his friend had been posted. It seems to
have been a move they'd planned together. He arrives... Oh, go on,
have your head, then! Is there another gibbet round here you've taken
a fancy to? Go on, sir, laugh away. Oh yes, very funny I'm sure!... he arrives. But it was written on high that for all the precautions they took

to conceal the delight they felt when they saw each other again, and despite the care they took to ensure that the one approached the other with a visible display of the deference a peasant shows an adjutant, it was written that a group of soldiers and a handful of officers would happen to be there when they met who knew all about their goings-on, would become suspicious, and report what they'd seen to their commanding officer.

The garrison Commander, a prudent man, smiled when he was told what was afoot. Nevertheless, he did not leave the matter there but treated it with all the seriousness it warranted. He set men to spy on the adjutant. First reports said that he rarely left his quarters and that the peasant never went out at all. Now, it was impossible for the two of them to stay cooped up together for a week without their odd behaviour reasserting itself. Which is exactly what happened.

I hope, Reader, you're noticing how considerate I'm being? Had I a mind to, I could easily order a touch of the whip to be laid on the backs of the horses drawing the black-hung hearse, show Jacques, his Master, the Excise men (or mounted constables), and the rest of the cortège assembled outside the nearest stopping-place, interrupt the story of Jacques's Captain, and keep you dangling for as long as I liked. But to do that, I should have to lie, and I don't like lying, unless it's useful or I have my back against a wall. The fact is that Jacques and his Master never saw the black-clad hearse again and that Jacques, still worrying about the way his horse was behaving, carried on with his tale:

Jacques. One day, spies reported to the Commander that there had been a violent argument between the adjutant and the peasant. They had then both gone out, the peasant leading off and the officer following very reluctantly, and both had gone into the office of a banker in town. They were still there.

It later emerged that, giving up all hope of ever seeing each other again, they had decided to fight a duel to the death. Highly conscious of the obligations of true friendship, even at his most unspeakably ferocious, my Captain, who was a rich man as I've mentioned... I sincerely hope, sir, you're not going to make me travel the rest of the way on a horse that's mad... my Captain, who was rich, had insisted that his friend should accept a bill of exchange for 24,000 livres which would provide him with the wherewithal to live abroad if he got killed, declaring that he wouldn't fight unless this was agreed first. To this offer, his comrade had replied: 'And do you think, old friend, that if I kill you I shall survive you for long?'

They left the banker's and were heading for the gates of the town when they were suddenly surrounded by the Commander and several officers. Though it looked like a chance meeting, both friends—or enemies, whichever you prefer—were not taken in. The peasant said who he was. They spent that night in an isolated house. Next day, at first light, my Captain embraced his friend several times, left, and never saw him again. Within days of reaching his native heath, he was dead.

Master. And who told you he was dead?

Jacques. What about the coffin? And the hearse with his coat of arms on the door? My poor Captain is dead, of that I am certain.

Master. But what about the priest, with his hands tied behind his back? What about the servants, also with their hands tied behind their backs? And the Excise men, or possibly the mounted constables? And the about-turn which brought the cortège heading back towards the town? No, your Captain is alive, of that I am certain. But do you have any information about his friend?

Jacques. The story of his friend has a line all to itself in the great scroll, in other words in what is written on high.

Master. I hope...

Jacques's horse did not give the Master time to finish. It shot off like lightning, veering neither right nor left, but careered straight down the road. Soon Jacques was out of sight and his Master, assuming that his headlong course would end at a gibbet, laughed until his ribs ached.

Now, Reader, since Jacques and his Master are no good on their own and very poor value when separated—like Don Quixote without Sancho, or Richardet without Ferragus, which is something that neither the continuator of Cervantes nor the imitator of Ariosto, Monsignor Forti-Guerra, ever understood properly*—let's chat among ourselves until they are back together again.

If you're thinking that the story of Jacques's Captain is made up, you're wrong.* I here declare that the tale Jacques has just spun for his Master was the story I heard at the Invalides in I forget which year, though it was on the feast of Saint Louis* and I was dining with a Monsieur de Saint-Étienne, who was then in charge.* The story was told, in the presence of several other resident officers who knew the facts, by a sober-sided man who did not give the least impression of being a wag. So I repeat, both on this occasion and for the future: be circumspect if you wish to avoid, in the conversations that take place between Jacques and his Master, accepting as true what is false and rejecting as false what is true. You can't say you haven't been warned, and I wash my hands of the matter.

But, you'll say, they are such an unusual pair!

Is that what's making you suspicious? Let me say in the first place that nature is so varied, especially in the area of human instinct and character, that there's no oddity dreamed up by the imagination of writers for which experience and observation cannot provide a real-life model. I myself have met the real-life counterpart of *Le Médecin malgré lui*, which I had previously regarded as the most extravagant and farcical of fabrications.

You mean the counterpart of the man whose wife says to him: 'I've got three children on my hands' and he says 'So? Put them on the floor, then.' 'But they keep asking for bread.' 'So give them a taste of the whip'?*

The very same. Here's how he spoke to my wife:

'Is that you, Monsieur Gousse?'*

'Well, it's not anybody else.'

'Where have you come from?'

'Back from where I've just been.'

'And what did you do when you were there?'

'I mended a windmill that wasn't working properly.'

'Who's mill was it?'

'No idea. I wasn't there to mend the miller.'

'You're looking very smart. That's not like you. But why are you wearing a dirty shirt under that clean coat?'

'I only have the one.'

'And why have you only got one shirt?'

'Because I've only got one body at a time.'

'My husband isn't in, but there's no reason why you shouldn't stay to dinner.'

'There is: I haven't said he could take charge of my stomach, nor my appetite neither.'

'Is your wife well?'

'As well as she wants to be. That's her business.'

'And the children?'

'Getting on famously.'

'And your little boy, with the beautiful eyes and chubby cheeks and such lovely smooth skin?'

'He's doing much better than the others. He's dead.'

'What are you teaching them?'

'Nothing, Madame.'

'What? Not reading or writing or the catechism?'

'No reading, no writing, no catechism.'

'Why is that?'

'Because no one ever taught me anything and I'm not any the more ignorant for it. If they're clever, they'll do what I did. If they're stupid, then whatever I taught them would only make them even more stupid...'

If you ever come across this peculiar specimen, you don't need to have been introduced to strike up an acquaintance with him. Just take him into a tavern, tell him what job you need doing, ask him to travel a hundred miles with you, and he'll go. Then when he's finished the job send him packing without offering him a penny, and he'll trot off as happy as a sandboy.

Did you ever hear of a man named Prémontval who used to give public mathematics lessons in Paris? He was a friend of his... But maybe Jacques and his Master have met up again: do you want to go back to them or stay with me?...

Gousse and Prémontval ran the school between them. Among the pupils who turned up in large numbers was a young woman, a Mademoiselle Pigeon, the daughter of the very clever mathematician who designed the two very fine planispheres which were transferred from the Jardin du Roi to the galleries of the Academy of Sciences.* Mademoiselle Pigeon went every day with her portfolio under her arm and her case of mathematical instruments in her muff. One of the teachers, Prémontval, fell in love with his pupil and in the midst of propositions concerning solid bodies inscribed within a sphere, a child was conceived. Now old Pigeon was not the sort of man to sit back and wait for the corollary of this truth to appear. The couple's situation became embarrassing. They talked about what they should do. But having no money, not a penny, what could be the outcome of their discussions? They turned to their friend Gousse for help. He, without hesitating, sold everything he owned, linen, suits, instruments, furniture, books, got a sum of money together, bundled the two love-birds into a carriage, and accompanied them at a gallop as far as the Alps. There, he emptied his purse of what little remained in it, gave it to them, hugged them both, wished them good speed, and then set out on the return journey on foot, surviving on charity as far as Lyons, where he earned enough money from painting the walls of a monastery cloister to get him back to Paris without having to beg.

That's admirable.

Yes it is. And I suppose that having witnessed this act of heroic selflessness you're now thinking that Gousse was liberally supplied with moral virtue? Well, you can think again. There was no more moral virtue in him than in the brain of a pike.

It's not possible.

Oh yes it is. I found something for him to do for me. I gave him a note for eighty livres to be drawn against my account. The sum was written in figures. What does he do? He adds a nought and pays himself eight hundred.

That's terrible!

He's no more dishonest when he robs me than honest when he robs himself to give to a friend. He's an odd bird and has absolutely no principles. The eighty francs weren't enough for him, so with a stroke of the pen he got his hands on the eight hundred he needed. And what about the rare books he's given me for nothing?

What books might they...?

But what about Jacques and his Master? What about Jacques's love-life? Ah, Reader, your patience in listening to me only shows how little interest you take in my two characters. I've half a mind to leave them where they are.

I needed a rare book. He brings it to me. Soon after, I needed another rare book: he brings that too. I try to pay him but he won't take the money. Then I needed a third rare tome.

'You can't have it,' said he, 'you should have asked earlier. The book-worm I knew in the Sorbonne has upped and died.'

'And what has the death of a Sorbonne scholar to do with the book I want? Did you just take the other two from his library?'

'Of course.'

'Without his permission?'

'Oh, I didn't need it for a spot of justified redistribution. All I did was to find a better home for the books by transferring them from one place where they served no purpose at all to another where someone would make use of them.'

After that, I challenge you to come to any conclusion about the way people behave. But the best is the story of Gousse and his wife...

All right, I hear you. You've had enough, and your view is that we should rejoin our two travellers. Reader, you treat me as if I were a machine, which is not very polite. 'Tell the story of Jacques's love-life.' 'Don't tell the story of Jacques's love-life.' 'I want you to tell me about Gousse.' 'That's enough of him'... I quite see that I must follow your whims sometimes, but I must also follow mine—not forgetting that any listener who allows me to start a story commits himself to hearing the end of it.

A while back I said 'in the first place'. Now an 'in the first place' is a prelude to at least an 'in the second place'. So, in the second place...

Listen or don't listen, I shall go on talking to myself...

Jacques's Captain and his friend could have been riven by violent, unconscious feelings of jealousy: friendship does not always rule out jealousy. Nothing is harder to forgive in others than merit. Was not each of them afraid the other might be promoted over his head, which would have offended both of them? Unknowingly they were trying to remove a dangerous competitor from the running: they were limbering up for the confrontation to come.

But how can anyone think such a thing of the one who so generously surrendered his post of adjutant to his impoverished friend? He stood down, it's true, but if he'd been denied the posting, he might have supported his own claim to it with the point of his sword. In the army, an unfair promotion does no honour to the soldier to whose advantage it falls and it dishonours his rival. But let's not go into that any further. Let's just say that it was their own brand of folly. Do we not all have our quirks? The folly of those two officers was for several centuries the folly of the whole of Europe: it was called the spirit of chivalry. The brilliant, multitudinous cohort of men armed from head to foot, sporting assorted tokens of love, prancing on palfreys, lances under their arms, visors raised or lowered, proudly glaring around them, sizing each other up at a glance, issuing challenges, biting the dust, littering the field of one vast jousting match with splinters of broken weapons— were nothing more than friends jealously wedded to the particular style of merit that was then the fashion. At the instant they couched their lances, each at his end of the lists, at the moment they dug their spurs into the ribs of their chargers, these friends turned into the most terrible enemies. They bore down on each other with as much fury as if they were on the field of battle.

Well, our two officers were simply two knights of yore, born into our own times but with the outlook of the olde worlde. Every virtue and every vice comes into fashion and goes out of fashion. Physical strength had its day, and skill at arms likewise. The spirit of derring-do is valued in one era and undervalued the next: the more common it is, the less arrogant men are and the less fuss they make of it. If you examine the impulses which drive them, you'll find some who were clearly born too late. They belong in another century. And what's to stop us believing that these two soldiers had engaged in dangerous duels every day for no other reason than because each wished to find his rival's weak spot and establish his superiority? Duels occur endlessly in society in all sorts of forms—between priests, between politicians, between writers, between philosophers. Every group and condition of men has its lances and its champions, and our most serious or amusing gatherings are in reality small-scale jousts in which love-tokens are worn in the heart if not on the sleeve. The larger the audience, the livelier the combat. The presence of women stokes the heat of battle and the combative spirit to absurd heights, and the shame of coming to grief while the ladies are watching is something that's rarely forgotten.

But what about Jacques? Jacques, passing through the gates of the town, raced along the streets to the whoops of children, sped out of the gate at the other end of town, and into the streets beyond. As his horse plunged through a low, narrow gateway, there was between the lintel of the gateway and Jacques's head a terrible confrontation which required that either the lintel would yield or that Jacques would be knocked backwards off his mount. It was, as you correctly surmise, the latter which occurred. Jacques fell, bleeding from his head and unconscious. He was picked up, taken indoors, and brought round with spirituous liquors—I do believe he was even bled by the man who owned the house.

This man was a surgeon, then?

No. Meanwhile, his Master had arrived and was asking everyone he met for news of him: 'Have you seen a tall, thin man riding a piebald horse?'

'Just passed this way. Going as if the devil himself was at his heels. He'll have got back to his master's by now.'

'Who's his master?'

'The hangman.'

'The hangman?'

'Yes. It's his horse.'

'Where does the hangman live?'

'It's a fair way, but I shouldn't bother going there. Here come his servants who look as if they're bringing the thin man you were asking for. We thought he was one of the stable-boys.'

And who was the man who was talking like this to Jacques's Master? An innkeeper at whose door he had halted. He couldn't have been anything else. He was short and round as a barrel, had his shirtsleeves rolled up to the elbow, a cotton bonnet on his head, a kitchen apron wound round his middle, and a large knife stuck in his belt.

'Look lively there, make up a bed for the poor lad,' Jacques's Master said to him. 'And send for a surgeon, a doctor, an apothecary...'

Meanwhile, Jacques had been laid at his feet. His head was swathed in an enormous, thick compress and his eyes were shut.

Master. Jacques? Jacques?

Jacques. Is that you, sir?

Master. Yes, it's me. Look at me.

Jacques. I can't.

Master. What happened to you?

Jacques. Ah! It was that horse, that damned horse! I'll tell you all about it tomorrow if I don't die in the night.

And while he was being moved and carried up to his room, his Master directed operations exclaiming: 'Watch it, go gently... gently, I said, by God! you'll hurt him. You, the one who's got him by the legs, turn right! You, the one holding his head, left turn!'

And Jacques kept muttering: 'All this was written, up there, on high...!'

The moment Jacques was in bed he fell into a deep sleep. His Master spent the whole night at his side, taking his pulse and regularly damping the compress with a healing balm. When he woke, Jacques caught his Master in the act and said: 'What's that you're doing?'

Master. I've been sitting up with you. You look after me whether I'm fit or under the weather. But when you're not well, then I look after you.

Jacques. It's very nice to know you're human. It's not a quality you often find in the way masters treat their servants.

Master. How's the head?

Jacques. As sound as the beam it had the argument with.

Master. Put this end of the sheet between your teeth and bite hard. Does that hurt?

Jacques. No. It looks like the old jug's not cracked.

Master. That's a relief. I imagine you'll be wanting to get up.

Jacques. What do you expect me to do in bed?

Master. I want you to rest.

Jacques. And if you want my opinion, I think we should have a bite to eat here and then be on our way.

Master. What about your horse?

Jacques. I left it with its owner, a good man, an honourable man, who bought it back for what we paid him for it.

Master. And do you know who this good and honourable man is?

Jacques. No.

Master. I'll tell you when we're back on the road.

Jacques. Why not tell me now? Is it a secret?

Master. Whether it's a secret or not, is there anything that says you need to know now or some other time?

Jacques. No.

Master. But you do need a horse.

Jacques. Perhaps the landlord of this hostelry would be only to happy to let us have one of his.

Master. Sleep a little longer and I'll go and see to it.

Jacques's Master goes downstairs, orders a meal, buys a horse, comes back up again, and finds Jacques dressed. Now they've eaten their dinner and they're on their way, with Jacques protesting that it was most uncivil to leave without paying a courtesy call on the man who owned the gate which had almost brained him and who had so obligingly extended the hand of kindness to him. The Master quieted his misgivings on that score by assuring him that he had generously rewarded the men who had carried him to the inn. Jacques argued that money given to the servants did not cancel his debt to the master; that this was exactly how men learned to regret their charitable impulses and be chary of repeating them; and that such proceedings made the recipient look exceedingly ungrateful. 'Sir, I can hear everything he must be thinking about me because I know what I'd be thinking about him if I were in his shoes and he in mine.'

They had just left the town limits when they overtook a tall, vigorous man, wearing a hat with a fringe and a coat braided at every seam, walking alone*—alone, that is, if you discount two large dogs which ran on ahead of him. No sooner did Jacques see him than the actions of jumping off his horse, shouting 'It's him!', and flinging both arms round the man's neck, were the work of a moment. The man with the two dogs seemed highly embarrassed by Jacques's effusions, disengaged himself gingerly, and said: 'Sir, you overwhelm me.'

'Not at all, I owe you my life and I can never thank you enough.'

'You don't know who I am.'

'Are you not the philanthropic citizen who came to my assistance, who bled me, who bandaged my wounds when my horse...?'

'I am.'

'Are you not one and the same as the honest citizen who bought the horse back for the same price he got for it?'

'I am.'

Whereupon Jacques again kissed him on both cheeks, his Master smiled, and the two dogs stood stock still with their noses in the air as though amazed by a spectacle they were seeing for the very first time. To these demonstrations of gratitude Jacques added a series of deep bows which his benefactor did not acknowledge, and a stream of good wishes which were stonily received. Then he got back on his horse and said to his Master: 'I have the greatest respect, nay veneration for that man. You must tell me who he is.'

Master. And why, Jacques, in your view, is he a man to be revered?

Jacques. Because by attaching no importance whatsoever to the kindness he does, it must follow that he is philanthropic by nature and that with him the habit of charity is of long standing.

Master. And how can you tell that?

Jacques. By the cold, distant way he responded to my thanks. He did not acknowledge me, didn't say a single word, didn't even seem to know who I was. Perhaps at this moment he's shaking his head in sorrow and saying to himself: 'Yonder traveller must be a stranger to kindness and clearly finds justice in others difficult to deal with: only that can explain why he was so deeply grateful...' What's so funny about what I'm saying that makes you laugh like a drain? But never mind that now, just tell me the man's name so I can write it down in my little book.

Master. No problem. Ready?

Jacques. Fire away.

Master. Write: The man for whom I have the greatest respect, nay veneration...

Jacques. ... nay veneration.

Master. Is...

Jacques. Is...

Master. The hangman of the town of ———.

Jacques. The hangman?

Master. That's right, the hangman.

Jacques. Would you please tell me what's the point of this little joke?

Master. It's not a joke. Just follow your chain back a couple of links. You need a horse. Fate directs you to a stranger on the road. The stranger is a hangman. On two occasions the horse deposits you under a gibbet, and on the third it takes you to a hangman. There you collapse in a senseless heap. From there you are carried—where? To an inn, a tavern, a common lodging-house. Jacques, do you know the story of the death of Socrates?

Jacques. No.

Master. Socrates was an Athenian sage. It's been true for rather a long time that being a wise man among fools is a dangerous occupation. His fellow citizens sentenced him to drink hemlock. Well now, Socrates did exactly what you have just done. He treated the public executioner who gave him the cup of hemlock as courteously as you did your man. Jacques, you are a philosopher of sorts—don't deny it. I'm well aware that philosophers are a breed who are anathema to powerful men to whom they refuse to kneel. Anathema to magistrates, who are the licensed defenders of the very abuses philosophers attack. Anathema to priests who rarely observe them bowing down at their altars. Anathema to poets, who are unprincipled men who stupidly regard philosophy as the hammer which will destroy art, not to mention those of them who, by engaging in the odious practice of satire, have never been anything other than vile flatterers. Anathema to the peoples who are permanently enslaved by the tyrants who oppress them, the rogues who cheat them, and the jesters who keep them amused. So you see, I know all about the dangers of your profession and the significance of the admission I now ask you to give. I shan't give your secret away. Jacques, my friend, you are a philosopher and I am genuinely sorry for you. If I may presume to use present events to anticipate what will some day come to pass, and if what is written on high is sometimes revealed to men long before the event, then I predict that you will die a philosophical death and that you put your head in the noose with as much good grace as Socrates took the cup of hemlock.

Jacques. Sir, a soothsayer couldn't have put it better, but fortunately...

Master. You don't really believe me. That only strengthens my premonitions.

Jacques. And you believe it, sir?

Master. I do. But even if I didn't, it wouldn't matter.

Jacques. Why?

Master. Because there's danger only for those who open their mouths, and I intend to keep mine shut.

Jacques. And premonitions generally?

Master. I pooh-pooh them, though I admit I can never do so without going slightly weak at the knees. Some of the things we dream are so overpowering! We are brought up to believe these things from an early age. If you've had five or six dreams come true and then you dream your best friend is dead, you'll be round at his house first thing next morning to see if it's true. But the premonitions which are hardest to ignore are the ones you get when what you dream really happens somewhere else, far away. Then they seem to have some symbolic meaning.

Jacques. There are times when what you say is so deep and so far-sighted that I've no idea what you're talking about. Couldn't you lighten my darkness with an example?

Master. Nothing easier. A woman lived in the country with her husband, who was eighty and suffered agonies from kidney stones. The husband says goodbye to his wife and travels to town to have the operation. The night before he is to be operated on, he writes to his wife: 'When you get this letter, I shall be under the knife of Frère Cosme...'* Now you know those wedding rings which are divided into two, which have the name of the husband engraved on one part and the wife's on the other? Well, the wife was wearing just such a ring on her finger when she opened the letter from her husband. At that very moment, the two parts of her ring came apart. The one with her name on stayed on her finger, and the one with her husband's name snapped off and fell on to the letter she was reading... Tell me, Jacques, do you think that anyone would be sufficiently strong-minded or have enough inner certainty not to be affected to some extent by having such a thing happen to them in similar circumstances? The wife was in a terrible state which lasted until the next post, when she received a letter from her husband saying the operation had been a success, that he was out of danger, and that he hoped to give her a great big kiss before the end of the month.

Jacques. And did he give her a great big kiss?

Master. Oh yes.

Jacques. I asked because I've noticed on several occasions that Destiny is a tricky customer. At first you say it got it wrong, but later you say it got it right after all. Anyway, sir, the top and bottom of it is that you believe I've been fingered by a symbolic premonition and, against your better judgement, you think I am threatened with the same death as that philosopher?

Master. I won't pretend otherwise. But to take your mind off such a gloomy prospect, couldn't you...

Jacques. Carry on with the story of my loves?

So Jacques resumed the story of his love-life. We had left him, as I recall, talking to the surgeon.

Surgeon. I'm afraid it'll take more than one day to sort your knee out.

Jacques. It'll take exactly as long as the time that's allowed in what's written on high. So what?

Surgeon. At so much a day for bed, board, and treatment, it'll mount up.

Jacques. Doctor, we don't need bother about how much it'll come to for whatever time it takes, only about how much per day.

Surgeon. Twenty-five sous. Is that too much?

Jacques. Far too much. Look, doctor, I'm poor and I'm down-and-out. So let's knock a half off and then you can start thinking about how soon you can have me moved to your house.

Surgeon. Twelve and a half, that's not a lot. You couldn't make it thirteen?

Jacques. Twelve and a half, thirteen... Done!

Surgeon. And you'll pay each day?

Jacques. That's what we agreed.

Surgeon. The problem is that my wife's a tigress, you see, and she doesn't like being messed about.

Jacques. Well, then, doctor, have me carted off to your tigerish wife at once.

Surgeon. A month at thirteen sous a day, that's nineteen and a half livres. You couldn't make it twenty?

Jacques. Twenty francs it is.

Surgeon. You want to be well fed, well looked after, and cured quickly. In addition to room, board, and medical attention, there may be medicines, and perhaps bandages and dressings and...

Jacques. So?

Surgeon. Well, all that could come to twenty-four francs.

Jacques. All right. Twenty-four francs—but no tampering with the figures.

Surgeon. One month at twenty-four francs. Two months will come to forty-eight and three months will be seventy-two. Oh, my lady wife would be ever so pleased if you could see your way, the minute you set foot in the house, to handing over half the seventy-two francs on account!

Jacques. I agree.

Surgeon. She'd be even more pleased...

Jacques. If I paid the full quarter? I'll pay it.

Jacques added: The surgeon rejoined my host and his wife, told them about our arrangement, and the next moment the husband, his wife, and their children had all gathered round my bed looking very cheerful. They asked endless questions about how I felt and how my knee was. They were generous in their praise of their friend the surgeon and his wife. They expressed their good wishes till good wishes were coming out of my ears. They were all smiles, they took such an interest! They couldn't say how happy they'd be to do whatever they could for me! In the meantime, the surgeon hadn't mentioned the fact that I had a little money, but they knew him of old: he was taking me to stay with him and they knew what that meant. I paid the man and wife what I owed and gave the children a little something which their father and mother immediately took off them. It was morning. The husband left to go to the fields, the wife put her wicker basket on her back and went her way, and the children, surly and resentful at having been deprived of what was theirs, disappeared. So when it came to getting me out of bed, dressing me, and settling me on a stretcher, there was no one left except the doctor, who began yelling his head off. Not that there was anyone to hear.

Master. And in all likelihood Jacques, who is so fond of talking to himself, said: 'Never pay in advance if you want decent service!'

Jacques. No, sir, it wasn't the time for making moral observations but it was the time for losing my temper and swearing. I lost my temper, I swore, and only then did I make moral observations, and while I was making them the doctor, who had gone away and left me by myself, returned with two peasants he'd hired to cart me off—at my expense, as he did not fail to point out. The men attended to the preliminaries of laying me on a makeshift stretcher which they fashioned with a mattress stretched over two poles.

Master. Heaven be praised! There you are, settled in the surgeon's house and in love with the wife or possibly the daughter of the doctor.

Jacques. I do believe, sir, that you're wrong.

Master. If you imagine I'm going to spend three months in the doctor's house without hearing a single word about your love-life, you can think again! Listen, Jacques, you may well be right, but do me a favour: spare me a description of the house, the doctor's character, the doctor's wife's bad moods, and the progress of your cure. Skip. Take all that as read. Let's get to the nub. Right then, your leg's almost completely better, you're more or less fit again and you're in love.

Jacques. All right, I'm in love, since you're in a hurry.

Master. Who are you in love with?

Jacques. A tall girl of eighteen, with dark hair, lovely figure, big black eyes, a small mouth with coral lips, fine arms, and pretty hands... Oh sir, such pretty hands!... Those hands...

Master. You're imagining you're still holding them.

Jacques. Sir, you yourself have reached for and held those selfsame hands more than once, on the sly, and if those hands had been willing then you could have done whatever you wanted.

Master. By God, Jacques, I wasn't expecting that.

Jacques. Nor me.

Master. I'm thinking... but I'm damned if I can recall a tall girl with dark hair nor any pretty hands. Try and explain.

Jacques. Very well, but only on condition that we backtrack and bide a while in the surgeon's house.

Master. Do you think it's written on high that we will?

Jacques. That's up to you to say. But here below it's written: *chi va piano va sano*.

Master. Also: *chi va sano va lontano*,* and I'm anxious to get to wherever all this is leading.

Jacques. Well, what have you decided?

Master. Whatever you want.

Jacques. In that case we're back at the surgeon's, and so it was, after all, written on high that we would be. The doctor, his wife, and his children joined forces so effectively to empty my purse by dipping their sticky fingers into it, that they all but succeeded in no time at all. My knee seemed to be coming along nicely, though it wasn't really. The wound had almost healed up, I could go out with the help of crutches, and I still had eighteen francs left. Now no one likes talking more than people who stammer, and no one likes walking more than a man with a limp. One autumn day, it was a fine afternoon, I decided to go for a longish stroll. It was about eight or nine miles from the village where I was staying to the next.

Master. And the name of this village?

Jacques. Ah! if I told you that, you'd know everything. When I got there, I went into a tavern, sat down, and had something to drink. The light began to fade and I was getting ready to return to my lodging when, from the room in the inn where I was sitting, I heard a woman screaming, very loud. I went out into the street. A crowd had gathered round her. She was lying on the ground, tearing her hair, and, pointing to the shattered remains of a large earthenware pitcher, saying: 'Now I've got nothing, no money for a month! And who will feed my poor children all that time? That steward has a heart that's solid flint and he'll want his money down to the last penny. Oh, I'm so wretched. I'm ruined! Ruined!!'

Everyone felt sorry for her and on all sides I heard them muttering 'Poor woman!' but nobody put his hand in his pocket. Without more ado, I went up to her and said: 'My good woman, what's happened here?'

'What's happened? Can't you see? I was sent to fetch a pitcher of oil. I tripped and fell, the pitcher broke, and here's all the oil that was in it...'

Just then, the woman's young children appeared. They were practically naked and their mother's ragged clothes showed just how poor the whole family was. Then both mother and infants started bawling their eyes out. True as I'm standing here now, it wouldn't have taken a tenth as much to move me to tears. My innards churned with compassion and tears came to my eyes. Brokenly, I asked the woman how much the oil in her pitcher had been worth.

'How much was it worth?' she said, raising her arms to heaven. 'It was worth nine francs—more than I can earn in a month.'

I immediately opened my purse and tossed two crowns to her: 'Here,' said I, 'there's twelve,' and not stopping to hear her thanks I headed back towards my village.

Master. That was a damned fine thing you did there, Jacques.

Jacques. With respect, I did a very stupid thing. I hadn't gone a hundred yards before I began thinking I'd been a fool; I hadn't got halfway home before I was saying it out loud. When I got back to the surgeon's house with an empty purse, I was even more acutely aware of it.

Master. You may be right and my praise could very well be as misplaced as your compassion. But no. No, Jacques, I'll not go back on my initial reaction, for the main merit in what you did is the fact that you put your own need second. I can see the consequences: you'll be subjected to the cruelty of your unfeeling surgeon and his wife, they'll kick you out, but even though you were to die on a dung-heap at their gate, you would lie dying on that dung-heap feeling mighty pleased with yourself.

Jacques. Sir, I'm not made of such stern stuff. I was limping along and, since I must confess it, was regretting my twelve francs, which were well and truly given and couldn't be ungiven, and letting my regrets take the bloom off the good deed I had done. I'd got about halfway between the two villages and by then it was quite dark, when three robbers sprang out of the bushes that lined the road, leaped on me, knocked me to the ground, went through my pockets, and were very surprised to find that I had so little money on me. They'd been counting on richer pickings. They'd seen me dole out charity in the village and reasoned that anyone who could give half a louis away so freely must have another twenty about his person. They were furious: their hopes had been dashed and now they'd exposed themselves to having their bones broken on a scaffold for the sake of a handful of copper coins if I chose to report them and they were caught and I identified them. They spent a while deciding whether or not to murder me. Fortunately, they heard a noise and ran off, and I escaped with no more than a few bruises from my fall and a few more which I got as I was being robbed. Once they'd gone, I made my way back to my village as best I could. I arrived at two in the morning, white-faced, done-in, with the pain in my knee a great deal worse, and aching all over as a result of the beating I'd been given. The doctor... Sir, what's wrong now? You're gritting your teeth and stiffening your sinews as if you'd just come face to face with an enemy.

Master. As a matter of fact I have. I've got my sword in my hand, I'm rushing your robbers, and I'm avenging you. Tell me, how is it that whoever composed the great scroll could bring himself to write that this would be the reward you got for your selfless action? Why is it that I, a nobody, a collection of human failings, spring to your defence, while He, who is said to be the embodiment of all perfections, can sit back coolly and watch you being attacked and trampled underfoot?

Jacques. Hush, sir. That sort of talk has a devilish whiff of heresy about it.

Master. Why are you looking round like that?

Jacques. I'm just looking to see if there's anybody about who might have heard you...* The doctor felt my pulse and found I had a temperature. I went to bed without mentioning my adventure and lay there thinking, knowing I had to deal with two people—and God, what people!—without a penny to my name and having no doubt whatsoever that when I woke next morning I'd be asked to hand over the daily sum as agreed.

At this point the Master threw his arms around his servant's neck, exclaiming: 'Poor Jacques, what will you do? What'll happen to you? I fear for you in this predicament!'

Jacques. Sir, calm yourself, I'm here.

Master. I wasn't thinking. I'd got to the next day, I was by your side in the doctor's house when you wake up and they come asking for money.

Jacques. Sir, in this life we never know what we should be cheering and what we should be grieving over. Good leads to evil and evil to good. We stumble along in the dark beneath what is written on high, as crazily yoked to our desires as to our joys and our sorrows. When I weep, I often end up feeling foolish.

Master. And when you laugh?

Jacques. I also feel foolish. But I can't help weeping and laughing, and it makes me very angry. I've tried hundreds of times... I didn't sleep a wink that night.

Master. No, no, tell me what you tried.

Jacques. Not giving a damn about anything. Oh, if I'd only been able to do that!

Master. Why? What good would that have done you?

Jacques. It would have helped me to stop worrying, to stop needing anything, to be captain of my soul, to think I was as well off sleeping with my head on a milestone at some street corner as on a soft pillow. I'm like that sometimes, but the problem is that it doesn't last. There are occasions when I stand as firm and solid as a rock, but as often as not it doesn't take much more than a piddling complication, something really trivial, to knock me off my perch. Oh I could kick myself! I've given up trying and have decided to settle for being what I am. I've noticed, when I've thought about it, that it all boils down to more or less the same in the end, and I say to myself 'What's it matter what we're like?' It's just another form of resignation, only not as difficult and much easier to live with.

Master. Easier is right, that's for sure.

Jacques. Early next morning, the surgeon draws back my bed curtains and says: 'Look lively, friend, let me see your knee. I've got a long way to go today.'

'Doctor,' I said in a voice racked with pain, 'I must sleep.'

'I'm glad to hear it. It's a good sign.'

'Let me sleep. I'm not bothered about having my leg dressed.'

'It won't come to any great harm. Go back to sleep, then.'

And so saying, he closes my curtains but I don't sleep. An hour later, his lady wife pulls back the bed curtains and says: 'Come on, lad, here's your nice sugared toast.'

'Madame,' said I dolefully, 'I'm not hungry.'

'Eat it up. It won't cost you any more nor, come to think of it, less.'

'But I don't feel like eating.'

'Fair enough. The children and I will have it.'

And so saying, she closes the curtains round my bed, calls for her children to come, and without more ado they make short work of my sugared toast.

Reader, I would very much like to know what you'd think if I were to break off at this point and return to the story of the man who only had one shirt because he only had one body at a time. Perhaps you'd think I've got myself into an impasse, as Voltaire would say, or more crudely am stuck up a dead-end* with nowhere to go, that I'd launch into some made-up yarn to gain enough time to find some way out of the tale I've started. Well, Reader, you'd be quite wrong. I know exactly how Jacques will get out of the hole he's in and what I'm going to tell you about Gousse, the man who only had one shirt at a time, isn't a made-up yarn at all.

One morning—it was Whitsuntide—I received a note from Gousse in which he begged me to visit him in a prison where he was being held. As I dressed, I wondered how he had got there and imagined that his tailor, his baker, his wine-merchant, or his landlord had applied for and obtained an order for his arrest. When I get there, I find him sharing a room with a number of other sinister-looking prisoners. I asked him who they were.

'The old man you see there with the glasses perched on the end of his nose is a very clever man with advanced transferable skills in adding up and taking away. He's currently trying to make the ledgers he's copying into tally with his accounts. It's not easy. We've discussed it. I have no doubt that he'll do it.'

'And that one there?'

'He's a fool.'

'Meaning?'

'A fool who invented a machine for making counterfeit banknotes. But it was no good, it was defective and went wrong in all sorts of ways.'

'And the third man, in the servant's livery, the one playing the bass viol?'

'He's only being held here temporarily. Tonight or tomorrow morning, because he's not charged with anything serious, he'll be transferred to Bicêtre.'*

'What about you?'

'Me? I'm in here for something even less serious.'

When he'd said this, he stood up, put his cotton cap on his bed, and immediately his three fellow-prisoners disappeared. When I'd got there, I'd found Gousse in his dressing-gown sitting at a small table, busying himself with geometry and getting on with his work as happily as if he'd been at home. When we're alone, I say: 'And what exactly are you doing here?'

'Me? Working, as you see.'

'No, I mean who had you put away?'

'I did.'

'You did? Really?'

'Yes, sir, I did.'

'And how did you manage that?'

'The same way I'd have managed it with anybody else. I served a writ on myself, I won my case, and as a result of the judgement I obtained against me and the sentence which followed, I was arrested and brought here.'

'Are you mad?'

'No. I'm just telling you the facts.'

'Couldn't you start a different case against yourself, win it, and as the result of a different judgement and another sentence, get yourself released?'

'No, sir.'

Gousse had a pretty maidservant who did duty as his better half more often than his better half herself. This unequal division had introduced discord into the domestic hearth. Now, though it was the most difficult thing in the world to ruffle his equanimity, for no one was less sensitive to strife, he decided to leave his wife and live with his servant. But all he owned was tied up in furniture, instruments, drawings, tools, and other personal effects, and he made up his mind that he'd much rather leave his wife with nothing at all than depart empty-handed. To this end, he devised the following plan.

He arranged for credit notes to be made out payable to the maidservant. She would then sue for repayment and obtain an order for his goods and chattels to be seized and sold. The said goods and chattels would then be conveyed from the Pont Saint-Michel, where he lived, to the house where he proposed to set up with her.

He was very pleased with this cunning plan. He drew up the notes, issued a summons against himself, hired two lawyers, went rushing from the one to the other, prosecuting himself with unbounded zeal, mounting excellent attacks and putting up the weakest of defences. He was sentenced to pay up or else be subject to the penalties laid down by the law. Already, he began to imagine getting his hands on everything in his house. But things did not turn out like that at all. He had come up against a very crafty minx who, instead of seeking to distrain his effects, went for him instead, had him arrested and jailed. So, although the puzzling replies he had given me might seem peculiar, they were in fact quite true.

While I've been telling you this story, which you'll assume I've made up...

What about the man in the livery who was scraping away on the bass viol?

Reader, you shall have it, I promise. You have my word on it. You won't be sold short. But please let me get back now to Jacques and his Master.

Jacques and his Master had reached the place where they were to spend the night. It was late, the gates were all shut, and they'd been forced to stop at an inn outside the town's walls. There I can hear a great hullabaloo...

You can *hear*? But you weren't there. How could you have heard anything?

You're right. So Jacques... his Master... er... a terrible hullabaloo is heard. I see two men...

You don't *see* anything of the kind. This has nothing to do with you. You weren't there.

True enough. There were two men chatting quietly at a table outside the door of their room. A woman, hands on hips, was heaping a torrent of abuse on their heads, and Jacques was trying to calm her down while she paid no more attention to his peaceful remonstrations than the two men she was shouting at paid to her fulminations.

'Come, come, my good woman,' said Jacques, 'a little patience, calm down. Now what's all this about? These two persons look like gentlemen...'

'Them? Gentlemen? They're brutes, men who have no hearts, no human feelings, nor feelings of any other sort. Whatever harm did poor Nicole ever do to them that they should treat her so badly? She might be crippled for the rest of her life.'

'Perhaps it's not as bad as you think.'

'She took a terrible wallop, I tell you. It'll leave her crippled.'

'We'll have to see. We must send for a surgeon.'

'Somebody's gone for one.'

'She should be put to bed.'

'She's in bed and she's howling fit to break your heart. Poor Nicole!'

While all these lamentations were in progress, guests here were ringing for service and customers there were calling: 'Landlady, some

wine!...' To which she answered: 'I'm coming.' More bells rang and
someone shouted:

'Landlady, what about my sheets?'

She answered: 'Just coming.'

'The chops and the duck!'

'Coming!'

'Bring a tankard! Bring a chamber-pot!'

'Coming! Coming!'

And from another room in the inn, a man was yelling furiously:

'You infuriating chatterbox! You damned gossip! What are you
poking your nose into now? Are you going to keep me waiting until
tomorrow? Jacques! Jacques!'

The landlady, beginning to get over her distress and rage, said to
Jacques:

'Sir, I'll be all right now, you're very kind.'

'Jacques! Jacques!'

'You'd better run along. Oh, if you knew all the dreadful things that
have happened to her, poor thing!'

'Jacques! Jacques!'

'Go on, now. I think that's your master calling you.'

'Jacques! Jacques!'

It was indeed Jacques's Master, who had got undressed all by himself, was dying of hunger, and was extremely put out that his dinner
had not been brought. Jacques went up the stairs and a moment later
was followed by the landlady, who looked thoroughly contrite.

'Sir,' she said to Jacques's Master, 'beg pardon I'm sure. But there
are things that happen in this life that stick in your gullet. What would
you like? I've got chicken, pigeon, an excellent saddle of hare, and
rabbit: the rabbits round here are the best. Or would you prefer a fowl
from the river?'

Jacques ordered supper for his Master as if it were for himself, as he
always did. It was brought, and while they were setting about it heartily
the Master said to Jacques: 'What the devil were you doing downstairs?'

Jacques. Maybe some good, maybe some harm, who knows?

Master. And what exactly was this good or possibly harm that you
were doing down there?

Jacques. Preventing that woman getting knocked about by two men
downstairs who at the very least have broken her serving-wench's arm.

Master. Maybe it would have done her good to get knocked about a bit.

Jacques. And for ten reasons, each better than the one before. One of the very best things that ever happened to me, personally, to myself, in the whole of my life...

Master. Was to have been knocked about? Pour me some wine.

Jacques. Yes, sir, knocked about. Knocked about on the road, that night, as I was limping back from the village, as I was telling you, after committing the folly, say I, the good deed, say you, of giving all my money away.

Master. I remember. More wine. And how did it all start, I mean the squabble you sorted out downstairs and the brutal treatment handed out to the landlady's daughter, or was it her serving-wench?

Jacques. I've no idea.

Master. You've no idea what an argument is about and yet you go rushing blindly in! Jacques, that's unwise from the standpoint of prudence, justice, and moral principle... More wine.

Jacques. I've no idea what moral principles are either, unless it means the rules you lay down for others to obey for your own benefit. I believe one thing but I can't help behaving in a way that contradicts it. All sermons are like the preambles to royal edicts. All moralists would like us to practise what they preach because we might be the better for it, but it never applies to them of course... Virtue...

Master. Virtue, Jacques, is an excellent thing. Both good people and wicked people speak very highly of it... More wine.

Jacques. That's because both get something out of it.

Master. But how do you reckon it was such a good thing for you to get knocked about?

Jacques. It's late. You've put away a large supper and so have I. We're both tired. So if you want my advice, we'll go to bed.

Master. We can't do that. The landlady hasn't brought everything yet. While we're waiting, go on with the story of your love-life.

Jacques. Where was I? Please sir, may I ask you now and in the future to point me in the right direction?

Master. I'll see to it. And now, taking up my duties as prompter, I recall you were in bed, with no money, not knowing which way to turn, while the doctor's wife and her children were munching your sugared toast.

Jacques. At that moment, there came the sound of a carriage drawing up outside the front door. A servant comes in and says: 'Is this the house where a poor man lives, a soldier who walks with a crutch, who limped back from the next village last night?'

'It is,' said the doctor's wife. 'What do you want with him?'

'To put him in the carriage outside and take him away with us.'

'He's in that bed. Draw the curtains aside and you can ask him yourself.'

Jacques had got this far when the landlady came in and said: 'What do you want for dessert?'

Master. Whatever you've got.

The landlady, not bothering to go back downstairs, shouted from their room: 'Nanon! bring us up some fruit, biscuits, and jam.'

On hearing the name Nanon, Jacques muttered to himself: 'Ah! so it must have been her daughter who was knocked about. Oh, it would take less than that to make anyone angry...'

And his Master said to the landlady: 'You sounded very cross a while back.'

Landlady. And who wouldn't have been angry? The poor creature hadn't done them any harm. She'd no sooner gone into their room when I heard her howling, and when I say howling, I mean howling... But thank the Lord, I'm easier in my mind now. The surgeon reckons she'll be all right. Still, she's got two enormous bruises, one on the head and the other on her shoulder.

Master. Has she been with you long?

Landlady. Not more than a fortnight. She was abandoned at the next post-house on the road.

Master. What do you mean, abandoned?

Landlady. Lordy, that's exactly what she was. Some people are harder than nails. She very near drowned when she was trying to get across the river that runs just across the way. It was a miracle she ever got here, and I took her in out of charity.

Master. How old is she?

Landlady. I think she must be about eighteen months.

On hearing this, Jacques burst out laughing and exclaimed: 'It's a dog!'

Landlady. Prettiest little thing you ever saw. I wouldn't take ten louis for Nicole if it was offered. Poor Nicole.

Master. You have a very kind heart.

Landlady. That I have. I'm very fond of my animals, and of the servants too.

Master. Quite right. And who are the men who treated Nicole so badly?

Landlady. A couple of gentlemen from town. They've never stopped whispering in each other's ear. They think nobody knows what they're saying and nobody knows their story. But they've not been here three hours and there's nothing I don't know about their business. It would make you laugh, and if you weren't even more anxious to get to bed than I am, I'd tell you the whole story, just as their servant told it to my serving-girl who, it turns out, comes from the same part of the world as him, and she told it to my husband who told it to me. The mother-in-law of the younger one passed through here about three months back. She was on her way, very much against her will, to a convent out in the sticks where she didn't sit around waiting to make old bones but upped and died. That's why both the young men are wearing mourning. Oh, look at me, without noticing I've made a start of telling you all about it. I'll leave you gentlemen. Goodnight. Did you like the wine?

Master. It was very good.

Landlady. Was the supper all right?

Master. Excellent. The spinach was slightly over-salted.

Landlady. I'm a bit heavy-handed sometimes. You'll find your beds comfy. The sheets are clean. We never use them twice here.

And so saying the landlady went away, and as Jacques and his Master got into bed, they laughed heartily not only at the misunderstanding which had led them to mistake a dog for the landlady's daughter or servant, but also at the landlady's extreme attachment to a stray dog she'd had for two weeks. As Jacques tied the draw-string of his Master's nightcap, he said to him:

'I'd be willing to bet that of all the creatures that live and breathe under her roof, Nicole is the only one the landlady really loves.'

His Master replied: 'You could be right, Jacques. But now let's get some sleep.'

While Jacques and his Master sleep, I shall fulfil the promise I made by giving you the tale of the man in prison who was scraping away on his bass viol, I mean friend Gousse's comrade:

'The third man,' he told me, 'is the steward of a large, well-to-do house. He fell in love with the wife of a pastry-cook in the rue de l'Université.* This pastry-cook was a good man who spent more time looking into his oven than into his wife's behaviour. It wasn't his jealousy which cramped the lovers' style so much as his uxoriousness. What did they do to free themselves of this curb on their activities? The steward presented to his master a written statement to the effect that the pastry-cook was a man with low morals, a drunkard rarely seen outside of a tavern, a violent brute given to beating his wife, who was the most virtuous and unfortunate of women. On the strength of this statement he obtained a *lettre de cachet*,* and this warrant, which would end the husband's freedom, was placed in the hands of an officer of the watch to be executed without delay.

Now it so happened that the officer concerned was a friend of the pastry-cook. Every so often they'd repair to their regular hostelry together: the pastry-cook would bring some of his pies and the officer would buy the wine. The officer, armed with the *lettre de cachet*, walked by the pastry-cook's shop and gave him the nod as usual. When they were tucking into the pies and washing them down with the wine, the officer asked his friend how business was.

Pretty good.

Was he in any bother?

No.

Did he have any enemies?

Not that he knew of.

How did he get on with his relations, his neighbours, his wife?

All sweetness and light.

'So how is it, then,' said the officer, 'that I've got orders to arrest you? If I were to do my duty, I'd grab you by the collar, there'd be a carriage waiting outside, and I'd deliver you to the place specified in this *lettre de cachet*. Here, read it.'

The pastry-cook read it and turned pale. The officer said:

'Not to worry. Let's just put our heads together and work out what's the best way of keeping you and me out of trouble. Now, who comes calling at your house?'

'Nobody.'

'Your wife's pretty and she flirts.'

'I don't pay any heed to her.'

'Anybody got his eye on her?'

'Good God no—unless it's that steward who turns up from time to time and holds her hand and talks a lot of silly nonsense to her. But it's always in the shop when I'm around, when the apprentices are there too. I don't think there's anything between them that isn't open and above board.'

'You're a very decent sort.'

'That's as maybe. But the best policy always is to believe your wife is honest. That's what I do.'

'And whose steward is he?'

'Monsieur de Saint-Florentin's.'*

'And from whose office do you think this *lettre de cachet* came?'

'Not the office of Monsieur de Saint-Florentin, by any chance?'

'The very same.'

'Oh, eating my cakes, seducing my wife, and wanting to have me locked up—it's too sordid! I can't believe it.'

'You really are a good man! How has your wife been behaving these last couple of days?'

'Not so cheerful as usual.'

'And the steward. Is it long since you saw him?'

'Yesterday, I think. Yes, yesterday.'

'Did you notice anything?'

'I'm not very good at noticing things, though it did seem to me that when they were saying goodbye, they sort of nodded their heads at each other, as if one was saying yes and the other was saying no.'

'Which head nodded yes?'

'The steward's.'

'They're either innocent or they're in this together. Listen, old friend, don't go home. Find somewhere safe and stay there, the Temple, say, or the Abbaye,* wherever you like. Meantime, leave it all to me. And above all, remember...'

'Not to show my face and to keep my mouth shut.'

'Exactly.'

Even as they spoke, the pastry-cook's premises were being surrounded by police spies. Informers wearing all manner of disguises spoke to the pastry-cook's wife and asked where he was.

She tells one that he's ill.

She tells another he's gone to a reception, and says to a third that he's at a wedding.

When will he be back?

She doesn't know.

On the third day, at about two in the morning, an informer alerts the officer that a man, his face muffled by a cloak, had been seen carefully opening the street door and slipping quietly into the pastry-cook's house. Immediately the officer, accompanied by a constable, a locksmith, a cab, and several men of the watch, hurries off to the scene. They force the lock. The officer and the constable make their way up the stairs on tiptoe. They knock at the door of the pastry-cook's wife's bedroom: no reply. They knock again: still no reply. At the third knock, a voice answers:

'Who is it?'

'Open up!'

'Who is it?'

'Open in the name of the King!'

'It's all right,' says the steward to the pastry-cook's wife, who was with him in bed, 'there's nothing to worry about. It's the officer of the watch who's here to execute the warrant. Open the door. I'll tell them who I am, he'll go away, and it'll be all over.'

The pastry-cook's wife, in her nightdress, unlocks the door and gets back into bed.

Officer. Where's your husband?

Pastry-cook's wife. He's not here.

Officer [*drawing back the bed-curtains*]. Then who's this?

Steward. It's me. I'm Monsieur de Saint-Florentin's steward.

Officer. You're lying. You're the pastry-cook, because the pastry-cook is the man who sleeps with the pastry-cook's wife. On your feet and get dressed. You're coming with me.

He had no choice but to obey and he was brought here. The Minister, apprised of his steward's scurrilous behaviour, has approved the conduct of the officer, who is due here at dusk to take him from this prison and transfer him to Bicêtre where, thanks to the money-minded administrators who run it, he'll get a quarter of a loaf of bad bread and an ounce of beef each a day and can scrape away at his bass viol from morning to night.

Now how about if I too get my head down for a while until Jacques and his Master wake up? What do you say?

Next morning Jacques got out of bed when it was still very early, put his head out of the window to find out what the weather was doing, saw that it was doing appalling things, went back to bed, and let his Master and me sleep on for as long as we liked.

Jacques, his Master, and the other travellers who were staying at the same inn thought the sky might lighten by midday. But it didn't, and the rain from the downpour had so swollen the stream separating the old town from the new town that had grown up outside the walls that it would have been dangerous to try to cross it. So those whose road lay in that direction decided to write off that day and wait. Some began to chat, others moved about, poking their noses out of doors, watching the sky, then coming back in again swearing and stamping their feet. Others argued about politics and drank, many played cards, and the rest smoked, dozed, or did nothing.

The Master said to Jacques: 'I hope Jacques will go on with the tale of his love-life and that Heaven, having decided to grant me the satisfaction of hearing how it ends, has sent this foul weather to keep us here for that very purpose.'

Jacques. Heaven having decided! You never know what Heaven wants or doesn't want, and maybe it doesn't know itself. My poor Captain, who is dead, told me that many a time, and the older I get, the more I see he was right. Do your stuff, sir.

Master. Right you are. Now, you'd got to the bit about the carriage and the servant who'd been told by the doctor's wife to open your bed-curtains and ask you himself.

Jacques. The servant comes up to my bed and says: 'Come on, friend, up you get, put your clothes on and we'll be off.'

From under the sheets and the blankets I'd pulled over my head, I said without looking at him or being seen: 'Let me sleep, friend. Go away.'

The man answers that he has orders from his master and must carry them out.

'And has your master, who orders me about like this though he doesn't know me, also given orders that what I owe here should be paid in full?'

'All taken care of. Get a move on. They're all waiting for you at the chateau, where I guarantee you'll be a lot better off than here, if the rest of the tale lives up to expectation. They're very curious about you.'

I allow myself to be prevailed upon, I get out of bed, dress, and am led away by the arm. I'd said my goodbyes to the doctor's wife and was making my way to the carriage, when she comes up to me, tugs at my sleeve, and asks will I step aside into a corner of the room because she has something to say to me.

'There now, lad,' says she, 'I don't think you've got any reason to complain about what we've done for you, have you? The doctor saved your leg and I've seen to your every need. I hope you won't forget that when you get to the chateau.'

'What can I do for you there?'

'Say you want my husband to come and change your dressing. They're ever so grand there! Best customers in the area! The gentleman who owns the chateau is very generous and pays well. You can make our fortune. My husband has tried to get a foot in the door several times but it's never worked.'

'But, Madame, isn't there a resident surgeon at the chateau?'

'Of course.'

'And if this resident surgeon were your husband, would you be happy if someone went behind his back and had him kicked out?'

'But you don't owe that surgeon anything, whereas it seems to me that you are in my husband's debt. If you're walking on two legs now as you did before, it's him you've got to thank for it.'

'And because your husband has done good by me, must I do another man harm? Now I'm not saying that if there was a vacancy for a surgeon...'

Jacques was about to go on when the landlady came in holding Nicole tightly wrapped in a shawl, kissing her, saying never mind, stroking her, and talking to her like a child: 'Poor Nicole, she only barked once all night. And you, gentlemen, did you sleep well?'

Master. Very well.

Landlady. The weather's all out of sorts.

Jacques. We're not best pleased.

Landlady. Are you going far, gentlemen?

Jacques. We've no idea.

Landlady. Are you following somebody?

Jacques. We're not following anybody.

Landlady. So you move on and stop as and when your business requires along your way?

Jacques. We don't have any business.

Landlady. So you're travelling for pleasure?

Jacques. Or for our pains.

Landlady. I hope it's pleasure.

Jacques. What you hope doesn't come into it. It all depends whether or not it's written up there, on high.

Landlady. Oh, you mean a wedding?

Jacques. Maybe, maybe not.

Landlady. Be careful, gentlemen. That man downstairs, the one who was so nasty to my ickle Nicole, he got married, and a peculiar affair it was too. Come on, you poor little thing, come and give me a kiss. I promise he won't hurt you again. Look, she's all of a tremble!

Master. And what was peculiar about this man's marriage?

Just as Jacques's Master was asking this question, the landlady said: 'I can hear ructions downstairs. I'll go down and tell them what to do. Then I'll come back and tell you all about it.'

Her husband, who'd grown tired of shouting: 'Wife! Wife!', now comes up the stairs followed, unbeknownst to him, by a peasant of his acquaintance. He says to his wife: 'What the devil are you doing here?' Then he turns round and, spotting the peasant, asks: 'Have you brought the money?'

Peasant. No. You know I've got no money.

Landlord. Got no money? Then I'll get it myself. I'll sell up your plough, your horses, your oxen, and your bed! Why, you good-for-nothing...!

Peasant. I'm not a good-for-nothing.

Landlord. What are you, then? You're destitute, you don't know where to get the wherewithal to buy seed to plant your fields. Your landlord is fed up with advancing you money and won't give you another penny. So you come to me, and my wife here, the damned busybody who's the reason for all the stupid things I've ever done in my life, speaks up for you, persuades me to make you a loan. I make the loan, you promise to pay me back, and this is the tenth time you've let me down. But I'm telling you, I won't let you down, not lightly anyway. Get out!

Jacques and his Master were girding up their loins to speak on the poor man's behalf, when the landlady, putting one finger to her lips, gestured to them to hold their tongues.

Landlord. Get out!

Peasant. Everything you say is quite true, as true as it is that the bailiffs are round at my place and that any minute now my daughter, my boy, and I will be turned out of doors.

Landlord. It's no more than you deserve. What do you mean, coming here at this time of morning? I leave off in the middle of bottling my wine, I come up from the cellar, and you're not there like you should have been. I've told you: get out.

Peasant. I did come, but I was afraid of the reception I'd get, so I went away and I'll go away again now.

Landlord. You'd better.

Peasant. So poor little Marguerite, who is so good and so pretty, will have to go into service in Paris.

Landlord. Go into service! In Paris? Do you want to ruin her life?

Peasant. It's not me that wants it. It's the unfeeling brute I'm talking to.

Landlord. Me, unfeeling? I'm not unfeeling, never have been, as you know very well.

Peasant. I can no longer support my daughter nor my boy. My daughter will have to go into service and the boy will enlist.

Landlord. And it'll all be my fault? I won't have that. You're a hard man and you'll be the cross I bear as long as I live. Come on, let's see what we can do for you.

Peasant. You can't do anything for me. I'm truly sorry I owe you money and if I had my way I wouldn't ever owe you another penny ever again. You do more harm by shouting than good with your help. If I had the money, I'd throw it in your face, but I don't. So my girl will turn into whatever it pleases God to make her, my boy will have to get himself killed if he must, and as for me, I shall go begging—but not at your door. Never again, no never, will I be obliged to a man as hard-hearted as you. Take whatever you can get for my oxen, my horses, and my tools, and much good may it do you. You're the sort of man who makes people ungrateful and that's not what I want to be. Goodbye!

Landlord. Stop him, woman! He's going!

Landlady. Don't be like that, man. Let's see how we can help.

Peasant. I don't want your help. The price is too high.

The landlord kept whispering to his wife: 'Don't let him go, stop him. His daughter in Paris! His boy in the army! Him a burden on the parish! I couldn't bear it!'

Meanwhile, his wife was getting nowhere. The peasant, who had spirit, wouldn't accept anything, and it took all four of them to keep him there. The landlord, with tears in his eyes, turned to Jacques and his Master and said: 'Gentlemen, try and talk him out of it!'

Jacques and his Master joined in. They all spoke at the same time, appealing to the peasant. If I ever saw...

If *you* ever saw? But you weren't there. Say 'If ever a man was seen'.

Oh very well. If ever a man was seen so flattened by a refusal, and then so overjoyed that someone would take his money, it was that landlord. He hugged his wife, he hugged Jacques and his Master, and cried: 'Send somebody round to boot those blasted bailiffs out of his house!'

Peasant. But you will agree...

Landlord. I'll agree that I've made a hash of everything. But what did you expect? The way you see me is the way I am. Nature made me the hardest and the softest of men. I'm no good at saying yes and no good at saying no.

Peasant. Can't you behave any differently?

Landlord. I've got to the age when people rarely change for the better. But if, when people first started coming to me for help, they'd jumped down my throat the way you just did, then maybe I'd have been the better for it. Friend, thanks for the lesson, maybe I'll learn from it... Look alive, woman, go downstairs and give him what he needs. Come along, don't just stand there, for God's sake! Shape yourself! You'll... My dear, may I ask you, please, to move a little more quickly and not keep him waiting. Then you can come back and stay with these gentlemen. I can see you're getting along with them like a house on fire.

The landlady and the peasant went downstairs. The landlord remained a moment longer and then, when he had gone, Jacques said to his Master: 'What an odd man! But what does Heaven, which sent the foul weather that's keeping us here because it wanted you to hear about my love-life, want now?'

The Master, stretching out in his chair, yawning, tapping his snuff-box, answered: 'Jacques, we have more than one day left to be together, unless...'

Jacques. You mean that, for today, Heaven wants me to keep my tongue still or, putting it another way, that it wants the landlady to speak. She's got a tongue on her and would be delighted to. So let her speak...

Master. You sound cross.

Jacques. Well, I like talking too.

Master. Your turn will come.

Jacques. Or not.

I can hear you, Reader. This, you're saying, is the real denouement of *Le Bourru bienfaisant!** I think you're right. Now if I'd been the author of that play, I'd have added a character who would have been called episodic but wouldn't have been. This character would have come on from time to time and there would always be a motive for it. On the first occasion, he comes to ask for more time to pay but, fearing he'll get a dusty answer, goes away again before Géronte arrives. Hard-pressed by the sudden appearance of the bailiffs in his house, he plucks up courage a second time to face Géronte, but Géronte refuses to see him. Finally, I'd have brought him into the denouement where he'd have played exactly the same role as the peasant with the landlord. Like the peasant, he would have a daughter and would be trying to find work for her as an assistant in a dressmaker's shop, and a son he was about to remove from college and put into service. He himself would have made up his mind to live as a beggar until such time as he was sick of life. You'd have seen the kindly curmudgeon fall at this man's feet, you'd have heard him being told home truths as he deserved, he would have been forced to explain himself to his whole family, who now gather round trying to persuade the debtor to yield and accept further help. The man who is both kindness and flint would get his comeuppance, he would promise to change his ways, but at the very moment he promises I'd show him reverting to type by losing his temper with all the characters on the stage who by then would be saying polite good-byes before taking their leave. Suddenly, he says: 'Devil take all this damned cerem...' But he stops short in the middle of the word and in a kinder tone of voice says to his nieces: 'Come, girls, give me your hand and let's go inside.'

And to tie this character into the general situation, you'd make him some sort of dependant or protégé of Géronte's nephew?

Why, yes!

And it would be at the nephew's insistence that the uncle lent the money?

Brilliant!

And this loan would have been the reason why the uncle had fallen out with his nephew?

That's it exactly.

And I suppose the climax of this charming little drama would be a general re-enactment with the whole family gathered together of what he had said previously to each of them separately?

You're absolutely right.

If I ever meet Monsieur Goldoni, I shall recite to him the scene at the inn.

Do. He's more than clever enough to make something interesting of it.

The landlady came back up the stairs, still clutching Nicole in her arms, and said:

'I think there'll be a good dinner for you. The poacher's just come. His lordship's gamekeeper won't be far behind him...'

And so saying, she pulls a chair forward. Now she's sitting and her story begins:

Landlady. You've got to keep a close eye on servants. They're a master's worst enemy.

Jacques. Madame, that's nonsense. There are good servants and bad servants, and it could be that there are more good servants than good masters.

Master. Just listen to yourself for a moment—you're making the same kind of sweeping generalization you're objecting to.

Jacques. The fact is that masters...

Master. The fact is that servants...

Well, Reader? What's to prevent me starting a violent quarrel between the three of them, having Jacques grab the landlady by the neck and bundle her out of the room, or having the Master grab Jacques by the neck and bundle him out of the room, or making one storm off in this direction and the other in the opposite direction, thereby ensuring that you get to hear neither the landlady's story nor the rest of the tale of Jacques's love-life? Rest assured: I won't do anything of the sort. The landlady went on:

'You've got to admit that if there are some very nasty men about, you also get some very nasty women too.'

Jacques. Quite right. And you don't have to go far to find them.

Landlady. Keep your nose out of this. I'm a woman and I can say whatever I please about women. I don't need your approval.

Jacques. My approval is as good as anybody else's.

Landlady. Sir, you've got a very knowing manservant who's not as respectful to you as he might be. I've got servants too, but just let them...

Master. Jacques, shut up and let Madame speak.

The landlady, encouraged by Jacques's Master's intervention, gets up, bears down on Jacques, stands with both hands on hips, forgets that she's holding Nicole, drops her so that Nicole ends up on the floor, her feelings hurt, struggling in her shawl, barking her head off, with the landlady adding her shrieks to Nicole's yelps, Jacques adding loud laughter to Nicole's yelps and the landlady's screeching, and Jacques's Master opening his snuffbox, taking his pinch of snuff, and unable to suppress a smile. The whole hostelry is in an uproar:

'Nanon? Nanon? Come quick! Bring the brandy bottle... My poor Nicole is dying... Untangle her from that shawl... Oh you're so clumsy!'

'I'm doing my best.'

'Why is she whimpering like that?... Get out of the way, let me do it... She's dead!... That's right, snigger, you great booby! What's there to laugh about?... Poor Nicole is dead!'

'No, Madame, I think she'll come out of it—yes, she's moving!'

Whereupon Nanon dabs brandy on the dog's nose and forces a few drops down her throat; the landlady wrings her hands and unleashes her venom against impertinent servants; and Nanon says: 'There, Madame, she's opening her eyes. See, she's looking at you.'

'Poor thing! She's talking to me! Who wouldn't feel sorry for her?'

'Madame, give her a little cuddle, say something to her.'

'That's it, poor Nicole, my pet, growl away if it makes you feel better. There's a power that looks after doggies just as there is for people. It takes good care of the lazy, greedy good-for-nothings who snarl and snap, and it makes life a misery for the sweetest little pet that ever was.'

'Madame's quite right. There's no justice in this world.'

'Be quiet, wrap that shawl round her again, go and settle her on my pillow, and remember that the first squeak I hear from her I'll take out on you. Come here, my sweet, give me a kiss before she takes you away. Closer, you silly thing. Dogs are such lovely creatures, they're better...'

Jacques. Than mothers, brothers, sisters, children, servants, husbands...

Landlady. Of course they are, and there's no need to laugh. Dogs are innocent, they don't let you down, they never do you any harm, whereas everybody else...

Jacques. Let's hear it for dogs! The finest creatures the sun ever shone on!

Landlady. If there's anything finer, it's certainly not people. If only you'd seen the miller's dog. He's my Nicole's boyfriend. There's not a man alive, not among the whole lot of you, that he wouldn't put to shame. He comes four miles at first light, sits down under this window, and howls fit to break your heart. Whatever the weather's like, he won't budge. The rain soaks him, he sinks into the mud, you can hardly make out his ears or the end of his nose.* Would you do as much for the woman you loved best in all the world?

Master. It's certainly very chivalrous behaviour.

Jacques. But where's the woman who is as deserving of such attentions as your Nicole?

The landlady's fondness for dumb animals was not, however, her dominant passion, as you might think: it was talking. The more pleasure and patience you showed in listening to her, the better a person you were in her eyes. So she did not have to be asked twice to resume the interrupted story of the peculiar marriage, though she did lay down one condition: that Jacques would shut up. The Master promised that Jacques would hold his tongue. Jacques sprawled in a chair in one corner, eyes closed, with his cotton cap pulled well down over his ears and his back half-turned to the landlady. The Master coughed, spat, blew his nose, took out his watch, looked at the time, felt for his snuffbox, tapped the lid, and took a pinch. The landlady settled down to taste the delights of holding forth.

She was about to begin when she heard her dog bark.

'Nanon, go and see what's the matter with my little angel... That's mixed me all up. I can't remember where I'd got to.'

Jacques. You hadn't started.

Landlady. The two men I was going on at about poor Nicole when you arrived, sir...

Jacques. Say 'gentlemen'.

Landlady. Why?

Jacques. You've done us the courtesy thus far and I've got used to it. My Master calls me Jacques but everybody else says Monsieur Jacques.

Landlady. I'm not going to call you Jacques or Monsieur Jacques. I'm not talking to you.

'Madame?'
'What is it now?'
'The bill for number five.'
'Look on the corner of the mantelpiece.'

Landlady. They're two very proper gentlemen. They're from Paris and are making their way to the estate of the older one.

Jacques. Who says so?

Landlady. They did.

Jacques. That doesn't prove a thing.

The Master made a gesture to the landlady by which she understood that Jacques was not all there. The landlady responded to the Master's gesture with a sympathetic shrug of her shoulders and said: 'And at his age too! Such a pity!'

Jacques. It's a great pity that none of us ever knows where we're going.

Landlady. The older one is called the Marquis des Arcis. He was a ladies' man, was very attractive, and he took a very dim view of female virtue...

Jacques. He was right.

Landlady. Monsieur Jacques, you're interrupting.

Jacques. Madame, proprietress of the Stag Inn, I wasn't talking to you.

Landlady. Even so, the Marquis found one woman sufficiently out of the ordinary to resist his advances. Madame de La Pommeraye was her name. She was a widow who lived by strict principles, was well born and possessed of wealth and a forthright manner. Monsieur des Arcis broke with all his acquaintance, ignored everyone except her, paid court with the greatest assiduity, made all the sacrifices conceivable to prove that he loved her. He even proposed marriage. But the widow had been so unhappy with her first husband that...

'Madame?'
'What?'

'Where's the key to the bin where you keep the oats?'
'Look on the nail. If it's not there, try the lid of the bin.'

... with her first husband that she would have sooner have exposed herself to the most horrible dangers than to the perils of a second marriage.

Jacques. Ah, but what if it had been written on high?

Landlady. The lady lived a very retired life. The Marquis had been a friend of her husband and had been a frequent visitor at her house. She continued to receive him. If she overlooked his unbridled taste for the company of women, it was because he was what is known as an honourable gentleman. The constant attentions of the Marquis, which were reinforced by his personal qualities, his youth, his looks, the indications he gave of being truly in love, the lonely life she led, her need for affection, in a word, everything which makes us yield to the attractions of a man...

'Madame?'
'What?'
'The post's come.'
'Put it in the green room and distribute it as usual.'

... worked its usual magic and Madame de La Pommeraye, after holding out for some months against the Marquis and her better judgement, and demanding the solemn oaths that custom requires, finally made the Marquis a happy man. His fate would have been sunnier had he been able to sustain for his mistress the feelings he had sworn he had for her and which she sincerely had for him. Believe me, sir, only women know what love is: men don't understand the first thing about it...

'Madame?'
'What?'
'The brother from the monastery is here, collecting.'
'Give him twelve sous from these gentlemen and six from me and let him take his bowl round the other rooms.'

Within a year or two, the Marquis was beginning to find life with Madame de La Pommeraye too tedious. He intimated that they might see more of society: she agreed. He suggested she might receive mixed company: she agreed. He proposed that she host a grand dinner-party:

she agreed. Then imperceptibly, a day would go by, two days, when he did not call on her. Imperceptibly, he began failing to put in an appearance at the dinner-parties he had arranged. Imperceptibly, he made his visits shorter. He claimed engagements which called him elsewhere. When he did come, he would not speak but sprawled in an armchair, picked up a book, threw it aside, talked to her dog, or fell asleep. In the evenings, his health, which was making his life a misery, required him to retire early: it was what Tronchin* had ordered. "Tronchin's a great man. By God, I'm convinced he'll pull that friend of yours round, even though all the other doctors have given up on her!" And so saying, he would reach for his cane and his hat and go out, sometimes forgetting to embrace her. Madame de La Pommeraye...

'Madame?'
'What now?'
'It's the cooper.'
'Tell him to go down to the cellar and say he's to have a look at the two barrels in the corner.'

Madame de La Pommeraye began to sense that she was longer loved. She had to know if it were so and this is how she set about finding out...

'Madame?'
'All right, I'm coming!'
The landlady, weary of these constant interruptions, went downstairs and apparently found a way of putting a stop to them.

Landlady. One day, after dinner, she said to the Marquis: 'My dear, you seem preoccupied.'
'And your mind seems to be elsewhere too.'
'It is, and it's full of sad thoughts.'
'What's the matter?'
'Nothing.'
'That's not true. Come, Marquise,' said he with a yawn, 'tell me about it. It will help pass the time for both of us.'
'Are you bored, then?'
'No. But there are days...'
'When you're bored?'
'You're wrong, my dear, I swear that you're quite, quite wrong. It's just that there are days... It's hard to say why it should be.'

'My dear, I've been wanting to say something to you for some time, only I'm afraid I'll hurt you.'

'You? Hurt me?'

'Perhaps. But Heaven will bear witness to my innocence...'

'Madame? Madame? Madame?'

'I told you not to call me for anybody or anything. Call my husband.'

'He's not here.'

'I do apologize, gentlemen, I shall be back in a moment.'

She goes down, comes back up again, and begins again where she left off:

Landlady. 'It all came about without my wanting it, without my even being aware of it, through the fatal mischance which seems to hang over the lives of the whole human race, since I myself have not escaped it.'

'Ah! This concerns you!... I was afraid... But what is it?'

'Marquis, it's... I am so ashamed. It would only distress you. All things considered I think it best if I say no more.'

'No, no, my dear, tell me. Is there something in a secret corner of your heart you're keeping from me? Was not the first rule we agreed upon that we should be completely open and frank with each other?'

'It was, and that is what hangs heavy on me. The weight of it makes the burden of my guilt complete. Have you not noticed that I am not as cheerful in spirit as I was formerly? I have lost my appetite, I eat and drink only because I tell myself I should, and I cannot sleep. I find the company of our closest friends irksome. At night, I lie awake and wonder: Has he grown less adorable? No. Have you any complaint to make against him? No. Have you cause to reproach him for placing his affections elsewhere? No. Does he love you less? No. Then why is it that if the man who loves you is the same, your feelings have altered? For they have, and you cannot hide the fact. You no longer wait for him to come with the same impatience, you no longer take the same pleasure in seeing him, or experience the old anxiety when he is late returning, that thrill of pleasure when you hear the sound of his carriage or his name when he is announced and appears at last—you no longer feel any of these things.'

'What does this mean, Madame?'

Madame de La Pommeraye covered her eyes with her hands, bowed her head, and paused for a moment. Then she resumed:

'Marquis, I knew that you would be very shocked and know all the bitter things you will now say to me. Spare me this, Marquis... or rather do not spare me. Speak your words of reproach and I shall be an acquiescent listener, for I deserve every one of them. Yes, dear Marquis, it is true... Yes, I am... Yet is it not bad enough that it has happened, without my further adding to it the shame and contumely of deceit by pretending that things are other than what they seem? You are the same, but the woman who loves you has changed. She adores you and respects you as much, nay more, than ever. But... but a woman as accustomed as I am to ponder the secret motions of my innermost feelings, and am never anything but honest with myself, cannot fail to acknowledge that the love I felt has fled. It is the most dreadful discovery to make, but it is no less real for that. I, Marquise de La Pommeraye, fickle? inconstant?... Marquis, do not stay your anger, think of the most odious names—I have already applied them to my case—and call me by them, for I am ready to accept them all... all of them, I say, but do not call me unfaithful in my affections. This you will, I hope, spare me, for in truth I am not such a woman.'

'Wife?'
'What is it?'
'Nothing.'

'There's never a minute's peace in this place, even on days when we've hardly any customers and you'd think there was nothing to do. A woman in my position doesn't have it easy, especially with a husband as stupid as mine.'

Landlady. So saying, Madame de La Pommeraye sinks back into her armchair and begins to weep. At once, the Marquis falls to his knees before her and says:

'You are a wonderful, an adorable woman, and I know no other to compare with you. I am confounded by your candour and honesty which fill me with shame. Ah! how infinitely superior you are to me at this moment! How tall you stand in my eyes and how small I feel! You were the first to speak and yet it was I who was guilty first. My dear, your sincerity is contagious. I would be a monster if it were not, and I will confess that the history of your heart is also the history of mine, to the letter. Everything you have ruminated upon I have ruminated upon myself, but I said nothing, suffered in silence, and cannot say when I would have found the courage to speak...'

'Is this true, my dear?'

'Quite true, and it only remains for us to offer each other mutual congratulations that at the same instant we should both relinquish the fragile and illusory bond which united us.'

'Indeed, for how terrible for me if my love had persisted when yours had died!'

'Or if my feelings had been the first to change.'

'You are right, I know.'

'You never seemed to me more adorable or more beautiful than you are at this moment and, had past experience not taught me to be circumspect in these matters, I could almost believe I loved you more than ever.'

And as he spoke these words, the Marquis took her hands and kissed them...

'Wife?'

'What is it?'

'The hay merchant's here.'

'Look in the book.'

'Where's the book?... Oh, don't bother, I've got it.'

Landlady. Madame de La Pommeraye, concealing the aching despair that tore at her, now spoke again, saying:

'So, Marquis? What shall we do?'

'We have neither of us abused the good faith of the other. You will of course continue to have my respect and admiration, and I believe I have not entirely forfeited the claim I had to yours. We shall continue to see each other, we shall share confidences the way old friends do. We shall be spared the petty irritations, the minor betrayals, the reproaches, the ill-tempered outbursts which normally accompany relationships when they end. We shall be like no other couple. You will regain your liberty and you will return mine to me. We will go abroad into fashionable society arm in arm. I will be the confidant of your conquests and shall keep you fully informed of mine—should I attempt any such ventures, which I very much doubt, for you have given me high expectations in that line. It will be delicious. You will guide me with your advice; I shall not refuse you mine when you are beset by perilous circumstances and believe you might need it. Who knows what may happen?'

Jacques. No one does.

Landlady. 'There is every likelihood that the more I venture forth, the more you will gain by comparison with other women, and that I shall return to you more passionate, more tender and more convinced than ever that Madame de La Pommeraye is the only woman alive who could ever make me happy. And when I do return, there is every chance that I will remain yours until the end of my life.'

'But what, perchance, if you were to return to me and find I was no longer there? For the truth is, Marquis, people do not always behave fairly, and it is not beyond the bounds of possibility that I might be taken by a whim, a fancy, even a full-blown passion for another man, though he did not compare with you?'

'I should most assuredly be very sorry for it, but I should have no cause for complaint. I should merely blame the fate which drove us apart when we were close and brought us together again when the time was past when we could be united.'

After this exchange of views, they began to discuss the fickleness of the human heart, the emptiness of lovers' pledges, the bonds of marriage...

'Madame?'

'What is it?'

'The coach is here.'

'Gentlemen,' said the landlady, 'I must go. This evening, when I've got through all my chores, I'll come back and finish the story, if you're curious to know the rest.'

'Madame?'

'Wife?'

'Landlady?'

'Coming, coming, coming!'

When she'd gone, the Master said to his servant: 'Did you notice something?'

Jacques. What?

Master. That woman tells a much better story than you'd expect from the usual run of innkeeper's wives.

Jacques. Quite true. All those interruptions from the servants and whatnot downstairs made me feel cross more than once.

Master. Me too.

And you, Reader, feel free to speak your mind, for as you observe, we are in the mood for frank and open exchanges. Do you want to abandon the loquacious, voluble landlady with her elegant turns of phrase and go back to Jacques's love-life? I myself don't mind one way or the other. When she comes back up yet again, Jacques the Garrulous would ask for nothing better than to resume his role: he'd shut the door in her face and say through the keyhole: 'Goodnight, Madame. My Master's asleep and I'm just about to turn in. The rest will have to wait until next time we pass this way.'

The first time those two creatures of flesh and blood swore undying love to each other was at the foot of a crumbling crag. They bore witness to their constancy beneath the canopy of heaven which is constant only in changing. They themselves were changing even as they spoke and all changed around them, and they believed that their feelings were immune to change! Children! Eternal children!...

I'm not sure who made these observations: Jacques? His Master? Me? But it's obvious it must have been one of us three and that the aforesaid remarks were preceded and followed by many others of the same ilk which would have seen Jacques, his Master, and me clear through until after supper, until the landlady got back, if Jacques had not said to his Master:

Jacques. Look here, sir, the lofty thoughts you voiced just now out of the blue are all very well, but they don't compare with an old fable people used to tell in my village on autumn evenings.

Master. What fable was that?

Jacques. The fable of the Sheath and the Knife. One day, the Sheath and the Knife began to quarrel. The Knife said to the Sheath:

'Sheath, my love, you are a fickle jade, for every day you accommodate new knives.'

The Sheath answered the Knife: 'Knife, my dear, you are a faithless knave, for every day you change sheaths.'

'Sheath, that is not what you promised me.'

'Knife, you deceived me first.'

This quarrel occurred at table. The man sitting between the Sheath and the Knife spoke up saying:

'You, Sheath, and you, Knife, were both right to change, since change is what suits the both of you. But you were quite wrong to promise that you would not change. Knife, can you not see that God made you to fit more than one Sheath? And you, Sheath, to accommodate more than one Knife? You thought certain knives were mad when they vowed to dispense altogether with sheaths, and you thought certain sheaths mad when they vowed to remain closed to all knives. But you did not think that you were just as mad as they when you, Sheath, swore to limit yourself to one Knife, and you, Knife, never to look beyond one Sheath'

The Master said to Jacques: 'Your fable isn't very decent but it's colourful. You'll never guess what an odd thought I've just had. I'm imagining you married to the landlady and wondering how a husband who likes the sound of his own voice gets on with a woman who never stops talking.'

Jacques. A similar thing happened to me for the first twelve years of my life, when I was living with my grandfather and my grandmother.
Master. What were they called? What did they do for a living?
Jacques. They had a shop that sold second-hand clothes. My grandfather Jason had several children. The whole family were very earnest. They got up, dressed, went about their business. They came home at midday, ate, and went back to work again without saying a word. In the evening, they would just sit around. The mother and the girls would spin, sew, and knit without speaking, the boys snoozed, and the father read the Old Testament.
Master. And what did you do?
Jacques. I ran around the room with a gag on.
Master. A gag!
Jacques. Yes, over my mouth. And it's all due to that damned gag that I have this terrible urge to talk. A whole week would go by sometimes without anyone saying anything in the Jason household. All her life, which was a long one, all my grandmother ever said was 'Hats for sale,' while the only words spoken by my grandfather, who was only ever seen standing up in front of his ledgers, straight as a ramrod, with both hands tucked into his frock-coat, was 'One sou'. There were days when he was tempted not to believe the Bible.
Master. Why was that?
Jacques. Because it repeated itself. He thought that was a form of loose talk unworthy of the Holy Spirit. He used to say that people who repeat themselves were fools who took people who listened to them for fools.
Master. Jacques, what if, to make up for the long silence you were forced to keep for those twelve years when you lived with a gag over

your mouth in your grandfather's house, and while the landlady is downstairs gabbing...

Jacques. What if I went on with the story of my love-life?

Master. No, with the other one you never finished, the one about that friend of your Captain.

Jacques. Oh sir, what a cruel memory you have!

Master. Oh Jacques! My dear Jacques!

Jacques. What are you laughing at?

Master. At something that will make me laugh more than once in future—at the thought of you when you were a boy in your grand-father's house with a gag over your mouth!

Jacques. My grandmother used to take it off when there was no-body around, and when my grandfather noticed, he wasn't happy. He'd say: 'Carry on like that, and the lad will turn into the biggest prattlebox that ever was!' His words have come true.

Master. Come along, Jacques, dear old Jacques, let's have the story of the friend of your Captain.

Jacques. I won't say no, but you're not going to believe it.

Master. Is it, then, a tall story?

Jacques. No, because it also happened to somebody else, a French army officer by the name, if memory serves, of Monsieur de Guerchy.

Master. Well, I shall say to you what a French poet, who had turned a rather fine epigram, once remarked when a man claimed in his pres-ence to have made it up himself: 'And why shouldn't this gentleman have made it up? I managed it.' Why shouldn't Jacques's story have hap-pened to his Captain's friend, since it happened to the French officer named de Guerchy? But when you tell it, you'll be killing two birds with one stone: tell me the story of both these men, for I never heard either.

Jacques. That's fine by me. But you have to swear you don't know it.

Master. I swear.

Reader, I'm quite tempted to ask you to swear too, but I'll settle for merely pointing out a singularity in Jacques's character which he seems to have inherited from his grandfather Jason, the uncommu-nicative second-hand clothes dealer, which is that, unlike truly garrul-ous people, although he loved talking, he hated repeating what he had already said. For this reason, he would sometimes say to his Master: 'I'm storing up a lot of trouble for myself. What'll I do when I've got nothing left to say?'

Master. You'll begin again from the beginning.

Jacques. What! Jacques, begin again! The very opposite is written on high. And if I did start all over again, I wouldn't be able to stop myself saying out loud: 'Ah! If your grandfather could only hear you now!' and I'd reach for the gag.

Master. You mean the gag he used to put over your mouth?

Jacques. In the days when gambling was allowed at the fairs of Saint-Germain and Saint-Laurent...*

Master. But that's Paris, and your Captain's friend was adjutant in a frontier garrison.

Jacques. For God's sake, sir, just let me get on with it... A number of officers stepped into a booth and inside came across another officer who was talking to the woman who ran it. One of them challenged him to a game of dice—ten-up, actually—for you should know that after the death of my Captain, his friend had been left well off and had taken to gambling. So he, or perhaps it was Monsieur de Guerchy, accepts. Fate willed it that his opponent should have first throw and he goes ten-up, and does it again and again and again, with no likelihood that he'd ever stop. The game began to hot up, and they played three games, then doubled the stakes, then another three games ditto and another three games and were set fair to continue in the same vein when one of the officers who were watching spoke up and told Monsieur de Guerchy, or my Captain's friend, whichever, that he'd best call it a day and stop playing, because his opponent obviously knew more about dice than he did. When he heard this remark, which was only intended as a joke, my Captain's friend, or possibly Monsieur de Guerchy, believed that he was up against a man who cheated. He put one hand quietly into his pocket, took out a knife, and when his opponent reached for the dice to put them in the dice-box, stabbed the blade clean through his hand, nailing it fast to the table, saying: 'If these dice are loaded, you're a scoundrel. If they're not, I'm in the wrong.'

There was nothing the matter with the dice. Monsieur de Guerchy said: 'I regret this and offer whatever reparation you care to name.'

That was not what the friend of my Captain said. He said: 'I've lost my money, I've skewered a gentleman through the hand, but in return I've rediscovered the joy of fighting till my arm drops off if I like.'

The officer with the knife through his hand withdrew to get it seen to. When he was better again, he called on the skewerer and demanded satisfaction. This officer, that is, Monsieur de Guerchy, found the challenge reasonable.

The other, I mean my Captain's friend, threw his arms around his neck and said: 'I can't tell you how impatient I've been for you to come!'

Off they go to the place appointed. The skewerer, Monsieur de Guerchy or maybe the friend of my Captain, takes a thrust clean through his body. The skeweree picks him up, carts him back to his quarters, and says: 'Sir, we shall meet again.'

Monsieur de Guerchy said nothing.

The friend of my Captain said: 'Sir, I am counting on it.'

They fought a second time, and a third, then eight or ten times, and on each occasion the skewerer gets the worst of it. They were both distinguished officers, both with sterling qualities. The story got out and the Minister stepped in. One of them was confined to Paris and the other was ordered back to his post. Monsieur de Guerchy bowed to His Majesty's command but the friend of my Captain took it hard. And there you have the difference between these two men, neither lacking in natural courage: one was reasonable and the other touched with a whiff of madness.

Thus far, the feud between Monsieur de Guerchy and the friend of my Captain is common to both, for it is the same feud, and that is why I kept mentioning them both by name, if you follow me, sir. I shall now separate them and from now on will tell you only about the friend of my Captain, for the rest concerns him alone. Oh sir! In what follows, you shall see how little control we have over our own destinies and how many strange things are inscribed in the great scroll!

My Captain's friend, alias the skewerer, asks for leave to visit his province. It is granted. His way lies through Paris. He takes his seat in a stagecoach. At three in the morning the coach trundles past the Opéra as people are leaving a ball. Three or four young blades in masks flag down the coach and say they intend to have their breakfast with the passengers. It is daybreak when they reach the inn where breakfast awaits. Who was amazed? Why the skewerer when he recognized the skeweree, who gives him his hand, embraces him, and says how absolutely delighted he is that they should meet by such a lucky chance. Immediately they go behind a barn and draw their swords, the one wearing a frock-coat and the other still wearing his mask. The skewerer, that is the friend of my Captain, ends up on the ground once again. His opponent sees that he's taken care of, then sits down with his friends and the other coach passengers, and eats and drinks in the best of spirits.

The passengers were making ready to continue their journey and the others to return to the capital in their fancy dress on hired horses...

... when the landlady reappeared and cut off Jacques's story in mid-sentence. Yes she's back and I warn you—it is no longer in my power to send her away.

Why not?

Because she's come with two bottles of champagne, one in each hand, and because it's written on high that any person intending to hold forth who approaches Jacques with a preamble of that kind will of necessity have his whole attention.

She comes in, puts her two bottles on the table, and says: 'What do you say, Monsieur Jacques, shall we let bygones be bygones?'

Now the landlady was not exactly in the first flush of youth. She was a large woman, solidly built but light on her feet, glowing with rude health, well upholstered, mouth slightly too big but full-cheeked, with good teeth, prominent eyes, a square brow, the smoothest skin, and an open face, very quick and lively, a bosom you could spend a weekend in, arms a little on the beefy side, but finely shaped hands—the sort that always appeal to a painter or sculptor. Jacques grabbed her round the waist and kissed her hard. However resentful he felt, he could never hold out against a decent bottle of wine and a good-looking woman: this was written on high about him, as it is about you, Reader, and me, and a good many others too.

'Sir,' said she to the Master, 'you're not going to sit there and let us get on with it by ourselves? Listen, you could go another five hundred miles and you'd not find a better tipple anywhere along your road.'

And so saying, she put one of the two bottles between her knees, pulled the cork, and slid one thumb over the top of the bottle with such practised ease that none of the wine escaped.

'Look sharp,' she said to Jacques, 'hurry, give us your glass.'

Jacques holds out his glass. The landlady moves her thumb slightly to one side, releases the pressure, and Jacques gets froth all over his face. He had seen it coming and had gone along with it. The landlady laughed and Jacques and his Master laughed. They sank a few quick glassfuls one after the other just to make sure the wine was all right, then the landlady said:

'They've all gone to bed, thank God, so I'll not be interrupted any more and can get on with the story.'

Jacques, staring at her with eyes whose natural sparkle had been enhanced by the champagne, said to her, or maybe to his Master:

'Our landlady must have been as pretty as a picture. What do you say, sir?'

Master. Must have been? By God, Jacques, she still is!

Jacques. You're right, sir. But I wasn't comparing her to another woman, but to herself when she was younger.

Landlady. Oh, I'm no oil-painting these days. But time was when a man could circle my waist with his two hands. That's when you should have seen me. People would come fifteen miles out of their way to stay here. But let's not dwell on all the wise and foolish heads I've turned in my time, and get back to Madame de La Pommeraye.

Jacques. How about having a little toast first, to the foolish heads you've turned, or to my good health?

Landlady. Good idea. Some of the heads I've turned were worth it, including or excluding yours. Did you know I was banker to the military for ten years, true as I'm sitting here? I advanced cash to quite a few soldiers who wouldn't have got through their campaigns if it hadn't been for me. They were good lads and I've got nothing against them, nor they against me neither. I never asked for security. They kept me waiting sometimes two, three, four years, but I always got my money back.

Whereupon she starts listing the officers who had done her the honour of dipping into her purse. There was X, a colonel in regiment A, and Y, a captain in regiment B... and suddenly Jacques bursts out: 'He was my Captain! My poor, dead Captain! You knew him?'

Landlady. Did I know him! Tall, well-built, not much fat on him, aristocratic-looking and stern, nice legs, two small red marks on his right temple. So you were in the army?

Jacques. Was I in the army!

Landlady. You've gone up in my estimation. Some of the good habits you learned in his service must surely have rubbed off on you. Let's drink to the health of your Captain.

Jacques. If he's still alive.

Landlady. Dead or alive, it's all the same. Aren't soldiers supposed to get killed? After making it through ten sieges and five or six battles, they must get hopping mad to find themselves stretched on their deathbed surrounded by a crowd of black-cassocked vultures?... But back to the story. Let's have another drink.

Master. By God, Madame, you're right there.

Landlady. You're referring to my wine? Well, you're right again. Now, can you remember where we'd got to?

Master. Yes, they'd just finished their confiding, and very wicked they both were too.

Landlady. The Marquis des Arcis and Madame de La Pommeraye embraced, saying how very relieved they were, then went their separate ways. The tighter the rein the lady had kept on her feelings when he was there, the more violent was her reaction when he had gone. 'So, it's true,' she cried, 'he doesn't love me any more!'

I won't go into details of the wild and foolish thoughts that run through women's heads when they've been deserted, it would make you men more vain than you are already. I have said the lady was proud, but she could also be very vindictive. When the first rush of fury had subsided and was replaced by a mood of cold indignation, her thoughts turned to revenge, a cruel revenge, a revenge such as would serve to put the fear of God into any man who might thereafter feel tempted to seduce and betray an honest woman. And she did avenge herself, she avenged herself in the cruellest way, and her vengeance was highly publicized and it mended nobody's ways. Since then, women have not been any less vilely seduced and betrayed.

Jacques. That might be so with other women, but surely not you?

Landlady. Ah! Me even more than the rest. Oh, we women are so stupid! And it's not even as though the men who are so wicked come out of it any better! But let's not dwell on that. So, what will she do? She doesn't know yet. She'll put her mind to it. She puts her mind to it.

Jacques. And while she's putting her mind to it...

Landlady. Well said. But both bottles are empty.

'Jean!'
'Madame?'
'Fetch us up a couple of bottles, from my special store, at the far end.'
'Righty-ho!'

She gave the matter considerable thought and this was what she hit upon. She had once met a woman who had come up from the country to Paris for a lawsuit, and with her she had brought a daughter who was young, pretty, and well-brought-up. She had subsequently learned that this woman, ruined by the loss of her lawsuit, had been reduced to running a bawdy-house. Men came to the establishment, played cards, had supper, and usually one or more of the customers would stay and spend the night with Madame or her daughter, as their fancy took them. Madame de La Pommeraye sent one of her servants to track them down. They were found and invited to call on Madame de La Pommeraye, whom they hardly remembered. They were now known as Madame and Mademoiselle d'Aisnon and did not have to be asked twice. The very next day, the mother turns up at Madame de La Pommeraye's front door. After the usual exchange of courtesies, Madame de La Pommeraye enquires of Madame what she had been doing, how she had managed since losing her case.

'To be perfectly frank,' said Madame d'Aisnon, 'I am involved in a dangerous, shameful business. It pays badly and I hate it, but needs must when the devil drives. I had almost made up my mind to put my daughter on the stage at the Opéra,* but she has only a small voice and never danced very well. Both during and after the trial, I did the rounds with her of the magistrates, great personages, prelates, and bankers, who all took her on for a while and then dropped her. It's not that she isn't a very pretty girl or that she lacks wit and grace, but she has no gift for sex, absolutely no talent for rousing desire in jaded men. I run an establishment where anyone can come and gamble and eat and, after hours, can stay the night if they want to. But what didn't help was that she went and fell for an aristocratic little abbé, an atheistical, non-believing, philandering, anti-philosophical hypocrite. I won't mention his name, but he is the vilest example of the type who aim at a bishop's mitre and take the route to it which is both the shortest and requires the least talent.* I don't know what he told my daughter but he used to come round every morning and read out what he'd scribbled down over dinner and supper the night before. Will he, won't he end up a bishop? Fortunately, they've fallen out. One day, my daughter asked him if he knew the people he wrote about, and he said no. When she asked if his views were any different from those of the people he lampooned, he said no, and she promptly let fly at him and told him in no uncertain terms that what he was doing made him the most vicious, two-faced man alive.'

Madame de La Pommeraye asked her if she and her daughter were well known.

'Much too well known, unfortunately.'

'Am I to take it, then, that you are not anxious to continue as you are?'

'Absolutely. There's not a day goes by without my daughter saying that the lot of the meanest of God's creatures would be preferable to hers. She's become so morose that men won't go anywhere near her.'

'So if I decided to make both your fortunes, you would not object?'

'I'd agree to much less.'

'But first I must know if you are willing to promise to let yourselves be guided by me and do exactly what I say.'

'Whatever you advise, you can count on us.'

'And you will obey my instructions whenever I give them?'

'We should await them eagerly.'

'That is all I need to know. Now go home. It will not be long before you hear from me. Meanwhile, get rid of all your possessions, sell everything, keep none of your clothes, especially if they are loud and vulgar, for they would not suit my plans.'

Jacques, who was beginning to get interested, asked the landlady: 'What if we drank the health of Madame de La Pommeraye?'

Landlady. All right.

Jacques. And the health of Madame d'Aisnon?

Landlady. Here's to her.

Jacques. And you won't refuse to do the same for Mademoiselle d'Aisnon who has a small voice, was never much of a dancer, and has fallen into a state of melancholy that reduces her to the sad necessity of accepting a new lover every night of the week?

Landlady. Don't mock. Mocking is the cruellest thing you can do. If you knew what torture it is when you're not in love...

Jacques. To Mademoiselle d'Aisnon and her torture.

Landlady. Get on with you.

Jacques. Are you in love with your husband, Madame?

Landlady. I wouldn't say that.

Jacques. Then I'm very sorry for you, for he seems a very healthy specimen to me.

Landlady. All that glistens is not gold.

Jacques. To the landlord's rude good health!

Landlady. You can drink to that by yourself.

Master. Jacques, Jacques, you're going at it too fast.

Landlady. Never fear, sir, it's good stuff is this champagne. He'll not feel it in the morning.

Jacques. Since I won't feel it in the morning and because I'm not bothered about whether I'm making good sense or not tonight, I give you, sir, and you, lovely landlady, another toast, a toast I absolutely insist on: let's drink to Mademoiselle d'Aisnon's abbé!

Landlady. Ah! no Monsieur Jacques, not to an ambitious, ignorant, slanderous, intolerant bigot! I believe that's what they call people who would like to slit the throats of anyone who doesn't think the way they do.

Master. There's something you don't know, Madame, which is that Jacques here is a philosopher of sorts. He's always very eager to stand up for insignificant numskulls who bring dishonour on both themselves and the causes they defend so badly. He says his Captain used to say people like them were the antidote to people like Huet, Nicole, and Bossuet.* He never understood what that meant, no more than you do... Has your husband gone to bed?

Landlady. Ages ago.

Master. And he lets you sit up talking like this?

Landlady. I've got him trained... Madame de La Pommeraye gets into her carriage, drives round the part of town furthest away from where Madame d'Aisnon lived, rents a small apartment in a respectable house a stone's throw from a church, furnishes it as sparsely as possible, invites Madame d'Aisnon and her daughter to dinner, and settles them in the same day, or maybe a day or two later, leaving a list of instructions they were to abide by.

Jacques. Madame, we forgot to drink the health of Madame de La Pommeraye and the Marquis des Arcis. It's not right!

Landlady. Go ahead, Monsieur Jacques, the cellar's not empty yet... These were the instructions, or what I can remember of them:

You will not walk out in public places, because you must not be recognized.

You will entertain nobody, not even neighbours or their wives, because you must be seen to live retiring lives.

From tomorrow, you will dress like devout, churchgoing ladies, because that is what you must be thought to be.

You will not keep in your apartment any books other than devotional works, because there must be nothing in your surroundings that might give us away.

You will attend every church service with the utmost assiduity, on Sundays and on every day of the week.

You will find a way of gaining regular access to the parlour of a convent: the tittle-tattle of nuns will do us no harm.

You will become closely acquainted with the curé and the other priests in the parish, for I may need them as witnesses.

You will not allow any of them to call on you regularly.

You will go to confession and you will take communion at least twice each month.

You will revert to your family name, because it is a respectable one and because sooner or later enquiries will be made about you in your province.

From time to time, you will make small donations to charity, but you will not yourselves accept charity in any circumstances. It must be thought that you are neither poor nor rich.

You will spin, sew, knit, and embroider, and you will give everything you make to the Sisters of Charity, to be sold.

You will live very frugally: you may have two small meals sent in from a tavern, but that is all.

Your daughter must never go out without you, nor you without her. And whenever the opportunity arises to be seen to do good works, for a small outlay of money, you will be sure to take it.

And you must never, I repeat, never receive visits from priests, monks, or persons with religious convictions.

You will keep your eyes fixed on the ground whenever you walk abroad. In church, you will have eyes only for God.

'I fully admit that you will find life austere, but it will not last long and I promise that you shall be handsomely rewarded. I want you to consider my offer. If what I ask is beyond your capacity for self-discipline, tell me now. I shall not be offended or surprised. I omitted to mention that it would be useful if you could master the gaseous language of mysticism and familiarize yourself with the Old and New Testaments so that people will think your piety is of long standing. Say you are Jansenists or Molinists,* I do not mind which, though it would be best to be of the same persuasion as your parish priest. Miss no opportunity, whether it's appropriate or not, whatever the occasion, to denounce the *philosophes*. Say Voltaire is the Antichrist, learn your abbé's little tract by heart, and hawk it round the streets if you have to.' Madame de La Pommeraye added: 'I will not come to call on you, for I am not fit company for two such saintly ladies. But don't worry. You may come here from time to time, secretly, and the three of us shall more than make up for your life of penance. But take good care that in the process of faking the symptoms of religion you do not catch the disease. As for your modest household expenses, I shall take care of them. If my plan succeeds, you will soon cease to have need of me. If it fails through no fault of yours, I am rich enough to provide you with a good future, one that is far better than the life you gave up for me. But the key word is obedience, absolute, unlimited obedience to my will. Without it, I refuse to answer for the present and make no promises for the future.'

Master [*tapping the lid of his snuffbox and glancing at his watch to see the time*]. What a damnable woman! Pray God I never meet one like her!

Landlady. Just be patient, you haven't heard the half of it yet.

Jacques. Meanwhile, you sweet, you gorgeous creature, what say we consult the bottle?

Landlady. Monsieur Jacques, this champagne of mine puts my beauty in your beholding eye.

Master. I've been dying to ask you a question for ages, which you may find indiscreet, but I can't hold it back any longer.

Landlady. Ask away.

Master. I'm convinced you weren't born in a tavern.

Landlady. You're right.

Master. And that you were brought down to it from a higher station as the result of some quite extraordinary turn of events?

Landlady. That is so.

Master. So what if we were to suspend the story of Madame de La Pommeraye for a little while and...?

Landlady. Out of the question. I'm always ready to talk about the things that happen to other people but not about myself. All I'm prepared to say is that I was educated at Saint-Cyr* where I didn't spend much time reading the gospels but got through a large number of novels. It's a far cry from a royal abbey there to the tavern I now run.

Master. We'll leave it at that, then. Carry on as if I'd never spoken.

Landlady. While our two pious ladies went about edifying the neighbourhood, and the odour of their sanctity and Christian endeavour spread far and wide, Madame de La Pommeraye maintained with the Marquis an outward show of respect, friendship, and total trust. Always welcome, never scolded, never sulked at, he would tell her all about his little conquests and she appeared to enjoy hearing about them. When one of his affairs was not going smoothly, she would offer her advice and sometimes brought up the subject of marriage, but in such a casual manner that no one could have suspected her of speaking with her own interests at heart. If the Marquis came out with the kind of tender, gallant sentiments which a man who has been on the most intimate terms with a woman can scarcely avoid, she either smiled or ignored him. To judge by what she said, her heart was at peace and, though she would have never thought it possible, she gave the impression that having a friend like him was all she needed in life to be perfectly and completely happy. Besides, she was no longer a girl and her desires had lost their edge.

'You mean you've no secrets to share with me?'

'None at all.'

'But what about that friend of mine, the Count, who was so attentive in the days when I ruled your heart?'

'My door is closed to him. I never see him now.'

'How very odd! And why did you send him away?'

'Because I do not like him.'

'Ah, Madame! I think I see it all. The fact is you still love me!'

'Perhaps.'

'You're hoping that I will come back to you.'

'Why not?'

'And you are building up your moral credit by behaving blamelessly.'

'I do believe I am.'

'And were I to be so fortunate or unfortunate to pick up where we left off, you would make a virtue of never referring to my regrettable escapades?'

'You know me to be utterly discreet and very forgiving.'

'My dear, after what you have done, there is no act of heroism of which you are not capable.'

'I am not unhappy that you should think so.'

'Upon my soul, I do believe you are a danger to me.'

Jacques. I think so too.

Landlady. They had remained on this same footing for three months when Madame de La Pommeraye judged the time had come to set the wheels in motion. One fine summer's day when she was expecting the Marquis to lunch with her, she sent word to Madame d'Aisnon and her daughter they were to pay a visit to the Jardin du Roi.* The Marquis came, lunch was served early, lunch now is eaten and eaten in rare good spirits. Afterwards, Madame de La Pommeraye suggested to the Marquis that they might go out, if, that is, he had nothing more agreeable planned. That day, the Opera and the theatres were closed, as indeed the Marquis himself pointed out. With a view to making up for the absence of a frivolous entertainment with an alternative which was both amusing and instructive, chance would have it that the Marquis himself proposed to the Marquise that they might visit the Cabinet du Roi. The suggestion was not rejected, as you might guess. At once the horses are harnessed, they set off, they reach the Jardin du Roi, and mingle with the crowds, looking at everything and seeing nothing, just like everyone else.

Reader, I've forgotten to describe the setting, I mean the poses and positions of my three characters, Jacques, his Master, and the Landlady. Through my carelessness in this matter, you've heard them speak but you were not able to see them. Better late than never. The Master, on the left, in his nightcap and dressing-gown, reclining comfortably in a high-backed chair with a tapestry seat, his handkerchief hanging over one of the arms and his snuffbox in his hand. The landlady, upstage, facing the door, at the table, with her glass in front of her. Jacques, hatless, on her right, both elbows on the table, head down between two bottles and the other two on the floor beside him.*

Landlady. When they'd visited the Cabinet du Roi, the Marquis and the lady he regarded as his friend took a turn in the gardens. They were strolling along the first avenue on the right as you go in, close by the arboretum, when Madame de La Pommeraye gave a start of surprise and said:

'If I'm not very much mistaken, I think it's... Yes, it's them!'

And she promptly abandons the Marquis and rushes on ahead to meet our two pious ladies. The d'Aisnon girl looked quite ravishing in a simple dress which did not draw the eye directly but fixed the attention of the beholder on her whole person.

'It can't be... it's not you, Madame, is it?' said Madame de La Pommeraye.

'It is!'

'But how are you? Whatever became of you? It's been an age!'

'You are acquainted with our troubles. We have resigned ourselves to living simply, as our new circumstances dictated, and have ceased to go abroad in society since we can no longer appear in it to advantage.'

'But why break off relations with me? I have no connection with fashionable society and always had wit enough to see it for the dreary sham it is!'

'One of the disadvantages of a want of fortune is the mistrust it generates. Those who have no money fear they will quickly outstay their welcome.'

'You, outstay your welcome with me? I find the very thought hurtful.'

'Madame, I am not to blame. I've reminded Mama a score of times but she would always say: child, Madame de La Pommeraye has forgotten all about us.'

'But that is monstrously unfair. Come, sit down and we'll talk. This is a friend, the Marquis des Arcis, and you can speak freely in front of him. But how your daughter has grown! She has become quite a beauty since last we met.'

'There's one thing to be said for our present plight: it places all those things which are so bad for the health beyond our reach. Look at her face, her arms. That's what you gain from a frugal life, regular habits, plenty of sleep, work, and a good conscience, and that is something worth having...'

They sat down and chatted like old friends. Madame d'Aisnon spoke well, her daughter said little. Their tone exuded piety but they were relaxed and unprudish. Dusk was still some way off when both Christian ladies got to their feet. It was pointed out to them that it was still early. Madame d'Aisnon said in a loud whisper to Madame de La Pommeraye that they still had one further pious duty to perform and that they could not stay any longer. They were already some distance away when Madame de La Pommeraye took herself to task for not asking where they lived and for failing to give them her address.

'An act of thoughtlessness,' she added. 'There was a time when I would not have been so remiss.'

The Marquis ran after them to retrieve the situation. They accepted Madame de La Pommeraye's address but, though he tried everything he knew to persuade them, he could not obtain theirs. He did not dare offer them his carriage, though he confessed to Madame de La Pommeraye that he had been tempted.

The Marquis wasted no time in asking Madame de La Pommeraye who and what these two women were.

'Two unfortunates who are more fortunate than we are. Did you observe how well they looked? The serenity in their faces? The candour and propriety which dictate everything they say? In the company we keep I do not see or hear anything to compare with that. We pity the zealots and they pity us but, all things considered, I am inclined to think it is they who are right.'

'My dear Marquise, you're not tempted to take to religion?'

'And why not?'

'Have a care, for I would not wish the end of our affair, if it is indeed ended, to bring you to that.'

'And would you rather have me reopen my door to your friend the Count?'

'Much.'

'Is that what you recommend?'

'Without reservation'

Madame de La Pommeraye told the Marquis what she knew of her pious friend and her daughter, their name, which part of the country they came from, what they had been, and about their lost lawsuit, injecting as much drama and pathos as she could manage. After which she said:

'They are both very worthy ladies, the daughter in particular. You will agree that no woman as well endowed as she would want for anything if she set her mind to converting her beauty into a bankable asset. But they have preferred an honest competency to an easy life of shame. What they have left is so little that I really cannot imagine how they manage to survive at all. They must work day and night. Enduring a life of poverty when you are born into it is something many people can do. But to move from great wealth to the most reduced of circumstances, to accept it and find joy in it, is beyond my comprehension. That is what religion does. Your modern philosophers can say what they like, religion is a good thing.'

'Especially for the poor.'

'And which of us is not poor in one way or another?'

'Damn me! I do believe you're catching religion!'

'What's so dreadful about that? This life is such a trifling thing when compared to the life that is to come.'

'You already sound like a missionary.'

'I sound like a woman who has seen the light. Come, Marquis, be truthful. Would you not count wealth as dross if we were all more aware of the rewards we can expect and the punishments we must fear in the afterlife? Would any man seduce a young woman or a wife who loves her husband if he thought he might die in her arms and be instantly plunged into the eternal torments of hell's fires? Surely you see that he would be mad to attempt it.'

'But it happens every day.'

'Only because people have no faith, because they know not what they do.'

'No, it's because our religious beliefs have no influence on the way we behave. Really, my dear, I'll swear you are rushing headlong to the nearest confessional box.'

'I could do far worse.'

'Come, you've taken leave of your senses. You still have twenty years of delicious sinning ahead of you. Don't waste the opportunity. You can repent afterwards and flaunt it all at the feet of some priest, if you've a mind to... But this conversation is taking a serious turn. Your head is filling with dark, brooding nonsense, it's the effect of the damned solitary life you insist on leading. If you want my advice, you'll summon the Count to return at once, you'll stop seeing hell and damnation everywhere, and you will revert to your former, charming self. Perhaps you are afraid I will hold your past against you if we ever reconcile our differences. But we may never be reconciled and then you will have deprived yourself of the sweetest pleasures in life, and all for fears which may or may not be real. To be perfectly frank, the honour of being my moral superior is not worth the sacrifice.'

'What you say is perfectly true, which is why that's not holding me back...'

Landlady. Then they talked of many other things which I do not remember.

Jacques. Madame, let's have a drink. Drinking refreshes the memory.

Landlady. Let's have one, then... After a few more turns around the gardens, Madame de La Pommeraye and the Marquis got into their carriage. Madame de La Pommeraye said:

'She makes me feel quite old. When they first came to Paris, she was just a girl.'

'You mean the daughter of the lady we met in the gardens?'

'Yes. It's just like a flower-bed: the roses that fade are replaced by new ones. Did you get a good look at her?'

'Didn't miss a thing.'

'What did you make of her?'

'The head of a Raphael Madonna on the body of his Galatea.* And such sweetness in her voice!'

'Such modesty in her glance!'

'So demure in the way she moved!'

'And so proper in all she said—I never noticed a more proper tone in any other young woman I ever met. That's what education does for you.'

'When it is put to work on a good-natured disposition.'

The Marquis deposited Madame de La Pommeraye at her door. And Madame de La Pommeraye made it her first task to inform her two pious protégées that she was satisfied with how they had played their roles.

Jacques. If they carry on the way they've started, then, Monsieur des Arcis, Marquis or no Marquis, you'll not escape their clutches, no, not if you were the Devil himself.

Master. I'd very much like to know what they're up to exactly.

Jacques. I wouldn't. I'd be cross. It would spoil everything.

Landlady. From that day forth, the Marquis became an assiduous visitor at the house of Madame de La Pommeraye, who duly noticed but did not ask him the reason for it. She was never the first to mention the two devout ladies but always waited for the Marquis to bring the subject up, which he always did with some impatience and an ill-disguised air of feigned indifference.

'Have you seen those two friends of yours?'

'No.'

'It's not right, you know. You're rich, they're in queer street, and yet you don't even invite them along to dinner now and then.'

Mme de La Pommeraye. I thought you knew me better than that, Marquis. With the eyes of love, you once exaggerated my virtues; now, with the eyes of a friend, you detect faults. I have already invited them a dozen times but have not managed to persuade them once. They refuse to come here, and whenever I go to them they insist I leave my carriage at the end of the street and that I dress very plain, without rouge or jewellery. We must not be too surprised they should be so careful: it would only take a rumour to alienate a good number of charitable souls and deprive them of the help on which they depend. It seems, Marquis, that a high price is demanded by those who do good works.

Marquis. And the bigots are the most exacting of all.

Mme de La Pommeraye. Quite, they need only the flimsiest excuse to free them of their Christian duty. If it were to leak out that I take an interest in my friends, people would say: Madame de La Pommeraye is looking after them, so they don't need anything. Which means no more charity.

Marquis. Charity!

Mme de La Pommeraye. Yes, charity.

Marquis. You know them and yet they live on charity?

Mme de La Pommeraye. I repeat, Marquis, that it is clear that you no longer love me, since much of your respect for me has obviously vanished along with your affection. Who told you that if these two ladies have been forced on to the mercies of the parish, it was my fault?

Marquis. Pray forgive me, Madame, it was quite wrong of me. But what reason do they give for refusing the kind offices of a friend?

Mme de La Pommeraye. Ah, Marquis, we men and women of the world know nothing of the delicate scruples of such sensitive souls! They do not consider it proper to receive help from just anyone, without distinction.

Marquis. But that robs us of our best chance to redeem our follies and excesses.

Mme de La Pommeraye. Not at all. Let's suppose, for example, that the Marquis des Arcis were to feel sorry for them. Now, why should he not convey his largesse to them through a third party more worthy than he?

Marquis. But less reliable.

Mme de La Pommeraye. That might well be so.

Marquis. Tell me, if I were to send them twenty louis or so, do you think they would refuse to accept it?

Mme de La Pommeraye. I am certain they would. And would you find a refusal so inappropriate, coming as it would from a mother who has such a charming daughter?

Marquis. You know, I've been tempted to go and see them.

Mme de La Pommeraye. I can believe it. But have a care, Marquis! This charitable impulse of yours is very sudden and highly suspect.

Marquis. Be that as it may, do you think they would have received me?

Mme de La Pommeraye. Certainly not. The impression made by your carriage, clothes, and servants together with the young lady's undoubted charms would be more than enough to set the tongues of the neighbours and their wives wagging and bring ruination on them.

Marquis. You alarm me, for that was certainly not my intention. So I must give up all thought of helping and calling on them?

Mme de La Pommeraye. I would say so.

Marquis. But what if I were to channel my help through you?

Mme de La Pommeraye. I do not believe any help you offered would be sufficiently disinterested for me to take responsibility for conveying it.

Marquis. That is very hard.

Mme de La Pommeraye. Yes, hard is the right word.

Marquis. But how can you imagine such a thing? Marquise, you cannot be serious! A young girl I only ever saw once?

Mme de La Pommeraye. But she is one of the few women who are once seen and never forgotten.

Marquis. True, there are some faces that haunt the mind.

Mme de La Pommeraye. Marquis, you really must take care, for you are building up trouble for yourself. I would rather save you from it now than have to provide consolation later. Do not confuse this young woman with the others you have known, for she is not like them. She cannot be tempted, she cannot be seduced, she cannot be approached, she won't listen, and there is no overcoming her resistance.

After this conversation, the Marquis suddenly recalled that he had urgent business to attend to. He stood up hurriedly and left, looking very thoughtful.

A considerable period of time then followed during which the Marquis scarcely let a day go by without calling upon Madame de La Pommeraye. He would arrive, sit down, and not speak, leaving Madame de La Pommeraye to do all the talking. After a quarter of an hour, he would get up and go.

Then almost a whole month passed when he did not come at all. At the end of it, he reappeared looking very sad, very gloomy, and

extremely sorry for himself. When the Marquise saw him, she exclaimed: 'My, what a state you're in! Where have you been? Have you
spent all this time in some bawdy-house?'

Marquis. More or less, by God. I was desperate and flung myself
into an orgy of the most appalling debauchery.

Mme de La Pommeraye. How do you mean, desperate?

Marquis. I mean I was desperate.

Whereupon he began pacing up and down without speaking. He
stood at the window, he stared at the sky, he paused in front of Madame
de La Pommeraye. He went to the door, summoned the servants,
though he had no orders to give them, sent them away, came back,
stood over Madame de La Pommeraye, who went on with her work
and seemed not to notice, tried to say something, but did not dare. In
the end, Madame de La Pommeraye took pity on him and said: 'What
is it? You're not seen for a month, you reappear looking as if you'd returned from the grave, and you wander around the place like a soul in
torment.'

Marquis. I can't stand it any longer. I must tell you everything. Your
daughter's friend has made a deep impression on me. I have done
everything in my power, everything, to forget her. But the harder I've
tried, the more her memory haunts me. She is an angel and I am obsessed with her. There is something important I want you to do for me.

Mme de La Pommeraye. What is it?

Marquis. I must see her again and I can only do so through you. I
have had men out seeing how the land lies. They never go anywhere except to church and back again. I've waited on street corners a dozen
times for them to pass by, and they never even notice. I've hung around
outside their house with the same effect. The result was, first, to make
me as ruttish as an old goat and then holier than all the angels. I've not
missed mass once these last two weeks. Ah, Marquise! Such a face! She
is so beautiful!

Madame de La Pommeraye knew all this already.

Mme de La Pommeraye. In other words, first you did everything you
could to get over it and then you left no stone unturned to drive yourself mad. I take it that the latter strategy has succeeded?

Marquis. I cannot tell you how well it has succeeded! Will you not
take pity on me? May I have you to thank for the joy of seeing her again?

Mme de La Pommeraye. That will be difficult but I will see what I
can do—only on one condition, which is that you will leave the poor

creatures in peace and stop bothering them. I will not hide the fact that they have written to me complaining bitterly of the way you have been persecuting them. Here is their letter.

The letter she gave the Marquis to read had been concocted by all three of them. It appeared to have been written by the d'Aisnon girl at her mother's behest, and no effort had been spared to make it as honest, as sweet, as touching, as elegantly phrased, and as sensible as was required to turn the Marquis's head. Not surprisingly, he positively drooled over every word. He read each sentence several times, he wept tears of joy, and said to Madame de La Pommeraye: 'Come, Madame, surely you agree that no one could write a more perfect letter than that?'

Mme de La Pommeraye. Of course.

Marquis. Every line you read makes you feel the greatest admiration and the profoundest respect for women of such character!

Mme de La Pommeraye. That's as it should be.

Marquis. Very well, I give you my word. But be sure, I implore you, that you in turn will keep yours.

Mme de La Pommeraye. In all honesty, Marquis, I do believe I am just as addle-brained as you. You must still have the most dreadful hold over me. It's frightening.

Marquis. When shall I see her?

Mme de La Pommeraye. That I don't know. First I must try and find a way of managing it which does not arouse suspicion. They can hardly be unaware of your intentions, so you can imagine how my involvement would appear to them if they thought I was acting in league with you... But, Marquis, between you and me, do I need this complication? What concern is it of mine whether you are in love or not, or whether your wits have turned? You must straighten out this business yourself. The role you thrust on me is too bizarre, really it is.

Marquis. But, Marquise, if you abandon me, I am lost! I will say nothing of myself, for I should only offend you, but I beg you, for the sake of two fine and admirable women who are so dear to your heart! You know me! Save them from all the follies I am capable of committing. I shall go to their house, yes, I shall go, I warn you. I will break down their door, I shall force my way in, I shall sit down, I have no idea of what I shall say or do, but you know that in my present distraught state of mind you can fear the worst...!

Landlady. You will observe, gentlemen, that from the start of this story until this moment, the Marquis des Arcis has not said one word which was not like a dagger thrust into Madame de La Pommeraye's heart. She was choking with outrage and fury, which is why her voice faltered and almost broke as she replied:

Mme de La Pommeraye. You are right, of course. Ah! had I been loved like that, perhaps... But we'll say no more of that... Very well, but I shall not be doing it for you. And I assume at least, Marquis, that you will give me time.

Marquis. As little as I can.

Jacques. Landlady, this woman's a fiend in a skirt! Lucifer couldn't hold a candle to her! She's made me go weak at the knees. I'd better have a drink to put me to rights... You're not going to let me drink all by myself?

Landlady. She doesn't scare me... Madame de La Pommeraye was thinking: 'I may be suffering but I shall not suffer alone. You are so cruel! I do not know how long my torment will last but I shall make yours drag out for eternity.'

She kept the Marquis waiting more than a month for the meeting she had promised. She left him all this time to suffer and grow even more besotted. Saying that it would help make the waiting easier to bear, she allowed him to speak of his passion.

Master. And strengthen it by going on and on about it.

Jacques. What a woman! What a demon! Madame, I'm getting more scared by the minute.

Landlady. So the Marquis came each day and talked to Madame de La Pommeraye who, with artful words, stoked him to fever pitch, strengthened his resolve, and completed his downfall. He instituted enquiries and learned of the origins, family, fortune, and ruin of both mother and daughter. He returned to the subject again and again and did not believe he was as fully informed and certainly not as moved by their fate as he might be. The Marquise helped make him aware of the progress of his own feelings and painted alluring pictures of how it all might end by issuing seemingly friendly warnings ostensibly intended to frighten him off.

'Marquis,' she would say, 'tread very carefully. A day might come when my friendship, on which you trespass so outrageously, will no longer be sufficient to justify my actions either in my eyes or yours. Of course, there are men who commit worse follies every day. But, Marquis, I fear that you will not get the girl except on conditions which, until now, have not been to your liking.'

When Madame de La Pommeraye judged that the Marquis was ripe for plucking, she arranged with the two women that they should lunch with her and, with the Marquis, that he should seem to call on her by chance, dressed for the country, so as to allay any suspicions they might have. This plan was put into effect.

The second course had been served when the Marquis was announced. The Marquis, Madame de La Pommeraye, and the d'Aisnons, mother and daughter, together rang all the changes of embarrassment to perfection.

'Madame,' said he to Madame de La Pommeraye, 'I am this moment back from my estates. It's too late for me to return for lunch in town, for I am not expected until tonight, and I was rather hoping you would not refuse me lunch.'

And so saying, he brought up a chair and settled down at the table which had been arranged in such a way that he found himself sitting next to the mother and opposite the daughter. He gave a grateful glance at Madame de La Pommeraye for this thoughtful attention to detail. Recovering from their initial confusion, our two puritans quickly regained their composure. The talk flowed freely and there was even laughter. The Marquis was extremely attentive to the mother and behaved with the greatest reserve and formality towards the daughter. It was a source of secret amusement to all three women that the Marquis should go to such lengths to say or do nothing which might shock their modesty. They were even so cruel as to make him discuss religion for three hours on end, and Madame de La Pommeraye observed:

'What you say reflects the greatest credit on your parents: the early lessons we are taught are never forgotten. You have such a clear understanding of the subtleties of divine love that anyone would think that you were raised entirely on a diet of Saint François de Sales.* You have never had Quietist leanings,* I suppose?'

'I really don't remember.'

There is no need to report that our two pious ladies contributed to the discussion with all the charm, intelligence, grace, and delicacy they could muster. In the course of the conversation, the subject of the passions cropped up. Mademoiselle Duquênoi (that was her real name) argued that only one passion was truly dangerous. The Marquis concurred. Both women left between six and seven o'clock and could not be prevailed on to stay longer. Madame de La Pommeraye agreed with Madame Duquênoi that duty came first, for otherwise there could be no day, however agreeably spent, that was not spoiled by the pangs of an uneasy conscience. They take their leave, much to the regret of the Marquis, who remains alone with Madame de La Pommeraye.

Mme de La Pommeraye. Well, Marquis? Am I not all heart? I defy you to show me another woman in the whole of Paris who would have done as much for you.

Marquis [kneeling before her]. You are right, there is no one like you. You are generosity itself and I do not know what to say. You are the only true friend I have.

Mme de La Pommeraye. But can you say for certain that you will always feel as you do now about what I have done?

Marquis. I should be a monster of ingratitude were I to behave otherwise.

Mme de La Pommeraye. Let's speak no more of it. Now, what is the state of your feelings?

Marquis. Do you want me to be absolutely frank? I must have the girl or I shall die!

Mme de La Pommeraye. Oh, you shall have her. The question is, as what?

Marquis. We shall see.

Mme de La Pommeraye. Marquis, I know you. I also know them. It's all quite obvious.

The Marquis went two months without calling on Madame de La Pommeraye, and this is what he did in that time. He struck up an acquaintance with the confessor of both mother and daughter. This priest was a friend of the abbé I mentioned and, after raising all the hypocritical objections that can be put in the way of a dishonourable intention and selling the saintliness of his cloth for the highest price he could get for it, he finally agreed to everything the Marquis wanted.

The first villainy perpetrated by this man of God was to alienate the good opinion of the curé by persuading him that the two women Madame de La Pommeraye had taken under her wing were receiving parish charity at the expense of the poor, many of whom were in greater need than they. His aim was to make them do what he wanted by forcing them into destitution.

Next, using the weapon of the confessional, he proceeded to set mother against daughter. When he heard the mother complain of her daughter, he exaggerated the wrongs of the one and fomented the resentment of the other. If it was the daughter who complained of her mother, he insinuated that there was a limit to the power mothers and fathers have over their children and that, should her mother's persecution reach a certain point, it might not be impossible for the daughter to cast off the yoke of a tyrannical parent. Then, for her penance, he would tell her to come back to confession.

At other times he would say, with a twinkle in his eye, that she was a pretty girl, but added that beauty was one of the most dangerous gifts God could bestow upon a woman. He would mention the impression she had made on a certain gentleman whom he did not name but whose identity was not hard to guess. He moved from there to God's infinite mercy and the lenient view He took of sins which are unavoidable in certain circumstances; to the frailty of human nature which we can all find it in our hearts to forgive; to the violence and universality of feelings to which even the most saintly men have not been immune. He asked if she had ever felt certain desires, if the promptings of nature spoke to her through dreams, if the proximity of men disturbed her. He then raised the question of whether a woman should yield to a passionate man or resist, and thus sentence to death and damnation one for whose sake Jesus Christ shed His holy blood: this question he did not dare settle for her. Then he would sigh deeply, raise his eyes to Heaven, and pray for the peace of all souls in torment... The young woman gave him his head. Her mother and Madame de La Pommeraye, to whom she gave a faithful account of everything her confessor said, both suggested additional sins which she might confess and thus lead him further along this road.

Jacques. This Madame de La Pommeraye is a very wicked woman.

Master. That's easily said, Jacques. Where did she get her wickedness from? From the Marquis des Arcis. Give him back to her just as he swore he would be, and I defy you to find any fault in Madame de La Pommeraye. When we get back on the road, you can prosecute and I shall undertake her defence. As for the vile, interfering priest, you can say whatever you like about him.

Jacques. He's such a swine that after hearing about this business I'll never go to confession again. What do you think, Madame?

Landlady. Me? Oh, I shall continue to go to my old curé. He doesn't pry and only hears what you tell him.

Jacques. Shall we raise our glass to the health of your old curé?

Landlady. This time I'll go along with that, for he's a good man. He lets the young people dance on Sundays and holidays, and he doesn't mind if the grown-ups come here as long as they don't go home rolling drunk. I give you the curé!

Jacques. The curé!

Landlady. All three women were in no doubt that at any moment this man of God would venture to convey a letter to his penitent. And so it came to pass. But how circumspectly did he set about it! He did not know who it was from, though he was quite convinced it must have come from some kindly, philanthropic soul who had learned of their plight and was offering to help. This was not the first such letter he had passed on to women in such circumstances.

'In any case,' said he, 'you are a good girl and your mother is very sensible. I insist that you open it only in her presence.'

So Mademoiselle Duquênoi took the letter and gave it to her mother, who forwarded it immediately to Madame de La Pommeraye. Armed with the epistle, she sent for the priest, heaped reproaches on his head as he deserved, and threatened to inform his superiors if similar reports of his conduct ever came to her attention again.

When she had finished lecturing the priest, Madame de La Pommeraye summoned the Marquis, gave him to understand that his behaviour fell very short of what was expected of a gentleman, said that he had compromised her position, and brandishing the letter, informed him in no uncertain terms that, notwithstanding the genuine friendship that still bound them, she had no alternative but to forward it to the attention of the authorities or, failing that, should her daughter be tainted by any whiff of public scandal, give it to Madame Duquênoi.

'Ah, Marquis!' she said, 'love has corrupted you! You were surely born under an evil star, for Love, which inspires us to great deeds, prompts in you only the basest actions! What did these two poor ladies ever do to you that you would add shame to their poverty? Must you persecute the girl merely because she is pretty and wishes to remain virtuous? What gives you the right to make her loathe and detest the greatest gifts God has bestowed on her? What did I ever do to deserve to end up as your accomplice? You should get down on your knees, Marquis, beg my forgiveness, and swear you will leave my unfortunate friends in peace.'

The Marquis promised to do nothing further without consulting her, but repeated that he must have the girl, whatever the cost.

However, he proved to be quite untrue to his word. The mother was aware of how matters stood and he did not hesitate to approach her directly. He acknowledged that what he had planned was quite wrong. So he offered a large sum of money, dangled high hopes of what in time might come to pass, and with his letter sent a small case containing fine gems.

The three women conferred together. Both mother and daughter were minded to accept, but that was not what Madame de La Pommeraye wanted. She reminded them of the promise they had made her, threatened to reveal everything, and much to the regret of both our churchgoing ladies (the daughter most reluctantly removing a pair of earrings which suited her so well), both the jewel-case and the letter were returned along with a covering note which breathed injured pride and indignation.

Madame de La Pommeraye reproached the Marquis for giving her such little cause to believe his promises. As his excuse, he said it had been impossible for him to ask her to act for him in so indelicate a matter.

'Marquis,' she said, 'I have warned you once and I do so again: you have not got where you wanted to be. But the time for reading you moral lectures is past, it would be a waste of words, for there is no more to be done.'

The Marquis confessed that he shared her view but asked her permission to make one last effort. By this he meant settling a large sum on both women, sharing his fortune with them, and giving them title, for as long as they should live, to two houses which he owned, one in town and the other in the country.

'Certainly you may try,' said the Marquise. 'I draw the line only at violence. But you may take it from me, my dear Marquis, that honour and virtue in the true sense are without price in the eyes of those fortunate enough to possess them. Your new offer will succeed no better than the others. I would stake my life on it. I know these women.'

The new proposal is duly put.

The three women held another secret council. Mother and daughter waited in silence to hear what Madame de La Pommeraye had decided. For a moment, she paced up and down without speaking.

'No,' she told herself, 'my bitter heart shall not settle for so little.'

Whereupon she said the answer must be no, and thereupon both women burst into tears, fell at her feet, and told her how horrible it was for them to find themselves forced to turn down an immense fortune which they could accept without fearing the consequences. Madame de La Pommeraye replied tersely:

'You don't imagine I am doing all this for you? Who are you? What do I owe you? What is there to prevent me from sending you back to your miserable bawdy-shop? What is on offer may be more than enough for you, but it's too little for me. Take a pen, Madame, and write your reply which I shall now dictate. And I shall take care to see for myself that it is sent.'

Both ladies returned home much more in fear than in sorrow.

Jacques. This woman behaves as if she's possessed! What's she really after? You can't tell me that a lovers' tiff isn't adequately punished by the sacrifice of half a very large fortune?

Master. Jacques, you've never been a woman, let alone a virtuous woman, and you are judging by the dictates of your own character, which is not the same as Madame de La Pommeraye's. You want me to tell you? I'm very much afraid that the marriage of the Marquis des Arcis with a tart is written up there, on high.

Jacques. If it is written, it will happen.

Landlady. The Marquis wasted no time in calling upon Madame de La Pommeraye, who asked: 'Well, how goes your new offer?'

Marquis. Put and rejected. I don't know which way to turn. If I could tear this terrible obsession from my heart, I would. If I could tear my heart out I would. But I can't. Look at me, Marquise, and say if you don't see any physical resemblance between that young woman and myself?

Mme de La Pommeraye. I never mentioned it before but yes, I had noticed something of the sort. But that's neither here nor there.* What have you made up your mind to do?

Marquis. I can't make up my mind to do anything. Sometimes I feel I want to jump into a post-chaise and keep on going for as long as there's road to drive on. Then the next moment, I feel as weak as a kitten, too exhausted to move, my head spins, I cannot think straight and have no idea of what's to become of me.

Mme de La Pommeraye. Then I wouldn't advise you to take up travelling. It hardly seems worth while to get as far as Villejuif only to turn round and come back again.*

The next day the Marquis wrote to the Marquise informing her that he was going to the country, where he would remain for as long as he could. He begged her to further his cause with her two friends, should any occasion for it arise.

He did not stay away long.

He returned, having made up his mind to marry the girl.

Jacques. I feel very sorry for the Marquis.

Master. I don't.

Landlady. He stopped at Madame de La Pommeraye's house. She was out. When she returned, she discovered the Marquis ensconced in a large armchair, with his eyes closed, deeply lost in thought.

'Ah, Marquis! Back again? The country holds no lasting charms for you.'

Marquis. No, I cannot settle anywhere and I have returned with my mind made up to embark upon the greatest folly a man of my birth, age, and character could possibly commit. But I shall be better off marrying her than suffering like this. So I shall marry her.

Mme de La Pommeraye. But Marquis, this is a grave step and it deserves serious thought.

Marquis. I have only one thought, but a sound one, and it is this: I can never be more unhappy than I am now.

Mme de La Pommeraye. You might be mistaken.

Jacques. Oh, the snake in the grass!

Marquis. So here at last, my dear Marquise, is a piece of business I believe I can decently ask you to negotiate on my behalf. Go to see both the mother and the daughter. Question the mother, judge the daughter's feelings, and tell them what I propose.

Mme de La Pommeraye. Hold hard, Marquis. I thought I knew them well enough for the few dealings I have had with them. But now the future happiness of a friend is at stake, so you will allow me to scrutinize them more closely. I shall make enquiries in the place they came from, and I promise to uncover every move they have made since arriving in Paris.

Marquis. These precautions seem quite unnecessary to me. Women living in such straitened circumstances, who have refused the bait I have dangled under their noses, can be nothing less than persons of rare merit. Why, with the offers I have made them I could have brought a duchess to heel. Besides, did you not tell me yourself that...

Mme de La Pommeraye. Yes, I told you whatever you like, but even so, you will please allow me to satisfy myself.

Jacques. The bitch! The scheming, raging shrew! Why did he ever have anything to do with her?

Master. Why did he seduce and then desert her?

Landlady. Why did he stop loving her without rhyme or reason?

Jacques [*pointing to the sky above*]. Could it be, sir...?

Marquis. And why don't you get married?

Mme de La Pommeraye. And who, pray, should I marry?

Marquis. The Count. He has wit, comes of a good family, and he is rich.

Mme de La Pommeraye. But who will answer for his fidelity? You, Marquis?

Marquis. Certainly not. But it seems to me that a wife can manage well enough without a husband's fidelity.

Mme de La Pommeraye. That's true, but if mine were to be unfaithful to me, it might just occur to me to take offence: I am a vindictive woman.

Marquis. In that case, you would take your revenge, that goes without saying. But we could all move in together and the four of us would form the most amusing ménage.

Mme de La Pommeraye. That is all very well, but I have no intention of taking up matrimony. The only man I might have been tempted to marry...

Marquis. Is me?

Mme de La Pommeraye. I can confess it now that it no longer matters.

Marquis. But why did you never tell me?

Mme de La Pommeraye. In the event, I was right. The woman you are about to take to wife will suit you far better from every point of view.

Landlady. Madame de La Pommeraye pursued her investigations in all the detail and with all the speed she deemed necessary. She furnished the Marquis with the most flattering reports, some obtained in Paris and others from further afield. She asked him to promise her a delay of two weeks more, so that he might review his position once again. Those two weeks seemed an eternity to him. Finally, the Marquise had no choice but to yield to his entreaties and his pleading. The first interview took place in her friends' apartment. Everything is agreed, the bans are published, the marriage contract is signed. The Marquis makes a present of a superb diamond to Madame de La Pommeraye, and the marriage is celebrated.

Jacques. A web of deceit! What a revenge!

Master. I don't understand.

Jacques. If you put my mind at rest about what happened on the wedding night, I can't see much harm's been done thus far.

Master. Shut up, you fool.

Jacques. I was thinking...

Landlady. Just do what your Master's told you.

As she said this, she smiled, and as she smiled, she raised her hand to Jacques's face and tweaked his nose. 'But it was on the following day that...'

Jacques. Weren't things the same the next day as they were the day before?

Landlady. Not quite. Next morning, Madame de La Pommeraye wrote a note to the Marquis asking him to call at her house at his earliest convenience on a matter of some urgency. The Marquis did not keep her waiting. But when he got there, she received him with a face that was the picture of fury and indignation. What she said to him did not take long. This is what she said:

'Marquis,' she began, 'you are about to know me for what I am. If other women had a sufficiently good opinion of themselves to feel all the resentment I do, there would be fewer men like you. You acquired the love of a good woman but could not keep it. I was that woman and she has taken her revenge by providing you with a wife who is worthy of you. Get out of my house and drive to the Hôtel de Hambourg in the rue Traversière.* There you will be informed of the vile trade which both your wife and your mother-in-law plied there for ten years under the name of d'Aisnon.'

There are no words to describe the poor Marquis's surprise and dismay. He did not know what to think, but his uncertainty lasted only as long as it took him to drive from one end of town to the other.

He did not go home again that day but wandered the streets. Both his mother-in-law and his wife half suspected what had happened. At the first knock on the door, his mother-in-law fled to her room and locked herself in, leaving the Marquis's wife to wait alone.

As her husband came in, she could read in his face the towering rage which consumed him. She prostrated herself before him and remained face down on the floor, not speaking.

'Get out, you whore! Don't come anywhere near me!'

She tried to get up but collapsed and lay, with her face pressed to the floor and both arms stretched out, between the Marquis's feet.

'Sir,' said she, 'ride roughshod over me, trample me beneath your heel, it's no more than I deserve. Do what you like with me but spare my mother.'

'Get out!' repeated the Marquis, 'leave my house! It is enough that you have tarred me with shame: you can at least spare me the temptation of committing a crime!'

The wretched girl remained as she was and did not answer. The Marquis was sitting in an armchair, his head buried in his hands and his body arched forward over the foot of his bed, without looking at her and shouting at intervals: 'Get out!'

When she continued silent and unmoving, he was surprised and said again in an even louder voice: 'I want you to get out. Do you hear?'

Then he bent down, pushed her away roughly, and then realized that she was not merely senseless but almost lifeless. He took her round the waist, laid her on a couch, and stood for a moment looking down at her with an expression which went from pity to anger and back again. He rang and footmen appeared. He sent for maids and told them: 'Take your mistress. She is unwell. Carry her to her room and attend to her.'

After a while, he sent secretly to have news of her. He was told that she had recovered her senses but that new fainting-fits had followed hard on the heels of the first, and were so long and so frequent that no one would answer for her.

An hour or so after this, he again sent secretly for news. He was told that she was breathing with difficulty and that she was now afflicted with fits of choking which could be heard from the courtyard outside.

The third time, it was by then early morning, he learned that she had wept a great deal, that the choking-fits had ceased, and that it seemed she might sleep.

Later the same day the Marquis ordered the horses to be harnessed to his carriage and was not seen again for two weeks. No one knew where he had gone. But before leaving, he ensured that all the needs of mother and daughter were attended to and gave instructions that Madame's orders were to be obeyed as though they were his own.

During all this time both women remained closeted together, hardly speaking, the daughter sobbing, groaning at intervals, tearing her hair, and wringing her hands, so that her mother did not dare come near and console her. One wore the face of despair and the other of grim resolve. A score of times, the daughter told her mother: 'Mother! We must leave this place! We must escape!' and a score of times the mother opposed her, saying:

'No, my girl, we must stay, we must see how all this ends. He is not going to kill us.'

'Would to God', the daughter said, 'that he had already done so!'

To which her mother replied: 'You'd do more good by keeping silent than by talking such nonsense.'

On his return, the Marquis shut himself away in his study and wrote two letters, one to his wife and the other to his mother-in-law who, the same day, left the house and went directly to a Carmelite convent in the next town, where she died not a few days since. Her daughter dressed and dragged herself to her husband's apartment where, it seems, he had asked to see her. She was hardly through the door when she flung herself on her knees.

'Get up,' said the Marquis.

But she did not get up. Instead, she shuffled towards him on her knees, shaking uncontrollably, her hair uncombed, shoulders bowed, hands held at her sides, with her head raised and her eyes fixed on his, while the tears streamed down her cheeks.

'I think I sense', said she, a sob separating every word, 'that your rightful indignation has subsided and that perhaps, with time, I may yet be granted your mercy. Sir, I beg you, do not be quick to forgive me. Many honest girls have turned into dishonest women but perhaps I may provide an example of the contrary. I am not yet worthy that you should hold out your hand to me. Wait—but leave me with the hope of your pardon. Keep your distance from me. You shall observe my conduct and judge. Oh how happy I would be should you sometimes condescend to notice me! Choose some dark corner of your house and grant that I might live out my days there. I shall stay confined and never complain. Ah! If only I could expunge the name and title I was made to usurp and then die, you should have instant satisfaction! I have allowed myself to be led, by weakness, temptation, compulsion, and threats, to commit an infamous act. But you must not believe, sir, that I am wicked. I am not wicked, since I did not hesitate to come as soon as you sent for me and now dare to raise my eyes to meet yours and speak as I do. If only you could read what is in my heart, if only you could see how far my past faults are put behind me, how foreign to me are the ways of women of my sort! Corruption laid its hand upon me, but it did not keep me in its grip. I know what I am, but in one matter I do myself this much justice: by my tastes, my sentiments, and my character, I was born worthy of the happiness of being yours. Oh, had I been allowed to speak to you alone, I should have only needed to say one word, and I believe I should have had the courage to say it. Sir, do with me what you will. Call your servants, let them strip me naked and turn me out into the street when it is night, I will not resist. Whatever fate you have in mind for me, I shall submit to it. A distant province or the obscurity of a convent will remove me from your sight for ever. Say the word and I shall go. Your happiness is not lost beyond hope, for you will forget me.'

'Get up,' said the Marquis gently, 'I have forgiven you. Even as the outrage was inflicted I never forgot you were my wife and respected you as such. Not one word intended to humiliate you escaped my lips, or if it did I am truly sorry for it and swear that you will never hear another that demeans you. For bear in mind that a wife cannot make a husband unhappy without making herself unhappy. Be honest, be happy, and make me happy too. Please get up now, you are my wife, get up and embrace me. Stand up, Marquise, the floor is no place for you. Rise, Madame des Arcis!'

While he spoke, she had remained where she was, her face hidden by her hands and her head against the Marquis's knees. But when he said 'my wife', when he said 'Madame des Arcis', she leaped to her feet and threw herself at him, holding him fast, hardly able to breathe for anguish and joy. Then she released him, fell to the ground, and kissed his feet.

'Ah!' said the Marquis, 'I have forgiven you, I told you so, but I see you do not believe me.'

'That is how it must be,' she replied. 'I must never believe you.'

The Marquis went on: 'And I believe that I regret none of this. Moreover, I believe that this Pommeraye woman, far from having her revenge, has done me a great service. And now, Madame des Arcis, you must dress and meanwhile your trunks shall be packed. We will go and stay at my estate and there we shall remain until such time as we may show ourselves here again without disagreeable consequences for either of us.'

They were absent from Paris for almost three years.

Jacques. I'd bet good money that those three years passed in a flash and that the Marquis des Arcis was one of the best husbands that ever lived and had one of the best wives who ever breathed.

Master. And I'd go halves with you, though I really can't think why, because I wasn't at all happy with the girl all through the time when Madame de La Pommeraye and her mother were deviously plotting. Never felt afraid for one moment, gave no sign that she was unsure of herself or that she felt any remorse. I did not see her protesting against her role throughout the whole ghastly business. She did not hesitate to do whatever was required of her. She goes to confession, takes communion, makes a mockery of religion and its ministers. To me, she seemed as deceitful, as contemptible, as wicked as both the others... Madame, you tell a very good story, but you are not yet sufficiently skilled in the art of drama. If you really wanted us to feel for the girl, you should have made her more outspoken and shown her as the innocent victim forced into what she did by her mother and Madame de La Pommeraye. You needed to demonstrate that it was because she was cruelly used that she went along, against her will, with a succession of crimes spread over a whole year. That way you would have prepared the ground for her reconciliation with her husband. When you bring a character on stage, that character must be consistent. Now, I ask you, dear lady, is the young woman who plotted with those two wicked females the same as the wife we saw pleading at her husband's feet? You have infringed the rules of Aristotle, Horace, Vida, and Le Bossu.*

Landlady. Bossy? Who's being bossy? I told you the story exactly as it happened. I didn't leave anything out and I didn't put anything in. Anyway, who knows what went on in the girl's mind? Who can say that when she seemed to be throwing herself enthusiastically into the plot, she wasn't eaten up by some secret misgivings?

Jacques. Madame, this time I must agree with my Master—I'm sure he won't mind since it doesn't happen very often—about this Bossu man, who I never heard of, and the other three he mentioned, though I don't know them either. If Mademoiselle d'Aisnon, née Duquênoi, had been a sweet little thing, I'm sure it would have come out.

Landlady. Whether she was a sweet little thing or no, the fact remains that she's a model wife, that her husband's pleased as punch with her, and that he wouldn't swap her for another one.

Master. I congratulate him. He was more lucky than wise.

Landlady. And I shall bid you goodnight. It's late and I'm always the last in bed and the first up. It's no life running an inn. Goodnight to you both. I promised, in connection with what I can't remember, to tell you the story of a peculiar marriage, and I believe I've kept my word. Monsieur Jacques, I don't think you'll have any trouble getting to sleep. Your eyes are closing already. Goodnight, Monsieur Jacques.

Master. So there's no way of hearing about your own adventures, Madame?

Landlady. No.

Jacques. You've got an awful appetite for stories!

Master. So I have. They both instruct and amuse me.* Someone who can tell a good story is a rare bird.

Jacques. Now that's exactly why I don't like stories, unless I'm the one who's telling them.

Master. You'd rather spout a lot of nonsense than keep your mouth shut.

Jacques. That's true.

Master. And I'd rather hear a lot of nonsense being spouted than hear nothing at all.

Jacques. It's Jack Sprat and his wife.

I've no idea where the landlady, Jacques, and his Master had put their brains not to have come up with even one of the many things that could be said in Mademoiselle Duquênoi's favour. Did she have any idea of what wily Madame de La Pommeraye was up to before the grand finale? Wouldn't she have preferred to accept the Marquis's blandishments than his offer of marriage, and been happier to have him as a lover than as a husband? Wasn't she constantly threatened and dominated by the Marquise? Can she be blamed for hating her old sordid, degrading life? And if you want to take her side and think better of her, could you really expect her to have shown much more delicacy and finer scruples in her choice of a means of extricating herself from it?

And, Reader, do you think it would be any harder to make a case for Madame de La Pommeraye? Maybe you'd have found it more amusing to hear Jacques and his Master on the subject, but they had so many other and more interesting things to talk about that it's quite likely they might never have got round to this particular topic. So allow me a moment to do it instead.

You foam at the mouth at the very mention of the name of Madame de La Pommeraye. You shriek: 'Oh, what a horrible woman! The hypocrite! The harridan!' Please, no shrieking, no foaming, no taking sides. Let's think about this calmly. Blacker crimes than hers are committed every day of the week, but they are not touched by genius. You may hate Madame de La Pommeraye, you may fear her, but you do not despise her. Her revenge was savage, but it was not contaminated by any motive of base self-interest. You weren't told that she threw the large diamond the Marquis gave her right back in his face, but that is what she did, I have it on the very best authority. She wasn't interested in increasing her wealth or acquiring honours or titles. Just think. If she'd been married and had worked as hard to ensure her husband was given his due for his service to the public good, or if she'd slept with a government minister or even a first secretary to get him a decoration or a regiment, or with the keeper of ecclesiastical preferments to lay her hands on a rich abbey, you'd think it was all pretty straightforward. Conventional wisdom would be on your side. Yet when she takes her revenge for being callously betrayed, you turn against her instead of seeing that her vindictiveness revolts you because either you are incapable of feeling vindictive on the same scale, or else place a very low value on the honour of women. Have you given any thought at all to what Madame de La Pommeraye sacrificed for the Marquis? I won't dwell on the fact that her purse had been his to use whenever he needed money and that for several years he slept under no roof and ate at no table except hers, for you'd dismiss it with a shake of your head. But she did give in to his every whim, went along with his tastes, and turned her life upside down to please him. She was highly respected in society for the purity of her morals, and she stooped to join the common herd. When at last she granted the Marquis some return for his attentions, people said: 'Ah! so the perfect Madame de La Pommeraye is no better than us after all!' She was aware of sarcastic smiles on people's faces, heard their jokes, and she had blushed and looked away. She had drained the cup of bitterness which is always handed to women whose blameless lives have for too long drawn attention to the immoral conduct of other women around them. She had endured the furious blast of scandal, which is the customary revenge exacted against foolish prudes who make an ostentatious show of virtue. She was a proud woman and would rather have died of shame than continue to appear in society humiliated by the knowledge that she had surrendered her honour and would suffer the common fate of a woman spurned, which is to be ridiculous. She had almost reached the age where a woman may find that the loss of a lover can never be made good. It was in her character that this unfortunate episode should drive her to frustration and solitude. A man can run his sword through another for a gesture or a denial. So why should a woman who has been ruined, dishonoured, and betrayed not be allowed to throw the man who has used her so cruelly into the arms of a courtesan? Ah, Reader, you are free with your praises but how quick you are to condemn!*

But I hear you say: 'What I've got against the Marquise is not so much what she did but rather the way she did it. I can't accept the idea of a grudge that lasts for so long, a tissue of lies and deceit that is spread over almost a whole year.'

Neither can I, nor can Jacques, his Master, and the landlady. But look, you readily forgive what's done in the heat of the moment. Well, let me point out that whereas the heat of the moment cools quickly for other people, in the case of Madame de La Pommeraye and women of her character, it lasts a very long time indeed. In some cases, they go on feeling for the rest of their lives exactly as they felt the day they were spurned. And where's the harm, what's so unjust about that? It seems to me that if it happened more often fewer women would be abandoned. Indeed, I'd like to see a law that forced any man who seduced and deserted an honest women to marry a tart. Pair off communal men with communal women.

But while I've been prattling on, Jacques's Master is snoring as if he'd been listening to every word, and Jacques, no longer in control of his leg muscles, is staggering around the room in his nightshirt and bare feet, falling over the furniture and finally waking his Master who growls through the bed-curtains: 'Jacques, you're drunk.'

Jacques. Or very nearly.

Master. What time do you intend to go to bed?

Jacques. Soon, sir. It's just that... just that there's...

Master. Just what?

Jacques. Just a drop left in this bottle... it's going flat... I hate half-empty bottles. I'll remember when I'm in bed, and it would take a lot less to stop me getting to sleep. By God, that landlady is a splendid woman, and her champagne's splendid too. Be a pity to let it go flat... I know where I'll put it... There, it won't get any flatter now.

And while he babbled on, bare-footed in his nightshirt, Jacques took two or three good pulls at the wine, without inserting commas, as he put it, that is, in one unbroken movement from bottle to glass and from glass to mouth.

There are two versions of what happened after he'd put the lights out. Some state that he began feeling his way round the walls but could not locate his bed, and that he said: 'By God, it's gone, or if it's still there it's written on high that I shan't find it. Either way, I'll have to do without,' and thereupon he decided to stretch out on a couple of chairs. According to others, it was written on high that his legs would get entangled in the chairs, that he would fall over and lie where he fell. Of these two versions, you can take your time, tomorrow or the day after, to choose the one you like best.

Next morning our two travellers, who had gone to bed late and rather the worse for drink, slept late, Jacques either on the floor or on two chairs according to the version you preferred, and his Master rather more comfortably in his bed. The landlady came up to let them know that the day would not be fine and that, were they minded to be on their way, they would be risking their lives and in any case they would be stopped by the swollen waters of the little river they had to cross. She said that several mounted travellers who had chosen not to take her word for it had been forced to turn back. The Master said to Jacques: 'Jacques, what'll we do?' and Jacques replied: 'First we'll have some lunch with our landlady. That might give us some ideas.' The landlady said that this was a very sensible decision. Victuals were brought. The landlady was only too delighted to have an opportunity to enjoy herself, Jacques's Master was ready to join in, but Jacques began to feel unwell. He toyed with his food, drank little, and said nothing.

This latter symptom was particularly irritating. It was the effect of the bad night he'd spent and the uncomfortable bed he'd spent it on. He complained of pains in his arms and legs, and his hoarse voice indicated the onset of a sore throat. His Master advised him to go back to bed but he wouldn't. The landlady offered to make him a bowl of onion soup. He asked for a fire to be laid in the room, for he felt shivery, wanted a pot of herb tea to be made and a bottle of white wine to be brought up, which was all seen to immediately.

The landlady takes herself off, leaving Jacques alone with his Master.

The Master stood by the window and said: 'What atrocious weather!', took out his watch—for it was the only timepiece he trusted—to see what time it was, and had a pinch of snuff. These actions he repeated every hour on the hour and each time he would exclaim: 'What atrocious weather!', then turn to Jacques and add: 'This is a good opportunity to carry on and conclude the story of your love-life. Still, you can't talk properly about love or anything else when you're off colour. So, see how you feel. If you can carry on, all well and good. Otherwise, drink up your herb tea and get some sleep.'

Jacques reckoned that silence was bad for him, that he was a chattering animal, and that the major advantage of his present employment, the one that mattered most to him, was the freedom he had to make up for the twelve years he'd spent gagged when he'd lived with his grandfather, God rest his soul.

Master. Go ahead and talk, then. We'd both enjoy it. You'd reached the point when the surgeon's wife was making some improper suggestion or other. If memory serves, she wanted you to have the surgeon who was resident in the chateau kicked out and replaced by her husband.

Jacques. I'm with you. But just a moment, if you don't mind. Got to wet the old whistle.

Jacques filled a large tumbler with herb tea, added a small quantity of white wine, and drank it. It was a recipe he'd got from his Captain. Monsieur Tissot, who got it from Jacques, recommends it in his book about common ailments.* White wine, according to both Jacques and Monsieur Tissot, relaxes the bladder, has diuretic virtues, disguises the insipid taste of the tea, and acts as a tonic on the stomach and the intestines. When Jacques had swallowed the last of his herb tea, he went on:

Jacques. So, I've left the surgeon's house, I've been in the carriage, I've arrived at the chateau, and I'm surrounded by all who dwell therein.

Master. Were you known to them?

Jacques. Of course. Do you remember that woman with the pitcher of oil?

Master. I most certainly do.

Jacques. Well, she was employed to run all sorts of errands for the steward and the servants. Jeanne had gone round the chateau telling everybody about the very kind turn I'd done her. News of my good deed had reached the ears of the lord of the manor, who had not been allowed to continue in ignorance of the kicks and thumps with which it had been nocturnally rewarded on the road. He had given orders that I should be found and brought to him. So there I am. I'm stared at, questioned, and praised. Jeanne kissed me and expressed her thanks.

'Give him a comfortable room,' the master told his servants, 'and see that he wants for nothing.'

To the resident surgeon, he said: 'You will keep a close eye on him.'

His instructions were followed to the letter.

So you see, sir, who can know what is written on high? Tell me now if it's a good thing or a bad thing to give your money away, and if it's a disaster to be beaten up? If neither of those two events had happened, Monsieur Desglands would never have heard of Jacques.

Master. Not Monsieur Desglands, Seigneur de Miremont! You mean to say you're at the Chateau de Miremont! At the house of my old friend, the father of Monsieur Desforges, the provincial governor?

Jacques. Exactly. And the girl with the dark hair and slim waist and black eyes...?

Master. Is Denise, Jeanne's daughter?

Jacques. The very same.

Master. You're right. She was one of the prettiest and most honest girls for fifty miles round about. I and most of the men who ever stayed with Desglands all tried our damnedest to get her into bed but we never succeeded. There wasn't a man among us who wouldn't have done anything for her if only she'd done one little thing for him.

When Jacques stopped saying anything at this point, his Master said: 'What are you thinking? What are you doing?'

Jacques. Saying my prayer.

Master. Do you pray?

Jacques. Now and then.

Master. And what do you say?

Jacques. I say: 'Thou who didst make the great scroll, whoever or whatever thou art, and whose hand didst write on high that which is written therein, thou hast since the beginning of time known my every need. Thy will be done. Amen.'

Master. Wouldn't it be better if you just kept mum?

Jacques. Maybe it would and maybe it wouldn't. I pray because you never know. But whatever might happen to me, I wouldn't either cheer or complain as long as I can remain in charge of myself. Basically I'm inconsistent. I rush to extremes and forget both my principles and the lessons my Captain taught me. As a result I laugh and cry like a moron.

Master. Didn't your Captain ever cry? Didn't he laugh?

Jacques. Not often... Jeanne brought her daughter to see me one morning. Up she piped saying: 'Sir, you're all right now you're in a grand chateau. You'll be a bit more comfortable here than at the surgeon's. You'll be really well looked after, especially to begin with. But I know the servants—I've been here long enough—and gradually they'll stop bothering. Their masters above stairs will stop worrying about you, and if you don't get better quickly you'll be forgotten, completely and utterly forgotten, so that if you took a fancy to starve yourself to death, you'd succeed.'

Then turning to her daughter, she said: 'Listen, Denise, I want you to look in on this gentleman four times a day: in the morning, at midday, at five, and again at supper-time. I want you to obey him just as if it was me telling you what to do.'

Master. Do you know what happened to poor Desglands?

Jacques. No I don't sir, but if all the good wishes I offered up for his prosperity went unanswered, it wasn't because they weren't sincere. He it was who got me taken on by Monsieur de la Boulaye, the Knight Commander, who died on his way to Malta. It was Monsieur de la Boulaye who passed me on to his oldest brother, the Captain of the same name, who may as we speak be dead of the fistula. It was the Captain who passed me on to his youngest brother, the Advocate-General of Toulouse, who went mad and was locked up by his family. It was the Advocate-General of Toulouse, Monsieur Pascal, who passed me on to the Count de Tourville, who preferred letting his beard grow under the cowl of a Capuchin monk to risking his neck under a soldier's helmet. It was the Count de Tourville who passed me on to the Marquise de Belloy, who ran away to London with some foreigner or other. It was the Marquise de Belloy who passed me on to a cousin of hers who ruined himself with women and then shipped himself off to the Indies. It was this same cousin who passed me on to a usurer named Hérissant who made loans with money belonging to Monsieur de Rusai, a Sorbonne theologian, who passed me on to Mademoiselle Isselin, a lady of the town then in your keeping, and she passed me on to you, and it's you I'll have to thank for having a crust to eat when I'm old, for you promised to see me all right if I stayed with you, and it doesn't look as if we'll ever go our separate ways. Jacques was made for you and you were made for Jacques.*

Master. But Jacques, you seem to have run through a large number of employers in a rather short time.

Jacques. True. Sometimes I was dismissed.

Master. Why was that?

Jacques. I've always been on the talkative side, and all my employers preferred me to keep my mouth shut. It wasn't the same as it is with you. You'd send me packing tomorrow if I stopped talking. I had the exact failing that suited you. But what did happen to Monsieur Desglands? Tell me while I'm making another cup of my herb tea.

Master. You mean you lived in his chateau and you never heard about his patch?

Jacques. No.

Master. We'll keep the story of his patch for when we're on the road. But there's another one that's shorter. He'd made his fortune from gambling. He was attracted to a woman you might have caught sight of at the chateau, very clever, but strict, taciturn, rather difficult and very unforgiving. One day, she said to him: 'Either you love me more than you love gambling, in which case give me your word of honour that you'll never gamble again, or you love gambling more than me, in which case you can stop telling me how much you love me and gamble as much as you like.'

Desglands swore on his honour that he'd never gamble again.

'No matter how large or small the stakes are?'

'No matter how large or small the stakes are.'

They'd been living together for twenty years at the chateau which you know when Desglands was summoned to town on important business. Unfortunately for him, he ran into an old gambling crony at his notary's who dragged him off for a bite to eat in a low gaming-house where in one session he lost everything he owned. His mistress was inflexible. She was wealthy, she made Desglands a modest allowance, and said goodbye to him for ever.

Jacques. I'm sorry to hear it. He was a fine gentleman.

Master. How's the throat?

Jacques. Hurting.

Master. That's because you're talking too much and not drinking enough.

Jacques. That's because I don't like herb tea but I do like talking.

Master. Anyway, Jacques, so there you are, under Desglands's roof, Denise is within reach, and Denise has been authorized by her mother to come to your room at least four times a day. The trollop! To think she would go for someone like Jacques!

Jacques. Someone like Jacques? I'll have you know, sir, that a Jacques is as much a man as the rest.

Master. You're wrong, Jacques. A Jacques isn't as much a man as the rest.

Jacques. Sometimes he's better than the rest.

Master. Jacques, you're getting above yourself. Just get on with the story of your love-life, and remember that you are not and never will be anything other than a Jacques.

Jacques. When we were at the inn where we encountered the bandits, if Jacques hadn't been a bit more of a man than his Master...

Master. Jacques, don't be impertinent. You're taking advantage of my good nature. If I was fool enough to promote you above your station, I can easily demote you again. Now, pick up your bottle and your tea-kettle, Jacques, and take yourself off below stairs.

Jacques. You can say what you please, sir, but I'm very happy here. I'm not going anywhere.

Master. You will go below stairs, I tell you.

Jacques. I'm sure you don't really mean this, sir. What! After accustoming me these past ten years to living with you as your companion on an equal footing...

Master. I've decided to put a stop to all that.

Jacques. After putting up with all my cheek...

Master. I won't put up with it any more.

Jacques. After seating me next to you at table and calling me your friend...

Master. You don't understand the meaning of the word friend when it is used by a superior to his inferior.

Jacques. When everybody knows that your orders are like wind in a chimney until they've been confirmed by Jacques, when your name has been so closely linked with mine that the one is inseparable from the other and everybody always says 'Jacques and his Master', after all that, you suddenly want to uncouple them! No, sir, it can't be done. It is written on high that so long as Jacques shall live, so long as his Master shall live, and even after they're both dead, people will go on saying 'Jacques and his Master'.

Master. And I'm telling you, Jacques, you will go downstairs and you will go now, because I'm ordering you to.

Jacques. If you want me to obey you, sir, order me to do something else.

At this point, Jacques's Master got to his feet, grabbed Jacques by the lapels, and said grimly: 'Go!'

Jacques answered coolly:

'I'm not going.'

His Master shook him hard and said:

'Shift your bones, you insolent dog! Do what I tell you!'

Jacques, more coolly still, replied:

'Call me an insolent dog if you like, but this is one insolent dog who isn't going anywhere. Listen, sir, my legs, as they say, don't always do what my head tells them to. You're getting all worked up for nothing: Jacques will stay where he is and won't go down the stairs.'

Then Jacques and his Master, having remained relatively calm up to this point, both fly off the handle at the same time and start yelling:

'Get downstairs!'

'I won't!'

'You shall!'

'Shan't!'

Hearing the hullabaloo, the landlady came up and asked whatever was the matter. But neither replied immediately since they both went on yelling: 'You shall!' and 'Shan't!' Then the Master, visibly upset, paced round the room muttering: 'Did anyone ever see the like of it?'

The landlady stood there in amazement and then said: 'Gentlemen, please! Now what's all this about?'

Still keeping cool, Jacques said: 'My Master's having a brainstorm. He's gone mad.'

Master. Don't you mean gone soft in the head?

Jacques. Whatever you say.

Master [*to the landlady*]. Did you hear that?

Landlady. He shouldn't have said it, but calm down the pair of you. Out with it, and I don't mind which of you tells me. Then I'll know what this is all about.

Master [*to Jacques*]. You tell her, you villain.

Jacques [*to his Master*]. Tell her yourself.

Landlady [*to Jacques*]. Come on, Monsieur Jacques, tell me like your Master said. When all's said and done, a Master is a Master.

So Jacques explained to the landlady what had happened. When she'd heard him out, she said: 'Gentlemen, would you like me to arbitrate?'

Jacques and his Master [*together*]. Yes, Madame, willingly.

Landlady. And do you swear on your honour to abide by the ruling of the court?

Jacques and his Master [*together*]. I swear.

Thereupon, the landlady sat behind the table and with the grave tone and sober deliberation of a judge said:

Landlady. Having heard the statement made by Monsieur Jacques and taking cognizance of the evidence which suggests that his Master is a good, a very good, an overly good master and that Jacques is not a bad servant, though a little too inclined to confuse the absolute and inalienable rights of noble persons with the impermanent and limited rights of commoners, I hereby declare null and void the equal standing which has been established between them by dint of lapse of time, and I furthermore hereby reinstate it with immediate effect. Jacques will go downstairs. When he has gone downstairs he will come back up again and enter fully once more into the prerogatives which he has enjoyed up to and including the present time. His Master will shake his hand and remark in a friendly manner: 'Good-day to you, Jacques, I am heartily pleased to see you again.' And Jacques shall reply: 'And I, sir, am heartily glad to see you.' I forbid any subsequent mention of this matter to be made by either party or the subject of the rights of either Master or Servant ever to be raised from this day forth. It is our judgement that one shall give orders and that the other shall obey them, each to the best of his abilities, and that the matter of what the one can do and what the other must do shall remain in the same state of undefined uncertainty as heretofore.

And so she concluded her judgement, which she had culled from some report or other published around that time of an almost identical squabble in which a master had been heard from one end of the kingdom to the other yelling at his servant: 'Down you go!' and the servant shouting back: 'Shan't!'* Then she turned to Jacques and said:

'Come along, give me your arm and let's have no more arguing.'

Jacques wailed: 'So it was written that I would go down the stairs!'

Landlady [*to Jacques*]. It was written on high that whoever serves a master will go down, up, forward, backward, or stay in the same place, and that this shall be so without the feet being free to refuse to do the bidding of the head. Now give me your arm so that the ruling of the court may be carried out.

Jacques gave the landlady his arm, but they had hardly stepped through the door of the room when the Master threw himself on Jacques and hugged him, then let Jacques go and hugged the landlady, and as he hugged them both in turn he said: 'It is written on high that I shall never be able to rid myself of this obstreperous man and that for as long as I live he will be my master and I shall be his servant!'

To which the landlady added: 'And to judge by the way the wind's blowing, it'll do neither of you any harm.'

The landlady, having put an end to their quarrel, which she assumed was the first, though in fact there had been more than a hundred like it, and having secured Jacques's reinstatement, then went about her business while the Master said to Jacques: 'I'd say we've calmed down and can consider these matters objectively. What do you say?'

Jacques. What I say is that when a man has given his word of honour, he ought to keep it. Since we swore to the judge on our honour that we wouldn't bring the matter up again, we must say no more of it.

Master. You're right.

Jacques. But without bringing the matter up again as such, couldn't we prevent many more like it cropping up by coming to some sensible arrangement?

Master. I agree.

Jacques. So, whereas it is agreed that: first, given that it is written on high that I am indispensable to you, and that I feel, nay know, that you cannot manage without me, I shall abuse my advantage each and every time the opportunity arises.

Master. But Jacques, nothing like that was ever agreed.

Jacques. Agreed or not, it's always been so, remains so today and shall continue to be so for as long as the world goes on turning. You don't think that other masters have never tried to escape this decree of fate, just as you're doing now? Put the thought out of your mind and submit to the rule of a necessity which it is not in your power to avoid.

Whereas it is agreed, secondly, that it is as impossible for Jacques to read his stars and know what power he has over his Master as it is for his Master to be ignorant of his weakness and to put aside his natural tolerance, Jacques has no choice but to be impertinent and that, if peace is to break out between them, his Master has no option but to turn a blind eye. All that has been arranged without our being informed—it was all signed and sealed on high at the moment nature

created both Jacques and his Master. It was decreed that you would
have the name and that I should have the thing. If you wish to do battle
with the will of nature, you might just as well try poking a hole in water
with a stick.

Master. So by your reckoning, your lot is preferable to mine?

Jacques. Who's arguing?

Master. But by your reckoning, I should take your place and put
you in mine.

Jacques. If you did, do you know what would happen? You'd lose
the name and you wouldn't get the thing. So let's stay as we are—we're
both pretty well off the way things stand—and let's spend the rest of
our lives creating a new proverb.

Master. What proverb's that?

Jacques. 'Jacques leads his Master.' We shall be the first it's said
about, though it will thereafter be said of many others who are better
men than we are.

Master. That seems very hard to me, very hard.

Jacques. Sir, my dear Master, knock your head against a brick wall
for long enough and it will fall on you. So, that's what has been agreed
between us.

Master. But does a law that is necessary require our consent?

Jacques. Of course. Don't you think it would be helpful to know
once and for all, to be sure and certain exactly where we stand? All the
times we've fallen out up to now have only come about because we've
never really admitted to each other that you were my Master in name
and that I was yours in fact. But now that's cleared up, we can carry on
accordingly.

Master. Where the devil did you learn all this?

Jacques. In the Great Book. Oh sir, you can ruminate, ponder and
study all the books ever written till you're blue in the face, but you'll
never be more than a beginner if you haven't read the Great Book.

In the afternoon the sun came out. Several travellers reported that
the little river was fordable. Jacques went downstairs. His Master paid
their landlady very handsomely. At the door of the inn was gathered a
sizeable knot of travellers who had been detained by the bad weather
and were now preparing to continue their several journeys.

Among these travellers are Jacques and his Master, and the man
who had got married in peculiar circumstances and his companion.

The foot-travellers take their sticks and shoulder their packs. Others settle themselves into covered carts or carriages. The riders are mounted and taking a stirrup cup for the road. The landlady, ever hospitable, holds a bottle, hands out glasses and fills them, not forgetting one for herself. She is thanked most graciously and she replies with courteous good cheer. Then they spur their mounts, say their goodbyes, and they're off.

Now it so happened that Jacques and his Master, and the Marquis des Arcis and his young companion were going the same way. Of these four characters, only the last is not known to you. He was not much more than twenty-two or twenty-three years of age. He was very shy and it showed in his face. He held his head inclined slightly over his left shoulder, did not speak, and was not used to being in company. When he bowed, he did so from the waist only, without moving his feet. When he was seated, he had a habit of taking both tails of his coat and crossing them over his legs, keeping his hands firmly in his pockets, and listening to whoever was speaking with his eyes almost completely shut. His odd bearing gave Jacques a clue and, moving closer to his Master, said: 'I'd wager that young man has worn a monk's robes.'

Master. Why do you say that, Jacques?
Jacques. You'll see.

Our four travellers ambled along together, discussing the rain, the day that had turned out fine, the landlady, the landlord, and the argument the Marquis des Arcis had had over Nicole. She had been hungry and was filthy, and she kept rubbing herself on his stockings. After trying to shoo her away with his napkin several times, he had become exasperated and lashed out with his boot... Whereupon the conversation immediately turned to the way women dote on pets. Each gave his view of the matter. Jacques's Master turned to him and said: 'How about you, Jacques? What do you make of it?'

Jacques asked his Master if he'd ever noticed that however badly off poor people were, not even having anything to eat, they all had dogs, and whether he'd observed that their dogs, having been taught to perform tricks, such as walking on their hind legs, dancing, fetching, doing somersaults when the name of the king or queen was shouted out, and playing dead, had been turned by all this training into the most unfortunate of all brute creatures. The conclusion he drew was that every man enjoys lording it over another man, and since animals occupy a place immediately beneath the lowest class of citizens who are ordered about by all the other classes, poor people keep a dog so they too have someone to order about.

Jacques. Well, everybody's got a dog. The prime minister is the king's dog. The first secretary is the prime minister's dog. A wife is a husband's dog, or a husband is a wife's dog. Favourite is Madame So-and-so's dog and Thibaut is the man on the corner's dog. When my Master tells me to talk when I'd prefer not to, which to be honest doesn't happen very often, when he tells me to shut up when I feel like talking, which I find very difficult, when he asks me to tell the story of my love-life and then keeps interrupting, what am I if not his dog? Weak men are the dogs of strong men.*

Master. But Jacques, I don't observe this fondness for pets only among poor people. I know titled ladies who surround themselves with a whole pack of dogs, to say nothing of cats, parrots, and chirruping birds.

Jacques. A menagerie that makes them and all their friends look ridiculous. They don't love anybody, nobody loves them, and they throw all the feelings they don't know what else to do with to their dogs.

Marquis des Arcis. To love animals or to throw your heart to the dogs—that's a peculiar way of looking at things.

Master. What they give to their dogs would feed two or three poor men.

Jacques. Does that surprise you now?

Master. No.

The Marquis des Arcis turned to look at Jacques, smiled at his ideas, and then said to his Master: 'Your man here is a rather unusual sort of servant.'

Master. A servant! You are very kind but it's I who am his servant. He damn near proved it in writing no later than this very morning.

Still talking, they arrived at the inn where they were to spend the night. They all shared a room. Jacques's Master and the Marquis des Arcis supped together, and Jacques and the young man ate at a separate table. The Master furnished the Marquis with a brief account of Jacques's history and fatalistic outlook. The Marquis gave an account of the young man who was with him. He had been a Premonstrant* and had left his order as the result of a strange adventure. Friends had recommended him and he had employed him as his secretary until something better should come along.

Jacques's Master said: 'Quite amusing really.'

Marquis des Arcis. What's amusing about it?

Master. I was thinking about Jacques. We'd hardly set foot in the inn we left this afternoon when Jacques whispered in my ear: 'Sir, do you see that young man? I'd wager he's been a monk.'

Marquis des Arcis. He guessed right, though how I don't know. Do you usually turn in early?

Master. Not as a rule, and tonight I'm even less inclined to, given the fact we've only put in a half-day's travel.

Marquis des Arcis. If you've got nothing to do that's more important or amusing, I'll tell you the story of my secretary. It's rather unusual.

Master. I'll be all ears.

I hear you, Reader. You're saying: 'What about Jacques's love-life?'

Don't you think I'm not just as curious as you are? Have you forgotten that Jacques liked talking, especially about himself? It's a compulsion commonly found in people of his class, a mania that lifts them out of their dull, mean lives, thrusts them into the limelight, and makes them suddenly seem interesting. Now what, in your opinion, is the motive that attracts ordinary people to public executions?*

Sheer callousness.

You're wrong. People aren't callous. They congregate around the scaffold, but if they could they'd forcibly remove the poor unfortunate from the clutches of justice. No, they turn up at the Place de Grève* for the drama, so that they can tell their friends all about it when they get home. It doesn't have to be an execution, that's not important, anything will do provided it gives them a role to play, makes the neighbours come running, and guarantees them an audience. Stage some sensational public entertainment on the boulevards and you'd find that the place of execution was deserted. People love spectacle and flock to anything like that, because they're entertained when they're there and even more entertained by talking about it when it's over. When the populace is roused, it can get very angry, but it doesn't last. Being poor, they've learned to be compassionate, they avert their eyes from the horrible sight they've come to see, they are moved to pity, and they go home with tears running down their cheeks...

Everything I've just been telling you, Reader, I got from Jacques. I admit it, because I don't like taking credit for other people's ideas. Jacques did not acknowledge the word 'vice' nor the word 'virtue'. He claimed that people are born lucky or unlucky. Whenever he heard the words 'reward' and 'punishment', he'd give a shrug. In his view, rewards are meant as an incentive for good people, and punishments are intended to frighten bad people. 'What else can they be for,' he would say, 'if we are not free to choose and our destiny is written up there, on high?' He believed that a man heads as necessarily towards glory or shame as a rock with an awareness of itself careers down the side of a mountain. It was his view that if we had a clear sight of the chain of causes and effects which shape a man's life from the moment he is born until his dying day, we would be convinced that everything he had done was what he had no choice but to do.

I've tried arguing the opposite with him several times but it did no good and I got nowhere. Indeed, there's not much you can say when someone tells you: 'Whatever you take to be the sum total of the elements of which I am composed, I am one and indivisible. Now, one cause produces only one effect. I have always been a cause in the singular, and I have never had more than one effect to produce. Therefore my life's span is a succession of necessary effects.' That's how Jacques used to argue following the line taken by his Captain. The distinction between the physical world and the moral world was without meaning for him.

His Captain had stuffed Jacques's head with his opinions which he had got from Spinoza,* who he knew by heart. Now if you apply this philosophy, you might well think that nothing ever made Jacques happy or sad. But that wasn't the way of it. He behaved more or less as you or I do. He said thank you to anyone who extended a helping hand, so that the helping hand might be extended again in the future. He got angry with any man who was unjust, and when people told him that he was like the dog which bites the stone which was thrown at it, he'd say: 'Not at all. The stone bitten by the dog cannot improve, whereas the man who is unjust can be modified by a stick.' He was often inconsistent, just like you or me, and inclined to forget his principles, except in some circumstances where his philosophy clearly had the upper hand. It was at such times that he'd say: 'Such and such had to happen, for it was written on high that it would.' He tried to prevent bad things happening and acted prudently while at the same time despising prudence. When the worst happened, he took up his old refrain and was consoled. As to the rest, he was a good man, candid, honest, brave, loyal, faithful, very obstinate, even more loquacious, and no less vexed than you and I to discover that he had embarked upon the story of his loves with almost no hope of ever finishing it.

Therefore, gentle Reader, I advise you to make up your mind, in the absence of Jacques's love-life, to settle for the adventures of the Marquis des Arcis's secretary. In any case, I can see poor Jacques now, with a large scarf wound round his neck and his flask, once full of good wine but now containing only herb tea, coughing, taking in vain the name of the landlady they'd left behind together with her champagne, which is something he wouldn't have done if he had remembered that everything is written on high, including his cold.

But, Reader, why must there always be love stories? I've already written you one, two, three, four love stories and you're due another three or four and that's a lot of love stories. Still, on the other hand, since I'm writing this for you, I must either proceed without your approval or give you what you want. And the fact is that you have a decided taste for love stories. All those tales in prose and verse you're so fond of are invariably love stories. Nearly all your poems, elegies, eclogues, idylls, lyrical ballads, epistles, comedies, tragedies and operas are love stories. Nearly all your paintings and statues are basically love stories. All you've ever wanted since the day you were born was to gobble up love stories and you never get tired of them. You've been fed a diet of them and you'll be kept on it for a long time yet—men and women, old and young—and you'll never ever get sick of it. It really is astounding! I wish the story of the Marquis des Arcis was another love story, but I'm afraid it isn't and you'll get bored with it. It's bad news for the Marquis des Arcis, for Jacques's Master, for you, Reader, and for me.

'There comes a time when every girl and every boy turns melancholy. They are troubled by a vague unease which colours everything and is not to be assuaged. They want to be on their own, they weep, the silence of cloisters affects them deeply, they are drawn to the image of peace which seems to rule convents and monasteries. They make the error of hearing the voice of God in the first stirrings of developing adulthood, and it is at the very moment when nature presses them hardest that they embrace a life which denies the voice of nature. The error does not last. Nature speaks more clearly, it is recognized, and the cloistered captive is overcome by regrets, languor, vapours, madness, or despair.'*

Thus spake the Marquis des Arcis by way of preamble.

'Alienated from the world at the age of seventeen, Richard—such was the name of my secretary—fled his father's house and donned the robe of a Premonstrant.'

Master. A Premonstrant? I'm glad to hear it. They're as pure as the driven snow.* There was only one thing their founder, Saint Norbert, left out of the rules of his order.

Marquis des Arcis. And that was to provide each of his followers with a bedding couch as standard equipment.

Master. If it wasn't traditional to represent Cupid as a naked cherub, he could be shown dressed in the habit of a Premonstrant. The order lays down some very odd rules. You're permitted duchesses, marquises, countesses, the wives of judges, councillors, and even bankers, but you're not allowed anywhere near the womenfolk of the middle classes. However pretty a shopkeeper's wife might be, you'll never find a Premonstrant in her shop.

Marquis des Arcis. That's just what Richard told me. He would have taken his vows after his two years as a novice if his parents had not stepped in. His father insisted that he should come home where, he said, Richard could test his vocation by observing all the rules of monastic discipline for a year. This agreement was scrupulously observed by both parties. When the year he spent verifying his call under the eye of his family was over, Richard asked to take his vows. His father replied:

'I granted you a year so that you could reach a final decision. I trust you will not refuse me a further year for the same motive. All I stipulate is that you spend it wherever you like.'

While Richard waited for this second deferment to end, the Abbot of the Order took him under his wing and it was during this time that he was implicated in one of those scandals which only happen in monasteries.

One of the abbeys of the Order was at that time headed by a superior of quite extraordinary character, Père Hudson. Père Hudson was a very handsome man: wide brow, oval face, aquiline nose, large blue eyes, strong cheekbones, wide mouth, good teeth, an engaging smile, a thatch of thick white hair which lent gravitas and a certain magnetism to his features, witty, cultured, humorous, dignified in speech and manner, with a taste for discipline and hard work, but also a man of fiery temperament, with an unbridled lust for pleasure and women, a highly developed genius for intrigue, and the most dissolute morals, who ruled his abbey with a rod of iron. When he was given charge of it, it was riddled with ignorant Jansenism: its studies were neglected, its temporal affairs were in disarray, religious observance had decayed, divine service was celebrated with scant respect, and any spare accommodation was occupied by dissolute boarders. Père Hudson either converted or expelled the Jansenists, took personal charge of the instruction that was given and received in the abbey, put its temporal affairs on a sound footing, enforced the rule of religion, removed the disreputable boarders, brought decorum and propriety to the celebration of divine service, and transformed the community into one of the most respected in the Order.

But the austerity which he forced on others he did not apply to himself, for he was not so foolish as to wish to undergo the full rigour of the strict rule to which he subjected his underlings. They, as a consequence, harboured feelings of bitter resentment against Hudson which were all the stronger and more dangerous for being suppressed. Every one of them was an enemy and a spy, each kept a record of his secret excesses, each had sworn to bring him down. He could not make a move that was not watched, and his plots were no sooner laid than they were common knowledge.

The Abbot lived in a house which abutted the monastery. It had two doors, one opening on to the street, and the other into the cloister. Hudson had broken the locks, the abbey's church had become the setting for nocturnal orgies, and the Abbot's bed had been transformed into a pleasure couch. It was by the street door, late at night, that he let women of every rank and condition into the Abbot's quarters, and it was there that he gave exquisite supper parties. Hudson heard confessions and he had corrupted any penitent female whom he thought had possibilities. Among these women was the wife of a confectioner who was well known in the locality as a pretty little flirt. Hudson, who could not go to her house, kept her shut up in his harem.

Now what was in effect a kidnapping could hardly take place without raising suspicions in the minds of her parents and her husband. They went to see him. Hudson received them with a show of concern. As these good people were in the process of telling him of their anxieties, the abbey bell began to ring. It was six in the evening. Hudson enjoins them to be silent, removes his hat, stands, makes a large sign of the cross, and says in the most melting and sincerest tones: 'Angelus Domini nuntiavit Mariae.'* And lo! the father and the brothers of the confectioner's wife blush for suspecting him and, as they leave by the stairs, speak on this wise unto the husband:

'You, son-in-law, are a fool.'

'You, brother-in-law, should be ashamed of yourself. A man who says the Angelus! A saint!'

One winter's evening, as he was returning to the abbey, the Abbot was approached by one of those creatures who solicit for custom on the streets. She was pretty and he went home with her. But he was scarcely through her door when the officers of the watch burst in. This incident would have been the ruin of a lesser man, but Hudson was resourceful and the episode earned him the goodwill and protection of the lieutenant of police. When brought before him, this is what he said:

'My name is Hudson and I am the Superior of my abbey. When I was appointed, it was totally run down. There was no learning, no discipline and the moral tone was lax to a degree. Spiritual matters had been scandalously neglected and the finances were such that there was an immediate threat of ruin. I have restored everything to a sound footing. Yet I am a man, and I preferred to approach a depraved harlot rather than an honest woman. You may now deal with me as you think fit.'

The magistrate told him to be more careful in future, agreed to treat the matter in confidence, and indicated that he would like to be better acquainted with him.

But the enemies who surrounded him had all written separate accounts setting out what they knew of Hudson's wicked ways and had sent them to the Vicar-General of the Order. When these reports were compared, they seemed all the more compelling. The Vicar-General was a Jansenist and therefore inclined to look for revenge for the persecution Hudson had meted out to those who shared his beliefs. He would have been only too delighted to extend a charge of depravity brought against one defender of the Papal Bull *Unigenitus** and laxism to cover the entire sect. He therefore handed all the accounts of Hudson's exploits to two commissioners whom he sent secretly with orders to investigate and obtain the evidence needed for formal charges to be made, instructing them to proceed in this matter with the greatest possible circumspection, for this was the only way of bringing the culprit to justice quickly and of removing him from the protection of the Court and Mirepoix,* for whom Jansenism was the most heinous crime of all and acceptance of *Unigenitus* the greatest of all the virtues. Richard, my secretary, was one of the two commissioners.

The two men left the quarters where they were lodged as novices, moved to Hudson's abbey, and began to make discreet enquiries. Soon they had a list of more misdeeds than would have been needed to put fifty monks behind bars. They had stayed for a long time, but their manner of proceeding had been so discreet that no hint of what they were doing leaked out. Clever though he was, Hudson was teetering on the brink of ruin and was blissfully unaware of the danger. Even so, the fact that the newcomers had been in no hurry to pay him their court, that they had not disclosed the reason for their journey, that they had frequent discussions with the other monks, that they frequently went out, together or separately, this, when added to the sort of people they visited and by whom they were visited, all made him uneasy. He watched them, had them watched by others, and soon the purpose of their coming became all too clear. He was not alarmed but made his first priority to find a way, not of escaping the gathering storm which threatened to engulf him, but of redirecting it on to the heads of the two commissioners. This is the very extraordinary plan he decided to implement.

He had seduced a young woman whom he kept hidden in a small apartment near Saint-Médard.* He now hurried to her and said:

'My child, all is discovered! We are lost! Before the week is out, you will be in prison and I do not know what will become of me. But do not despair, let's have no weeping, get a grip on yourself. Listen, do what I tell you, exactly as I tell you, and leave the rest to me. Tomorrow I am going to the country. While I'm away, go and find two monks whose names I shall give you,' and here he named the two commissioners. 'Ask to speak to them in private. When you're alone with them, get down on bended knees, beg them to help you, beg them for justice, beg them to act as your channel to the Vicar-General, for you should know they have great influence with him. Cry your eyes out, sob, tear your hair, and while you're crying your eyes out, sobbing, and tearing your hair, tell them all about us, and tell them in such a way that it generates pity for you and horror for me.'

'You mean, sir, that I'm to say...?'

'Yes. You will tell them who you are, who your parents are, how I seduced you when you came to say confession, how I stole you away from the loving care of your family and set you up in this apartment. Tell them that after I robbed you of your honour and forced you into a life of crime, I abandoned you to destitution. Say you don't know what's to become of you.'

'But Father...'

'Do exactly what I've told you and what I am about to tell you, or make up your mind to be the ruin of the both of us. The two monks will fall over themselves to be sympathetic, they'll promise to help and ask for a second meeting, which you will agree to. They will make enquiries about you and your relatives but since you won't have told them anything that isn't strictly true, they won't suspect you. When you've got through the first and second interviews, I'll tell you what you must do at the third. Just keep your mind on the role you have to play.'

Everything happened exactly as Hudson had planned. He went out of town a second time, the commissioners informed the girl, and she returned to the abbey. They asked her to repeat her unhappy tale. While she told it to one, the other made notes. They deplored her fate, informed her that her parents were devastated, which was only too true, and said they would guarantee her personal safety and prompt action against the man who had seduced her, provided she signed a full statement.

At first she seemed reluctant to do what they asked, but they pressed her and finally she agreed. All that remained was to settle the hour, day, and place for drawing up the statement. That would take time and privacy.

'We can't do it here. If the Abbot returned and saw me... Perhaps my place, but no, I wouldn't dare suggest it.'

The girl and the commissioners then went their separate ways, giving each other enough time to resolve these difficulties.

Père Hudson was informed of what had happened the same day. He felt exultant, for he was about to achieve his victory. It wouldn't be long now before he showed these two amateurs what sort of man they were up against.

'Take this pen,' he told the girl, 'and arrange to meet them in the place I'll name for you. I'm sure it will suit them. It's a respectable house and the woman who lives there has an excellent reputation with her neighbours and the other tenants.'

But this woman was one of those underhand, scheming creatures who pretend to be pious, insinuate themselves into the best households, speak honeyed, kindly, smooth-tongued words, and extract confidences from mothers and daughters with a view to leading them into wicked ways. It was for just this purpose that Hudson used her services: she procured for him. Did he, or did he not let her into the secret? That I do not know.

The Vicar-General's two agents agreed to the meeting as planned. They arrive. The scheming woman leaves. They are about to begin drawing up the statement, when all of a sudden there is uproar in the house.

'Who do you want to see?'

'We want to see Madame Simion.' (That was the scheming woman's name.)

'You've come to the right place.'

There is a violent knocking on the door.

'Oh sirs,' whispered the girl to the two monks, 'shall I answer?'

'I know you're in there!'

'Shall I let them in?'

'Open this door!'

The man shouting outside was a police officer with whom Hudson was on the closest terms—who did he not know? He had told him of the danger he was in and had given him his instructions.

'Aha! What's this?' said the police officer as he stepped into the room, 'two monks closeted with a tart? And not a bad-looking one either.'

The girl was so provocatively dressed that there was no mistaking what she did for a living or what she might be doing there with two monks, the older of whom was not yet thirty. Both protested their innocence. The police officer laughed and put his hand under the chin of the girl, who had thrown herself at his feet and was begging for mercy.

'This is a respectable house,' both monks clamoured.

'Oh yes. Very respectable.'

They said they were there on important business.

'We know all about the important business you're here on. Now, Mademoiselle, what have you got to say for yourself?'

'Sir, what these gentlemen say is perfectly true.'

But it was now the inspector's turn to take down statements, and since there was nothing in his report that was not a plain, unvarnished account of the facts, the two monks had no choice but to sign it.

As they went down the stairs, they found all the tenants on the landings outside their rooms, a large crowd at the door, a carriage, and a squad of constables who pushed them into the carriage to a barrage of insults and jeers. They hid their faces in their robes and felt very sorry for themselves. The villainous inspector shouted:

'Look here, what do men of the cloth like yourselves want with places like this and women like them? But don't you worry, nothing much will come of this. I've got special orders to hand you over to your Superior, who's a decent sort, very understanding. He won't make more of this business than it warrants. I don't think they deal with these things in your order as severely as the Capuchins do. Now if it was the Capuchins you were up against, by God I'd be really sorry for you!'

While the inspector was talking to them, the carriage set off for the abbey. The crowd swelled, surrounded the vehicle, ran on ahead, and trotted behind it.

Here someone said: 'What's up?'

There someone answered: 'A couple of monks.'

'What they do?'

'Arrested in a brothel.'

'What! Premonstrants going with tarts?'

''Sright. They've set up in competition with the Carmelites and the Cordeliers!'

They arrive. The police inspector gets out, knocks at the abbey gate, knocks again and then a third time, and in the end it opens. The Abbot, Père Hudson, is informed and he keeps them waiting a good half-hour, to ensure that the light of the scandal is not hidden under a bushel. Finally, he makes an appearance.

The inspector whispers in his ear. It looks as if the inspector is pleading and that Hudson is having none of it. Eventually the Abbot, looking very stern and speaking very firmly, tells him:

'I have no dissolute monks under my roof. These two men are strangers whom I do not know. Perhaps they are a couple of rogues in disguise. You must deal with them as you think fit.'

And on these words, the abbey gates swung shut.

The inspector climbed back into the coach and said to our two wretches, who were more dead than alive:

'I did everything I could. I'd never have thought Père Hudson was so strict. Anyway, what made you go looking for tarts?'

'If the young woman you found us with is what you say she is, it wasn't debauchery that took us to see her.'

'Oh come, come! You're not going to take that line with an old police hand like me? Who are you?'

'We are monks, and the robes we're wearing are our own.'

'Very well, but just remember that this little business of yours will all come out. Tell me the truth and maybe I'll be able to help.'

'We have told the truth... But where are we going?'

'The Petit-Châtelet.'*

'The Petit-Châtelet!'

'To prison!'

'I'm very sorry...'

And there indeed Richard and his companion were deposited.

But it was not Hudson's intention that they should stay there. He got into a post-chaise and drove at once to Versailles. He spoke to the Minister, to whom he related what had happened, colouring his account to suit his own purposes.

'And there, Your Grace, you see the dangers which lie in wait for any man who seeks to reform a degenerate institution and expels its heretics. Had I not acted at once, I would have been utterly disgraced. But the persecution will not stop there. The foulest accusations that can be heaped on the head of an upright man will reach your ears, but I sincerely hope, Your Grace, that you will recall that our Vicar-General...'

'Yes, yes, I know, and I am heartily sorry for you. The services you have rendered the Church and your Order shall not be forgotten. The Lord's elect have in every age been exposed to opprobrium. But they bore the strain and you must learn to do likewise. You may count on the generosity and protection of the King. Monks! Ah! I was a monk once and know by experience to what depths they can sink!'

'If, as the good of Church and State requires, Your Eminence should outlive me, I would persist with my work and fear nothing.'

'I'll soon have you out of this little difficulty. Now leave me.'

'No, Your Grace, I shall not leave without a written order...'

'For the release of those two unruly monks? I see that the honour of your faith and of the robe you wear is so strong in you that it blots out all sense of personal injury. That is a most Christian sentiment and I am edified though not surprised, since it comes from a man such as you. This affair shall make no noise in the world.'

'Ah, your Grace, you fill my soul with joy! In this dark hour, that was my greatest fear.'

'I shall see to it at once.'

Hudson received the order for their release that same evening. The next morning, at first light, Richard and his companion were eighty miles from Paris, in the keeping of a constable who delivered them to their mother house. The constable was also entrusted with a letter ordering the Vicar-General to terminate all such investigations and to impose the appropriate monastic punishment on both men.

This incident sowed panic among Hudson's enemies. There was not a single monk in the abbey who did not quake at a glance from him.

A few months later he was given the preferment of a rich abbey. The Vicar-General reacted by conceiving a deep loathing for him. He was old and had good reason to fear that Hudson might well succeed him. He was fond of Richard.

'My dear boy,' he said to him one day, 'what would happen to you if you were ever to come under the thumb of that blackguard Hudson? The very thought alarms me. You are not yet fully committed to the Order, and if you want my advice you would be wise to leave it.'

Richard took his advice and returned to his family, who lived not far from the abbey which Hudson had been given.

Hudson and Richard were invited to the same houses and it was impossible that they would never meet. And meet they did.

One day Richard was at the home of a gentlewoman who owned a country seat situated between Châlons and Saint-Dizier, only nearer Saint-Dizier than Châlons.* The lady said:

'We sometimes see your old Abbot. He is most engaging, But, tell me, what is he really like?'

'The best of friends and the worst of enemies.'

'Would you like to meet him?'

'No.'

Hardly were the words out of his mouth when the sound of a carriage was heard entering the courtyard, and out of it stepped Hudson and one of the handsomest women for miles around.

'Well, whether you want to or not,' said the lady, 'you shall, for here he is.'

The hostess and Richard sally forth to welcome the lady who had come in the carriage with Père Hudson. The women embrace. Hudson steps forward to greet Richard, recognizes him, and exclaims:

'Aha! it's you, Richard, my dear boy. You tried to ruin me but I forgive you. If you now forgive me your stay in the Petit Châtelet, we'll put it all behind us.'

'But you must admit, Abbot, that you were a great rogue.'

'You may be right.'

'And if justice had been done, then the one to see the inside of the Petit Châtelet ought by rights not to have been me but you.'

'Very possibly. But I do believe I can thank the danger I faced then for my altered way of life. Oh Richard! It made me think. I am a changed man.'

'The woman you've brought with you is really very delightful.'

'I have no eyes now for attractions of that sort.'

'A fine figure!'

'I no long care for such things.'

'So shapely!'

'A man wearies sooner or later of pleasures which are only to be enjoyed on a rooftop where the next move might end in a broken neck.'

'I never saw prettier hands.'

'I no longer have any use for them. A man with any sense will always return to the values of his true vocation, which is the only happiness that lasts.'

'And such eyes! And the sly way she turns to look at you! Come, you are a connoisseur of these things. Admit you never attracted eyes more sparkling and tender in your life! Such graceful movements, so light a step! What nobility of manner and bearing!'

'I have ceased to think of the vanities. I read the Scriptures and I study the early Church Fathers.'

'And on occasions the charms of this lady. Does she live far from Le Moncetz?* Is her husband young?'

Hudson, finally wearying of so many questions and having no doubt that Richard would ever believe he was a saint, suddenly said: 'My dear Richard, you think I'm a wicked old shit, don't you? Well, you're quite right.'

Dear, gentle Reader, pray forgive me the impropriety of the phrase and admit that here, as in any number of good stories (such, for instance, as the exchange between Piron and the late abbé Vatri), delicacy of language would ruin the effect.

What was this exchange between Piron and the abbé Vatri?

Go and ask the editor of Piron's works who did not dare write it down. You won't need to twist his arm to get him to tell you.*

Marquis des Arcis. All four of them then met up again inside the chateau. They lunched well, they lunched in the best of spirits, and it was nearly evening before they went their several ways, promising that they would see each other again soon.

But while the Marquis des Arcis was talking to Jacques's Master, Jacques for his part had not been reticent with his secretary, Richard, who found a refreshing quirkiness in him. This is something which would be a far commoner trait in people if, first, education and, secondly, extended contact with polite society did not knock off their rough edges, as happens with coins which, passing from hand to hand, are rubbed smooth and lose their definition.

It was late. The clock informed both masters and their attendants that it was time for rest and they heeded its advice.

As Jacques undressed his Master, he said:

Jacques. Sir, do you like pictures?

Master. Yes, but only word pictures. Pictures which are just colour on canvas, though I can pronounce on them as authoritatively as any connoisseur, I confess I don't understand at all. I'd be hard put to tell one school from another. You could show me a Boucher and say it was a Rubens or a Raphael.* I couldn't see the difference between a bad copy and a brilliant original. I'd put a price of a three thousand livres on a daub worth six francs, and offer six francs for a masterpiece worth three thousand livres. I freely admit that all the paintings I ever bought I got on the Pont-Neuf, from a man named Tremblin, who in my day was a lifeline for struggling artists, a supplier of dirty pictures, and the ruination of the talent of Vanloo's young pupils.*

Jacques. How do you mean?

Master. What's it to you? Just tell me about this picture of yours and keep it short. I'm falling asleep.

Jacques. Imagine you're standing in front of the fountain of the Innocents or by the Porte Saint-Denis.* They'd both make suitable backgrounds and add depth to the composition.

Master. I'm there.

Jacques. In the middle of the street you can see an overturned coach with its roof stove in.

Master. I see it.

Jacques. A monk and two whores have got out of it. The monk is making off as fast as his legs will carry him. The coachman is hurrying to get down from the driving seat. His dog is running after the monk and has him by the tail of his jerkin. The monk is struggling to get free of the dog. One of the girls is bare-breasted and she is holding her sides laughing. The other girl, who has taken a knock on the temple, is leaning against one door holding her head in both hands. Meanwhile a crowd has gathered. Ragged children come running and start yelling, shopkeepers and their wives stand in their shop doorways, and assorted spectators are hanging out of their windows.

Master. By God, Jacques, your picture is damned cunningly composed. It's busy, amusing, varied, and full of movement. When we get back to Paris go and give this subject to Fragonard and you'll see if he don't make something of it.*

Jacques. After what you have admitted about how little you know about painting, I can accept your elogious remarks without having to pretend to be modest.

Master. I'll wager it was something that happened to Père Hudson.

Jacques. Indeed it was.

Now, Reader, while all these good people are asleep, I have a little query I'd like to put to you and hereby lay it on your pillow for your consideration. It is this: What would a child born to Père Hudson and Madame de La Pommeraye be like?

Maybe he would be an upright citizen.

Maybe he would be an out-and-out villain.

You can tell me the answer in the morning.

Well, it's morning and our travellers have separated, for the Marquis des Arcis was now to take a different road from Jacques and his Master.

Does that mean we're going back to the story of Jacques's love-life?

I do hope so, but what at least is certain is that the Master knows what time it is, that he has taken a pinch of snuff, and that he has said to Jacques: 'Well now, what about this love-life of yours?'

Instead of answering this question, Jacques said: 'It's a very queer business, you know. People are always going on morning, noon and night about how terrible life is, but they can't bring themselves to put an end to it. Could it be that this life, all things considered, isn't so bad after all? Or is it that they're afraid that the next one will be worse?'

Master. Both, I should say. Incidentally, Jacques, do you believe in the afterlife?

Jacques. I neither believe nor disbelieve. I never think about it. I make the most of the one we've been given, like making withdrawals against future expectations.

Master. Personally, I think of myself as a chrysalis and like to believe that the butterfly, in other words my soul, will one day wriggle out of its case and fly up in the direction of divine justice.

Jacques. The image is delightful.

Master. It's not mine. I came across it, I think, in an Italian poet name of Dante, who wrote something called *The Comedy of Hell, Purgatory, and Paradise.**

Jacques. That's a rum subject to write a comedy about.

Master. Even so there are some very good things in it, especially Hell. He shuts heretics up inside flaming tombs from which tongues of fire leap out and spread devastation all round about.* He puts caitiff traitors in places where they shed tears that freeze upon their cheeks.* Slothful souls he puts in holes and says that blood gushes from their veins and is lapped up by disdainful worms below...* But what prompted you to say all that about complaining about the life we are afraid to lose?

Jacques. Something the Marquis des Arcis's secretary told me about the husband of the pretty lady who came in the carriage.

Master. She's a widow.

Jacques. It seems she lost her husband during a trip she made to Paris and the wretched man refused to have anything to do with the last rites. The lady who owns the chateau where Richard met up with Père Hudson was given the task of reconciling him to accepting his woolly blanket.

Master. Woolly blanket?

Jacques. The one they wrap round the heads of newborn babies, for comfort.

Master. Ah, I'm with you. And how did she set about pulling wool over his eyes?

Jacques. They gathered in a semicircle round the fire. The doctor took the patient's pulse, which was very weak, and then sat down with the others. The lady in question sat near his bed and asked a series of questions in a voice that never sank below the level required for him to catch every word of what she wanted him to hear. Then began a discussion which involved the lady, the doctor, and a few others there present. This is how it went:

Lady. Well, Doctor, do give us the latest news of Madame de Parme.*

Doctor. I have just come from a house where I was confidently told that she is so ill that they despair of her.

Lady. The Princess has always been a stickler for religious observance. The moment she felt she was in mortal danger, she asked to be confessed and have the sacraments administered.

Doctor. The curé of Saint-Roch* is to take a relic to her at Versailles, but it'll get there too late.

Lady. Madame Infanta is not the only one who sets such a good example. The Duke de Chevreuse,* when he was so ill, didn't wait for anyone to mention the sacraments. He called for them himself, which was a great comfort to all his family.

Doctor. He's much better now.

Family Friend. One thing's clear. The last rites don't make you die, rather the opposite.

Lady. In fact, everyone should attend to such matters as soon as there's any hint of danger. It would seem that patients have little understanding of how hard it is for those who sit at their bedsides, and yet how essential it is to raise these matters with them.

Doctor. I've just left a patient who asked me, not two days ago: 'Doctor, how do you reckon I am?'

'You have a high fever, sir, and the attacks are becoming more frequent.'

'Do you think I shall have another one soon?'

'No, but I am fearful for tonight.'

'Since that's the way of it, I shall send word to a man I am negotiating some business with, so I can get it over while I still have my wits about me.'

He was given confession and received the last rites. I went back that evening, but there was no further attack. Yesterday he was better and today he is out of danger. In the course of my practice I have seen the same effect produced by the sacraments many, many times.

Patient [*to his servant*]. Bring me chicken.

Jacques. They bring him chicken. He tries to cut it but doesn't have the strength. They cut it up very small for him. He asks for bread, attacks it desperately, tries his best to chew a mouthful, but is unable to swallow it and spits it out into his napkin. He asks for wine, wets his lips with it, and says: 'I feel fine.' Maybe he did, but half an hour later he was dead.

Master. Still, the lady went the right way about it... But what about your love-life?

Jacques. Do you remember the condition you agreed to?

Master. I do... You've been settled into the Chateau Desglands and Jeanne, who fetches and carries for everyone, has ordered her daughter Denise to call in on you four times a day and look after you. But before you get any further, tell me: did Denise still have her virginity?

Jacques [*coughs*]. I believe so.

Master. And you?

Jacques. Oh, mine had been over the hills and far away for some time before then.

Master. So this wasn't the first time you'd fallen in love?

Jacques. Why do you ask?

Master. Because men love the women they give their virginity to and are loved by women whose virginity they take away.

Jacques. Maybe, maybe not.

Master. And how did you lose yours?

Jacques. I didn't lose it. I swapped it.

Master. Tell me how you swapped it.

Jacques. It would be like Luke, Chapter 1, a never-ending string of 'begats', starting with the first and ending with Denise, who was the last.*

Master. And who believed she was your first but wasn't.

Jacques. And before Denise, so did a couple of our neighbours' wives.

Master. Who also believed they were your first but weren't.

Jacques. That's right.

Master. It wasn't very clever of either of them to miss out on your virginity.

Jacques. Look, sir, I can see from the way your right lip is curling and your left nostril is twitching, that I'd better just plough on and tell you the whole story rather than wait to be asked, especially since I can feel my throat getting worse and because the rest of my love-life will take some time and I don't think I can manage much more than a couple of short episodes.

Master. If Jacques really wanted to indulge me...

Jacques. What would he do?

Master. He'd start by telling me how he lost his virginity. Shall I be frank? I've always been rather partial to accounts of how it happens—it's a big occasion in anyone's life.

Jacques. But why?

Master. Because among all the stories that are told about that sort of thing, they're the only kind that are of any interest whatsoever. The rest are no more than common re-enactments and pale imitations. I feel sure that of all the lapses pretty young sinners can confess, their confessor is only seriously bothered about the first.

Jacques. Oh sir, sir, you've got a twisted mind. I wouldn't be surprised if the devil himself doesn't come to you on your deathbed and reveal himself in the same form and guise as he did to Ferragus.*

Master. Maybe he will. But I'd bet you were deflowered by some lewd old hag in your village.

Jacques. Don't bet on it, you'd lose.

Master. Or by your curé's housekeeper?

Jacques. Don't bet on that either, you'd lose again.

Master. Was it his niece, then?

Jacques. His niece was spite and piety on legs. They are qualities which go quite well together, but they don't go with me.

Master. This time I think I've got it.

Jacques. I doubt it.

Master. Once upon a time, there was a fair on or maybe it was market-day...

Jacques. There wasn't a fair and it wasn't market-day.

Master. You went to town...

Jacques. I didn't go to town.

Master. And it was written on high that you'd be in a tavern where you'd meet one of those accommodating girls, get her drunk...

Jacques. In fact, I hadn't had anything to eat or drink and what was written on high was that today, as we speak, you would be racking your brains making wrong assumptions and pick up a bad habit you've broken me of: the mania for guessing and getting it wrong. The man who stands before you, sir, was once baptized...

Master. If you intend to take the story of the loss of your virginity all the way back to the font, we won't get to it for ages.

Jacques. And I had a godfather and a godmother. Monsieur Buger, the best wheelwright in the village, had a son. Monsieur Buger was my godfather and his son was my friend. When we were both eighteen or nineteen, we both fell for a sweet little seamstress called Justine. She wasn't reckoned to be very hard to get, but she decided she'd change all that by breaking a heart. For this purpose, she chose mine.

Master. There you have an instance of the strange ways of women which we men find incomprehensible.

Jacques. Monsieur Buger, the wheelwright who was also my god-father, lived in a place which consisted of his workshop and, directly above it, a loft. He slept in the back of the shop. His son, my friend, slept in the loft. You got to the loft by climbing up a little ladder, the foot of which was equidistant from his father's bed and the door of the shop. When my godfather Buger was asleep, my friend Buger would open the door quietly and Justine would climb up the little ladder into the loft. Next morning, as soon as it was light and before Monsieur Buger was awake, young Buger would come down from the loft, open the door, and Justine would slip out the way she'd come.

Master. Presumably to climb into another loft, either hers or somebody else's.

Jacques. Why not? Buger and Justine got on very well together, but it was inevitable that there'd be trouble—it was written on high. And trouble there was.

Master. From the father?

Jacques. No.

Master. From the mother?

Jacques. No. She was dead.

Master. From a rival?

Jacques. No, dammit, no! Sir, it is written on high that you shall go bumbling on in this vein for as long as you live. I repeat: until the day you die you will keep trying to guess the answer, and you will keep on guessing wrong.

Anyway, one morning my friend Buger, feeling wearier than usual either from his labours of the previous day or the pleasures of the night, was slumbering peacefully in the arms of his Justine. All of a sudden there was a great bellow from the foot of the ladder: 'Buger! you hound! you lazy young Buger! The Angelus has rung, it's almost half-past five, and you're still in the loft! Are you reckoning on staying there till noon? If I have to come up there, I'll pitch you out of it faster than you'll like! Buger! Look alive!'

'Coming, father.'

'There's the axle that farmer's waiting for. He's like a bear with a sore head. Do you want him coming back and causing more ructions?'

'His axle is ready. He'll have it in a quarter of an hour.'

I leave you to picture Justine and my poor friend Buger shivering in their shoes.

Master. I'm sure Justine vowed she'd never go up to the loft again and that the next night she was there again. But how did she manage to get away that morning?

Jacques. Since you insist on trying to guess, I won't say... Meantime, my friend Buger jumped out of bed naked, his breeches in one hand and his jerkin over his arm. While he's getting dressed, Buger senior mutters between his teeth:

'Ever since he's been knocking around with that trollop, everything's gone to pot. It's got to stop, this can't go on, I'm getting fed up with it. It wouldn't be so bad if she was worth it, but she's no good, by God, a creature like that! Ah! if his poor dead mother, who was honest to her fingertips, was here to see it, she'd have given the boy a damn good hiding long ago and scratched that hussy's eyes out after mass, in the church porch, in front of everybody, because nothing would have stopped her! But if they believe I've been too easy on them up to now and think I intend to carry on the same way, they're making a big mistake.'

Master. And did Justine hear him from the loft?

Jacques. I don't doubt it for a moment. Meanwhile, my friend Buger had gone off to the farmer with the axle slung over his shoulder, and Buger senior had started work. After swinging his adze a few times, his nose requests a pinch of snuff. He feels for his snuffbox in his pockets, looks by the side of his bed, but can't find it.

'It's that damned layabout,' said he, 'he's gone off with it, as usual. Let's have a look and see if he's left it in the loft.'

Whereupon he climbs up into the loft. A minute later he realizes he hasn't got his pipe and his knife, so up he goes again.

Master. What about Justine?

Jacques. She'd quickly gathered up her clothes and had hidden under the bed, where she lay flat on her face more dead than alive.

Master. And what about your friend, Buger junior?

Jacques. When he'd delivered the axle, fitted it, and been paid, he hurried over to my house and told me of the awful fix he'd got himself into. After I'd had a bit of a laugh, I said:

'Listen, Buger, go and walk round the village, it doesn't matter where, and I'll get you out of this. I only ask one thing, just give me time.'

Sir, you're smiling. What's so funny?

Master. Oh, nothing.

Jacques. Off my friend Buger goes. I get dressed, because I was still in bed. I go round to his father's. The minute he claps eyes on me he gives a whoop of surprise and delight and says:

'Why, it's my godson! Where have you been? What are you doing here so early in the morning?'

My godfather Buger was genuinely fond of me and so I was frank:

'Knowing where I've been is less important than how I'm going to get into our house.'

'Ah, lad, you're turning into a rake. I'm afraid you and your friend Buger are a right pair. You've not been home all night.'

'With that sort of thing, my father just won't listen to reason.'

'My boy, your father's right not to want to discuss it. But we'll start by having some breakfast. Let's see if the answer's in a bottle.'

Master. Jacques, there's a man with the right idea!

Jacques. I told him I didn't need or want anything to eat or drink. I said I was almost out on my feet and nearly asleep. Old Buger, who in his day had been as much of a tearaway as my father, said with a leer:

'So, lad, she was a pretty girl and you got your oats, eh? Listen. Your friend Buger's gone out. Climb up to the loft and get your head down on his bed... But just a word before he comes back. He's your friend. When the pair of you are alone together, tell him I'm not pleased, not at all pleased. There's this lass, Justine, you must know her, all the lads in the village know her, and she's turned his head. You'd be doing me a big favour if you could get her claws out of him. Before, he used to be what you'd call a good boy, but since he took up with that trollop... You're not listening, your eyes are closing. Up you go and get some rest.'

I climb up, get undressed, pull back the blanket and the sheets, I feel all around: no Justine. Meanwhile, my godfather Buger was muttering: 'Children, damned children! There's another one who'll grieve his father's heart!'

Since Justine wasn't in the bed, I deduced she must be under it. It was very dark up there. I bend down, reach out with my hands, feel one of her arms, grab it, and pull her towards me. She crawls out all of a tremble. I kiss her, say everything's all right, and motioned her to get into bed. She puts both hands together, kneels at my feet, and clasps me round the knees. If the loft had been light enough for me to see her, perhaps I mightn't have been unable to resist her unspoken pleading. But if the dark doesn't make you afraid, it makes you feel bold. Besides, I hadn't forgotten the way she'd given me the elbow. My answer was to push her towards the top of the ladder that led down to the shop. She gave a frightened squawk. Old Buger heard and said: 'He must be dreaming.' Justine faints, her legs buckle under her, and through her panic she says in a hoarse whisper:

'He's going to come... he's coming... I can hear him on the ladder... I'm lost!'

'No,' said I, also in a whisper, 'just get a grip on yourself, don't say anything, and get into bed.'

This she stubbornly refused to do. I hold firm, she resigns herself, and there we are stretched out side by side.

Master. You dog! You swine! Do you know what a dreadful thing it is you are about to do? You're going to have your way with the girl if not by force then through fear. If you were brought before the bench for it, you'd be treated with the full rigour which the law lays down for rapists.

Jacques. I'm not sure if I raped her, but I do know I never hurt her and she did me no harm. At first, she avoided my lips, put her mouth to my ear, and whispered: 'No, no, Jacques, don't...' whereupon I pretended to get out of bed and make for the top of the ladder. But she held me back and whispered in my ear:

'I'd never have thought you could be so nasty. I see I can't expect any pity from you, but at least, promise me, swear that...'

'What?'

'Buger will never know.'

Master. So you promised, you swore, and it all went well?

Jacques. Yes, and then it went well again.

Master. And then it went well again?

Jacques. Exactly, it's as if you'd been there yourself. Meanwhile my friend Buger, impatient, anxious, and tired of skulking around his house without seeing me, returns to his father who snaps at him:

'You took long enough about it.'

To which Buger snaps back:

'I had to plane down both ends of that bloody axle, didn't I? It was too big.'

'I warned you, but you just won't take telling.'

'Axles are a lot easier to take off than to put back on again.'

'Take this rim and finish it off outside the door.'

'Why outside the door?'

'Because the noise of your hammer would wake your friend Jacques.'

'Jacques?'

'Yes, Jacques. He's up in the loft, getting some sleep. Oh! you should feel sorry for fathers. If it isn't one thing, it's another. Come on, shift yourself! Standing there like a halfwit. Head lolling, mouth open, and arms dangling—that's not going to get the work done, is it?'

My friend Buger, fuming, makes a beeline for the ladder. My godfather Buger grabs him and says:

'Where d'you think you're going? Let the poor devil sleep. He's worn out. If you were in his shoes, would you be pleased to have your rest disturbed?'

Master. And Justine heard all that too?

Jacques. As clearly as you're hearing me now.'

Master. And what were you doing?

Jacques. Laughing.

Master. And Justine?

Jacques. She'd pulled her mob-cap off, and was tearing her hair and raising her eyes to heaven—at least I presume she was—and wringing her hands.

Master. Jacques, you're a barbarian, you've got a heart like flint.

Jacques. Absolutely not, sir. I'm very sensitive, but I keep my sensitivity by me for more suitable occasions. It's a treasure which people spend like sailors, whereas really they should be economical with it. The result is that when they should be splashing out they find it's all gone... Meanwhile I get dressed and come down. Old Buger says:

'You needed that, it's done you a power of good. When you came you looked like death, and here you are as fresh and pink-cheeked as a babe at the breast. Wonderful thing, sleep!... Buger, go down the cellar and fetch us up a bottle. It's time for breakfast. And you, my boy, will you have a bite of something?'

'I'd be glad to.'

The bottle arrives and is now standing on the bench. We stand around it. Old Buger fills his glass and mine. My friend Buger moves his to one side and says fiercely:

'Me, I got no craving for it this early.'

'You don't want a drink?'

'No.'

'Ah, I know what's the matter! I tell you, Jacques, that Justine's at the bottom of this. He's been round to her house and either she wasn't there or he caught her with somebody else. Taking against the bottle like this, it's not natural, I tell you.'

Me. You might just have hit the nail on the head.

Buger Jr. Jacques, cut out the jokes. I don't care if they're deserved or not, I don't like them.

Buger Sr. Just because he won't take a glass is no reason why we shouldn't. Your very good health, godson.

Me. And yours, godfather. Come on Buger, old pal, have a drink with us. You're worrying far too much about nothing.

Buger Jr. I told you once. I'm not drinking.

Me. Oh come on. If your father guessed right, so what? You'll see her again, you have it out with her, and you'll end up admitting you're in the wrong.

Buger Sr. Oh, leave him be. It's only fair if that damned wench punishes him for all the trouble he causes me. Here, have another, and we'll think about your problem. I suppose I'd better take you home to your father. But what do you want me to tell him?

Me. Whatever you like—tell him all the things you've heard him say when he's brought your lad back to you.

Buger Sr. Let's go, then.

He goes out, I follow, we get to the front door of our house. I let him go in first by himself. Being curious to hear what old Buger and my father have got to say to each other, I hide in a corner, behind a thin partition. There I don't miss a word.

Buger Sr. Come on, old friend, you're going to have to forgive him this time too.'

'Forgive him? What for?'

'Don't pretend you don't know.'

'I'm not pretending. I honestly don't.'

'You're angry, and you've good reason to be.'

'I'm not angry.'

'You are, I tell you.'

'If you really want me to get angry, that's fine by me, but before I do just tell me what he's been getting up to this time.'

'All right. So it's been three, maybe four times, but that doesn't make it a habit. You get together with a gang of lads and lasses, you drink, have a few laughs, dance, the time whizzes by, and before you know it your front door's been locked...'

Here Buger lowered his voiced and added:

'They can't hear us, so be honest: were we any wiser at their age? Do you know what a bad father is? A bad father is a man who's forgotten the follies of his own youth. Tell me, did we ever stay out all night?'

'All right, Buger, old friend, but did we ever go around with girls our parents disapproved of?'

'That's exactly why I make out I'm more cross than I feel. You should do the same.'

'But Jacques didn't stay out all night, at least not last night, I'm sure of it.'

'All right, if it wasn't last night, it was another night. But the top and bottom of it is that you're not angry with the lad?'

'No.'

'And you won't take your belt to the boy after I've gone?'

'No.'

'Will you give me your word?'

'You have it.'

'Your word of honour?'

'My word of honour.'

'There's no more to say. I'll be off, then.'

My godfather Buger had got to the door when my father tapped him on the shoulder and said:

'Buger, old friend, I smell a rat. Your lad and mine are cunning little devils and I'm afraid that they've put one over on us today. But it'll all come out in time. Goodbye, old friend.'

Master. How did the business between your friend Buger and Justine end?

Jacques. Predictably. He got angry; she got even angrier. She cried; he weakened. She swore that I was the best friend he had; I swore that she was the most decent girl in the village. He believed us and said he was sorry. We went up in his estimation and he thought all the more of the both of us. And that's the beginning, the middle, and the end of the story of how I lost my virginity. And now, sir, I'd be glad if you could tell me the moral of this ribald tale.

Master. It teaches us to know women better.

Jacques. You need to be taught that lesson?

Master. Well then, to know our friends better?

Jacques. Have you ever seriously believed you had a friend who'd say no to your wife or daughter, if either of them made up her mind to have him?

Master. To know fathers and sons better?

Jacques. But surely, sir, they have always been each other's dupes and will go on being so forever?

Master. These things you say are eternal verities, and they cannot be said too often. I have no idea what tale you promised me after that one, but you can be sure that only a fool would not find something to learn from it. So, lay on.

Reader, a sudden unease tugs at my conscience. The fact is I have given Jacques and his Master the honour of making a series of observations which, properly speaking, should be your province. If that is indeed the case, then feel free to say your piece now. Jacques and his Master won't raise any objections.

I also think I sense that you're not too happy with this name, Buger. I can't think why. It was the real name of my wheelwright's family. Their records of baptism, death certificates, and marriage lines are all made out in the name of Buger. Buger's descendants, who still occupy his premises today, are called Buger. When their children, who are pretty little things, walk down the street, people say: 'There go the little Bugers.'

When you say the name Boulle,* you commemorate the greatest cabinetmaker who ever lived. Even today, where the Bugers come from, no one mentions the name Buger without recalling the greatest wheelwright in living memory. The man whose name figures at the end of all the devotional prayer-books published around the start of the century was a relative of his. If ever some grand-nephew of Buger were to distinguish himself by some great action, the name Buger will impress you just as much as 'Caesar' or 'Condé'.*

For there's Buger and Buger just as there's William and William. If I just say William, I don't mean the Conqueror of England nor the draper in the play of Maître-Pathelin.* By itself, the name William is neither heroic nor common. It's exactly the same with Buger. By itself, Buger is neither the famous wheelwright nor any one of his dull ancestors or his boring descendants. In all conscience, can a person's name be tasteful or tasteless? The streets are full of dogs called Pompey. So put away your false prudery, or I shall say to you what Lord Chatham said to members of Parliament: 'Sh... ugar, sugar, sugar: what do you find so funny about that?'* And I in turn ask you: 'Buger, Buger, Buger: why shouldn't people be called Buger?' The fact of the matter is that, as one of the Great Condé's officers once remarked to him, there are proud Bugers, like Buger the wheelwright, decent Bugers, like you and me, and Bugers who are just as dull as any number of other people.

Jacques. One day, there was a wedding: Frère Jean had found a husband for the daughter of one of our neighbours. I was a groom. I'd been put on a table between the two biggest wags in the parish. I gave the impression I was a bit wet behind the ears, though I wasn't quite as green as they thought. They asked me a few questions about the bride on her wedding night to which I gave some rather silly answers. They had a good laugh and the wives of the two jokers called out:

'What are you saying? You seem to be having a good time at that end of the table.'

'It's too funny for words,' replied one of the husbands to his wife. 'I'll tell you all about it tonight.'

The other wife, who was just as inquisitive, asked her husband the same question and he gave her the same answer. The wedding breakfast went on, as did the questions, my stupid answers, the bursts of laughter, and the curiosity of the ladies. When the meal was over there was dancing, and after the dancing, bride and groom were lit to their wedding couch, the bride's garter was tossed to the crowd, I retired to my bed and both wags to theirs, where they told their wives it was incomprehensible, unbelievable that, though I was twenty-two, fully grown and lusty, reasonably good-looking, alert, and no fool, I could be so ignorant, as ignorant as the day I emerged from my mother's womb. The two women was no less amazed than their husbands. But the following day Suzanne, who lived next door, called me over and said:

'Jacques, are you doing anything?'

'No. Is there something I can do for you?'

'I'd like you... I'd like you to...'

And repeating 'I'd like you to', she squeezed my hand and gave me a very odd look.

'... I'd like you to get our billhook and come to the common with me and help me cut two or three bundles of firewood. It's far too heavy a job for me to do by myself.'

'I'd be glad to, Madame Suzanne.'

I fetch their billhook and off we go. As we went along, Suzanne allowed her head to rest on my shoulder, stroked my chin, pinched my ears, and tickled me in the ribs. We reach the common, which was on a slope. Suzanne lies down flat at the top of it with her legs spread wide and her arms under her head. I was lower down swinging at the bushes with the billhook. Suzanne bent her legs, drew her heels in close to her body, and her raised knees also raised her skirts. I was still swinging the billhook, though I was not looking at what I was swinging it at, and missing more often than not. Eventually, Suzanne says:

'Jacques, will you be finished soon?'

To which I replied:

'I'll stop whenever you say, Madame Suzanne.'

'Can't you see,' she said in a half-whisper, 'that I want you to stop now?'

So I stopped, got my breath back, and put the billhook down. Then Suzanne...

Master. Removed the virginity you no longer had?

Jacques. That's it, though Suzanne wasn't fooled for a moment, for she smiled and said:

'You pulled the wool over my husband's eyes and no mistake. You're a rogue.'

'Whatever can you mean, Madame Suzanne?'

'Nothing, but you know what I'm talking about. But if you pull the same trick on me another couple of times, I'll forgive you...'

I tied up her bundles of sticks, slung them over my shoulder, and we went home, she to hers and I to mine.

Master. Without stopping once along the way?

Jacques. No.

Master. So it wasn't very far from the common to the village?

Jacques. Exactly the same distance as from the village to the common.

Master. And she wasn't worth stopping for?

Jacques. A different man on another day might have thought her worth stopping for. Each moment has its own value.

A little while after this, Madame Marguerite, who was the wife of the other wag, had a sack of grain she wanted ground but didn't have time to go to the mill herself. She came and asked my father for the loan of one of his sons who would go for her. As I was the biggest, she assumed that my father would choose me, and so it turned out. Madame Marguerite leaves and I follow. I load the sack on to the mule and drive it to the mill. The grain is ground and the mule and I set off back again, both feeling hard done by, for I was thinking I'd get nothing for my pains. I was wrong.

Between the village and the mill, the way led through a small copse. There I found Madame Marguerite sitting by the side of the road. The light was beginning to fade.

'Jacques, there you are at last! Do you realize I've been waiting for you for an hour that has seemed an eternity?'

Reader, you're far too pernickety. Agreed, 'an hour that seems an eternity' is for smart ladies in town. 'An hour and more' is what Madame Marguerite would say.

Jacques. The river was low, the mill turned slowly, the miller was drunk, and though I was as quick as I could, I couldn't have got back any sooner.

Marguerite. Sit down here and we'll have a little chat.

Jacques. I don't mind if I do.

I sat down beside her for a little chat. Yet neither of us said anything. In the end I ventured:

Jacques. Madame Marguerite. You're not saying anything and we're not chatting.

Marguerite. I was thinking of something my husband said about you.

Jacques. You mustn't believe what your husband told you, he's all mouth and trousers.

Marguerite. He told me you've never been in love.

Jacques. Oh, on that score what he said was quite right.

Marguerite. What, never?

Jacques. In my life.

Marguerite. Really? A lad of your age doesn't know what a woman is?

Jacques. I'm sorry, Madame Marguerite.

Marguerite. And what do you think a woman is?

Jacques. A woman?

Marguerite. Yes, a woman.

Jacques. A woman... wait a sec... a woman's a man who wears a petticoat and a mob-cap and has got big jugs.

Master. You rogue!

Jacques. The first one hadn't been fooled but I wanted this one to be. When she heard my answer, Madame Marguerite roared with laughter and couldn't stop. I looked suitably dismayed and asked her why she was laughing so much. She said she was laughing because I was so simple:

'What! Doesn't a grown lad like you know any more than that?'

'No, Madame Marguerite.'

Whereupon she fell silent and so did I.

'But, Madame Marguerite,' I went on, 'we sat down for a little chat and you're not saying anything and we're not chatting. What's the matter? What are you thinking about?'

Marguerite. You're right, I'm... I'm thinking... I'm thinking that...

While she was saying 'I'm thinking', her bosom heaved, her voice faltered, her limbs trembled, her eyes closed, and her mouth half opened. She gave a deep sigh and fell back in a faint. I pretended I thought she was dead, and in a panic I started calling to her:

'Madame Marguerite! Madame Marguerite! say something! Are you ill?'

Marguerite. No, it's all right, lad. Just leave me alone for a moment... I don't know what came over me... It happened so quickly.

Master. She was lying.

Jacques. Of course she was lying.

Marguerite. I was thinking...

Me. Do you have thoughts like that at night when you're in bed with your husband?

Marguerite. Now and then.

Me. I expect he gets scared.

Marguerite. He's used to it.

Marguerite began to get over her faint and said:

Marguerite. I was thinking back to the wedding last week. My husband and Suzanne's made fun of you. I was ever so sorry for you and it made me feel awful.

Me. It's kind of you to say so

Marguerite. I hate it when people are made fun of. I was thinking that they'll start on you again whenever they get the chance and then I'd feel even worse.

Me. If you wanted to, you could make sure you never felt awful again.

Marguerite. How?

Me. By teaching me...

Marguerite. What?

Me. Whatever it is I don't know, whatever your husband and Madame Suzanne's husband found so funny, and then they wouldn't find it funny any more.

Marguerite. Oh I couldn't do that. I know you're a good lad and wouldn't say a word to anybody, but I wouldn't dare.

Me. Why not?

Marguerite. I just wouldn't.

Me. Oh come on, Madame Marguerite, teach me! Please! I'd be ever so grateful. Teach me.

As I said this, I squeezed her hands and she squeezed mine back. I kissed her eyes and she kissed my mouth. By now it was quite dark. So I said:

Me. I can see, Madame Marguerite, that you're not so sorry for me that you want to teach me, and I'm very hurt. Come on, up with you, we ought to be getting back.

She didn't say anything but took one of my hands. I'm not quite sure where she put it, but I do know I exclaimed:

Me. Why, there's nothing there!

Master. You villain! You villain! You're doing it again!

Jacques. The fact was that she was half-undressed and so was I. In fact my hand was still where she didn't have anything, and she had put hers where the same thing could not be said of me. In fact I was lying under her and, consequently, she was lying on top of me. In fact since I was contributing nothing to the business, she had to do everything herself. In fact she set about my education with such a will that at one moment I thought it would kill her. In fact I got as overwrought as her, and not knowing what I was saying I cried out:

'Oh, Madame Suzanne, you're making me feel so go–ood!'

Master. Don't you mean Madame Marguerite?

Jacques. No. In fact I got the names mixed up and instead of saying Madame Marguerite, I said Madame Suzanne. In fact I admitted to Madame Marguerite that what she thought she'd been teaching me that day, Madame Suzanne had already taught me three or four days before, though her lesson had been slightly different, it's true. In fact she said:

'You mean, it was Suzanne and not me who...'

To which, in fact, I replied:

'In fact it wasn't either of you.'

In fact while she was busy seeing that the laugh was on herself, on Suzanne, and on both husbands, and heaping little insults on me, I ended up on top of her with her, consequently, under me, and then, admitting that she had enjoyed it very much but not as much as the other way, she found herself on top of me again with me, consequently, under her. In fact, after a brief pause filled by rest and silence, it finished up in such a way that she wasn't under me nor I on top of her, nor she on top of me and I under her, for we were lying side by side, she leaning her head forward and her hindquarters firmly in my lap. In fact, if I had been less advanced in these matters, kind Madame Marguerite would have taught me everything there is to know. In fact, we had a hard time of it getting back to the village. In fact, my throat has come on a lot worse and it looks as if it'll be a fortnight before I can talk again.

Master. And you never saw the two women again?

Jacques. I'm sorry to say I did. More than once.

Master. Both of them?

Jacques. Oh yes.

Master. Didn't they fall out?

Jacques. Since they knew certain things about each other, they got on even more famously than before.

Master. Wives in town would have done exactly the same, but there, every woman to her own man... But why are you laughing?

Jacques. Every time I remember that witless gnome, shouting, swearing, fuming, wagging his head, waving feet, hands, his whole body about, and ready at any moment to fling himself out of the hayloft and not caring whether he killed himself or not, I just can't help laughing.

Master. What witless gnome? Madame Suzanne's husband?

Jacques. No.

Master. Madame Marguerite's husband?

Jacques. No. He's still a gnome and a gnome he'll stay until the day he dies.

Master. Who was he, then?

When Jacques didn't answer, his Master went on:

Master. Go on, tell me who the witless gnome was.

Jacques. One day, there was this little boy who was sitting under the counter in a laundry, crying his eyes out. The laundryman's wife got tired of the noise, so she said:

'Come, child, what are you crying for?'

'Because they want me to say A.'

'And why don't you want to say A?'

'Because the minute I've said A, they'll want me to say B.'

The minute I tell you the name of the witless gnome, I'll have to tell you the rest.

Master. Perhaps.

Jacques. No perhaps about it.

Master. Go on, Jacques, dear Jacques, do tell me the witless gnome's name. You're dying to, aren't you? Give in to it.

Jacques. He was a sort of dwarf, a knock-kneed, stuttering, one-eyed hunchback, very jealous and lecherous,* and he was in love with Suzanne who maybe was in love with him. He was the village curate.

Jacques and that little boy in the laundry were as alike as two peas, except that since getting his sore throat, it was very difficult to get him to say A, though once he was launched, he'd run right through the alphabet without further prompting.

Jacques. I was with Suzanne in her barn. We were alone.

Master. And you weren't there without a reason?

Jacques. Correct. And when the curate arrived, he flew off the handle and started going on, demanding that Suzanne should tell him what she thought she was doing alone with the lewdest of all the village louts in the part of the farm that was farthest away from the house...

Master. So I see you already had something of a reputation.

Jacques. It was thoroughly deserved. He was absolutely furious. While he was about it, he made a number of other rude comments. Then I got angry too. After trading insults, we came to blows. I grabbed a pitchfork, poked it between his legs, waggled the prongs, and forked him up into the hayloft, like a bale of straw.

Master. How high was the loft?

Jacques. At least ten feet. The stupid oaf couldn't have got down without breaking his neck.

Master. What happened next?

Jacques. Next I removed the scarf Suzanne wore round her shoulders, put my hand on her breasts, and stroked them. She didn't put up much resistance. There was a pack-saddle which had come in handy on previous occasions. I pushed her on to it.

Master. You pulled her skirts up.

Jacques. I pulled her skirts up.

Master. Was the curate able to see what was happening?

Jacques. As clearly as I can see you.

Master. And was he speechless?

Jacques. Absolutely not. Unable to contain his rage, he started shouting: 'M-m-murder! F-f-fie... f-f-fire! Huh-huh-help!' Whereupon her husband, who we thought was miles away, came running.

Master. I'm sorry to hear it. I don't care for priests.

Jacques. In that case you'll be delighted to know that right under this one's nose...

Master. Absolutely delighted.

Jacques. Suzanne has just enough time to get to her feet. I adjust my clothes, make myself scarce, and afterwards Suzanne told me what happened next. Her husband spots the curate perched up in the hayloft and bursts out laughing. The curate said:

'G-g-go on and l-l-laugh, you s-s-stupid cuc-cuc-clod.'

Her husband did what he was told, laughed even louder, and asked him who it was had pitchforked him up there.

'G-g-get me d-d-down from huh-huh-here!'

Her husband laughed some more and asks him how exactly he is to set about doing it.

'The w-w-way I g-g-got up, w-w-with a p-p-pitchf-f-fork.'

'By the Virgin and all the saints, you're right! That's what book-learning does for you.'

Her husband grabs the fork, holds it out to the curate, who puts it between his legs the way I had. Then the farmer marches round the barn a couple of times with him on the end of it, intoning a sort of dirge as he goes, with the curate screeching: 'L-l-let m-me d-d-down, you gray-gray-great oh-oh-oaf! P-p-put m-me d-d-down at wuh-wuh-once!'

And Suzanne's husband said: 'Reverend, what's to stop me parading you like this through every street in the village? Folks won't have seen another procession like it ever.'

But the curate was let off with a fright, for her husband set him down on terra firma. I don't know what he said to the farmer, because Suzanne had made off by then, but I did catch the following myself:

'Y-you r-r-wretch! S-s-strike a pup-pup-priest would y-you! I e-e-excommunicate you! Y-you'll bub-bub-burn in huh-huh-hell!'

It was the small oaf who was saying this while the great oaf of a farmer chased him, swatting him with the pitchfork. I was still a good way off when he spotted me. He stopped his good work with the pitchfork and called out to me: 'Come here you!'

Master. What about Suzanne?

Jacques. She managed.

Master. How? Badly?

Jacques. No, women always manage as long as they aren't actually caught *in flagrante delicto*... Why are you laughing?

Master. At something that will make me chuckle, just as you do, every time I remember the pint-sized curate stuck on the end of the husband's pitchfork.

Jacques. It wasn't very long after this episode, which soon came to the ears of my father who also had a good laugh, that I enlisted, as I've already told you.*

After a few moments which Jacques spent in silence or coughing, as some say, or laughing, as others claim, the Master turned to Jacques and said:

'What about the story of your love-life?'

Jacques shook his head and did not answer.

What does a grown man, an intelligent man, an honest and decent man who fancies himself as a philosopher, think he's playing at, telling disgusting stories like this?

First of all, Reader, they aren't stories. This is a chronicle, and I don't feel any more guilty—perhaps less—when I write down Jacques's follies than Suetonius when he chronicled the debauched life of Tiberius for us.* Yet you read Suetonius and you don't complain about him. Why don't you glower at Catullus, Martial, Horace, Juvenal, Petronius, La Fontaine, and many, many more?* Why don't you tell Seneca the Stoic: 'We're not interested in your loathsome slaves and their magnifying mirrors'?* Why is it that you only make allowances for dead authors? If you stop a moment and think about this one-sided view of yours, you'll see that it's based on a false premiss. If you are pure in heart, you will not read my book; if you are depraved, you will not be affected by reading me. But if you are not convinced by this argument, have a look at what Jean-Baptiste Rousseau says in the preface to his works and there you will find the case for my defence.* Which of you would dare take Voltaire to task for writing *La Pucelle*?* Not one of you. Doesn't it follow, therefore, that you use two different sets of scales for judging men's actions?

But, you say, *La Pucelle* is a masterpiece.

Good. That means more people will read it.

Whereas your *Jacques* is a tasteless mishmash of things that happen, some of them true, others made up, written without style and served up like a dog's breakfast.

Good. That means not many people will read *Jacques*.

Look, Reader, whichever view you take, you get it wrong. If my book is any good, you'll like it; if it's bad, it won't do you any harm. There is no book more innocent than a bad book. I rather enjoy—pausing only to change the names—writing down the stupid things you do. Your follies make me laugh, but what I write offends you. To be perfectly frank, Reader, I'd say that of the two of us the more unkind is not me. I'd be only too happy if it were as easy for me to defend myself against your aspersions as it is for you to defend yourself against being bored or imperilled by my book. Just leave me alone, you miserable hypocrites. Carry on fucking like rabbits, but you've got to let me say fuck: I grant you the action and you let me have the word. Words like 'kill' and 'rob' and 'betray' come boldly to your lips, but you don't dare speak *that* word out loud, you just say it under your breath. Could it be that the fewer so-called obscenities you come out with, the more numerous they remain in your thoughts? What harm were you ever done by something as natural, necessary, and right as genital activity, that you should wish to exclude all mention of it from your conversation and imagine that your mouth and eyes and ears would be polluted if it weren't? It is good that the words which are spoken the most often, written the least frequently, and the most effectively curbed should be the best known and the most widely used—as such indeed is the case. For *futuo** is no less common than the word 'bread'. It is known to every age and idiom, there are countless synonyms for it in every tongue known to man, it looms large in every language but is never directly expressed, being without voice or outward shape, and the sex which indulges the thing most is the one accustomed to say the word least.

I can still hear you objecting: 'Oh, what a cynic! The impudence! This is sophistry!'

That's right, go ahead—insult a revered author who you are forever reading and of whom I am here merely the mouthpiece: I mean Montaigne.* You might say that the freedom of his language is the guarantee of the purity of my morals. *Lasciva est nobis pagina, vita proba.**

Jacques and his Master spent the rest of the day not speaking. Jacques coughed a lot and his Master would say: 'That's a very bad cough!', and then look at his watch to see what time it was without realizing what he was doing, open his snuffbox without thinking, and take a pinch without being aware of it. My justification for saying this is that he repeated these actions three or four times and always in the same order. The next moment Jacques would cough again and his Master would say: 'What a rotten cough! Look, you tanked yourself up to your Adam's apple with the landlady's wine, you didn't stint yourself last night with Richard the secretary—you fell up the stairs and didn't know what you were saying—and today you keep starting and stopping. I'll wager there's not a drop left in your gourd.' Then he would start muttering to himself, look at his watch, and indulge his nostrils.

I omitted to mention, dear Reader, that Jacques never went anywhere without a wicker-covered flask of good stuff, which he called his gourd and kept hanging from the pommel of his saddle. Each time his Master interrupted his flow with one of his extended questions, he would unhook it, throw back his head, pour the contents down his throat without the bottle touching his lips, and only put it back over his pommel when his Master had stopped talking.

I also forgot to mention that whenever anything cropped up that required serious thought, the first thing he did was to consult his gourd. Whether it was some moral issue that needed to be decided, an incident to be discussed, whether to take this road or that, or begin, pursue, or abandon some course of action, weigh the advantages and disadvantages of a great point of politics or some commercial or financial venture, the wisdom or folly of a law, the outcome of a war, the choice of an inn, the choice of a room at the inn, the choice of a bed in the room at the inn, the first thing he always said was: 'Let's see what my gourd has to say', and the last was: 'The gourd has spoken and so say I.'

Whenever the voice of Destiny was silent in his head, it spoke through his gourd: it was a kind of portable Pythia which dried up as soon as it was empty. At Delphi Pythia, her skirts hitched up, sitting bare-bottomed on her three-legged stool, received her inspiration from below, whence it rose upward. Jacques, sitting on his horse, with his head back, his gourd uncorked, and its neck pointing at his mouth, received his inspiration from on high, whence it flowed downwards. When Pythia and Jacques announced their oracles, both were drunk.*

Jacques claimed that the Holy Spirit had descended on the apostles in a gourd: he called Whitsun the Festival of the Gourd.* Indeed, he had composed a short treatise on divinations of this kind,* a profound work in which he gives his preference to oracles pronounced by Bacbuc, or the gourd. He disagreed on this subject with the curé of Meudon,* though he venerated him, for the curé consulted the divine Bacbuc only insofar as he was given to cracking a bottle or two.* 'I'm fond of Rabelais,' said he, 'but I'm fonder of truth than I am of Rabelais.' He called him a heretical Engastrimyth,* and advanced many reasons, each more compelling than the one before, to prove that the true oracles of Bacbuc or the divine gourd could only be heard through the neck of the bottle. Among the distinguished devotees of Bacbuc and those most truly inspired by the gourd in recent centuries, he placed Rabelais, La Fare, Chapelle, Chaulieu, La Fontaine, Molière, Panard, Gallet, and Vadé.* To his mind, Plato and Jean-Jacques Rousseau, who championed wine-drinking but did not drink themselves, were two false followers of the gourd. In time of yore, the gourd was enshrined in a number of celebrated sanctuaries, the Pomme de Pin, the Temple, and the *guinguette*,* of which places of worship he was writing a separate history. He described in the most graphic terms the enthusiasm, the warmth, the heat with which the Bacbucians or the Périgour*d*ins were—and indeed still are—fired when they sat with their elbows on the table at the end of a meal and the divine Bacbuc, or the sacred gourd, appeared unto them, descended in their midst, hissed, spurted froth far and wide, and covered its disciples with its prophetic droplets. His manuscript is illustrated with two portraits, underneath which is written: 'Anacreon and Rabelais, supreme pontiffs of the Gourd, one an Ancient, the other a Modern.'*

Do you really mean Jacques used the word 'engastrimyth'?

Why not, Reader? Jacques's Captain was a Bacbucian and he might well have known the term. And since Jacques lapped up everything he said, he could easily have remembered it. But to be honest, 'engastrimyth' is mine. It was 'ventriloquist' in the original text.

That's all very well, you add, but what about Jacques's love-life?

Only Jacques knows the tale of his love-life, and he's come down with a sore throat which has left his Master with only his watch and snuffbox, a privation which he finds no less distressing than you do.

So where does that leave us, then?

To be frank, I haven't a clue. This might be a good moment to consult sacred Bacbuc or the holy gourd, but the faith is declining and its temples are deserted. Just as the oracles of the pagans ceased when our divine Saviour was born, so the oracles of Bacbuc fell silent when Gallet died.* Which means no more great poems, no more outpourings of sublime eloquence, no more masterpieces stamped by the intoxication of genius: everything has become reasoned, encompassed, academic, and very, very flat. O holy Bacbuc! O sacred gourd! O Divinity worshipped by Jacques! Return to our midst!

Reader, the urge has come upon me to tell you of the birth of the divine Bacbuc, of the prodigies which attended it and proceeded from it, of the miracles of her reign and the disasters which followed her retirement. And if the sore throat which has struck Jacques lasts and his Master stubbornly persists in not speaking, then you'll just have to make do with my account of it. I shall endeavour to spin it out until Jacques is fully recovered and can resume the story of his loves.

There is at this point a most regrettable gap in the conversation of Jacques and his Master. Some day, a descendant of Nodot, the Président des Brosses, Freinshémius, or Père Brottier might fill it, and the descendants of Jacques or his Master, whichever own the manuscript, will doubtless find it hilarious.*

It would appear that Jacques, reduced to silence by his sore throat, suspended the tale of his love-life and that his Master began the story of his. This is only a conjecture, and I offer it for what it is worth. After several dotted lines indicating that there is a gap in the text, we read: 'There is no sadder fate in all the world than to be stupid.' Was it Jacques who proffered this thought? Or was it his Master? It could make the subject of a protracted and prickly debate. If Jacques was sufficiently impertinent to be capable of addressing his remark to his Master, his Master was also sufficiently honest to be capable of addressing it to himself. Whatever the long and the short of this, it is clear that it is the Master who continues:

Master. The next day was her birthday and I had no money. The Chevalier de Saint-Ouin, my best friend, was never outfaced by anything. He said:

'So you've got no money?'

'No.'

'Well, all we need to do is to make some.'

'Do you know how to make money?'

'Of course.'

He gets dressed, we go out, and he leads me down various backstreets to a small, dark house. Inside, we go up a flight of dirty stairs to the third floor. There I step into a very spacious and strangely furnished apartment. Among its contents were three chests of drawers, side by side, each in a different style. Behind the one in the middle there was a tall mirror with a moulding that was too high for the ceiling, so that a good six inches of it was hidden by the chest. On these three chests were all manner of disparate objects, including two backgammon boards. All round the room were a good number of rather handsome chairs, though no two were alike. At the end of a bed which had no curtains there was a superb day-couch. Against one window stood a bird-cage which was new but without a tenant, and in front of another a chandelier hung from a broom-handle which rested at either end on the backs of two broken-down chairs with straw seats. And right, left, and centre were pictures, some on the walls and the rest stacked on top of each other.

Jacques. You can smell a shady operator a mile away.

Master. You've got it straight off. Next thing my Chevalier and Monsieur Le Brun—which was the name of our curio-dealer and moneylender's go-between—had flung their arms around each other.

'Why, it's you, Chevalier!'

'Indeed it is, my dear Le Brun.'

'But where have you been keeping yourself? I haven't seen you for ages. These are sorry times we live in, wouldn't you say?'

'Indeed they are, Le Brun. But that's neither here nor there. Listen, I need a word in your ear.'

Master. I sat down. The Chevalier and Le Brun withdrew to a corner to talk. All I can report of their conversation are a few stray snatches which I caught from time to time:

'Is he good?'

'Excellent.'

'Is he of age?'

'Well past it.'

'He's the son?'

'Correct.'

'Do you realize that our last two operations...'

'Keep your voice down.'

'The father?'

'Wealthy.'

'Old?'

'And failing fast.'

Then Le Brun said aloud:

'Look, Chevalier, I don't want to get mixed up in anything else. It always leads to trouble. All right, so he's your friend, and he looks a thoroughly honest gentleman, but...'

'Come now, Le Brun!'

'I've got no money.'

'But you've got contacts.'

'They're all rogues and black-hearted thieves. Chevalier, aren't you tired of dealing with such people?'

'Needs must when the devil drives.'

'The devil that drives you is a queer joker—a hand of cards, a roll of the dice, a girl...'

'Oh come now!'

'It's always me you turn to and I'm an easy touch. And as for you, I don't know any man alive you couldn't persuade to go back on his word. Oh all right, ring the bell so I can find out if Fourgeot is in... No, don't ring, Fourgeot can take you to see Merval.'

'Why not take me yourself?'

'Me! I swore that rogue Merval would never work for me again nor for any of my friends. You'll have to answer for this gentleman, who may be and certainly is an honest man, I shall have to answer for you to Fourgeot, and Fourgeot will have to answer for me to Merval.'

Meanwhile his maid had come in. 'Is it to go to Monsieur Fourgeot's?' she said.

Le Brun told her: 'No, you're not going anywhere... Look Chevalier, I can't, I really can't.'

The Chevalier flung his arms around him and spoke to him very nicely: 'My dear Le Brun! Old friend!...'

I joined them and added my voice to that of the Chevalier: 'Monsieur Le Brun! My dear sir!...'

Le Brun allowed himself to be persuaded.

The maid, who had observed all this mummery with a smirk on her face, left the room and in no time was back with a little man who limped. He was dressed in black, walked with a stick, and stammered. His face was wizened and wrinkled but his eyes were sharp. The Chevalier turned to him and said:

'Ah, Monsieur Mathieu de Fourgeot! We haven't a moment to lose. Take us there at once.'

Fourgeot, without seeming to hear him, undid a small chamois-leather purse.

'Don't be ridiculous,' the Chevalier to Fourgeot, 'we'll take care of that.'

I stepped forward, reaching for a half-crown which I slipped to the Chevalier who gave it to the maid, tilting her head up with his hand as he did so. Meanwhile, Le Brun was saying to Fourgeot:

Le Brun. I won't have it. You mustn't take these gentlemen there.

Fourgeot. Why ever not, Monsieur Le Brun?

Le Brun. Because he's a rogue and a villain.

Fourgeot. I'm quite aware that Monsieur de Merval... but there's no sin but should find mercy. Besides, he's the only man I know who's got any money just now.

Le Brun. Monsieur Fourgeot, do what you please. Gentlemen, I wash my hands of the whole business.

Fourgeot. Aren't you coming with us, Monsieur Le Brun?

Le Brun. Me? God forbid! He is odious and I mean never to set eyes on him again for as long as I live.

Fourgeot. But we won't get anywhere without you.

Chevalier. That's true. Come, my dear Le Brun. If you want to help me, if you want to oblige a gentleman who is pretty hard-pressed, you won't refuse me this and you'll come.

Le Brun. Me, go to a man like Merval?

Chevalier. Yes. You'll come for my sake.

After a great deal of urging, Le Brun allowed himself to be persuaded and next thing Le Brun, the Chevalier, Mathieu de Fourgeot, and I set off. The Chevalier patted Le Brun's hand in the most friendly way as he said to me:

Chevalier. He's all heart, the most obliging of men, a better friend you could not have.

Le Brun. I do believe the Chevalier could talk me into making counterfeit money.

We arrived at Merval's house.

Jacques. Mathieu de Fourgeot...

Master. Spit it out. What do you mean?

Jacques. Mathieu de Fourgeot... What I mean is that the Chevalier de Saint-Ouin knows these men by name, even by their Christian name, and is therefore a rogue who is working hand in glove with the rest of the gang.

Master. You could be right... But you couldn't wish to meet a kinder, more courteous, honest, civil, human, sympathetic, and disinterested man than Monsieur de Merval. When he was satisfied I had reached my majority and was solvent, Monsieur de Merval looked very concerned and pained. He told us gravely that he was very sorry but that very morning he had been forced to oblige a friend of his who was in the direst straits. As a consequence, he was completely cleaned out. He then turned to me and added:

'Sir, you needn't regret you did not come to see me sooner. I would have been sorry to turn you down, but I would have done it. Loyalty to one's friends must come first...'

We were all quite speechless. The Chevalier, even Le Brun and Fourgeot flung themselves at Merval's feet. Merval said:

'Gentlemen, you all know me. I like nothing better than to oblige and always endeavour to avoid tarnishing the service I provide by making people beg for it. On my word as a gentleman, there aren't four louis in the house.'

As I stood there in their midst, I felt like a sick man on whom a death sentence has just been pronounced. I said to the Chevalier:

'Chevalier, let's get out of here since these gentlemen can do nothing for me.'

The Chevalier took me to one side and whispered:

'Don't even think of it. It's her birthday tomorrow. I warn you, I've set it all up and she's expecting you to come up with a suitable offering. You know how she is. It's not that she's self-interested, but she's like all other women—they don't like having their hopes dashed. She may already have boasted about it to her father, mother, aunts, and girlfriends and then, when it turns out she's got nothing to show them, she'll be mortified.'

And so he turned back to Merval and pressed him even harder. After allowing himself to be plagued for some time, Merval said:

'I've got the softest heart in all the world. I hate to see people in difficulty. I'm thinking... I've got an idea.'

Chevalier. What idea?

Merval. Have you anything against taking merchandise in lieu?

Chevalier. Have you got something that would do?

Merval. No, but I know a woman who'd see you right, a good sort and very honest.

Le Brun. Yes, the sort who'd let us have a lot of old rubbish at sky-high prices. We wouldn't make a penny.

Merval. Not at all. They'll be very fine materials, gems mounted in gold and silver, all sorts of silks, pearls, a few precious stones—you're not going to make a loss with merchandise like that. She's a kindly body who's quite happy with a small profit, provided she has good security. It's business stock which she got for next to nothing. Anyway, go and see. Looking won't cost anything.

I pointed out to Merval and the Chevalier that my rank in society did not allow me to engage in trade and that even if I had not found the arrangement distasteful, my situation did not leave me enough time to exploit the opportunity.* Obliging Le Brun and kindly Mathieu de Fourgeot spoke up with one voice:

'That's no problem, we'll sell it for you. It'll only take half a day.'

The meeting was adjourned until the afternoon when we would re-assemble at the house of Monsieur de Merval, who tapped me on the shoulder and said in a creamily sincere voice:

'Sir, I am delighted to oblige, but take my advice: don't make a habit of borrowing money on these terms, for it invariably leads to ruin. In this country, it would be a miracle if you were ever again to have dealings with men as honest as Monsieur Le Brun and Monsieur Mathieu de Fourgeot.'

Le Brun and Mathieu de Fourgeot (or Fourgeot de Mathieu) acknowledged the compliment with a bow and said that he was too kind, that they had always tried in the past to run their little business with a clear conscience, and that he had no cause to sing their praises.

Merval. You're wrong, gentlemen, for who has a clear conscience nowadays? Ask the Chevalier de Saint-Ouin. He knows exactly what I mean.

We were on our way out when Monsieur de Merval shouted down from the top of the stairs to ask if he could count on us and if he should send word to the woman with the business stock. We said yes, he could, and then all four of us went off to have lunch in a nearby inn until it was time to keep our appointment.

It was Mathieu de Fourgeot who ordered the lunch, and he ordered a good one. We had got to the dessert when two common street-women came up to our table with their hurdy-gurdies. Le Brun told them to sit down. They were given something to drink and encouraged to chat and then we got them to play for us. While my three companions were enjoying themselves taking liberties with one, the other, who was sitting next to me, said very quietly:

'Sir, these men you're with are a very bad lot. There isn't one of 'em whose name isn't familiar to the police.'

When it was time, we left the inn and returned to Monsieur de Merval's. I forgot to mention that the lunch had emptied both my purse and the Chevalier's, and that as we walked along Le Brun told the Chevalier, who repeated it to me, that Mathieu de Fourgeot wanted six louis as his commission and that this was the smallest sum he could decently be offered. If he was happy with that, we'd get the stock for a lower price and easily get the money back when we sold our goods.

So there we are at Merval's house, where we found the woman who had already arrived with her merchandise. Mademoiselle Bridoie was her name and she was lavish with compliments and courtesies. She spread out cloths, linen, lace, rings, jewels, and gold boxes. We took the lot. Le Brun, Mathieu de Fourgeot, and the Chevalier priced the goods while Merval kept a tally. In all, the total came to nineteen thousand, seven hundred, and seventy-five livres, for which I was about to sign my note when Mademoiselle Bridoie said to me, with a curtsey, for she never spoke to anyone without curtseying:

'Sir, is it your intention to repay your notes when they fall due?'

'Of course,' said I.

'In that case,' she went on, 'it won't matter to you whether you write me a credit note or a bill of exchange.'

The words 'bill of exchange' made me turn pale.* The Chevalier noticed and turned to Mademoiselle Bridoie:

'Bills of exchange, Mademoiselle? Bills of exchange do the rounds and you never know in whose hands they'll end up.'

'Really, Chevalier, one is ever mindful of the respect due to persons of your rank.' And then with a curtsey: 'Such bills stay in one's pocket-book and are not produced until they fall due. Here, look...' And then, with a curtsey, she produces her pocket-book from her skirts and reads out a multitude of names of all categories and classes of person. The Chevalier had stepped closer to me and said:

'Bills of exchange! This is devilish serious! Decide what you're going to do. This woman seems honest enough to me, and besides, by the due date you'll be in funds again, or I'll be.'

Jacques. And you signed the bills?

Master. I did.

Jacques. It's customary for fathers to read their sons a brief sermon when they leave home and set out for the capital: don't get into bad company, please your superiors by carrying out your duties punctually, do not neglect religion, avoid loose women and swindlers, and above all, never sign bills of exchange.

Master. What do you expect? I did as they all do: the first thing I forgot was everything my father told me. So there I was, supplied with goods to sell, though it was money we needed. There were several pairs of very fine lace cuffs. The Chevalier appropriated a couple at cost price, saying:

'There, that's some of your stock already gone, so that's something you'll not lose money on.'

Mathieu de Fourgeot took a watch and two gold boxes and went off at once to fetch the money to pay for them. Le Brun took the rest to store in his house. I pocketed, along with some of the lace cuffs, a superb diamond necklace which I intended as one of the highlights of the birthday present I had to give. Mathieu de Fourgeot returned post-haste with sixty louis. Of the sixty he kept ten for himself and I got the other fifty. He told me he hadn't sold either the watch or the two boxes but had pawned them.

Jacques. Pawned them?

Master. Yes.

Jacques. I know where.

Master. Where?

Jacques. In the shop which belonged to the unmarried lady of the curtseys, the Bridoie woman.

Master. Quite right. In addition to the diamond necklace and the lace cuffs, I also took a pretty ring and a gold-cased box for keeping my patches* in. I had fifty louis in my pocket and the Chevalier and I were in the best of spirits.

Jacques. That's all to the good. There's only one thing in all this that puzzles me, and that is the disinterestedness of the obliging Monsieur Le Brun. Didn't he get a share of the spoils?

Master. Come, come, Jacques, don't be naive. You don't know what Monsieur Le Brun was like. I suggested I might offer him something for his good offices. He got angry, said I must think he was another Mathieu de Fourgeot, and told me he'd never asked for anything.

'That's my friend Le Brun for you,' exclaimed the Chevalier. 'He never changes. But it would be embarrassing if he turned out to be more honest than us.'

Whereupon he rummaged through our stock and picked out two dozen handkerchiefs and a length of muslin which he made Le Brun take for his wife and daughter. Le Brun began examining the handkerchiefs, which he judged to be very pretty, and the muslin, which he said was very fine, adding that because the gifts had been offered with such good grace and since he would soon have the opportunity of paying us back by selling the stock we had left with him, he would allow himself to be prevailed upon.

And then we were gone and were soon bowling along as fast as our carriage would take us towards the house of the woman I loved and for whom the diamond necklace, the lace cuffs, and the ring were intended. The present was a great success. She was bewitching. She tried on the diamond necklace and the cuffs immediately and the ring seemed as if it had been made for her finger. We went in to supper and were very merry, as you might imagine.

Jacques. And you stayed the night?

Master. No.

Jacques. But the Chevalier did, eh?

Master. I believe so.

Jacques. At the rate they were taking you, your fifty louis couldn't have lasted long.

Master. No. A week later, we went back to Monsieur Le Brun to see how much the rest of our merchandise had made.

Jacques. Nothing at all, or very little. Le Brun was dejected. He spoke out in no uncertain terms against Merval and our Lady of the Curtseys, called them rogues, villains, thieves, swore there and then that he'd never have any more to do with them ever again, and handed over seven or eight hundred francs.

Master. Almost: eight hundred and seventy.

Jacques. So, if my maths are right, eight hundred and seventy livres from Le Brun, fifty louis from Merval or Fourgeot, the necklace, cuffs, and ring, let's say another fifty louis—and that's what remained of your nineteen thousand, seven hundred, and seventy-three livres' worth of merchandise. By God! there's honesty for you. Merval was right: it's not every day you're fortunate to have dealings with such honest people.

Master. You forgot to include the cuffs which the Chevalier walked off with at cost price.

Jacques. That's because he never mentioned them again.

Master. No he didn't. And you said nothing about the two gold boxes and the watch that Mathieu pawned.

Jacques. That was because I didn't know what to say.

Master. Meanwhile, the day when the bills of exchange fell due arrived.

Jacques. Unlike your funds or the Chevalier's.

Master. I was obliged to go into hiding. My parents were informed and one of my uncles came to Paris. He presented a written complaint against all these rogues to the police. The complaint was forwarded to a clerk. This clerk was in the pay of Merval. The official reply came that, since the affair was now in the hands of the court, the police could do nothing. The pawnbroker to whom Mathieu had passed the two gold boxes served a writ on him. I was dragged into the ensuing lawsuit. The legal costs were so high that after the watch and both boxes were sold, there was a shortfall of five or six hundred francs and consequently not enough to pay the bill in full.

You can't believe this, can you Reader? But what if I told you about a man who used to run a café just round the corner from my house, and died not long ago leaving two very young, motherless children. The police came to his premises and affixed seals to his property. The seals were removed, an inventory was drawn up, and everything was sold. The sale made eight or nine hundred francs. Once the legal costs were paid, of the eight or nine hundred francs there remained two sous for each orphan. They were both handed their two sous and were then taken away to the poorhouse.

Master. That's monstrous!

Jacques. And it's still going on.

Master. In the meantime, my father died. I paid off the bills of exchange and emerged from my hiding-place where, to be fair to the Chevalier and my lady friend, I must admit they had kept me pretty faithful company.

Jacques. And so you were just as struck as before with the Chevalier and your inamorata, the lady in question making you dance to her tune more than ever.

Master. Why should that be, Jacques?

Jacques. Why? Because now you were your own master and the possessor of a sizeable fortune, you had to be turned into a complete fool, viz. a husband.

Master. By God, I do believe that was what they had in mind. But their scheme didn't work.

Jacques. Either you were lucky, or they went about it the wrong way.

Master. I have the impression that your voice isn't as hoarse as it was, and you seem to be speaking more freely.

Jacques. That might be your impression, but it's not so.

Master. Couldn't you go on with the tale of your love-life?

Jacques. No.

Master. Is it your view, then, that I should go on with mine?

Jacques. My view is that we should stop for a while and raise the gourd.

Master. What! With your sore throat, you had your gourd filled?

Jacques. Yes, but devil take them, they filled it with herb tea. As a result, there's not an idea in my head, I feel stupid, and will go on feeling stupid as long as there's only herb tea in the gourd.

Master. What are you doing?

Jacques. Tipping the tea out on to the ground. I'm afraid it'll bring us bad luck.

Master. You're mad.

Jacques. Sane or mad, out it goes to the very last drop.

While Jacques empties his gourd on to the ground, his Master looks at his watch, opens his snuffbox, and gets ready to resume the story of his loves.

Speaking for myself, Reader, I'm tempted to shut him up by pointing out to him, in the distance, either an old soldier bent over the neck of his horse who was coming up fast, or a young peasant girl wearing a little straw hat and red petticoats who was proceeding on foot or on a mule. Now why shouldn't the old soldier turn out to be either Jacques's Captain or the friend of his Captain?

But he's dead.

You think so? Why shouldn't the young peasant girl be Madame Suzanne or Madame Marguerite or the landlady of the Stag Inn, or Jeanne, or even her daughter Denise? A novelist would never pass up such an opportunity, but I don't care for novels, unless they're by Richardson.* I'm writing a chronicle here. This story will either be interesting or it won't, though that's neither here nor there. My intention was to be true and in this I have succeeded. That is why I shan't be bringing back Frère Jean of Lisbon. The portly abbot now approaching in a fly with a pretty young woman next to him won't be Hudson.

But Hudson is dead.

You think so? Did you go to his funeral?

No.

Did you see him committed to the earth?

No.

Then he's alive or dead, as I decide. If I wanted to, I could bring the above-mentioned fly to a halt and from it decant the abbot, his companion, and a whole series of adventures which would ensure you'd never get to know about Jacques's love-life or his Master's. But I wouldn't stoop so low. It just seems obvious to me that with a little imagination and style, there's nothing easier than churning out a novel. We'll stick with the truth and, while we're waiting for Jacques to get over his sore throat, let's hear what his Master has got to say.

Master. One morning, the Chevalier looked particularly dispirited. We had spent the previous day in the country—the Chevalier, his girl or mine (or maybe she was both), her father, her mother, a lot of aunts and female cousins, and me. He asked if I had said or done anything in an unguarded moment which might have alerted them to the way I felt. He told me that both her mother and father, alarmed by my attentiveness, had questioned their daughter. They said that if my intentions were honest, then it was a straightforward matter for me to say so and they would be honoured to receive me at home on that understanding. But if within two weeks I did not explain what was in my mind, then I would be asked to stop my visits which were attracting attention, making tongues wag, and harming their daughter by discouraging other advantageous parties who might otherwise come forward because they were afraid of being turned down.

Jacques. Ah, does Jacques smell a rat, sir?

Master. The Chevalier went on: 'Two weeks! That's not long. You love her, she loves you. What'll you do when the two weeks are up?' I told the Chevalier at once that I would withdraw.

'Withdraw! So you're not in love with her?'

'I am fond of her, very fond. But I have a family, a name, a position to keep up and ambitions. I could never agree to bury all my advantages in the shop of a girl whose father's in trade.'

'Is that what I'm to tell them?'

'If you like. But, Chevalier, I'm surprised by this sudden onset of delicacy and scruple from these people. They allowed their daughter to accept the presents I gave her and have left me alone with her a score of times. She goes to balls, assemblies, and the theatre, and she drives out in the country and around town with the first man who comes along with a handsome carriage to put at her disposal. They sleep soundly in their beds while visitors make music and conversation downstairs. You go to the house whenever you like and, between ourselves, Chevalier, if you are allowed in there's no reason why I shouldn't be. Their daughter has a reputation. I neither believe nor deny what people say about her, but you must agree that her parents might have shown more concern for their daughter's honour long before this. Do you want me to be frank? I've been taken for some sort of simpleton who they thought they could lead by the nose all the way to the feet of the parish priest. They've made a big mistake. I find Mademoiselle Agathe very attractive, and she's turned my head, which is all too obvious, I think, from the huge expense I've gone to for her. I'm not saying I don't want it to continue, but if I do go on with it I must be sure that she'll prove rather less unyielding in future. It's not my intention to kneel at her feet for ever, wasting time, money, and sighs which could be more usefully employed elsewhere. You may repeat that last remark to Mademoiselle Agathe and you can convey what went before to her parents. Either our relationship is to end or else I must be accepted on a different footing and Mademoiselle Agathe must treat me rather better in future than she has up to now. When you introduced me to her, you will agree, Chevalier, that you led me to expect opportunities which have not been forthcoming.'

Chevalier. By God, I myself was the first to be taken in. Who the devil would have thought that with all her flightiness and the teasing, mischievous tongue she's got on her, the silly girl would turn out to be a dragon of virtue?

Jacques. By God, sir, that's coming it pretty strong! And for once in your life you showed what you were made of?

Master. There are days like that. I hadn't forgotten the episode with the moneylenders or my strategic withdrawal to Saint-Jean-de-Latran* on account of Mademoiselle Bridoie, but most of all I remembered the rigours of Mademoiselle Agathe. I was tired of being played along.

Jacques. And after speaking out so bravely to your dear friend the Chevalier de Saint-Ouin, what did you do next?

Master. I did what I said I would. I stopped my visits.

Jacques. Bravo! bravo, *mio caro maestro!*

Master. A fortnight went by when I heard nothing except through the Chevalier, who gave me faithful reports of the effect of my absence on the family and encouraged me to stand firm. He said:

'They're beginning to get worried. They exchange looks, they talk, they're wondering what they could have done to upset you. The girl is being very dignified. She tries to make out she doesn't care but it's easy to see she's definitely put out: "We never see him any more and it would appear he doesn't want us to see him. That's fine. It's his business." Whereupon she pirouettes, starts humming a song, goes and stands by the window, and then comes back all red-eyed and everyone can see she's been crying.'

'Crying!'

'Then she sits down, picks up her embroidery, tries to work but can't. The others talk but she says nothing. They try to cheer her up, but she doesn't respond. They suggest a game, a walk, a play, and she says yes. And then when they're all ready, she says she'd rather do something else and a moment later she doesn't want to do that either... Look, you mustn't let this get to you. I won't tell you any more.'

'Look, Chevalier, do you think then, if I were to put in an appearance...'

'I'd think you were a fool. You've got to stick to your guns, you must be brave. If you return before you're called back, you're lost. You've got to show these people you mean business.'

'But what if I'm not called back?'

'You will be.'

'But what if it takes a long time?'

'You'll be called back soon. Dammit, a man like you is not easily replaced. If you go back of your own accord, you'll get the cold treatment, you'll be made to pay heavily for overstepping the mark, you'll be made to toe whatever line is drawn for you, you'll have to do what you're told and bend the knee. Do you want to be master or a slave, and an ill-used slave at that? Choose. To be honest, you've behaved in a rather cavalier way—no one would think now that you're exactly lovesick. Still, what's done is done and if there's any way of retrieving the situation, you should try it.'

'She cried!'

'Well? So she cried. It's better that she cried than you.'

'But what if I'm not called back?'

'You will be, I tell you. Whenever I go there I never talk about you, as though you didn't exist. They turn the conversation and I allow it to be turned, and in the end I'm asked if I've seen anything of you. I reply casually yes or maybe no, and then we talk of other things, though it's not long before they return to your disappearance. The subject is always brought up first by her father, her mother, her aunt or Agathe herself, and they say:

' "After all we did to make him welcome!"

' "The concern we all felt over that business he was mixed up in recently!"

' "All the kindness my niece showed him!"

' "The regard I lavished on him!"

' "All those protestations of affection that he gave us!"

' "How can you trust any man after something like this!"

' "After this, are you going to open your house to whoever knocks on your door?"

' "Can you trust your friends?"

I said: 'What about Agathe?'

'They're all pretty cut up, I do assure you.'

'But Agathe?'

'Agathe takes me to one side and says: "Chevalier, what do you make of your friend's behaviour? You've told me so many times that he loved me. I expect you believed it, and why shouldn't you? I did!" Then she breaks off, her voice falters, and her eyes brim with tears... Aha! I see you're doing the same. I'm not going to say any more, that's for sure.

Since you were foolish enough to pull out for no good reason, I wouldn't want you to behave as stupidly again by throwing yourself at them. You've got to make the most of this business if you want to get anywhere with Mademoiselle Agathe. She must be made to understand that her hold over you is not so secure that she cannot possibly lose you, or she must at least see that she should make more effort to hang on to you. After all you've done, and you've not got past the hand-kissing stage! Look, Chevalier, put your hand on your heart, we're friends and you can tell me everything without being indiscreet. Is it true that you've never been granted more?'

'Yes.'

'You're lying. You're being shy.'

'I might be shy if I had cause, but unfortunately I can swear I'm not lying.'

'But it's unbelievable. You know your way around. You mean to say that she's never had a moment's weakness?'

'No.'

'There must have been such a moment, but you didn't notice and you missed your chance. I'm afraid you've been rather obtuse. Men who are honest, impressionable, and sensitive are prone to it.'

'But what about yourself, Chevalier? Why do you keep going there?'

'No reason.'

'You have no ambitions in that direction?'

'Oh, but I do, very much so. Indeed, I've had ambitions in that direction for some time, but then you came, you saw, and you conquered. I became aware that she was looking at you a great deal but could hardly spare a glance for me and I concluded that was that. We've remained good friends. She confides her little thoughts to me, sometimes takes my advice, and I decided to make the best of things by accepting the subordinate role to which you'd reduced me.'

Jacques. Sir, two comments. The first is that I've never been able to get on with my story without some demon or other butting in, and yet yours flows along uninterrupted. It's like life. One man can run through a blackberry hedge without getting scratched, while another, however carefully he places his feet, finds brambles in the middle of the widest road and is skinned alive by the time he gets to wherever he's going.

Master. Have you forgotten your refrain? What about the great scroll and what's written on high?

Jacques. My second comment is that I still believe your Chevalier de Saint-Ouin is a rogue, and that after sharing your money with Le Brun, Merval, Mathieu de Fourgeot (or Fourgeot de Mathieu), and that Bridoie female, he is now trying to saddle you with his mistress, openly and in good faith it goes without saying, with benefit of notary and priest, so that he can also share your wife with you... Oh! my throat!

Master. Do you know what you've just done? Something that's very common and very rude.

Jacques. I'm quite capable of being both.

Master. You complain about being interrupted and then you interrupt.

Jacques. That comes of the bad example you've set me. Mothers want to be able to flirt and have modest daughters. Fathers want to throw their money around and have sons who are thrifty. Masters want...

Master. To interrupt their servants, interrupt them all the livelong day, and not be interrupted by them.

Reader, aren't you afraid you are about to get a repeat of the scene in the inn when one kept shouting 'Get downstairs!' and the other shouted back 'Shan't!'? What's stopping me from letting you have a burst of 'I will interrupt!'—'Oh no you won't!'? It's obvious that if I provoke either Jacques or his Master, they'll start quarrelling, and once I let them start squabbling who knows where it will end? But the truth is that Jacques returned a soft answer to his Master: 'Sir, I'm not interrupting. I'm having a conversation with you, as you said I could.'

Master. We'll let it go, but that's not the end of it.

Jacques. In what other way have I been rude?

Master. You run on ahead of the storyteller and cheat him of the pleasure of surprising you. With a tasteless display of perceptiveness, you guess what he is about to say and leave him with no choice but to shut up—which is exactly what I shall do.

Jacques. Oh sir!

Master. Damn all clever people!

Jacques. Agreed. But you're not going to be so cruel as to...

Master. Admit you'd deserve it if I did.

Jacques. I admit it. But none of this will stop you looking at your watch to see what time it is and taking your pinch of snuff. You'll calm down and carry on with your tale.

Master. The damned rogue can twist me round his little finger... A few days after my talk with the Chevalier, he came back to see me looking very pleased with himself:

'Well, my friend,' said he, 'next time will you believe my predictions? I told you. We men are cleverer than they are. Here's a letter from her. That's right, a letter. From her.'

It was a very sweet letter, with reproaches, wailing, and the rest of it. But the upshot was that I was reinstated under her roof.

Reader, you've stopped reading. What's the matter? Ah! I think I have it! You want to see the letter! Madame Riccoboni* would not have failed to show it to you. I'm sure you felt aggrieved not to have had sight of that other letter, the one sent by Madame de La Pommeraye to the two puritan ladies. Although it would have been infinitely more difficult to write than the one sent by Agathe, and though I do not have limitless faith in my abilities, I do believe I could have pulled it off. But it wouldn't have been fresh or new. It would have been like those marvellous speeches you get in Livy's *History of Rome*, or in Cardinal Bentivoglio's *Wars of Flanders*:* you enjoy reading them but they destroy the illusion. A historian who puts into the mouths of historical figures speeches which they never made is also likely to invent actions for them which they never committed. I therefore ask if you might see your way to managing without the aforementioned letters and carry on reading?

Master. She asked me why I had dropped out of circulation. I gave some sort of answer. She was happy with it and everything began again on the same footing as before.

Jacques. That is, you went on digging into your pocket but the affairs of your heart did not prosper as a result.

Master. The Chevalier kept asking how it was going and seemed to be losing patience.

Jacques. Perhaps he really was losing patience.

Master. Why is that?

Jacques. Why? Because he...

Master. Finish your sentence.

Jacques. I wouldn't dream of it. The storyteller must be allowed...

Master. I'm pleased to see that you're learning from my lessons...

One day the Chevalier suggested an outing, just the two of us. We would spend the day in the country. We set off early. We had lunch at an inn and dinner too. The wine was excellent and we drank a lot of it, taking about politics, religion, and women. The Chevalier had never behaved towards me with such trust and friendliness. He gave me the full story of his life with the most unbelievable frankness, hiding neither the good nor the bad in it. He drank, shook my hand, wept tender tears. I drank, shook his hand, and wept in turn. In all his past conduct, there was only one action that weighed on his conscience and would be a source of regret until the day he died.

'Chevalier,' said I, 'get it off your chest, tell me, I'm your friend, you'll feel better. Well? What was it? Some peccadillo to which your scruples have attached more importance than it warrants?'

'No, no!' exclaimed the Chevalier, holding his head in both hands and hiding his face in shame, 'it is a black deed, for which there is no forgiveness. You will never believe it! I, Chevalier de Saint-Ouin, once betrayed—yes, betrayed—a friend!'

'How did it happen?'

'Well, we were both regular visitors at the same house, just like us. There was a girl like Mademoiselle Agathe. He was in love with her, but she loved me. He was ruining himself for her, but I was the one who enjoyed her favours. I never had the courage to admit it to his face, but if we ever meet up again I shall tell him everything. This horrible secret which is buried deep inside me is too much to bear. It is a burden from which I must be delivered.'

'It would be as well if you did tell him, Chevalier.'

'Is that your advice?'

'Absolutely, that's what I advise.'

'How do you think my friend would take it?'

'If he's really a friend, if he's a fair-minded man, he'll find an excuse for you, he'll be moved by your candour and your contrition, he'll throw his arms around you: he'll do exactly what I would do if I were in his place.'

'You honestly think so?'

'I do.'

'And that's how you'd react?'

'I'm certain of it.'

Whereupon the Chevalier gets to his feet, comes towards me, tears streaming from his eyes and both arms flung out wide, and says to me:

'Come, then, friend, and embrace me.'

'What's this, Chevalier,' said I. 'You mean it's you? It's me? It's that damned Agathe?'

'Yes. I again release you from your oath. You are free to deal with me as you wish. If, as I do, you think that my action is unforgivable, do not forgive me. Stand up, leave now, never look on me again except with scorn, and abandon me to my sorrow and my shame. Ah, dear friend! If you only knew what power that vixen had over me! I was born an honourable man. You can imagine, then, how I suffered in the degrading role I had consented to play, how often I turned my eyes away from her and looked at you, groaning inwardly at both her treachery and mine! It is hard to believe you never noticed.'

I just sat there without moving, as still as a statue. I hardly heard what the Chevalier said. I cried: 'Oh, the jade! But you, Chevalier! You! My friend!'

'Yes. I was your friend and I am still your friend. For I know a secret which is more hers than mine and it will free you from the clutches of that wicked creature. My only regret is that you never got anywhere with her, it would have been a compensation for all you've done for her.'

[*At this, Jacques starts to leer and jeer.*]

But this is exactly like Collé's *La Vérité dans le vin!**

Reader, you're way off target. By trying too hard to be clever, you're being very, very stupid. It's not *in vino veritas* at all. It's the very opposite: it's untruth in wine. But I was rude to you. I'm very sorry and do apologize.

Master. Gradually I stopped being angry. I embraced the Chevalier. He sat down again, putting elbows on the table, and pressing his fists against his eyes, for he dared not look me in the face.

Jacques. He was ever so miserable and you, out of the goodness of your heart, consoled him. [*Jacques starts sniggering again.*]

Master. It seemed to me that the best thing to do was to treat the whole thing as a joke. But every time I came out with some jaunty remark, the Chevalier, who was very embarrassed, said:

'There's not another man like you, you are unique, you're worth a hundred of me. I doubt if I'd have had the generosity or the strength to forgive you a similar wrong, but you, you make light of it! No man ever behaved so well. What can I do to make amends? No, it's not something anyone can ever put right. I shall never, never forget my offence or your

forbearance, for both are deeply etched in my heart. The first I will remember so that I shall hate myself; the second, so that I may admire
you and grow in my affection for you.'

'Come, Chevalier, don't give it another thought. You're making far
too much of what we both did, you and I. Your health, Chevalier! Well,
my health then, if you won't drink to yours.'

The Chevalier gradually regained his composure. He told me in detail how he had betrayed me and applied the most hair-raising epithets
to himself in the process. He laid into the whole family—the girl, her
mother, her father, her aunts—and portrayed them as riffraff who
were unworthy of me, though they were all too worthy of him. Those
were his exact words.

Jacques. And that's why I'd advise women never to sleep with
men who get drunk. I have an equally low opinion of your Chevalier
both as a feckless lover and as a treacherous friend. Dammit, all he
had to do was act like a gentleman and tell you everything from the
start. No, hold on, sir, I've started so I'll finish. The man's a snake, a
weasel. I've no idea how it will all turn out, but I'm afraid he's leading you on again by pretending to undeceive you. Get me out of there,
get yourself out of that inn and far away from the company of the
rogue.

Here, Jacques reached for his gourd again, forgetting that it contained neither herb tea or wine. His Master began to laugh. Jacques
embarked on a coughing fit which lasted for nearly ten minutes. His
Master took out his watch and his snuffbox and went on with his tale
which, if you're agreeable, I shall interrupt, for no very good reason
except to annoy Jacques by proving that it was not written on high, as
he believed, that he would go on being interrupted while his Master
never would be.

Master [*to the Chevalier*]: After what you've just said about these
people, I don't expect you'll ever want to see them again.

'Me, see them again? But there's one thing that grieves me: the
idea of abandoning them without having my revenge. They duped,
cheated, robbed, and made a fool of one gentleman and took advantage
of the tender feelings and weakness of another, for I still dare to think
of myself as a gentleman, in order to make him commit a series of the
most appalling actions. They left two friends exposed to the danger of
hating or even killing each other, for you will admit, old friend, that if

you had found out about my underhand dealings, you might, being a man of courage, have felt so aggrieved that...'

'No, things wouldn't have gone that far. Why should they? Who'd have been to blame? And what for? For some misdeed that nobody could put their hand on their heart and swear they'll never commit? Was she my wife? And what if she had been? Was she my daughter? No, she's a trollop, and if you think a trollop's worth... Oh, let's just drop the subject and have another drink. Agathe is young, vivacious, deliciously pale, shapely, with bulges in all the right places. Such firm flesh, wouldn't you say? And such silky skin? Bedding her must have been an experience, and I imagine that as you lay there in her arms you had other things on your mind than thinking about your friends.'

'If the lady's charms and the pleasure involved could in some way lessen the offence, then certainly there's not a man on earth less guilty than I am.'

'Just a minute, Chevalier. I'm going back on what I said. I hereby rescind my forbearance and set one condition on my overlooking your treachery.'

'Say the word, friend, command, speak! Shall I throw myself out of the window, string myself up, drown myself, stab myself through the heart with this knife?'

Whereupon the Chevalier picked up an old knife that lay on the table, undoes the collar of his shirt, bares his chest, and with a wild look in his eye, holds the point of the blade with his right hand against the hollow beneath his collar-bone on his left side, and keeps it there, as if waiting my signal to despatch himself, Roman style.

'I don't mean anything like that, Chevalier. Put that gruesome knife down.'

'I won't put it down. It's what I deserve. Just say the word.'

'Put it down, I said. I don't set such a high price on your atonement.'

Meanwhile, the point of the knife was still poised over the hollow beneath his collar-bone on his left side. I made a grab for his hand, took the knife from him, and flung it away. Then, pushing the bottle close to his glass, I filled it and said:

'Let's have a drink first, and then I'll tell you what terrible condition I set down for your pardon. So Agathe is a succulent morsel, very responsive?'

'I only wish, old friend, that you'd known her the way I've known her.'

'Wait. We'll order a bottle of champagne and then you can tell me about one of your nights with her. You irresistible deceiver, you: your absolution lies at the end of the tale. Right, away you go. Didn't you hear me?'

'I heard.'

'Do you think the condition is too harsh?'

'No.'

'What are you thinking?'

'Just thinking.'

'What did I ask?'

'For an account of a night I spent with Agathe.'

'That's it.'

As he spoke, the Chevalier was measuring me from head to toe and muttering:

'Same height, about the same age, and even though there are some differences, it'll be dark, she'll be expecting me, and she won't suspect a thing.'

'Chevalier, what on earth are you thinking now? Your glass is still full and you haven't made a start.'

'I was thinking, old friend, and now I've thought it through, it's all worked out. Take my hand on it, we shall be avenged, oh yes we shall. It's low and it's wicked and it's unworthy of me, but it's only too worthy of that little minx. So, you want to hear about one of my nights?'

'Yes. Is that asking too much?'

'No. But what if, instead of hearing about mine, I could arrange for you to have one of your own?'

'That would be an improvement.'

[Here Jacques starts to leer.]

Without more ado, the Chevalier produced two keys from his pocket, one small, the other large.

'The small one', he said, 'opens the front door, the big one is the key to Agathe's apartment. Take them, they're yours to use as you wish. If I tell you how I've been operating for the last six months or so, you can follow my routine. Her windows are at the front of the house, as you know. I walk up and down outside while there's still light in them. A pot of basil on the windowsill is the agreed signal. When it appears, I go straight to the front door, open it, go in, lock it behind me, and go upstairs as quietly as I can. I turn into the small corridor on the right, and the first door on the left is hers, as you also know. I open it with the

large key, step into the little dressing-room to the right, where a dim
night candle gives out enough light for me to get undressed in comfort.
Agathe leaves her bedroom door ajar, I go in, and join her in bed. Have
you got all that?'

'Understood.'

'Since there are people all around us, we don't talk.'

'In any case, I should think you have better things to do than chat.'

'If anything goes wrong, I can always jump out of bed and hide in
her dressing-room, though that's never happened. What we usually do
is to part company around four in the morning. If pleasure or sleep de-
tains us past the watershed, we both get out of bed. She goes downstairs and I stay put in the dressing-room where I dress, read, snooze,
and wait until it's time to put in an appearance. Then I go down, say
good morning, and kiss cheeks as if I'd only just got there that very
minute.'

'And are you expected tonight?'

'I'm expected every night.'

'And you're willing to let me go instead of you?'

'I'd be glad to. I won't mind if you prefer the night to the story of the
night, but what I would like is...'

'Go on. I can't think of much I wouldn't be bold enough to take on
to accommodate you.'

'... is for you to stay in bed with her until it was broad daylight. Then
I'd burst in and find you together.'

'Oh come, Chevalier, that would be a very nasty thing to do'.

'Nasty? I'm nowhere near as nasty as you think. Before bursting in,
I'd get undressed in her dressing-room...'

'Really, Chevalier, you've got the devil on your back. Anyway, it
wouldn't work. If you give me the keys, you won't have them any
more.'

'Now you're being obtuse!'

'Not entirely obtuse, I think.'

'Why shouldn't the two of us enter the house together? You'd go off
and find Agathe while I'd stay in the dressing-room until you gave me
a signal that we would agree beforehand?'

'By God, it's priceless, and so crazy that I'm tempted to say yes. But
all things considered, Chevalier, I'd prefer to postpone this little prank
until another night.'

'I get you: you intend to take your revenge more than once.'

'If you agree.'

'Absolutely.'

Jacques. Your Chevalier is upsetting all my ideas. I imagined...

Master. You imagined?

Jacques. Nothing, sir. Pray continue.

Master. We drank some more, we said many wild things about that night, the nights to come and the night when Agathe would find herself caught between the Chevalier and me. The Chevalier had regained his old high spirits and the tenor of our conversation was the opposite of grim. He explained the rules of nocturnal engagement, which were not all easy to follow, but since he had spent many such nights and put them to very good use, I felt I could uphold the Chevalier's honour on my debut, despite his giving the impression of believing himself peerless. Then he went on and on in detail about Agathe's talents, perfections, and accommodating nature. The Chevalier blended heady passion and the intoxicating effects of the wine with great artistry. The time to start on our adventure or revenge seemed to come all too slowly. However, we rose from the table. The Chevalier paid the bill—it was the first time he'd ever done so—and we staggered into our carriage. We were drunk. Our driver and the footmen were even drunker.

Reader, what's to prevent me tipping driver, horses, carriage, masters, and servants into the nearest ditch? If the ditch option scares you, why shouldn't I bring them back to town safe and sound and then crash their carriage into another containing other young men, also drunk. Curses would be exchanged, there'd be an argument, drawn swords, and a pitched brawl. If you don't care for brawls, what's to stop me replacing the young drunks with Mademoiselle Agathe and one of her aunts?

But nothing like that actually happened. The Chevalier and Jacques's Master got back to Paris. The latter puts on the clothes of the former. It is now midnight and they are standing under Agathe's window. The lights go out and the pot of basil is where it should be. They walk the complete length of the street one last time, while the Chevalier drills his friend in what he has to do. They go up to the door, the Chevalier opens it, ushers Jacques's Master inside, keeps the front-door key, gives him the key to the apartment, locks the front door, and leaves him to it.

After giving these details, which he passed over quickly, Jacques's Master went on:

Master. I knew my way about the house. I tiptoe upstairs, open the door to Agathe's boudoir, close it behind me, step into the dressing-room where I find the little night-light burning, and get undressed. The bedroom door is ajar, I go in, and make for the alcove where Agathe is not asleep. I pull back the curtains and immediately feel two naked arms round my neck pulling me down. I let myself go, slip into bed where I am smothered with kisses which I return. So there I am, the happiest man alive. I am still there when...

When Jacques's Master noticed that Jacques was asleep or pretending to be asleep. He said:

'You've nodded off, you barbarian, you've fallen asleep at the most interesting part of the story!'

This was exactly what Jacques had been expecting his Master to say:

'Will you wake up!'

'I don't think I'd better.'

'Why not?'

'Because if I wake up, my sore throat might wake up too and I think it would be better if both of us took a rest.'

And so saying, Jacques let his head fall on his chest.

'You'll break your neck if you ride like that.'

'So I will, if that is what's written on high. Aren't you happy to be lying in Mademoiselle Agathe's arms?'

'Yes.'

'You're happy like that?'

'Very.'

'Well stay as you are.'

'You mean it suits you if I stay where I am.'

'Stay there at least until I've heard the story of Desglands's patch.'

Master. You're getting your own back, you ruffian.

Jacques. Even if I am, sir, after you've chopped up the story of my love-life with all your questions and fanciful asides without a murmur of complaint from me, it seems only fair if I ask you to interrupt yours by telling me the story of Monsieur Desglands's patch. I owe him a great deal, for he it was who plucked me from the surgeon's house just when my money was running out and I had no idea what would happen to me. It was under his roof that I met Denise, and but for Denise I wouldn't have opened my mouth all the time we've been travelling. Sir, oh sir, let's have the story of Desglands's patch! Make it as short as you like, but while it's going on the drowsy numbness that's overcome me and about which I can do nothing will lift and then you can count on having my full attention.

Master [*with a shrug*]. There was, in the neighbourhood where Desglands lived, a charming widow who had numerous qualities in common with a celebrated courtesan of the last century, being chaste by policy, libertine by temperament, and repenting on the morrow the follies she had committed the night before.* She spent the whole of her life moving from pleasure to regret and from regret to pleasure, without the habit of pleasure ever overcoming her regrets and the habit of regret extinguishing her taste for pleasure. I knew her at the very end of her life, when she said that at last she was free of her two greatest enemies. Her husband, who tolerated the only failing he had to reproach her for, pitied her while she lived and mourned her sincerely for many years after her death.* He claimed that it would have been as absurd for him to try to stop his wife taking lovers as it would to prevent her quenching her thirst. He excused her innumerable conquests by saying she always showed such good taste in choosing them. She never accepted the attentions of stupid or wicked men, and her favours were a reward for talent or probity. To say of someone that he was or had been her lover was a guarantee that he was a man of integrity. Since she was well aware of the fickleness of her nature, she never promised anyone to be faithful. 'Only once in my life', she said, 'did I ever break my word: the first time.' You could fall out of love with her and she with you, but you would still go on being her friend. There was never a more striking example of the difference between goodness and morality. You couldn't say she was moral, but you had to admit that it would have been difficult to find anyone who was more honest.* Her priest rarely saw her kneeling at his altar, but he found her purse open at all hours for the relief of the poor of the parish. She would joke and say that religion and law made a pair of crutches that were best not taken away from people who could not walk unaided. Women who feared her influence on their husbands, sought it for their children.

Jacques [*mutters: 'I'll make you pay for this tedious description' then adds*]. And you were mad about her?

Master. I would certainly have been if Desglands hadn't got in first. He fell in love with her...

Jacques. Sir, are the story of his patch and the story of his love-life so intimately connected that they cannot be separated?

Master. They could be separated. The patch was an episode. The story is the tale of everything that happened while they were in love.

Jacques. Did a lot of things happen?

Master. Oh yes.

Jacques. In that case, if you give the same amount of space to each of them as you've given to describing the heroine, we won't be done before Whitsun, and we can forget all about your love-life and mine.

Master. In that case, why did you put me off what I was saying?... Now, when you were at Desglands's house, did you notice a little boy?

Jacques. A nasty, wilful, cheeky, and sickly boy? Yes, I remember him.

Master. He was the natural son of Desglands and the merry widow.

Jacques. That boy will bring him nothing but grief. He was an only child, a good reason for thinking he'd go to the bad. He knew he'd be rich, another good reason for thinking he'd go to the bad.

Master. And since he was so sickly, he wasn't taught anything or reprimanded or corrected, which was a third good reason for thinking he'd go to the bad.

Jacques. One night, the little devil set up a barely human hullabaloo. The whole house was in an uproar and everyone came running. He said he wanted his papa to get up.

'Your papa's asleep.'

'I don't care, I want him to get up, I do, I do!'

'He's ill.'

'I don't care, I want him to get up, I do, I do!'

They woke Desglands, who threw his dressing-gown over his shoulders and came.

'Well, my boy, here I am. What do you want?'

'I want you to make them come.'

'Who?'

'All the people in the chateau.'

They were all sent for, masters, servants, visitors, permanent fixtures, Jeanne, Denise, me with my painful knee, everyone, except an old crippled concierge who'd been pensioned off to a cottage about a mile from the chateau. He wanted her to be fetched.

'But it's midnight, my boy.'

'I want her, I do, I do!'

'She lives a long way away, you know.'

'I want her, I do, I do!'

'And she's very old and can't walk.'

'I want her, I do, I do!'

There was nothing for it: the poor old woman must come. She had to be carried, because, she said, she would sooner have eaten the road than walked it. When we were all finally assembled, he wanted to get up and be dressed. So he was got out of bed and they dressed him. He said we were all to go into the great big drawing-room. He said he wanted to be put in the middle in his papa's great big chair. Which was done. He said we were all to hold hands. We did it. He said we were to dance round him in a ring, and dance round him we did. But the unbelievable part is what came next.

Master. I hope you'll spare me what came next.

Jacques. Certainly not, sir, you're going to hear it. [*Mutters: 'If he thinks he can get away with inflicting on me a description of the boy's mother which was as long as my arm, he can think again.*]

Master. Jacques, I spoil you.

Jacques. That's too bad.

Master. You're cross about my long and tedious character study of the widow. But I'd say you've already more than paid me back for being bored by telling me this long and tedious story of the boy's tantrums.

Jacques. If that's what you think, then carry on with the story of his father—but no more character studies, sir. I loathe character studies.

Master. Why do you loathe character studies?

Jacques. Because they never seem true to life when you come face to face with the people they're supposed to describe. You can't recognize them. Show me what they do, tell me exactly what they say, and I'll know at once what sort of person I'm dealing with. A word, one gesture has sometimes taught me more than all the wagging tongues of a whole town.

Master. One day, Desglands...

Jacques. When you're out, I sometimes look in on your library and take down a book, usually a history book...

Master. One day, Desglands...

Jacques. I skip all the character descriptions.

Master. One day, Desglands...

Jacques. Sorry, sir, but the spring was wound up and I had to let it unwind.

Master. And has it?

Jacques. Completely.

Master. One day, Desglands invited the divine widow to dinner together with a few gentlemen who lived nearby. Desglands's star was beginning to wane and among the guests was a man who was beginning to catch her roving eye. They were at table, with Desglands and his rival sitting next to each other directly opposite the widow. Desglands was racking his brains to make the conversation sparkle. He said the most gallant things to her, but her mind seemed elsewhere. She didn't hear anything he said but kept her eyes fixed on his rival. Desglands was holding a fresh egg. A spasm of anger prompted by jealousy shook him, he clenched his fist, and the contents of the egg burst from its shell and spurted all over his neighbour's face. The man was about to raise his hand but Desglands grabbed his wrist, stopped him, and whispered: 'Sir, I consider your challenge to have been issued.'

This was followed by a profound silence, and the widow felt unwell. The meal was gloomy and short. As they got up from table, she called Desglands and his rival into a separate chamber. Everything a woman could have decently done to reconcile them, she did. She begged, she wept, she swooned quite genuinely. She pressed Desglands's hands and looked at the other man with tear-filled eyes.

To the latter, she said: 'But you love me!...'

And to the former: 'But you loved me once!...'

Then to the pair of them: '... and you are intent on ruining me, you mean to make me the talk, the scandal of the whole county, hated and despised by all! Whichever one of you kills his opponent, I shall never speak to him again. He is not a man I can have either as friend or lover, and I shall feel nothing but the deepest loathing for him until the day I die.'

Whereupon she fainted away again, and as she fainted she cried:

'Unfeeling brutes! Draw your swords and plunge them into my breast! If as I die I see you embrace each other, then I shall die without regret!'

Desglands and his rival stood stock-still, or perhaps they tried to revive her, and both had tears in their eyes. But the time came for them to go their separate ways. The beautiful widow was taken home more dead than alive.

Jacques. There, sir! You see? I didn't need the character study you drew me of the lady. I know for myself everything you said about her.

Master. The next day, Desglands called upon his charming, fickle mistress, only to find his rival there already. Which of them, the lady or his rival, do you think was the more surprised to see Desglands with his right cheek covered by a circle of black taffeta?

Widow. Whatever's that?

Desglands. It's nothing.

Rival. Got a swollen cheek?

Desglands. It'll pass.

After a moment's conversation Desglands left, and as he went he gave his rival a sign which was quite unambiguous. The rival followed him down the stairs. They marched down the street, one on one side, the other on the opposite side, joined up at the back of the merry widow's garden, crossed swords, and Desglands's rival ended up on the ground seriously but not mortally wounded. While he was carried back to his house, Desglands returned to the widow. He sat down and they again spoke of what had happened the previous day. She asked him what was the meaning of the enormous and very silly patch he had on his cheek. He stood up and looked at himself in a mirror.

'You're right,' he said, 'I think it's a bit too big.'

He picked up a pair of the lady's scissors, removed the taffeta patch, cut off a fraction of an inch all round, put it back on again, and said to the widow:

'Is that better?'

'Yes, but only a fraction better than before.'

'Still, it's something.'

Desglands's rival recovered. They fought a second duel, which Desglands also won, as he did another five times in a row, and after each encounter Desglands trimmed a narrow strip off his taffeta patch and then put the rest back on his cheek.

Jacques. And how did it all end? When I was taken to Desglands's chateau, I seem to think he was no longer wearing his black patch.

Master. No. It all came to an end when the merry widow died. The protracted worry it caused her undermined her health, which was delicate and fragile.

Jacques. And Desglands?

Master. One day we were strolling together when he was handed a note. He opened it and said: 'He was a very courageous man, but I can't pretend I'm sorry he's dead.' And he immediately reached for his cheek and pulled off what remained of the black taffeta, which as a result of his frequent attentions was by then not much bigger than an ordinary beauty patch. And that's the story of Desglands. Now is

Jacques satisfied? And may I hope that he will now either listen to the story of my loves or resume the story of his own?

Jacques. Neither the one nor the other.

Master. Why not?

Jacques. For the following reasons: it's hot, I'm tired, this is a very pleasant spot, we'll be out of the sun under those trees, and we can rest in the cool shade beside that stream.

Master. Agreed. But your cold...

Jacques. It's a fever and therefore hot, and doctors say that disordered states are cured by their opposites.

Master. That is as true of moral states as it is of physical states. I have observed a very odd phenomenon, which is that there's scarcely a single moral dictum that can't be turned into a medical saw and, conversely, few medical saws that can't be converted into a moral dictum.

Jacques. You're probably right.

They dismounted and stretched out on the grass. Jacques turned to his Master and said:

'Are you awake? Or are you sleeping? If you're going to stay awake, then I'll sleep. If you're going to sleep, I'll stay awake.'

His Master says: 'You sleep.'

'Can I rely on you to stay awake? Because this time, we might lose two horses.'

His Master took out his watch and his snuffbox. Jacques settled down to go to sleep but kept waking up with a start, raising both arms in the air, and clapping his hands. His Master said:

Master. What the devil's the matter?

Jacques. Flies and gnats are the matter. I wish someone would tell me what's the use of the annoying little beggars.

Master. And just because you don't know, you assume they have no use. Nature never made anything that was useless or unnecessary.

Jacques. I quite believe it, for if a thing is then it had to be.

Master. When you've got too much blood or bad blood, what do you do? You send for the surgeon who siphons off two or three basinfuls of the stuff. Well, these gnats you're grumbling about are a swarm of tiny winged surgeons who come armed with tiny lancets to bite you and draw your blood off drop by drop.

Jacques. Yes, but it's all hit and miss, for they've no idea if I've got too much or too little. Get someone who's all skin and bones and you'll observe that your tiny flying surgeons won't bother with him. They look out for themselves. Everything in nature looks out for itself and only itself. If it does harm to other creatures, so what, so long as it does them some good?

And so saying, he clapped his hands in the air and exclaimed:

Jacques. Damn and blast these tiny flying surgeons!

Master. Jacques, do you know the fable about Garo?*

Jacques. Yes.

Master. What do you make of it?

Jacques. It's bad.

Master. That's easily said.

Jacques. And easily demonstrated. If instead of acorns, oak trees produced pumpkins, would Garo the Bumpkin have gone for a snooze under one? And if he hadn't gone for a snooze under an oak tree, what difference would it have made to the shape of his nose if the tree had rained pumpkins or acorns? It's the sort of thing you should give children to read.

Master. A philosopher with your name won't hear of it.

Jacques. Two things: first, every one is entitled to his opinion, and second, Jean-Jacques is not the same as Jacques.*

Master. Well that's Jacques's hard luck.

Jacques. Nobody can say that until he's read the last word of the last line of the page devoted to him in the great scroll.

Master. What are you thinking?

Jacques. I was thinking that all the time you've been talking to me and I've been answering, you were talking without wanting to and I was answering without wanting to.

Master. And?

Jacques. And? That we were therefore a couple of living, thinking machines.*

Master. But what do you want at this moment?

Jacques. By God, it doesn't matter what I want. All wanting does is to activate another set of cogs in both our machines.

Master. Activate in what way?

Jacques. I'll be damned if I can conceive that cogs are activated for no reason. My Captain used to say: 'Postulate a cause and an effect will follow. A trivial cause will produce a trivial effect. A passing cause will produce a passing effect. An occasional cause will produce an occasional effect. A cause that is blocked will produce a reduced effect. When the cause stops, the effect is nil.

Master. But it seems to me that I can sense inside me that I am free, in the same way that I am aware that I am thinking.

Jacques. To that my Captain would say: 'No doubt, because at this minute you are not wanting anything. But what if you wanted to jump off your horse?'

Master. I'd jump off my horse.

Jacques. Gladly, without hesitating, without forcing yourself, as eagerly as you do when you're dismounting at the door of an inn?

Master. Not quite that, but what does it matter as long as I jump and prove that I'm free?

Jacques. My Captain would say: 'Come, come! Surely you can see that if I hadn't put the idea into your head, it would never have occurred to you to want to do anything so peculiar as break your neck? So in fact I'm the one who grabs your leg and heaves you out of your saddle. If your fall proves anything at all, it isn't that you are free but mad.' My Captain also used to say that exercising a freedom without the prompting of some motive is the true hallmark of a maniac.

Master. That's a bit strong to my sense, and despite everything you and your Captain say, I shall go on believing that I am capable of wanting whenever I want.

Jacques. But if you are able, and always have been, to exercise your will, how come you don't want to fall in love with some ugly hag now, and why didn't you stop loving Agathe every time you wanted to? Sir, we spend three-quarters of our lives wanting without doing.

Master. That's true.

Jacques. And doing without wanting.

Master. Could you demonstrate?

Jacques. If you permit.

Master. I permit.

Jacques. It will be done. But meanwhile, let's talk about something else.

After all this taradiddle and various other observations of the same ilk, they fell silent and Jacques pushed back the brim of his enormous hat—an umbrella in the rain, a sunshade on hot days, his headgear in all weathers, the mysterious sanctuary beneath which one of the finest minds that has ever existed would consult Destiny at critical moments.

When the brim of his hat was turned up, his face seemed to be in the middle of his body. When it was turned down, he could hardly see ten paces in front of him, so that he'd got into the habit of going around with his nose in the air, for which reason it might be said in connection with his hat:

> *Os illi sublime dedit, coelumque tueri*
> *Jussit, et erectos ad sidera tollere vultus.* *

Be that as it may, Jacques pushed up the brim of his enormous hat and, gazing into the distance, spied a ploughman who was setting about one of the horses that was harnessed to his plough, though with no visible effect. The horse, which was young and strong, had lain down in the furrow, and although the ploughman was yanking his bridle, urging him, stroking, threatening, cursing, and lashing him, the animal would not move and stubbornly refused to get up.

After pondering this scene for some time, Jacques said to his Master, whose attention had also been caught by it:

Jacques. Do you know what's going on over there?
Master. What do you think is going on over and above what I can see?
Jacques. Can't you see?
Master. No. What's your guess?
Jacques. I'd say that stupid, wilful, lazy animal is a denizen of the city and, being proud of its former glory as a saddle-horse, it despises the plough, or, to sum it up in a word, it's your horse, but also a symbolic manifestation of the Jacques who sits beside you and of so many other spineless weasels like him who forsook the land to enter domestic service in the capital and would rather beg for their daily bread in the streets, even starve to death, than return to agriculture, which is the most useful and honourable of all occupations.

His Master began to laugh while Jacques, addressing the ploughman who was too far away to hear, said:

Jacques. Go to it, you poor devil, lay into him, don't hold back! He's got into bad habits and you'll wear out more than one cracker on the end of your whip before you teach the no-good brute a modicum of true dignity and a taste for hard work!

His Master went on laughing. Jacques, partly from impatience and partly out of pity, got up, walked towards the ploughman, and had gone barely two hundred paces when he turned and began shouting to his Master:

Jacques. Over here, sir. It's your horse, it's your horse!

And so indeed it was. No sooner had the animal recognized Jacques and his Master than he got up without further prompting, shook his mane, whinnied, reared up on his hind legs, and nuzzled his erstwhile travelling companion, while an indignant Jacques muttered between his teeth:

Jacques. You miserable, misbegotten, lazy good-for-nothing piece of horse-meat! Is there any reason why I shouldn't let you feel the end of my boot?

On the other hand, the Master kissed him, ran one hand over his flank, patted him playfully on the rump with the other, and almost with tears of joy in his eyes, exclaimed:

Master. My horse! Poor old boy! So I've found you!

The ploughman couldn't make out what all the fuss was about.

'I can see', said he, 'that this horse used to belong to you, but I'm still the rightful owner. I paid good money for him at the last fair. Now if you want to buy him back for two-thirds of what he cost me, you'd be doing me a great service, because I can't do anything with him. When I go to get him out of the stable, he's the very devil. When I go to put his harness on, it's even worse. When he gets to the field, he lies down and would rather be beaten to death than pull on his collar or put up with having a sack on his back. Gentlemen, could you find it in your hearts to take the blasted animal off my hands? He's a handsome beast, but all he's good for is prancing about under a gentleman's saddle, and that's no good to me.'

They suggested he should exchange the horse for whichever of their two mounts suited him best. He agreed to this and our travellers strolled back to the place where they'd halted for a rest. From there, they observed with some relief that the horse they'd let the ploughman have was taking to his new role without raising any objection.

Jacques. Well, sir?

Master. Well, there's nothing surer than that you are inspired! But are you inspired by God, or by the Devil? I can't tell, but Jacques, my dear Jacques, I fear the Devil's got into you.

Jacques. Why the Devil?

Master. Because you perform miracles, but your doctrine is very suspect.

Jacques. But what connection is there between the doctrine a man professes and the marvels he performs?

Master. I can see you haven't read Dom La Taste.*

Jacques. And this Dom La Taste I've never read, what does he say?

Master. He says that both God and the Devil perform miracles.

Jacques. How does he know which are God's miracles and which are the Devil's?

Master. By the doctrine that goes with them. If the doctrine is good, then the miracles are God's. If the doctrine is bad, then they are the Devil's.

Here Jacques began to whistle sceptically. Then he added:

Jacques. And who will teach me, a poor, ignorant man, if the doctrine professed by the miracle-maker is good or bad? But come, sir, let's mount up. Why should you care if it was through the intervention of God or Beelzebub that your horse was found? Will he step out any less lively if you knew the answer to that?

Master. No. Still, if you are really possessed...

Jacques. What's the cure for it?

Master. The cure, failing a full exorcism, would be to restrict yourself to drinking nothing but holy water.

Jacques. Me, sir, drink water! Jacques on holy water! I'd rather have a thousand legions of devils take up permanent residence in my insides than touch a drop of water, holy or unholy. Haven't you ever noticed that I'm hydrophobic?

Just a moment! 'Hydrophobic'? Jacques said 'hydrophobic'?

No, Reader, he didn't. I confess the word wasn't his. But if you want to apply such high critical standards, I challenge you to read any scene from a comedy or a tragedy, one dialogue, however well-written, and not detect the voice of the author in the mouth of his characters. What Jacques actually said was: 'Haven't you ever noticed, sir, that the mere sight of water makes me jump backwards like a mad dog?...' There it is. In expressing it differently from him, I was true but more succinct.

They got back on their horses and Jacques said to his Master:

Jacques. You'd reached the point in the tale of your love-life when you'd found ecstasy twice and were perhaps ready to find it a third time...

Master. When all of a sudden the outer door to the boudoir burst open and the bedroom filled up with a crowd of people who surged forward. I saw lights, I heard men's voices and women's voices all talking at once. The bed-curtains were flung back and I was confronted by her mother, father, aunts, cousins of both sexes, and a police officer who intoned solemnly:

'Ladies and gentlemen, please be silent. Caught in the act! The gentleman is a man of honour. There is only one way of making amends and the gentleman will prefer to take it voluntarily rather than be forced to do so by law.'

With every word he spoke he was interrupted by the father and mother who heaped reproaches on me, by the aunts and female cousins who heaped the most unminced epithets on the head of Agathe, which she had hidden under the bedclothes.

I was dumbfounded and didn't know what to say. The officer turned to me and observed sarcastically:

'Sir, you look very comfortable there. But now you must be so good as to get up and dress.'

This I did, but in my own clothes which had been substituted for those of the Chevalier. A table was brought and the officer began drawing up the charge against me. Meanwhile the mother had to be held down by four people to stop her launching herself at her daughter, and the father kept saying:

'Calm down, my dear, not so warm. Even if you give your daughter a damned good hiding, the facts of the case will be the same. It'll all turn out for the best.'

The other people were scattered about the room on chairs in different poses expressive of grief, indignation, and anger. The father turned on his wife from time to time, saying:

'This is what comes of not keeping closer eye on your daughter's conduct.'

To which the mother replied: 'Who'd have thought the gentleman would do such a thing. He looked so good and honest.'

The others said nothing. When the charge had been drawn up, it was read out to me and, since it was no more than the truth, I signed it and went downstairs with the officer, who invited me very politely to step into a carriage which stood waiting at the door and thence conveyed me, accompanied by a sizeable escort, straight to For-L'Évêque.*

Jacques. To For-L'Évêque! To prison?

Master. To prison. And then the terms of a gruesome suit were put to me. What it involved was nothing less than marriage to Mademoiselle Agathe. Her parents refused to settle for anything less.

Next morning, the Chevalier appeared in my cell. He knew everything. Agathe was distraught and her parents furious. He'd been subjected to the most bitter recriminations for having introduced them to such a devious acquaintance. He it was who'd been the original cause of their misfortune and their daughter's disgrace. They were in a terrible state. He'd asked if he could speak to Agathe in private, and this had been granted, though only after considerable resistance. At first Agathe tried to scratch his eyes out and had called him the most odious names. He'd been expecting this and had waited until her fury blew itself out, after which he had tried to make her see reason.

'But then she said something to which', said the Chevalier, 'I'm not sure how I should respond.'

' "My father and my mother discovered me with your friend," she said. "Shall I tell them that though I was found in bed with him I thought I was in bed with you?"

' "But in all honesty," said I, "do you really think my friend should marry you?"

' "No," said she, "you're the one, you brute, who should be made to do it." '

I said to the Chevalier: 'You can get me out of this mess if you want.'

'How?'

'How? By making a clean breast of the whole business.'

'I threatened Agathe with that, but naturally I shan't do anything of the kind. It's far from certain that such a course of action would serve any useful purpose, but one thing is crystal clear: it would mean disgrace for all of us. Anyway, it was your fault.'

'My fault?'

'Yes, yours. If you'd gone along with the escapade as I originally put it to you, Agathe would have been found in bed with two men, and all this would have ended as one big joke. But it wasn't to be and now we've got to get you out of a fine old pickle.'

'But can you, Chevalier, explain one small thing to me? Why were my clothes removed from her dressing-room and yours put in their place? Damme, I've given it a lot of thought but it's still a mystery I can't solve. It's made me a mite suspicious of Agathe, for it strikes me she might have seen through our little subterfuge and there might have been some sort of conniving between her and her parents.'

'Perhaps you were seen going up to her apartment. But one thing's for sure: you'd hardly got undressed when my clothes were returned to me and I was asked to hand yours over.'

'It'll all come out in time.'

While the Chevalier and I were busy worrying, comforting ourselves, bandying accusations, exchanging insults, and begging each other's pardon, the officer of the watch came in. The Chevalier turned pale and left hurriedly. The officer was an honest man—a few of them are—who, as he reread the charge to me, recalled that once upon a time he had been a student with a young man who had the same name as mine. It occurred to him that I might be a relative or even the son of his old college friend, and so it proved. His first question was to ask me who was the man who had run away as he arrived.

'He didn't run away,' I said, 'he left. He's my best friend, the Chevalier de Saint-Ouin.'

'Your friend! Some friend he is! Were you aware, sir, that he was the one who came and tipped me the wink? The father and another relative were with him.'

'Him!'

'The very same.'

'Are you sure of that?'

'Quite certain. What did you call him?'

'The Chevalier de Saint-Ouin.'

'Ah! The Chevalier de Saint-Ouin! That's him! Are you also aware of what sort of man your friend, best friend, the Chevalier de Saint-Ouin, really is? He's a crook and well known to us for the many swindles he's pulled. The police only let men like him remain at liberty to roam the streets because they can sometimes come in useful. They are villains who inform on other villains. Overall, it seems, the good they do by preventing crimes and exposing criminals far outweighs the harm caused by their own criminal activities.'*

I told the officer the whole sorry story exactly as it had happened. He did not see it in a more favourable light than before, for none of the reasons why I should be found not guilty could be produced or proved in a court of law. However, he did agree to interview the girl's father and mother, to apply pressure on the girl herself, put my side of things to the judge, and omit nothing that would help to prove my innocence, though he warned me that if my accusers took good legal counsel, there was little the authorities could do.

'What! You mean I'll be forced to marry her?'

'Marry her? That would be very harsh and I don't think you need fear it will come to that. But there will be a claim for damages, and in your case they will be high.'

Jacques, you look as if you've got something to say.

Jacques. Yes, I wanted to say that clearly you were much worse off than I was: I paid for a night's-worth which I never got. All the same, I'll have heard it all if Agathe turns out to be pregnant.

Master. Don't be too hasty to discard that hypothesis just yet, for shortly after I'd been locked up, the officer told me that she had been round to see him to make a formal statement that she was pregnant.

Jacques. That's how you became the father of a child...

Master. Whose interest I've protected...

Jacques. But which you never sired.

Master. Neither the protection of the judge nor all the steps taken by the officer could prevent matters running their legal course. But since the girl and her parents were known to be bad characters, I did not have to marry her as a condition of my being released from prison. But I was sentenced to a hefty fine, and was required to pay for the birth and to contribute to the cost of raising and educating a child who had been brought into the world through the exploits of my friend, the Chevalier de Saint-Ouin, of whom he was an identical second but smaller edition. It was an uncomplicated birth between the seventh and eighth month, and it produced a strapping male who was put out to a buxom wet-nurse who I've been paying each month ever since.

Jacques. How old is your son, sir?

Master. He'll be ten soon. I've left him all this time in the country where the village schoolmaster has taught him reading, writing, and arithmetic. It's not far from where we're going and I shall take the opportunity to pay those good people what I owe, take him off their hands, and put him to a trade.

Jacques and his Master spent yet another night in a roadside bivouac. They were now too near the end of their travels for Jacques to resume the history of his love-life. Besides, he was a long way from being over his sore throat. The next day, they reached...

Where?

Not a clue, on my honour.

What business did they have wherever it was they were going to?

Anything you like. Do you think Jacques's Master told everybody his business? But whatever it was, it didn't take longer than a fortnight.

Did it go well? Did it go badly?

I don't know that either, but Jacques's sore throat cleared up as a result of two medicines which he detested: diet and rest.

One morning, the Master said to his servant:

Master. Jacques, bridle and saddle the horses and then fill your gourd. We've got to go you know where.

This was no sooner said than done, and in next to no time they were making their way to the place where for the last ten years the son of the Chevalier de Saint-Ouin had been raised at the expense of Jacques's Master. When they'd got some way from the inn where they'd spent the night, the Master turned to Jacques and spoke as follows:

Master. What did you make of my love-life?

Jacques. I think that there are some very odd things written up there, on high. A child gets born, God only knows how. Who can tell what role the poor motherless, fatherless infant will play in life? Who can say whether he was born to defend or to overthrow an empire?

Master. Neither. I'll make a good turner or clockmaker of him. He'll get married and have sons who'll go on making chair-legs for the whole world for ever after.

Jacques. Yes, but only if that is what's written on high. But why shouldn't a Cromwell emerge from a turner's shop? Didn't the man who had the head of his king chopped off come from a brewer's shop? And aren't people saying nowadays that...*

Master. Let's not go into that. You're fit again. You've heard the full story of my loves. If you have a conscience, you won't try to wriggle out of letting me have the rest of yours.

Jacques. Everything's against it. First, we don't have much further to go. Second, we can't remember where I was up to. Third, I have this awful feeling that my story will not get finished, that it's a tale that'll bring us bad luck, and that the minute I start up again I shall be interrupted by some disaster which might turn out well or badly.

Master. If it turns out well, that's all right.

Jacques. Agreed, but I have this feeling it won't.

Master. If it turns out badly, then so be it. But whether you tell your story or whether you don't, will it happen any the less?

Jacques. Who can say?

Master. You were born three centuries too late.

Jacques. No, sir. I was born at the right time, like everybody else.

Master. You'd have been a great soothsayer.

Jacques. I'm not exactly sure I know what a soothsayer is, nor do I care.

Master. One of the longest chapters in your treatise on divination is about soothsayers.

Jacques. No doubt, but it's such a long time since I wrote it that I can't remember a single word of it. But hold on a moment, sir, here's a chap who knows more than all the soothsayers, prophetic geese, and sacrificial chickens put together, I mean the gourd. Let's see what the gourd has to say.

Jacques took his gourd and asked it a lengthy question. His Master took out his watch and his snuffbox, saw what time it was, then took his pinch, by which time Jacques said:

Jacques. I have the impression that Destiny is not looking quite as black as it did. Tell me where I'd got to.

Master. You were at Desglands's chateau, your knee was a little better, and Denise had been told to look after you by her mother.

Jacques. Denise was very obedient. The wound in my knee had almost closed up, I'd even been able to dance in a ring on the night of the boy's tantrum, and yet from time to time I'd get the most excruciating shooting pains in it. It struck the surgeon who lived in the chateau and knew rather more about such things than his colleague, that these pains which had returned and would not shift, could only be caused by the presence of some foreign body which had remained in the wound after the bullet had been removed. So early one morning he came to my room and had a table brought next to my bed. When the bed-curtains were drawn, I saw the said table covered with sharp instruments, Denise sitting at the head of my bed weeping hot tears, her mother standing with her arms crossed and looking very grim, the surgeon with his coat off, his sleeves rolled up, and a lancet in his right hand.

Master. You're frightening me.

Jacques. I was terrified. 'Look, lad,' said the surgeon, 'have you had enough of being in pain?'

'More than enough.'

'Do you want the pain to stop and keep your leg?'

'Yes to both.'

'Then put it out over the side of the bed, so I can work on it more easily.'

I hold my leg out. The surgeon puts the handle of the lancet between his teeth, raises my leg over his left arm, holds it there firmly, takes the lancet from his mouth, inserts the point into the opening of my wound and makes a wide, deep incision. I didn't even blink, but Jeanne looked away, and Denise let out a shriek and felt faint.

At this point, Jacques paused in his narration and took another swig from his gourd. These pauses were more frequent as the distances grew shorter, or, as geometers says, they were in inverse proportion to the said distances. He judged the quantities so exactly that, while the gourd was full when he set out, it was empty to the last drop when he arrived. The men who run the roads could have used him as a first-rate odometer,* and generally speaking each pause had its sufficient reason.* On this occasion, the reason was to allow Denise to recover from her swoon and himself to get over the pain caused by the incision the surgeon had made in his knee. When Denise had recovered and he felt comforted, he continued:

Jacques. The very deep incision reopened the wound all the way down, and from deep inside it the surgeon, using a pair of tweezers, extracted a tiny remnant of the twill of my breeches which was still embedded in it. Its presence had been causing the shooting pains and had prevented the wound from healing over. Once this operation had been performed, I got better and better, thanks to the good care Denise took of me. No more shooting pains, no more temperature. I had a healthy appetite, I slept well, and my strength returned.

Denise changed my dressing regularly and was very gentle with me. If only you could have seen how gingerly, how deftly she removed my bandage, how afraid she was of causing me the smallest twinge of pain, how carefully she bathed my wound. I would sit on the edge of my bed, she would face me with one knee on the floor. My leg would rest on her thigh, to which I would sometimes apply faint pressure. I had one arm on her shoulder and would watch her work with a tenderness which I believe she shared. When I was bandaged up again, I took both her hands in mine, thanked her, though I didn't know what to say, I had no idea of what I could do to show her how grateful I was. She would stand there, staring at the ground, listening in silence to what I said. No pedlar ever called at the chateau without my buying something for her. Once it was a scarf, another time it was a few yards of calico or muslin, or a gold cross, a pair of cotton stockings, a ring, a garnet neck-lace. When I'd bought her something, I never knew how to give it to her and she never knew how to accept it. I'd start by showing it to her. If she said it was nice, then I'd say: 'Denise, I bought it for you.' If she accepted it, my hand would shake as I gave it to her, and her hand would shake as she took it.

One day, not knowing what to get her, I bought garters. They were silk, with white, red, and blue embroidery and a pretty pattern. That morning, before she came, I put them on the back of the chair next to my bed. As soon as Denise saw them she cried:

'What beautiful garters!'

'They're for the girl I love,' said I.

'So you've got a girl, then, Monsieur Jacques?'

'Of course. Didn't I ever tell you?'

'No. I expect she's pretty?'

'Very pretty.'

'And do you love her?'

'Heart and soul.'

'And does she love you?'

'I have no idea. These garters are for her. She's promised to do something for me, and if she does it, I think I'll go crazy.'

'What is it?'

'She said I could put one of these garters on her leg with my own hands.'

Denise blushed, misunderstood what I'd said, assumed the garters were intended for someone else, looked devastated, made one blunder after another, looked high and low for the things she needed to dress my leg, found them under her nose, spilled the wine which she'd heated, stood by my bed to attend to me, held my leg with her hand which shook, made a complete mess of unwinding the bandages, and,

when she was ready to bathe the wound, found she'd forgotten everything she needed. She went and got it, dressed my knee, and as she
dressed my knee I saw that she was crying.

'Denise, are you crying? What's the matter?'

'Nothing.'

'Has someone been unkind to you?'

'Yes.'

'Who's the brute who's been unkind to you?'

'You.'

'Me?'

'Yes.'

'But how on earth did I manage that?'

Instead of answering, she turned and looked at the garters.

'Ah!' said I, 'is that what's made you cry?'

'Yes.'

'Well, Denise, you can stop crying. I bought them for you.'

'Monsieur Jacques, is that true?'

'As true as true—so true that here they are.'

Whereupon I held out both of them to her, but kept one back. At
once a smile appeared through her tears. I took her by the arm, drew
her closer to where I lay, reached down for one of her feet which I
propped up on the side of the bed, bared her leg as far as her knee—
where she kept her skirts firmly clamped with both hands. I kissed her
leg, slipped on the garter I had kept back and it was no sooner in place
when her mother, Jeanne, came in.

Master. A badly timed entrance.

Jacques. Maybe, maybe not. Far from noticing how flustered we
both were, she saw only the garter her daughter was holding in her
hand.

'That's a pretty garter,' she said. 'But where's the other one?'

'On my leg,' replied Denise. 'He said he'd bought them for a girl
he's in love with, but I swore to him they were for me. It's only right,
isn't it, Mama, that since I've put one on, I should be allowed to keep
the other?'

'Oh, Monsieur Jacques, Denise is quite right. You can't have one
garter without the other. You wouldn't want to make her give back the
one she's already got!'

'Why not?'

'Because Denise wouldn't like it, nor me neither.'

'Well let's come to an arrangement. I'll put the other one on her leg in your presence.'

'No, no! You can't do that!'

'Then she'll have to give the pair of them back.'

'You can't do that either.'

Jacques and his Master are at this moment entering the village where they were going to see the boy and the foster-parents of the boy who was the son of the Chevalier de Saint-Ouin. Jacques fell silent. His Master said:

Master. Let's dismount and bide here a while.

Jacques. Why?

Master. Because all the signs are that you are approaching the end of the story of your love-life.

Jacques. Not quite yet.

Master. When a man gets to the knee, he's not got much further to go.

Jacques. Sir, Denise's thighs were a lot longer than a normal girl's thighs.

Master. Even so, let's dismount.

They dismount, Jacques first. He scurries round, cups hands to receive his master's boot. But no sooner does his Master put his foot on the stirrup than the leather belt holding it snaps and my rider slides backwards and would have fallen heavily to the ground if Jacques had not caught him in his arms.

Master. Dammit all, Jacques, is this how you look after me? I could have broken a rib or an arm, or cracked my skull or even been killed!

Jacques. That would have been no great loss, I'd say.

Master. What was that, villain? Just you wait! I'll teach you how to talk to your betters!

And the Master, pausing only to wind the lanyard of his whip twice round his wrist, began chasing Jacques, and Jacques ran round the horse roaring with laughter, and his Master swearing, cursing, fuming with rage, also ran round the horse, directing a stream of abuse at Jacques, and the chase went on until both of them, bathed in sweat and quite exhausted, came to a halt, one on one side of the horse, and the other on the other, Jacques panting and still laughing, and his Master panting and glaring at him furiously. They were just getting their breath back when Jacques said to his Master:

Jacques. Sir, surely you admit it now?

Master. What do you want me to admit, you dog, you cur, you swine? That you're the worst of all possible servants and that I am the most unfortunate of all Masters?

Jacques. Haven't we just given the clearest demonstration of the fact that most of the time we act without volition? Come, put your hand on your heart and tell me: in all we've been doing for the last half-hour, was there anything you consciously intended? Haven't you been my puppet, and wouldn't you have carried on in the same way for a month if I'd decided to continue pulling your strings?

Master. What! You mean that was all a game?

Jacques. Just a game.

Master. Did you know the belt would break?

Jacques. I nobbled it.

Master. And your insolent remark was premeditated?

Jacques. It was.

Master. And that was the string you attached to my head to make me dance to your tune?

Jacques. It was indeed.

Master. You're a dangerous villain.

Jacques. Why not say that I am, courtesy of my Captain who once pulled the same stunt on me, a tricky man to argue with.

Master. But what if I'd hurt myself?

Jacques. It was written on high and guaranteed by my foresight that such a thing would not happen.

Master. Oh let's sit down. We both need a rest.

As they sit down, Jacques mutters:

Jacques. Damnation, what a stupid clod!

Master. Am I to take it you're talking about yourself?

Jacques. Yes, I am, for not leaving enough in my gourd for an extra swig.

Master. You needn't regret it—I'd have drunk it myself. I'm dying of thirst.

Jacques. Damn me again for a blithering idiot for not leaving enough for two swigs!

His Master asks him to continue with his story, to help them forget how weary and thirsty they are. Jacques refuses. His Master sulks. Jacques lets him sulk. In the end, after he'd warned that some disaster would surely happen if he did, he went on, upon this wise, with the history of his loves:

Jacques. One day—it was a holiday—the master of the chateau was out hunting...

Having got this far, he suddenly breaks off and says:

Jacques. I can't do it. I can't go on. As I speak I seem to sense the hand of Destiny reaching for my throat and can feel it tightening its grip. For the love of God, sir, say I can stop.

Master. Oh very well, stop. Go and ask at the first cottage over there where the boy's foster-father lives.

The foster-father's house was further along. They head towards it, each holding his horse by its bridle. The door opens at once. A man appears. Jacques's Master utters a cry and reaches for his sword. The man does likewise. The horses take fright at the clash of steel, Jacques's mount snaps its bridle and escapes, and at the same moment the man his Master is fighting falls dead on the ground. The villagers come running. Jacques's Master leaps smartly into his saddle and gallops off as fast as he can go. Jacques is held, his hands are tied behind his back, and he is led away to the local justice who packs him off to prison.

The dead man was the Chevalier de Saint-Ouin, who on that very day had been brought by pure chance, with Agathe, to visit their son's wet-nurse. Agathe crouched over the corpse of her lover and tore her hair. Jacques's Master was already so far away that he was out of sight. Jacques, as he was being taken from the house of the justice to prison, said: 'This must have been written up there, on high.'

And there I shall call it a day, because I've told you everything I know about my two characters.

But what about Jacques's love-life?

Look, Jacques said over and over that it was written on high that he'd never finish the tale, and I now see that he was right. I can tell, Reader, that you are not best pleased. Well, why don't you pick up his story at the point where he left it yourself, and continue it as you think best? Or go and call on Mademoiselle Agathe, find out the name of the village where Jacques is being held, see Jacques, and question him. He won't need to be asked twice, it'll give him something to think about.

I suppose, by resorting to published memoirs (which I have good reason to believe are highly suspect*), that I could supply what's missing here, but what would be the point? You can only be interested in what you think is true. Still, since it would be somewhat rash, without proper examination, to pronounce judgement on the conversations of Jacques and his Master, which is the most important work to appear since *Pantagruel*, by François Rabelais, and the life and adventures of Compère Mathieu,* I shall reread the memoirs with all the impartiality I can muster and shall, one week from today, deliver a judgement which shall be definitive, though I reserve the right to retract if someone more intelligent can show where I've gone wrong.

[*The Editor writes*]: The week is up. I've now read the memoirs I mentioned. Of the three paragraphs which appear therein but not in the manuscript in my possession, the first and the last seem to me genuine, while the second is obviously an interpolation. I now give you the first, which supposes a second gap in the conversation between Jacques and his Master:

One day—it was a holiday— the master of the chateau was out hunting and the remaining denizens of the chateau had taken themselves off to mass in the parish church a good mile away. Jacques was out of bed and Denise was sitting next to him. They did not speak, looked as though they'd had a tiff, and a tiff is in fact what they'd had. Jacques had done everything to persuade Denise to make him a happy man but Denise had held firm. After this long silence, Jacques, weeping bitterly and with a hard, acrimonious edge to his voice, said to her:

'It's obvious you don't love me.'

Denise, clearly riled, stands up, takes him by the arms, drags him to the side of the bed, sits down, and says:

'So, Monsieur Jacques, I don't love you. Well then, Monsieur Jacques, you may do to unhappy Denise whatever you will.'

And so saying, she bursts into tears and chokes on her sobs.

Tell me, Reader, what would you have done if you'd been Jacques?'

Nothing.

Well, that's exactly what he did. He led Denise back to her chair, knelt at her feet, dried the tears which streamed down her cheeks, kissed her hands, comforted and reassured her, said he knew she loved him truly, and left it to her tender sentiments to decide the time when she would reward him for his. This manner of proceeding left Denise visibly moved.

Perhaps you will object that Jacques, kneeling at Denise's feet, was hardly in a position to dry her eyes... unless it was a very low chair. The manuscript doesn't specify, but we may assume that it was.

Here now is the second paragraph, which was copied out of *The Life and Opinions of Tristram Shandy*—unless, that is, the conversations of Jacques the Fatalist and his Master pre-date that work, in which case the Reverend Sterne is a plagiarist, though I don't believe that for one minute, for I have a particular regard for Monsieur Sterne, whom I set apart from most of the men of letters of his nation, whose regular custom is to steal from us and then hurl insults in our direction.

On another occasion—it was early one morning—Denise had come to dress Jacques's wound. Everyone else in the chateau was asleep. Denise trembled as she went to his room. When she reached the door, she stopped, unsure whether to go in or not. She entered, still trembling, and stood for some time at the side of Jacques's bed without drawing the bed-curtains. Then she opened them quietly, said good-morning to Jacques, still trembling, then trembled some more as she asked what sort of night he'd spent and how he felt. Jacques replied that he'd not slept a wink and that he was still suffering torments from his knee which was itching like blazes. Denise offered to make the itch go away. She took a small square of flannel, Jacques put his leg out of the bed, and Denise began rubbing away with her flannel just below the wound, first with one finger, then with two, then three, then four, and finally with her whole hand. Jacques watched her at work and love coursed hotly in his veins. Next, Denise, still with her flannel, began rubbing the wound itself where the scar still showed red, first with one finger, then with two, then three, then four, and finally with her whole hand. But curing the itch below the knee and on the knee was not enough. It had also to be stopped above the knee where it made its presence felt most strongly. Denise then applied her flannel above the wound, rubbing away very firmly, first with one finger, then with two, then three, then four, and finally with her whole hand. The emotion felt by Jacques, who had not taken his eyes off her for one moment, now expanded to such a pitch that, being incapable of holding out for a moment longer, he grabbed Denise's hand... and put it...

What leaves absolutely no doubt that this is indeed plagiary is what follows. The plagiarist adds: 'If you are not satisfied with what I have revealed to you of Jacques's loves, Reader, why not try to do better yourself, I shan't mind. But whichever way you set about it, I am certain that you will finish the tale as I have.'

'You're wrong, you slandering swine, I won't finish it the way you have. Denise was a good woman.'

'Who's saying different? Jacques grabbed her hand and put it to his lips: *his lips*. You're the one with the dirty mind, you hear things no one is saying.'

'Ah! so all he did was place her hand on his lips?'*

'Most certainly. Jacques was far too sensible to take advantage of a girl he had every intention of marrying and thus sow the seed for a spirit of mistrust which would have poisoned the rest of his life.'

'But in the previous paragraph, it states clearly that "Jacques had done everything to persuade Denise to make him a happy man".'

'Well, apparently at that point he hadn't yet made up his mind to marry her.'

The third paragraph shows Jacques, our unfortunate fatalist, manacled hand and foot, lying on prison straw in a dark cell, trying to remember all the principles he could recall of his Captain's philosophy and half-thinking that some day he might look back fondly on his gloomy, damp, filthy abode, where he was fed on black bread and water and had to defend his hands and feet from the attentions of the mice and rats. We are informed that while he was musing thus, the gates of the prison and the door to his cell were suddenly burst open, that he was set free along with a dozen footpads, and that he found himself enrolled as a member of Mandrin's gang.*

Meantime, mounted constables had gone in pursuit of his Master. They caught up with and arrested him and had him locked up in a different gaol. He had been released through the efforts of the same officer who had served him so well during his earlier escapade, and had been living quietly in Desglands's chateau for two or three months when chance restored to him a servant who was almost as crucial to his happiness as his watch and his snuffbox. He never took a pinch of snuff, never looked at his watch to see what time it was, without heaving a sigh and muttering:

'What ever became of my poor Jacques?'

One night, Desglands's chateau was attacked by Mandrin's bandits. Jacques recognized it: it was his benefactor's house, the place where his mistress lived. He intervened and prevented the chateau from being looted.

Then we read a snatch of text which gives moving details of the unexpected reunion of Jacques, his Master, Desglands, Denise, and Jeanne.

'Jacques, is that you?'

'Is that you, sir?'

'How did you manage to get mixed up with that rabble?'

'And how come I find you here? Is that you, Denise?'

'Is that you, Monsieur Jacques? Oh, how you made me cry!'

While all this was going on, Desglands called: 'Bring glasses and wine at once! And be quick about it! He's saved all our lives!...'

Within a few days, the aged chateau concierge died. Jacques was given his job and married Denise, with whom he set about raising disciples of Zeno and Spinoza,* loved by Desglands, cherished by his Master, and adored by his wife, for so it was written.

Up there.

On high.

People have tried to convince me that his Master and Desglands both fell in love with his wife. I have no information on that, but of one thing I am certain. Every evening, Jacques would say to himself:

'If it is written on high that she will be unfaithful, then whatever you do to prevent it, Jacques, unfaithful she will be. If on the other hand it is written on high that she will not be unfaithful, then whatever they do to make it happen, unfaithful she will not be. Go to sleep, friend.'

And he would go out like a light.

EXPLANATORY NOTES

3 *its billet*: the opening pages of *Jacques the Fatalist* carry strong echoes of the tale of Trim's knee, as told to Uncle Toby, in Sterne's *Tristram Shandy*, bk. viii, chs. 19–23. Trim too is a fatalist, but whereas Jacques follows the lead of his Captain in this matter, Sterne's corporal has the backing of William of Orange: 'The King of Bohemia with his queen and courtiers happening one fine summer's evening to walk out—Aye! there the word *happening* is right, Trim, cried my uncle Toby; for the King of Bohemia and his queen might have walk'd out or let it alone:—'twas a matter of contingency, which might happen, or not, just as chance ordered it.

'King William was of an opinion, an' please your honour, quoth Trim, that everything was predestined for us in this world; insomuch, that he would often say to his soldiers, that "every ball had its billet". He was a great man, said my uncle Toby—And I believe, continued Trim, to this day, that the shot which disabled me at the battle of Landen, was pointed at my knee for no other purpose, but to take me out of his service, and place me in your honour's. . .' (ch. 19).

battle commences: the battle at Fontenoy, in Belgium, fought on 11 May 1745, ended in a crushing victory by the French over a combined English and Austrian force.

in love?: 'Besides, said the corporal, resuming his discourse—but in a gayer accent—if it had not been for that single shot, I had never, an' please your honour, been in love.—So, thou wast once in love, Trim! said my uncle Toby, smiling. . .' (*Tristram Shandy*, bk. viii, ch. 19). Sterne allows Trim, with a few interruptions, to complete the story of his *amour* a few pages on. Diderot expands the incident into the longest of his fictions.

5 *what they are*: at the battle of Landen, 'the number of wounded was prodigious, and no one had any time to think of anything but his own safety. . . I was left upon the field, said the corporal. Thou wast so, poor fellow! replied my uncle Toby—So that it was noon the next day, continued the corporal, before I was exchanged, and put in a cart with thirteen or fourteen more, in order to be conveyed to our hospital.

'There is no part of the body, an' please your honour, where a wound occasions more intolerable anguish than upon the knee—

'Except the groin; said my uncle Toby. An' please your honour, replied the corporal, the knee, in my opinion, must certainly be the most acute, there being so many tendons and what-d'ye-call-'ems all about it.

'It is for that reason, quoth my uncle Toby, that the groin is infinitely more sensible—there being not only as many tendons and what-d'ye-call-'ems (for I know their names as little as thou dost)—about it but. . .' (ibid.).

6 *of his master*: by the 1770s a hackneyed theme of traditional comedy, the best example being Lesage's *Crispin rival de son maître* (1707). Though Diderot

consciously derides such ploys, he will nevertheless allow Jacques to be preferred by Denise whom the Master had met at the house of his friend
Desglands: this is the 'first time' of this teasing remark.

7 *and temples*: 'I was telling my sufferings to a young woman at a peasant's
house, where our cart, which was the last of the line, had halted; they'd
helped me in, and the young woman had taken a cordial out of her pocket
and dropp'd it upon some sugar, and seeing it had cheer'd me, she had given
it me a second and a third time.—So I was telling her, an' please your honour, the anguish I was in, and was saying it was so intolerable to me, that I
had much rather lie down on the bed, turning my face towards the one
which was in the corner of the room—and die, than go on—when, upon
her attempting to lead me to it, I fainted away in her arms. She was a good
soul! as your honour, said the corporal, wiping his eyes, will hear.

'I thought love had been a joyous thing, quoth my uncle Toby.

''Tis the most serious thing, an' please your honour (sometimes), that is
in the world.

'By the persuasion of the young woman, continued the corporal, the cart
with the wounded men set off without me: she had assured them I should
expire immediately if I was put into the cart. So when I came to myself—I
found myself in a still quiet cottage, with no one but the young woman, and
the peasant and his wife. I was laid across the bed in the corner of the room,
with my wounded leg upon a chair, and the young woman beside me, holding the corner of her handkerchief dipp'd in vinegar to my nose with one
hand, and rubbing my temples with the other.' (*Tristram Shandy*, bk. viii,
ch. 20).

8 *criminal population*: bad harvests and the failure of the royal administration
to control the price of bread after the introduction of free trade in grain in
1764, led to periodic outbreaks of unrest. One such crisis marked the years
1768–70, which saw an increase in the activities of highwaymen and
smugglers.

11 *Berg-op-Zoom and Port-Mahon*: Berg-op-Zoom, in the Netherlands, was
taken by the French in 1747. Port-Mahon, capital of Minorca, fell in 1756
to the Duke de Richelieu who, it is said, to mark the occasion ordered his
chef to prepare a new sauce which he called 'mahonnaise'. Diderot's casual
attitude to the chronology of his tale is nowhere more in evidence than here.
If Jacques's military career ended at Fontenoy in 1745, he cannot have been
in his Captain's service in 1756.

13 *her distaff*: a cleft stick about a metre long on which was wound wool, cotton, or flax to be spun into thread by women. It was superseded by the
spinning-wheel but was still used for flax in the eighteenth century.

with hats: Saint Roch (*c*.1293–1327), born at Montpellier, was a plague doctor. When he himself was stricken, he was found by a dog whose master
nursed him back to health. In church iconography he was usually shown
with three hats, whence a proverb meaning that of the many possessions we
have, a number are totally useless.

14 *observed to do*: Pierre Dufouart (1737–1813) and Antoine Louis (1723–92). Dr Louis, of the Hopital de La Charité hospital in Paris, wrote articles about surgery for Diderot's *Encyclopédie*. Laurent Versini identifies the general as the Marquis de Castries (1727–1801), who was wounded when the castle of Amoenebourg in Westphalia was taken in September 1762.

on the ship?: the question, repeated for comic effect, is spoken by Géronte in Molière's *Les Fourberies de Scapin* (1671), II. xi.

15 *between their riders*: perhaps an echo of the 'entire affection' of Rozinante and Sancho Panza's mule 'Dapple' in *Don Quixote* (Part II, ch. 12).

16 *your fall*: an echo of Diderot's interest in the problem of perception. He makes experience the source of our knowledge of things, and argues that the association of ideas, though a valid source of knowledge, is secondary in importance. This exchange also shows the modernity of his mind: it anticipates modern linguistics, which distinguishes between things and the words which signify them.

18 *times are hard*: an anticipation both of Robert Malthus's argument that population increases faster than the means of subsistence, and of the more modern view that population falls as living standards rise.

20 *what you mean*: though Diderot goes on to distance himself from allegory, the castle is clearly a symbolic attack on the corrupt *ancien régime*. The 'score of villains' are the royal ministers who congregated at Versailles (in 'the best rooms') and manipulated the *parlements* (the 'handul of fat-arses'), who used the 'larger number' of their kind (the legal profession) to carry out their bidding. Those who ask impertinent questions are the *philosophes*. Perhaps Diderot did not intend anything quite as specific, but the episode is clearly an aggressive political comment on a society which had been hijacked by absolutist monarchy and aristocratic privilege.

23 *Julien Le Roy*: a noted watchmaker (1686–1759).

24 *harvest time*: one of the few indications of the 'real' time of a narrative where time and place are made deliberately unspecific.

25 *Conches*: 17 km from Évreux, which suggests that the travels of Jacques and his Master are restricted to an area west of Paris.

31 *Cleveland*: the *Histoire de Clèveland, fils naturel de Cromwell, ou le Philosophe anglais* (1732–9), a novel by the abbé Prévost, which was strong on the melodrama and providential interventions which Diderot mocks in *Jacques*. Even so, knowing how much the public insists on love stories (p. 151), he would not have been surprised to know that Prévost's novel of tragic passion, *Manon Lescaut* (1731), has proved far more popular than his own fictions.

or Sedaine: Diderot singles out Molière (1622–73) for his portraits of obsessive psychology, and the playwright Regnard (1655–1709) for his interest in eccentric behaviour. He considered Sedaine (1719–97) the best practitioner of the *drame bourgeois* to which he himself was committed. He had unbounded admiration for the 'everyday realism' and moral values of Samuel Richardson (1689–1761), whose novels took France by storm in the 1750s and 1760s.

32 *Pondicherry*: it has been suggested that Diderot had in mind a poet named Vignier, author of an *Essai de poésies diverses* (1765).

33 *said that*: Horace, *Ars poetica*, 372–3: *Mediocribus esse poetis | Non homines, non di, non concessere columnae* ('Neither men, gods, nor bookseller's stalls allow poets to be mediocre').

35 *to Lisbon*: cf. *Tristram Shandy*, bk. viii, ch. 20: 'I took her at first for the daughter of the peasant (for it was no inn)—so had offer'd her a little purse with eighteen florins, which my poor brother Tom (here Trim wip'd his eyes) had sent me as a token, by a recruit, just before he set out for Lisbon.'

   my love-life: Sterne similarly defends his failure to begin the life of Tristram (who is not born until book iv, chapter 32), by his weakness for digressions which, 'incontestably, are the sunshine—they are the life, the soul of reading!—take them out of this book, for instance,—you might as well take the book along with them' (*Tristram Shandy*, bk. i, ch. 22).

   discalced Carmelite: Jean belonged to the mendicant Order of Notre Dame of Mount Carmel founded in Palestine in the twelfth century, introduced into France during the reign of Louis IX (1215–70) and reformed by Saint Teresa in the sixteenth century. Members of the order went barefoot.

36 *Eau des Carmes*: an alcoholic cordial made from lemon balm.

   Père Ange: the character recalls a cousin of Diderot, Frère Ange, also a Carmelite, who was bursar of his community. He was asked by Diderot's father to keep an eye on his son during his bohemian years in Paris. When Diderot, then in love with Anne-Toinette Champion, gave him the slip, he was convinced that Frère Ange, perhaps to avenge earlier slights, had orders to have him arrested, 'which he is only too anxious to see happen' (letter of Feb. 1743).

39 *earthquake*: Lisbon was devastated by an earthquake on 1 November 1755. The philosophical implications were felt throughout Europe. If God is good, how could he allow such destruction? If he is omnipotent, why did he not prevent it? It followed that God was at most one or the other, but not both. Voltaire expressed his anguish in his *Poème sur le désastre de Lisbonne* (1755), and returned to the subject in *Candide* (1759), which argued against philosophical optimism as an answer to the problem of evil. Diderot here is very close to the position adopted by Voltaire.

41 *Xanthippus*: the master of Aesop, the Greek fabulist who lived in the later half of the sixth century BC, was in fact Xanthus.

46 *Le Pelletier*: the character has been identified as Charles Le Pelletier (1681–1756). Diderot knew of him through a biography published by Mlle Alès de Corbet, Le Pelletier's god-daughter, in 1760.

53 *understood properly*: a continuation of part I of *Don Quixote* (1604–14), published in 1614, is attributed to an enemy of Cervantes, Luis Aliaga.

Ricciardetto, a mock-heroic poem by Niccolo Forteguerri (1664–1735), an Italian prelate, was published in 1738 and was translated into French as *Richardet* in 1766. It parodies themes and subjects from *Orlando furioso* (1516) by Ariosto (1474–1533). Richardet and Ferragus are knights of the court of Charlemagne.

you're wrong: Diderot later reveals (p. 99) that the tale of the duelling friends was prompted by Claude-Louis de Régnier, Comte de Guerchy (d. 1768), who saw active service in France's many wars and became France's ambassador in London in 1763.

feast of Saint Louis: 25 August.

in charge: in 1670 Louis XIV ordered the building of Les Invalides, a home for officers and men invalided out of the army, on the left bank of the Seine, just west of the Louvre. Work started in 1671 and ended in 1676, though the dome, begun in 1677, was not completed until 1735. There is no record that it was commanded by a Monsieur de Saint-Étienne.

54 *... of the whip'?*: the exchange, between Sganarelle and his wife Martine, occurs in Molière's *Le Médecin malgré lui* (*The Doctor Despite Himself*, 1666), I. i.

Monsieur Gousse: the character is based on Louis Goussier (1722–99), who drew plates for Diderot's *Encyclopédie*.

55 *Academy of Sciences*: Marie-Anne-Victoire Pigeon (1724–67) was the wife of Pierre Le Guay de Prémontval (1716–64), who began giving free, public lessons in mathematics in 1738. They fled Paris, not for the reasons Diderot gives here but because Prémontval's anti-religious views had brought him to the attention of the authorities. They settled for a while in Switzerland before moving to Prussia where Prémontval was elected to the Academy of Science in Berlin and his wife became Reader to Prince Henry of Prussia. Mlle Pigeon's father, Jean Pigeon d'Osanges (1654–1739), was a noted mathematician, and his celebrated planispheres were transferred from the King's Botanical Gardens (see note to p. 111) to the Academy of Sciences, founded by Louis XIV in 1666.

61 *walking alone*: public hangmen were not permitted to live within city limits and were treated as pariahs.

63 *Frère Cosme*: Diderot has in mind not Saint Cosmo, patron saint of surgeons, but Jean Baseilhac (1703–81), known as Frère Cosme, a Feuillantine monk, who was well known for his success in treating patients suffering from the stone. He founded a hospice near Diderot's own house in the rue Taranne, not far from the Porte Saint-Honoré, then Paris's most westerly gate.

67 *chi va ... va lontano*: an Italian proverb: he who goes gently goes surely; he who goes surely goes far.

69 *heard you*: that is, in case the Master's words should be reported to the authorities by police spies: see note to p. 227. Such anti-religious talk could be dangerous. In 1765 the Chevalier de la Barre had, in his cups, sung

irreverent songs and failed to raise his hat while a funeral procession passed by, for which crime he was burned at the stake.

71 *dead-end*: Voltaire considered the word *cul-de-sac* vulgar and recommended that it be replaced by *impasse*.

Bicêtre: built in 1632, in south-east Paris, Bicêtre was part of the city's scattered criminal and medical provision, the Hôpital Général. It was both prison and hospital, but was known—and feared—for its lunatic wards and the mercury treatment it dispensed to patients suffering from venereal disease.

78 *rue de l'Université*: this thoroughfare still runs parallel to the Seine on the left bank, starting at the Invalides and ending at the Eiffel Tower.

lettre de cachet: the essentially paternalistic legal system allowed individuals to make a personal application to the king to remove from circulation, without trial and for an unspecified period, individuals whose behaviour was judged to put families at risk: extravagant fathers, erring daughters, feckless sons. The *lettre de cachet* was seen to be arbitrary and open to abuse, and it came to symbolize the oppression and injustice of the *ancien régime*.

79 *Saint-Florentin's*: Louis Phélypeaux (1705–77), Duke de la Vrillière, Comte de Saint-Florentin had, since the 1720s, overseen France's religious affairs, notably matters relating to the Protestant community which had been outlawed since 1685. He was given ministerial office in 1761, with responsibility for the policing of the capital.

or the Abbaye: the Temple, in the north-east of the city, began as a monastery built by the Knights Templar in the twelfth century. Traditionally its grounds, like those of the Abbaye de Saint-Germain-des-Prés, on the left bank, offered the right of sanctuary.

86 *Bourru bienfaisant*: by Carlo Goldoni (1707–93), the Italian playwright who arrived in Paris in 1761. Diderot attended one of the first performances of *Le Bourru bienfaisant* in November 1771. The action shows how Géronte, the 'kindly curmudgeon' of the title, is unable to sustain his hard-heartedness when confronted by his own naturally compassionate nature. In rewriting Goldoni's play, Diderot cocks a snook at critics like Palissot and Fréron who had accused him of plagiarising the Italian playwright in both of his own plays, *Le Fils naturel* and *Le Père de famille*.

89 *his nose*: in a letter to Sophie Volland (2–8 Nov. 1760), Diderot takes Taupin, the dog of a local miller, as an instance of a love as great as those sung by the poets. Taupin has taken a fancy to Thisbe, Madame d'Aine's pet bitch. 'Now picture this: whatever the weather, every day without fail he turns up at the door and lies down in the ooze, with his nose resting on his paws, his eyes glued to our windows, never moving from his uncomfortable post, despite the rain bucketing down and the wind flapping his ears, and howl like blazes for Thisbe from morning till night.' Madame d'Aine concluded that 'it's not possible to analyse the most delicate feelings without finding something louche at the bottom of them'. Diderot concurred.

To Damilaville (3 Nov. 1760), he wrote: 'there is something testicular beneath our most sublime sentiments and purest emotions.'

92 *Tronchin*: Théodore Tronchin (1709–81), a celebrated Swiss doctor and a pioneer in the use of inoculation. He was Voltaire's doctor and a friend of Rousseau, who introduced him to Diderot.

100 *Saint-Germain and Saint-Laurent*: there were two almost permanent fairs in Paris which served a double purpose as markets and as places of popular entertainment. The Foire Saint-Germain was on the south bank of the Seine and ran from June to September, while the Foire Saint-Laurent was located near the Temple in the winter months.

105 *at the Opéra*: it has been estimated that by the 1770s one in seven Parisiennes was involved in prostitution, from the mistresses of rich and powerful men to common streetwalkers who were reduced to selling themselves to avoid starvation. Actresses were generally assumed to be sexually promiscuous and, of this group, the singers and dancers of the Opéra were the most notorious.

least talent: an abbé had studied for but never taken his vows. Though only loosely attached to the Church, abbés found employment as directors of conscience in rich households, where they were often suspected of abusing their influence. As a group, they were accused of preaching moral values they did not practice, and the *philosophes* regarded them as champions of the obscurantism they fought to overcome. A number of abbés published virulent denunciations of philosophic ideas (as Mademoiselle d'Aison's does) and, though Diderot may well have a particular individual in mind, his remarks are aimed at the type.

107 *Huet, Nicole, and Bossuet*: Daniel Huet (1630–1721), Bishop of Avranches, was a mathematician and noted Greek scholar, whom Diderot admired for his scepticism. Pierre Nicole (1625–95), the Jansenist scholar, taught Racine at Port-Royal. Jacques-Bénigne Bossuet (1627–1704), Bishop of Meaux, had been the voice of Catholic orthodoxy in the age of Louis XIV. Jacques's Captain's position is clear from this statement of support for those who attacked traditional Church doctrine, and he would have had the same opinion of Mademoiselle d'Aisnon's scribbling abbé as Diderot himself.

108 *Jansenists or Molinists*: Cornelius Jansen (1585–1638) taught that human beings cannot earn salvation without the benefit of divine grace, which is granted only to the few: Jansenists were bound by a strict doctrine of predestination which was declared heretical in 1713. The Spanish Jesuit, Luis Molina (1535–1600), advanced arguments to show that human will is compatible with God's providence. Jansenists were thought to be grim and fanatical, whereas Molinists were suspected of being over-lax in their moral standards. See also notes to pp. 121, 155.

109 *Saint-Cyr*: a school for the daughters of impoverished nobles founded in the royal convent of Saint Cyr, near Versailles, in 1687 by Mme de Maintenon and Louis XIV. In 1802 it was turned into one of France's most

prestigious military academies. That we never get to hear the landlady's biography is a further instance of Diderot's stance as master of the revels and his argument that narratives such as the one the landlady might be expected to tell imitate other novels, not life. But the aside is also intended to explain why the landlady tells a better story—and expresses it in the language of the contemporary novel of manners—than is commonly met with in an innkeeper's wife.

111 *Jardin du Roi*: on the site of the present Jardin des Plantes on the left bank of the Seine. Begun by Louis XIII in 1640, it was recognized as one of Europe's finest botanical gardens under the naturalist Buffon, who was its director between 1739 and 1788. Its noted collection of plants was known as the Cabinet du Roi.

beside him: Diderot regularly pauses to give the reader a 'tableau', a technique drawn from the narrative paintings he admired, which he also used in his dramas. By halting the action momentarily, he hoped to convey a strong visual impression of a scene, its setting, and especially its characters.

115 *Galatea*: Diderot greatly admired the religious and mythological works of Raphael (1483–1520). His *Galatea*, a large fresco in the Farnesina Palace in Rome, was completed between 1511 and 1514.

121 *Saint François de Sales*: François de Sales (1567–1622), Bishop of Geneva, founder of the female Order of the Visitation (1610) and author of the influential *Introduction à la vie dévote*.

Quietist leanings: Quietism placed Christian perfection in the love of God and an inactive soul. A branch of ascetic, mystical theology, it grew out of ideas propounded by Miguel Molinos (1640–96) in the middle of the seventeenth century. It was taken up in France in the 1690s by Mme Guyon and the Bishop of Cambrai, Fénelon. When his Quietist tendencies were attacked by Bossuet, and censured by the Pope in 1699, Fénelon withdrew his support and the movement never recovered.

126 *here nor there*: a reflection of Diderot's interest in physiognomy as a means of reading character, and in the 'elective affinity', which Goethe would later exploit more systematically in *Die Wahlverwandtschaften* (*Elective Affinities*, 1808–9).

back again: Villejuif, long since overtaken by urban sprawl, was then a village just a few miles south of Paris.

129 *rue Traversière*: on the site of the present rues de l'Échelle and Molière, this street joined the rue Saint-Honoré and the rue de Richelieu just west of the Palais Royal. Diderot knew it well, for he had lived there in about 1744.

133 *Aristotle ... Le Bossu*: Aristotle (384–322 BC), in the *Poetics*, insisted on unity of dramatic action. The *Ars poetica* of Horace (64–8 BC) was imitated by Boileau-Despréaux, 'the lawgiver of Parnassus', in his *Art poétique* (1674), which codified the rules of literature in the age of Racine. Jerome Vida (1485–1566), author of *Poeticorum libri III* (1527), was a follower of Virgil and one of the Italian poets and scholars who helped shape the theory

of French classicism. René Le Bossu (1631–89) argued, in an essay on epic poetry (1675), that the heroic subject should take precedence over the character of the hero. It may be that the first three were fresh in Diderot's mind, for the abbé Batteux, an Academician and celebrated classical scholar, published *Les Quatre Poétiques d'Aristote, d'Horace, de Vida, de Despréaux* in 1771. Le Bossu is included for the dreadful pun that follows.

134 *amuse me*: Horace's view (*Ars poetica*, 343) that the best writers are those who mix the useful with the agreeable (*utile dulci*) was still the justification for literature with a moral vocation.

136 *to condemn*: an echo of Diderot's defence of women, more fully stated in *La Religieuse* and an essay on women written in 1772.

138 *common ailments*: the *Avis au peuple sur sa santé* (1761), by Simon-André Tissot (1728–97).

140 *made for Jacques*: Diderot not only provides Jacques with a chain of employers, but takes the opportunity to mock a number of *bêtes noires*, though not all are identifiable. The inclusion of the brothers La Boulaye, Pascal, and Mlle Isselin may be private jokes, like Rusai (a homonym of *rusé*, sly). But the Comte de Tourville, the grandson of one of Louis XIV's generals, was real enough, as was the Marquise de Belloy, a patron of art. Hérissant was a publisher hostile to the *Encyclopédie*, and is lampooned here as a moneylender.

144 *'Shan't!'*: the quarrel between Jacques and his Master contains a clear political charge. Jacques defends his name because it was still associated with the old peasant uprisings known as the *jacqueries*, while his impertinence anticipates Figaro, who also remarked how few masters were capable of being servants (Beaumarchais, *Le Barbier de Séville* (1785), i. ii). But the reference to 'an almost identical squabble' is much more specific. It alludes to the intermittent confrontations, the latest in 1771, between the king and the *parlement* of Paris which, though primarily a legal body, made several attempts to reclaim the political power which Louis XIV had denied it. On each occasion the *parlement* was exiled but was later allowed to resume its functions, rather as Jacques is told to go downstairs and then is allowed to return as though nothing has happened.

148 *Weak . . . of strong men*: Diderot intends this observation upon human foibles, a commonplace in the literature of moral reflection, as another instance of Jacques's awareness of the chain of cause and effect to which all are subject.

a Premonstrant: member of an Augustinian religious order founded in 1119 by Saint Norbert at Prémontré, 20 km. north of Soissons. Once known for its strictness, the order had grown lax and in the eighteenth century was associated with a number of sexual scandals.

149 *public executions*: capital punishment took brutal forms, from hanging and breaking on the wheel, to quartering, as in the case of Damien who attempted to kill Louis XV in 1757. It had long been assumed that executions, to have a deterrent effect, should be public.

149 *Place de Grève*: the Place de Grève had been a place of public execution since 1310. It was there that the guillotine was first used on 25 April 1792. Called the Place de l'Hôtel de Ville since 1806, it was situated on the right bank of the Seine, opposite the present Pont d'Arcoli.

150 *Spinoza*: Baruch Spinoza (1631–77) argued that there is no difference between mind, as represented by God, and matter, as represented by Nature. Spirit and matter are thus reconciled as a single Substance, which is called God, and is reflected in man by the harmony between body and mind. In the *Ethics* he concludes that we have no free will, since we are dependent on causes outside us, and that the greatest good is knowledge of God's will. Spinoza was admired by the *philosophes* and by Diderot as having laid the foundations for atheistic materialism. However, Diderot, as a neo-*Spinoziste*, dispensed with God and defined determinism in terms of the unavoidable laws which govern the universe and organize matter into pre-progammed forms.

152 *or despair*: Diderot had provided a graphic demonstration of the dehumanizing effects of the convent system in *La Religeuse*.

driven snow: but only outwardly. Premonstrants wore wore white habits, made of wool, and no undershirt.

154 *'Angelus . . . Mariae'*: 'The Angel of the Lord brought the news to Mary.' Cf. Luke 1: 26 ff., which tells how the angel Gabriel announced the virgin birth. Père Hudson's stratagem recalls the hypocrisy of Molière's Tartuffe.

Unigenitus: in 1713 the Pope issued a Bull condemning a number of Jansenist propositions published in tract by le Père Quesnel. It established the doctrinal position of Rome, which rejected the austerity of Jansenist theology and approved a less rigorous creed which allowed, for example, pardon for sins and the possibility of redemption through good works. But the Bull did not end the divisions within the Church. There were highly publicized factional clashes in the 1730s and 1740s, and Jansenist fundamentalists (who complained of the freer, 'lax' theology of orthodox Catholicism) maintained their stance into the French Revolution and beyond.

155 *and Mirepoix*: Jean-François Boyer (1675–1755), Bishop of Mirepoix, a thorn in Voltaire's flesh and a fervent anti-Jansenist. He had been tutor to the Dauphin and almoner to the Dauphine, and his opinions were respected at court.

Saint-Médard: the church of Saint-Médard, in the south-east corner of Paris, became notorious in 1732 when the Jansenist faithful, who gathered round the grave of a pious cleric named Girard, quivered, shook, and shuddered under the influence of the Holy Spirit. Judging matters to have grown out of hand, the police closed the cemetery. The episode remained of blessed memory to Jansenists.

159 *Petit-Châtelet*: on the left bank, near the Petit-Pont. Once a fort, it was used principally as a debtors' prison.

160 *than Châlons*: the lady is the mother of Sophie Volland and the château the Volland family home at Isle, on the Marne just outside Vitry-le-François, which lies about halfway between St-Dizier and Châlons-sur-Marne, in Champagne, some 200 km. east of Paris.

161 *Le Moncetz?*: a village near Isle. Between 1752 and 1767, the superior of the Premonstrant abbey founded there in 1142 was François Durier, a frequent visitor at the house of Madame Volland and the inspiration for Père Hudson. Diderot was fascinated by the contrast between the strict discipline he imposed on his abbey and the laxity of his personal morals.

tell you: René Vatri (1697–1769) was a noted Hellenist. Alexis Piron (1689–1773), a successful comic and satirical playwright, was elected to the French Academy in 1753, but was prevented from taking his seat by Louis XV, who was scandalized by the licentious tone as a poet. His complete works were published in 1776 by Rigolet de Juvigny in a sanitized form. This aside confirms that Diderot continued to add to his manuscript after the main body of the text was completed by about 1774.

162 *a Raphael*: Diderot regularly denigrated the work of François Boucher (1703–70), the most influential and successful artist of the age of Louis XV. Though he occasionally admired certain of his painterly effects, he considered him very inferior to the great masters like Rubens (1577–1640) and Raphael (1483–1520).

young pupils: Carle Van Loo (1705–1765), director of the Royal Academy of Painting, whom Diderot greatly admired. The Pont-Neuf, the westernmost of the bridges crossing the Seine at the Île de la Cité, was built between 1578 and 1607. It was lined with shops of all kinds, the last of which disappeared only in the middle of the nineteenth century.

Porte Saint-Denis: the fountain, designed by Jean Goujon in 1549, stood at the entrance to the Cemetery of the Holy Innocents, near the junction of the rue Saint-Denis and the rue Saint-Honoré. The Porte Saint-Denis was the northernmost of the old city gates.

163 *something of it*: Jacques's 'composition' is based on an accident in the rue des Prouvelles which Diderot recounts in a letter to Sophie Volland of 7 October 1760. As an art critic, Diderot admired the draughtsmanship of Jean-Honoré Fragonard (1732–1806), though cared less for the sensuality of certain of his subjects.

164 *The Comedy . . . Paradise*: the epic vision of the afterlife by Dante (1265–1321). The image of the chrysalis is taken from *Purgatory* (x. 124–6): 'Perceive ye not we are of worm-like kind, | Born to bring forth the angel butterfly, | That soars to Judgement. . .' (Plumptre's translation).

round about: *Inferno*, ix. 112–32.

their cheeks: ibid., xxxi. 46–8. 'Their eyes, which erst within had tears deep pent, | Gushed downwards through the lids, and then the cold | Congealed the tears and stayed their free descent.'

164 *worms below*: ibid., iii. 67–9. 'And streams of blood down-trickled on each face, | And, mingled with their tears, beneath their feet, | Were licked by worms that wriggled foul and base.'

165 *Madame de Parme*: Princess Louise-Élisabeth of France (1727–59), eldest daughter of Louis XIV. As the wife of Philip, Prince of Parma, the heir to the Spanish throne, she was also known as Madame Infanta.

Saint-Roch: the church of Saint-Roch, in the Rue Saint-Honoré.

Duke de Chevreuse: Marie-Charles-Louis d'Albert (1717–81), Duke de Chevreuse, who made his reputation at the siege of Prague in 1741.

166 *the last*: the genealogy of Christ appears not in Luke but in the Gospel according to Matthew.

167 *Ferragus*: see note to p. 53. After violating a nun, Ferragus, castrated by Renaud, lives as a hermit. When he is dying, Lucifer comes to him brandishing 'the sorry remains of his lost virility' (Canto X).

175 *Boulle*: André-Charles Boulle (1642–1732), sculptor and cabinetmaker to Louis XIV. The 'Boule' or 'Buhl' style of furniture makes a heavy use of rich inlaid decoration.

Condé: Louis de Bourbon (1621–86), Prince de Condé, one of the most distinguished military commanders of the seventeenth century.

Maître-Pathelin: Guillaume Jousseaulme, in the anonymous *Farce de Maître Pathelin* (c.1460), the best-known of all medieval farces.

176 *about that?'*: Diderot puts his own gloss on what is more usually seen as an instance of the rhetorical power which William Pitt (1708–78), Earl of Chatham, exerted over the Commons. To finance the Seven Years War, he proposed to raise funds by requiring shopkeepers to buy a licence. The Treasury preferred a tax on sugar, a proposal which infuriated the West India Merchants. When Pitt rose to speak in a debate on 9 March 1759, he was greeted by 'a horse laugh' which he quelled by thundering: 'Sugar, Mr Speaker? Sugar, Mr Speaker? Sugar, Mr Speaker?', and then, as the hecklers fell silent: 'Who will laugh at sugar now?'

182 *and lecherous*: Sterne's man-midwife, if less lecherous, was built along similarly grotesque lines: 'Imagine to yourself a little squat, uncourtly figure of a Doctor Slop, of about four feet and a half perpendicular height, with a breadth of back, and a sesquipedality of belly, which might have done honour to a sergeant in the horse-guards' (*Tristram Shandy*, bk. i, ch.9).

184 *I told you*: see p. 3.

for us: Tiberius is the third of the *Twelve Caesars* of Suetonius (AD ?69–?141).

many more?: in this list of Roman authors who wrote freely, and in some cases very freely, of sexual matters, La Fontaine (1621–95) is included not for his *Fables* but for his collections of verse tales (1669–96) which revived the bawdy vein of Boccaccio.

magnifying mirrors'?: according to Seneca (*Questiones naturales*, i. 16), Hostius Quadra, a slave, made use of such mirrors in his relations with homosexual partners.

185 *my defence*: Jean-Baptiste Rousseau (1671–1741), the greatest lyric poet of the century, was forced into exile in 1707 for publishing obscene, scurrilous verses. He defended himself in the preface to an edition of his works published in 1712.

La Pucelle?: a mock-epic (1755) by Voltaire (1694–1778), notorious for its licentious treatment of Joan of Arc.

futuo: first person, present tense of Latin *futuere*, the etymological origin of *foutre*.

186 *Montaigne*: the text, from 'To be perfectly frank' to 'the words least', is transcribed almost literally from Montaigne (*Essais*, iii. 5).

Lasciva . . . vita proba: 'The page I write is licentious, but my life is pure.' The line is from the *Epigrams* (I. iv. 8) of Martial (AD 43–104).

187 *both were drunk*: Pythia was the title of the priestess of Apollo at Delphi. She was inspired by sulphurous vapours which escaped from an underground vent inside the temple. She sat, without benefit of nether-garments, on a three-legged stool, called the tripod, in which there was a small hole. The tripod stood directly above the vent and Pythia was thus admirably placed to (for want of a better word) inhale the said inspirational vapours. When seized by the spirit, she proceeded to speak oracles in hexameters, but not before washing herself in the sacred fountain, shaking a laurel tree, and observing the strict laws of temperance and chastity.

of the Gourd: the descent of the Holy Spirit on the day of Pentecost was announced by 'a rushing mighty wind' and 'cloven tongues like as of fire'. All present 'were confounded, because that every man heard them speak his own language'. In renaming the festival, Jacques shares the view of those who mocked, saying: 'These men are full of new wine' (Acts 2: 1–13).

of this kind: Diderot clearly has in mind the list of prophetic methods (from aeromancy to tephramancy) supplied by Herr Trippa to Panurge in the *Third Book of . . . Pantagruel* (ch. 25), by François Rabelais (c.1491–1553). Pantagruel sets out to visit Bacbuc, priestess of the sacred bottle, at the start of the *Fourth Book* but does not arrive until chapter 34 of the *Fifth Book*, when the verdict of the bottle is Trinch ('meaning drink') (ch. 45).

Meudon: a few miles west of Paris on the Seine, where Diderot had rented a small house since 1759.

a bottle or two: in the *Fifth Book of . . . Pantagruel* (ch. 44), Bacbuc leads Panurge into the presence of the Sacred Bottle, which speaks with a voice resembling the bursting of glass bottles when they are left too near a fire.

Engastrimyth: in ancient Greece, the term applied to women who delivered oracles 'through the belly'. The Latin equivalent has survived as 'ventriloquist'.

187 *Rabelais . . . Vadé*: a chronological list of writers known not only for their
liking for alcohol but also for their opposition to received ideas and the defence of the freedom to think.

Pomme de Pin. . . guinguette: the Pomme-de-Pin, one of the oldest taverns in
Paris, was on the Île de la Cité, in the shadow of Notre Dame. Villon was an
habitué in the fifteenth century, Rabelais in the sixteenth, and it was the
meeting-place of freethinkers in the first half of the seventeenth century
and of writers like Racine, Molière, and La Fontaine in the second. The
Temple (see note to p. 79) was the haunt of freethinkers at the end of the
reign of Louis XIV and during the Regency. The *guinguette* was the name
given to taverns in the outskirts of Paris which were frequented in summer
by workers and artisans.

. . . a Modern: Anacreon (*c*.560–*c*.478 BC), one of the finest of the Greek
lyric poets; but Diderot's reference is to the *Anacreonta*, a much later collection of verses attributed to Anacreon, and denoted to the celebration of
wine and beauty. By insisting that truth is found in writers so separate in
time, Diderot shows the artificiality of the Quarrel of the Ancients and the
Moderns, which had divided intellectual loyalties around the turn of the
century.

188 *Gallet died*: Gallet (1700–57), grocer, apothecary, and author of popular
verse, was a founder-member of the Société du Caveau, a literary and
drinking club which was set up in 1726. In 1751 he took refuge from his
creditors in the sanctuary of the Temple and died there of drink.

. . . find it hilarious: François Nodot (d. *c*.1700) published newly discovered
fragments of Petronius in 1693. Charles des Brosses (1709–77), President
of the *parlement* of Dijon, historian, philologist, and archaeologist, recon-
stituted a text by Sallust (1777). Jean Freinsheim (1608–60) published sup-
plements to Livy and Quintus Curtius. Gabriel Brottier (1723–89), a Jesuit,
was the editor of the works of Tacitus (1771) and Pliny the Elder (1779).

193 *the opportunity*: ever since aristocratic power had been broken by the civil
wars of the Fronde in the middle of the seventeenth century, etiquette and
custom dictated that nobles could not be involved in trade, commerce, and
industry without damaging their standing on which their social and often
financial position depended. At last we learn that Jacques's Master, a chevalier (p. 200), is nobly born.

194 *turn pale*: while a promissory note was repayable to the named creditor on
the due date, a bill of exchange was transferable. Such a bill might pass from
hand to hand and at some point prove embarrassing to the signatory.

196 *my patches*: small circles of taffeta worn on the face by both men and women
to enhance their attractiveness. Advanced patch-wearers observed a code
by which the position of the beauty spot conveyed a hidden signal.

199 *by Richardson*: see note to p. 31.

201 *Saint-Jean-de-Latran*: a church on the left bank of the Seine and a place of
sanctuary. Demolished during the French Revolution, it occupied a site

commemorated in the present rue de Latran, just north of the College de France in the fifth *arrondissement*.

205 *Madame Riccoboni*: Marie-Jeanne de Mézières (1714–92) began a stage career in 1734 and scored a number of successes in the plays of Marivaux. In 1735 she married the actor Antoine Riccoboni. After 1757 she turned to fiction with a series of epistolary novels which history has judged much more favourably than Diderot, with whom she corresponded.

Livy's History. . . Flanders: as a historian of Rome, Livy (59 BC–AD 19) is read more for his style than as a reliable chronicler. The history of the wars in Flanders (1644) by Guido Bentivoglio (1579–1644), papal nuncio to the court of Louis XIII, was translated into French in 1769.

207 *dans le vin*: the comedy *La vérité dans le vin, ou les désagréments de la galanterie* (*In vino veritas, or the Vexations of Gallantry*) by Charles Collé (1709–83), a satirist and member of the Caveau (see note to p. 188, on *Gallet*) was first performed in 1747. The plot deals, in comic terms, with a similar situation which Diderot, who had a taste for rewriting the work of others, adapts for his own purposes.

214 *night before*: Diderot has in mind Ninon de Lenclos (1620–1705), not only one of the most celebrated odalisques of her century, but an extremely cultivated woman whose salon was a meeting-place for writers and philosophers.

her death: Diderot seems to forget that he has made her a widow.

more honest: an example of Diderot's interest in the nature of moral actions which, like other materialists, he divorced from religion and rooted in our common humanity as, at most, a social code.

220 *about Garo?*: in La Fontaine's fable, 'The Acorn and the Pumpkin' (*Fables*, ix. 4), Garo, a peasant, cannot understand why God hung acorns, which are small, on oaks, which are large and clearly more suited to pumpkins. But he sees that God has ordered everything for the best when, having dozed off under an oak, he is woken by a falling acorn: if a pumpkin had fallen on him, he would not have got off so lightly.

as Jacques: in his treatise on education, *Émile* (1762, bk. ii), Jean-Jacques Rousseau argued that fables in general, and those of La Fontaine in particular, are expressed in language which is too sophisticated for children and offer unsuitable lessons, since they show that life is a war between the unscrupulous and the innocent in which the latter defend themselves with the methods of the former. Thus the wily fox cheats the vain crow out of the piece of cheese by complimenting him on his appearance. La Fontaine's moral seems to be a warning against flatterers, but for Rousseau it could also be read as a justification of flattery as an indispensable life-skill.

machines: Diderot was much taken with the suggestion made by materialist philosophers such as La Mettrie and d'Holbach that man is composed entirely of molecules arranged into patterns. We are made of base matter centrally organized by a nervous system which requires us to follow basic

instincts for the purpose of survival and procreation, and gives us knowledge of our surroundings by processing the data of our senses into ideas.
According to this view, there are no innate ideas and no God, and a man is a
bundle of nerve-ends which is pre-programmed to act and think in an entirely mechanical way. If animals, who have small brains, are machines, so
are people, though their brains are 'machinery' are more sophisticated.
Clearly one part of Jacques's 'fatalism' reflects this theory of 'philosophic'
(or physical) necessity which raises the question of free will. For if we are
bound by the automatic operations of the body, is the mind ever free to conceive ideas and wishes that are independent of it?

222 *tollere vultus*: by Ovid's account of the creation (*Metamorphoses*, i. 85–6),
the god who created all life made animals hang their heads but 'gave man a
face at the top of his body and commanded him to raise his eyes to heaven
and lift his head to the stars'. The line is slightly misquoted.

224 *La Taste*: Louis Bernard de La Taste (1692–1757), a Benedictine theologian who, between 1733 and 1740, published a series of theological letters
attacking the hysterical scenes at the cemetery of Saint-Médard: see note to
p. 000. He argued that the Devil too performs miracles, his purpose being
to tempt the faithful into sin.

226 *For-L'Évêque*: a prison on the right bank of the Seine, between the Châtelet
and the Louvre, for soldiers and unruly actors.

227 *criminal activities*: Paris, with a population of some 600,000 people, employed a force of 1,500 *archers*, or officers of the watch, to keep order. Crime
was not investigated in any recognizably modern sense, and evidence took
the form of information which came to light: confessions, eyewitness reports, information received, and thieves and murderers caught in the act.
The police thus relied heavily on paid spies. Householders informed on
their neighbours, servants on their masters, and whores in brothels compiled reports on their clients. In 1753 10,000 livres (a quarter of the police
budget) was earmarked for paying informers, and the practice was so widespread that many believed that one half of the population of Paris was actively employed spying on the other half.

229 *that. . .*: Robert (d. 1617), the father of Oliver Cromwell (1599–1659),
owned land on which there was a small brewery. Jacques is probably interrupted because he may be about to repeat dangerous rumours which made
Louis XIV's mistress, Madame du Barry, the illegitimate child of a monk
and a cook, or to repeat philosophic claims that Christ was the illegitimate
son of a Roman soldier.

231 *odometer*: from the Greek *hodos* (road) and *metron* (measure), an instrument
used for measuring distances covered by a wheeled vehicle, or in this case,
by Jacques's skill with the gourd.

sufficient reason: a term used in Leibniz's philosophical system to mean a
specific cause. The expression had been mocked mercilessly by Voltaire in
Candide (1759).

237 *highly suspect*: again Diderot attacks the conventions of fiction. To avoid the
term 'novel', denounced as 'frivolous' and 'dangerous' by moralists, authors preferred 'journal', 'letters', 'correspondence', and especially 'history' and 'memoirs', thus implying that their work was not invented but
authentic and true.

Compère Mathieu: *Le Compère Mathieu* (1766), by Henri-Joseph Laurens
(1719–97), a libertine novel which in its manner and frank treatment of sex
bears some comparison with *Jacques the Fatalist*.

239 *his lips*: Diderot is more indelicate than Sterne, who allows Trim to relate
the incident in these terms: 'It was a Sunday, in the afternoon . . . Everything was still and hush as midnight about the house . . . when the fair
Béguine came in to see me.

'My wound was then in a fair way of doing well—the inflammation had
been gone off for some time, but it was succeeded with an itching both
above and below my knee, so insufferable that I had not shut my eyes the
whole night for it.

'Let me see it, said she, kneeling down upon the ground parallel to my
knee, and laying her hand upon the part below it—it only wants rubbing a
little, said the *Béguine*; so covering it with the bed-clothes, she began with
the forefinger of her right hand to rub under my knee, guiding her
forefinger backwards and forwards by the edge of the flannel which she kept
on the dressing.

'In five or six minutes, I felt slightly the end of her second finger—and
presently it was laid flat with the other, and she continued rubbing in that
way round and round for a good while; it then came into my head, that I
should fall in love—I blush'd when I saw how white a hand she had—I
shall never an' please your honour, behold another hand so white whilst
I live—. . .

'The young *Béguine*, continued the corporal, perceiving it was of great
service to me—from rubbing some time, with two fingers—proceeded to
rub at length with three—till by little and little she brought down the
fourth, and then rubb'd with her whole hand: I will never say another word,
an' please your honour, upon hands again, but it was softer than sattin . . .

'The fair *Béguine*, said the corporal, continued rubbing with her whole
hand under my knee—till I feared her zeal would weary her—"I would do
a thousand times more," said she, "for the love of Christ"—In saying
which, she pass'd her hand across the flannel, to the part above my knee,
which I had equally complain'd of, and rubb'd it also—

'I perceived, then, I was beginning to be in love—

'As she continued rub-rub-rubbing—I felt it spread from under her
hand, an' please your honour, to every part of my frame,—

'The more she rubb'd, and the longer the strokes she took—the more the
fire kindled in my veins—till at length, by two or three strokes longer than
the rest—my passion rose to the highest pitch—I seiz'd her hand—

'—And then thou clapped'st it to thy lips, Trim, said my uncle Toby—
and madest a speech.

'Whether the corporal's amour terminated precisely in the way my uncle Toby described it, is not material; it is enough that it contained in it the essence of all the love romances which ever have been wrote since the beginning of the world' (*Tristram Shandy*, bk. viii, ch. 22).

239 *Mandrin's gang*: Louis Mandrin (1725–55), highwayman and smuggler, was as famous in France as Jonathan Wild or Jack Sheppard in England. His appearance is a further example of Diderot's carelessness with the chronology of his narrative.

240 *Zeno and Spinoza*: Zeno of Citium (*c.*335–*c.*264 BC), founder of Greek Stoicism. On Spinoza, see note to p. 150. In other words, Jacques will raise a brood of fatalists as resilient as himself.

The Oxford World's Classics Website

www.worldsclassics.co.uk

- Browse the full range of Oxford World's Classics online

- Sign up for our monthly e-alert to receive information on new titles

- Read extracts from the Introductions

- Listen to our editors and translators talk about the world's greatest literature with our Oxford World's Classics audio guides

- Join the conversation, follow us on Twitter at OWC_Oxford

- Teachers and lecturers can order inspection copies quickly and simply via our website

www.worldsclassics.co.uk

American Literature

British and Irish Literature

Children's Literature

Classics and Ancient Literature

Colonial Literature

Eastern Literature

European Literature

Gothic Literature

History

Medieval Literature

Oxford English Drama

Poetry

Philosophy

Politics

Religion

The Oxford Shakespeare

A complete list of Oxford World's Classics, including Authors in Context, Oxford English Drama, and the Oxford Shakespeare, is available in the UK from the Marketing Services Department, Oxford University Press, Great Clarendon Street, Oxford OX2 6DP, or visit the website at www.oup.com/uk/worldsclassics.

In the USA, visit www.oup.com/us/owc for a complete title list.

Oxford World's Classics are available from all good bookshops. In case of difficulty, customers in the UK should contact Oxford University Press Bookshop, 116 High Street, Oxford OX1 4BR.

	Eirik the Red and Other Icelandic Sagas
	The German-Jewish Dialogue
	The Kalevala
	The Poetic Edda
LUDOVICO ARIOSTO	Orlando Furioso
GIOVANNI BOCCACCIO	The Decameron
GEORG BÜCHNER	Danton's Death, Leonce and Lena, and Woyzeck
LUIS VAZ DE CAMÕES	The Lusiads
MIGUEL DE CERVANTES	Don Quixote Exemplary Stories
CARLO COLLODI	The Adventures of Pinocchio
DANTE ALIGHIERI	The Divine Comedy Vita Nuova
LOPE DE VEGA	Three Major Plays
J. W. VON GOETHE	Elective Affinities Erotic Poems Faust: Part One and Part Two The Flight to Italy
E. T. A. HOFFMANN	The Golden Pot and Other Tales
HENRIK IBSEN	An Enemy of the People, The Wild Duck, Rosmersholm Four Major Plays Peer Gynt
LEONARDO DA VINCI	Selections from the Notebooks
FEDERICO GARCIA LORCA	Four Major Plays
MICHELANGELO BUONARROTI	Life, Letters, and Poetry